In Clouds of Fire

a story of community

By

Elaine Stienon

Best wishes always
Elaine Stienon
July 25, 2004

This book is a work of fiction. Places, events, and situations in this story are purely fictional. Any resemblance to actual persons, living or dead, is coincidental.

First published by AuthorHouse 04/29/04

ISBN: 1-4184-5738-8 (e-book)
ISBN: 1-4184-4767-6 (Paperback)

Library of Congress Control Number: 2003099776

This book is printed on acid free paper.

Printed in the United States of America
Bloomington, IN

Books by
Elaine Stienon

Lightning in the Fog

Utah Spring

The Light of the Morning

1

"What do you mean—Mormonites?" Hannah, just nineteen, turned in the wagon seat to stare at her aunt. Her pale brown eyebrows drew together as she frowned. "I thought we were going to the Shakers first."

Elizabeth felt the impact of the look, made more forceful by the startling blue eyes and their expression of protest. The wagon hit a bump and both women pitched sideways. "Now, Hannah—what did I say about being argumentative? I simply changed my mind—that's all."

"But–"

"These Mormonites are poor, deluded, ignorant people. They need to be shown the error of their ways. And soon, before they make any more converts."

"But the Shakers–"

"The Shakers can wait. Right now this group needs us the most."

Hannah leaned back against the seat and sighed. Her aunt,

annoyed at the girl's show of impatience, gave her a sharp look. Hannah shrugged and tucked a wisp of auburn hair back under her bonnet. "I was looking forward to seeing the Shakers dance, is all."

Elizabeth brushed a pine needle from her lap. "You'll see them soon enough. We have this other falsehood to deal with first." She tried to brace herself as the wagon lurched again. "My stars. I was glad to get off that boat, but this is almost worse."

They'd hired the wagon to take them from Painesville to Mentor, where their host was meeting them. The driver, a short, stocky man, no longer young, had piled their belongings into the wagon without a word. He hadn't even offered to assist them up.

Hannah looked out at the side of the road. Elizabeth followed her glance—nothing but thick pine woods, dark with shadows. She shivered. Such a primitive, wild place—as far west as Elizabeth Brighton Manning had ever traveled. In her role as lecturer, writer, missionary and self-appointed advisor to the nation on matters of moral and spiritual welfare, she never dreamed she would cover such a distance to root out error.

Kirtland Mills, Ohio. Far from the gentle Pennsylvania hills of her youth. Even the trees seemed bigger than the ones back east—taller, closer together. She half-expected to see an Indian lurking behind one of them. Don't be foolish, she told herself. The Indians no longer posed a threat in these parts. But even if they had, she imagined she would be more than a match for them. Had she not been sent, under the banner of the Almighty, to root out error and combat ignorant superstition? And here, in this dark, wild place, there was apparently plenty of both.

"In fact," she remarked to Hannah. "The people with the strange nickname are even more interesting than the Shakers. You should know something about them before we get there."

"I know they're followers of Joseph Smith," Hannah said. "They consider him a prophet."

"Yes. And in such an enlightened age as this. Here it is, 1831, and this man is purporting to receive direct revelations from God. Do you realize what I'm saying, Hannah? He claims that God actually *speaks* to him, the way I'm talking to you now. Can you imagine anything more ridiculous?"

"I don't know," Hannah said. "Where does the Book of Mormon fit in?"

"That's the most ridiculous thing of all. The story is that an angel—can you imagine?—an *angel* showed him the location of some gold plates, buried in a hill. He went and dug them up, and even though he could hardly write English, he translated the words on the plates from some ancient language. 'Reformed Egyptian,' or some such nonsense."

"I see. Why did he call it the Book of Mormon?"

"Apparently it's the name of some ancient prophet who once lived on this land."

"You mean—before the Indians?"

"It claims the Indians were descendants of the house of Israel, or something like that."

Hannah raised her eyebrows. "Have you read it?"

"Of course not. I wouldn't waste my time with such things. Oh, look. Here we are."

So far to come, Elizabeth thought. If only the poor, deluded people had stayed in western New York, where the movement had started. A large group of them had all moved west just this past spring. It meant a longer journey for her. But she was forgetting about the Shakers, and how they'd planned to visit both communities. The wagon slowed to a stop.

"Who's meeting us this time?" Hannah asked.

"The local Presbyterian minister. I thought I told you. Now, this town should be Mentor. He'll take us into Kirtland Mills in the morning. Then we'll meet this so-called prophet."

"I do hope he's good-looking," Hannah said.

"Hannah, what a thing to say! I hope you don't really mean that."

Hannah sighed. "No, Aunt Elizabeth. I'm just joking. But I haven't seen a handsome man since we got off the boat. Maybe there aren't any out here."

"Hannah, you should be ashamed—Oh, hello," she said as a middle-aged man stepped toward them. "You must be the one who was to meet us."

"Miss Manning? Jacob T. Sherman, at your service." Dressed in black broadcloth, he was of medium height, red-faced, and definitely not what any young woman would call handsome. His nose was too long, and he kept sniffing and rubbing it, as if he had a cold.

Hannah stifled a yawn as she got out of the wagon. Elizabeth tried not to notice. "This is Miss Manning—my niece and traveling companion."

He made a little bow and sniffed again. "I'm delighted, ladies. We've been looking forward to your arrival. Let me just get your things in the buggy, and I'll take you to our home for a bit of rest. Then we can begin our tour tomorrow."

In the early morning they rode toward Kirtland in the buggy, listening as Reverend Sherman spoke.

"The one thing you have to remember is that these people believe in a restoration of the gospel—the ancient Old Jerusalem gospel. Now, so do the Campbellites—Alexander Campbell's followers. The Disciples of Christ. But the Mormonites, or whatever you want to call them, believe that their restoration was divinely instituted."

"I see," Elizabeth said. Hannah sighed audibly. The minister went on.

"In fact, the one thing this movement has done is to break the back of Campbellism in the Western Reserve. A great many Campbellites, you see, went over and joined them."

"That's interesting." Elizabeth was trying to think of a subtle way to nudge Hannah, who sat drumming her fingers on the side of the vehicle.

"One of the Campbellites' greatest preachers, a man named Sidney Rigdon, joined the Mormonites last year. He took most of his congregation with him—and it was a large one."

"Do they come from other faiths too?" Elizabeth asked.

"Oh, yes. Some from the Shakers, a great many from Methodist, Baptist, Presbyterian backgrounds. In fact, it's alarming. It must be stopped."

"I'm not sure what I can do," she said. "I can lecture, but I'm sure they won't invite me to do that. In a case like this, I can only try to talk with individual people."

Hannah yawned, leaning back in the seat. The minister said, "The thing we object to most is this—this business of direct revelation. Why, the very idea! God actually speaking to this young upstart, this Smith. Now he's set himself up at the head of this so-called church, and the people regard him as God's spokesman."

"Well, we'll see about that."

Hannah let out a little snore. Embarrassed, Elizabeth gave the girl a push with her foot. Hannah snorted and woke up. The reverend's voice trembled, as if he were trying to conceal his amusement. "Kirtland's just up ahead. Quite a bustling place right now. The stores and trade-shops are all along here. We have a grist-mill, a hotel, a post office—and, oh, yes. A Presbyterian and a Methodist church."

"Where are all the Mormonites?" Elizabeth asked.

"It's a good bet that anyone you see is one of them," he said unhappily. "You might try over at the general store there. They should be having meetings some time this morning. Classes and such—whatever they do."

They had arranged for Mr. Sherman to let them off in the main part of town. He helped them down, and they watched as he drove away. They would meet him over at the Presbyterian church later. The two women entered the building where the Mormonites were gathering, Elizabeth first, with Hannah close behind. People waited in little groups, talking. A young woman stood alone by the door. Tall and slender, she had black hair, intent, dark eyes, and a dignified bearing. In fact, she seemed so affable, with such a pleasing appearance, that Elizabeth had difficulty believing she was one of the deluded ones.

"Excuse me," Elizabeth said. "Could you tell me where I might find Joseph Smith?"

The young woman smiled. "He's just up in front, there. The tall one, telling jokes."

"Him?" Hannah exclaimed. "Why, he's too handsome to be a prophet!"

The young woman began to laugh. "He happens to be my husband. He'll enjoy that immensely." Hannah laughed too, but Elizabeth felt mortified. The prophet's wife said, "Just go on up and introduce yourselves. He's used to visitors—we have a great many."

Elizabeth wanted to ask more questions, but just then an older woman came up and touched Mrs. Smith on the arm. Clearly her attention was needed elsewhere.

Elizabeth had not expected these people to exhibit such warmth and kindness; it came as a kind of shock. She walked up to the tall young man. Hannah followed, the amused look still on her face. Smith was decidedly good-looking by any standard, with an open, forthright expression, his pale auburn hair brushed back from his high forehead. Elizabeth thought of her errand and tried to sound determined.

"Excuse me, sir. I understand you are Mr. Joseph Smith?"

He smiled. "You understand correctly." She felt his full attention on her, his blue eyes intent as he waited.

"Sir, I am Elizabeth Brighton Manning, the lecturer. We're visiting here for a few days."

"Oh, yes." He shook her hand, and looked kindly at Hannah as Elizabeth introduced her. "They warned—uh, they said you might be coming. I hope you enjoy your stay with us." His gaze lingered on Hannah. "We're going to have a meeting here in just a short while—a service of ordination. We're ordaining two young men to the priesthood."

"Priesthood?" Elizabeth said.

"The ministry. You see, we believe that the priesthood of old has been divinely restored. We have the same offices that were had in the New Testament church—deacons, teachers, priests, elders—and we believe that these men are called of God to serve in the office where they are best suited."

She listened. Best not to refute it right away. He said, "If you have any questions, I'll be glad to answer them. Right now we must get on with the service."

With another glance at Hannah, he excused himself and joined the group of men at the front of the room. Elizabeth and Hannah found seats on one of the wooden benches. Elizabeth whispered to Hannah, "Why did you have to keep smiling at him?"

"I like him."

"This man is a deluded, ignorant person. You can't take anything he says seriously."

"He made sense to me."

"That's because you have no experience in such matters, as I have. And you mustn't smile at him like that. After all, the man is married."

"He didn't seem to mind."

"Oh, you're impossible. Of all the–"

"Hush, Aunt Elizabeth. The service is beginning."

During the service, which consisted of hymns, prayers, and a brief talk by Smith, she could find nothing unchristian or contrary to the scriptures she knew. Maybe there wasn't as much error here as she'd suspected. Then she remembered how the man had set himself up as a prophet.

Time for the ordinations. The two young men, hardly out of their teens, sat facing the congregation. Four of the elders stood behind them, Smith among them. At the designated time, two of the ministers placed their hands on the head of the first young man. One of them spoke the words and the prayer which comprised his ordination to the office of teacher.

Elizabeth shifted in her seat, uncomfortable. The prayer was humble, to be sure, and the words uplifting. But she thought of her own Protestant faith—the long years spent in study before anyone could be considered ordained. For the second young man, about to become a priest, Joseph Smith was the spokesman.

Not a learned man, Smith nonetheless had his own brand of eloquence. "Take care that you do not hearken to the precepts of the world, for that way is folly, but if you are humble, with a contrite spirit, you will be taught from on high."

Elizabeth was beginning to understand. If they were convinced they were being taught from 'on high,' then they wouldn't see the need for the years of theological training.

A service of baptism followed in the nearby Chagrin River. Elizabeth attended with great interest. As she knew, there were many ways of performing the rite of baptism, and no two sects were in agreement. Some sprinkled, some doused, some dunked. Some dunked the candidate three times forward, and others three times back. Some, like the Quakers, had no baptism at all.

To her amazement, these people conducted their baptismal service with assurance and an air of authority, as if there were only one way to do it. The one doing the baptizing raised his hand toward heaven and spoke the candidate's name, saying, "...having been commissioned of Jesus Christ, I baptize you in the name of the Father and of the Son and of the Holy Ghost. Amen." The candidate was then lowered back into the water and up again.

The commissioning part...ridiculous, of course. To think they had any authority at all was laughable enough. But to assert that they had more than other ministers—that they were divinely commissioned—was sheer foolishness.

She told Joseph Smith as much afterward. He listened gravely. He seemed about to give her an answer when she said, "You don't have to answer me. I *know* what's right and what's acceptable. And I shall make no bones about expressing my opinions."

"Very well. I had hoped you would see things differently. As your mind is already made up, that makes it very difficult to explain our beliefs."

"Answer me one thing." She assumed what she thought was her most defiant air. "About the Book of Mormon—can you, sir, in the presence of Almighty God, give me your oath that an angel from heaven showed you the place of those plates? And that you took the things contained in the book from those plates?"

"Now, wait—"

"And at the direction of the angel, you returned those plates to where you had taken them?"

"My testimony is public record," he said. "And there are the testimonies of other witnesses—three of them saw the angel, and then eight others—"

"No, *you*. I want you to swear it before me now!"

He took a deep breath, and a look of weariness came over his face. His eyes were hard, a cold blue. "I don't see why I should swear at all."

A young woman about the age of Hannah had come up to him. She had light brown hair and a slight receding chin which trembled as she spoke. "Brother Joseph, my mother is in need of prayers for healing, and she particularly wanted you."

"Excuse me, Miss Manning." He started to turn away.

"Just a minute," Elizabeth said. "Have the courtesy to answer me, sir! Just what is this 'healing?'"

The young woman pushed her straggly hair back out of her eyes with a quick little gesture. "I'll answer for him. It's administration to the sick, through the laying on of hands. It's one of our ordinances. You know, like it says in *James.* If we have any sick among us, we're to call for the elders of the church."

"Is that a fact?" Elizabeth said. "I suppose they're healed, then, without further ado."

"Miss Manning," he said. "I can't answer that. It's the prayer of faith that heals the sick, and all healing comes from God."

The woman leaned forward, and her hair fell over her eyes again. "If you want to know about it, you go talk to Sister Johnson. There she is—the one with the white shawl. Go ask her."

Elizabeth looked at Mr. Smith. "How can you pretend to such things? You say you're a prophet, and now you claim healing. You, if I may say so, are no more than any ignorant plough-boy of our land."

He drew in his breath, then gave a slight smile. "It's true—I was raised a farmer. What can I say? Just that the gift has returned again—as in former times, to illiterate fishermen."

Elizabeth frowned. This person, though ignorant, was quick with words. The young woman said, "Please, Brother Joseph. My mother is waiting."

"Yes, of course." A gentler note came into his voice. "Where is she?"

"This way." The young woman put her hand on Mr. Smith's arm, then said to Elizabeth, "You go see Sister Johnson—she'll tell you."

2

Elsa Johnson had quick, bright eyes peering out of her wrinkled face, and a thin, pointed nose. She was not a tall woman. Elizabeth Manning had to lean down to ask her question.

"What's that, my dear? Speak up."

"I was told you could tell me something about the healing of the sick—that is, your beliefs concerning it."

"Healing of the sick?"

"Miraculous healings—like in the New Testament."

"Oh, my glory, child." Mrs. Johnson's smile seemed to light up her whole face, and for a moment Elizabeth imagined how handsome she must have been in her youth. "Sit down here—we have time. I'll tell you everything I know. Let's see—you want to know if such things happen today?"

Out of the corner of her eye Elizabeth saw Hannah talking with two young men. One of them, a tall blond giant with a scruffy beard, was showing her a book. "Yes. Tell me about healings today."

"Well, first let me begin by saying that if Christ's church has been restored, with all the same things that the original church had, then it stands to reason that the ancient gifts and blessings have been restored, too. The ministry of angels, miracles, healing—"

"Let's talk about the healing," Elizabeth said. Hannah was leaning close to the bearded young man, and they were laughing. Mrs. Johnson said, "Well, if you'd just have a little patience, I was about to tell you. You see, I've been healed. Wonderfully healed."

"How did it happen?"

Mrs. Johnson's dark eyes crinkled at the corners as she smiled again. "I was about to tell you that, too. You're just as bad as my sons. No patience at all. Now, you see this arm?"

Elizabeth nodded.

"A year ago I had arthritis so bad I couldn't even lift it. It came on me sudden-like, and for years I could hardly use it. Had to tote wood one-handed. Couldn't do my washing, did the cooking with one hand. If I hadn't had John and the boys to help me, I don't know what I would've done."

"And what happened? You asked for healing?"

"Now, wait, child. That's the strange part. I didn't even have to ask."

Elizabeth waited, trying to conceal her impatience. Mrs. Johnson gave a little cough.

"You see, we was a lot of us over at the Whitney home, folks just visiting and comin' to see Joseph and ask about the church. There was John—that's my husband, and myself, and Mr. Ezra Booth—he was a Methodist preacher from over in Mantua. Then there was his wife, and—oh, I don't know. Some other citizens of the place. We was all sitting down, talking. Joseph and the preacher—that's our friend, Mr. Booth—started talking about supernatural gifts, the kind they had back in the days of the apostles. Finally they got around to the subject of healing. The actual gift of healing, like you read about in the New Testament. And Brother Booth—'course he was Reverend Booth back then—well, he says..."

The strange thing was that Elizabeth could see it in her mind as Mrs. Johnson described it. The people crowded into the main room of the house, sitting anywhere they could find—chairs, the wooden settle—-the women silent as Reverend Booth asked his question.

"'Now, here is Mrs. Johnson with a lame arm. Has God given any power to men now on earth to heal her?'"

Elizabeth drew in her breath. Hannah and the young blond man were no longer in sight. She tried to give all her attention to Mrs. Johnson.

"In fact, my arm was so bad that day, I couldn't even raise it to my head. Well, folks started talking of other things—something completely different—I can't even remember what-all was said. As I recall, some moments passed. Joseph was just sitting there—he wasn't talking or anything. Suddenly he stood up, and I remember his face was very pale. He came over and took me by the hand—and if I live to be a hundred, I'll never forget his words and the way he said them. 'Woman,' he said in his solemn voice. 'In the name of the Lord Jesus Christ, I command thee to be whole.'

"Someone gasped, I remember. Joseph turned and left the room.

Then—then I lifted up my arm.

"Without pain!" she told Elizabeth. "There was no pain at all! You should've heard the rejoicing—the hosannas! I knew what had happened. The next day I could even do my washing without trouble or pain.

"Well, the whole bunch of them went and joined the church. They couldn't get into that water fast enough. Later, someone said that maybe the shock had done it—the presumption of the words had caused some sort of shock, and that's how I was healed. But it wasn't like that at all. I just lifted up my arm, and the pain was gone. It stayed gone, too."

Hannah was now nowhere to be seen. "So—you joined the church because your arm was healed."

"I did it because I knew then that everything Joseph Smith had said was true. All the ancient gifts and blessings had been restored. This truly is the church of Christ."

"I suppose you people don't believe in doctors."

"Of course we do. There're doctors among us. We believe in using all the medical knowledge we can find. But in some cases our knowledge only goes so far. That's when we have to put things in the hands of God."

Elizabeth was feeling uncomfortable, anxious about Hannah. "Well, thank you for your story."

"And now that I've told you, what do you make of it?"

"I—uh—don't know," Elizabeth said. "Excuse me. I've got to find my niece. Reverend Sherman will be waiting to take us home."

She actually had to look outside before she found Hannah. The girl was leaning on the porch railing, chatting, laughing with the young bearded man. Her smile faded when saw her aunt. "Oh, Aunt Elizabeth, come and meet Daniel Perry. His family came all the way from Broome County, in New York. Daniel, this is my aunt."

"I'm right pleased to meet you, ma'am."

Elizabeth ignored the hand he offered to her. She glared at Hannah. "Do you realize I've been inside waiting for you?"

Hannah blinked. "Oh, really? I—I thought you were busy interviewing someone. I'm truly sorry." She smiled again. "Daniel—Mr. Perry was telling me about the Book of Mormon."

"Really? I didn't realize it had so much humor in it."

Daniel Perry let his hand fall to his side. A troubled expression crossed his face, then faded as he looked at Hannah. Elizabeth felt tired, with a strange, nervous headache; she needed to get Hannah away from there. She took her by the arm. "You come along, now. Excuse us."

They went toward the next group of buildings. Hannah drew away from her aunt's grasp. "Why did you have to be so rude to him? He's a very nice person."

"It goes without saying that you shouldn't be talking to strangers."

"But—but I thought that's what we were supposed to do. To get their opinions and so forth."

"That's my duty—not yours."

"Well, I did find out some fascinating things. Don't you even want to hear?"

Elizabeth couldn't explain why she felt so disturbed, even disconcerted—as if the penetrating blue eyes of the prophet were still on her. She sighed. "What've they been telling you?"

"Well, you were right about Mormon being the name of an ancient prophet who once lived on this continent. He took a whole library of metal plates, full of the history of his people, and abridged them. He was the editor, so to speak. That's why the book is called after him."

"Indeed." Elizabeth tightened her lips together in an effort to conceal her agitation.

"But even more interesting is that he had a son—Moroni. He's the one who finished the record and hid the plates in a hill. And this Moroni was the same being who showed Joseph Smith where to find the plates, hundreds of years later."

"How could he? He must've died somewhere along the line."

"He came back as a resurrected being—an angel. He was the last person to engrave anything on the plates, and the one who hid them. They've been buried all this time."

Elizabeth sighed, tired of the subject. "And that's where they should've stayed."

Hannah turned and looked at her. "But you don't even know what's in the book. How can you come out here and pretend to teach them, when you won't even listen to their story?"

"I don't have to listen to know that it's foolishness."

"Aunt Elizabeth—wait. Do you know what he told me? It didn't sound foolish—he said it was about a migration of ancient Israelites, led out of the Old World by the hand of God. Several migrations, in fact. It tells of their journeys, and—and their wars, and how finally Jesus himself visited them, after his resurrection."

"How ridiculous! Why should he visit them?"

"Because they were some of the 'lost sheep' of the house of Israel."

Elizabeth started to retort angrily. Hannah put her hand to her face. Elizabeth saw with a pang how beautiful she was, her cheeks flushed with eagerness, her reddish hair falling about her shoulders—no longer a child, to be ordered around, but a young woman. No wonder young Perry hadn't been able to take his eyes off her.

"Look." Hannah produced a book from her pocket. "He even gave me a copy of it."

Elizabeth gasped. "You must get rid of it at once!"

"But why?"

"It's full of lies—obviously full of the devil."

"You haven't listened to one word I've said. It's a Christian book. It tells about their dealings with God—these ancient people."

"I don't care." Elizabeth reached for the book. "I shall burn it."

Hannah snatched it away. "At least let me read it first."

"No, Hannah." A sudden fear gripped her, for Hannah as well as herself. "You mustn't let it influence you in any way—you must trust me."

"Now, Aunt Elizabeth, I'm capable of thinking for myself. But even if you do burn it, I'll simply write to Mr. Perry and have him send me another copy."

What was to be done with the girl? Elizabeth sighed. "Your father has his hands full, I can see."

"He's given up. He says I'm on my own."

A mistake to have brought her? Perhaps. But Elizabeth had needed a traveling companion, and Hannah had been willing.

"Oh, Aunt Elizabeth—I'm afraid I left my shawl back in the meeting hall. I'll just run back—"

"No, you won't--we'll both go. And we'll walk, not run. Try to maintain some dignity."

As Elizabeth suspected, Mr. Perry hadn't left the front of the building. He raised his eyebrows as they started up the steps.

"Now, just get the shawl." Elizabeth tried to sound firm. "We really have to leave."

As Hannah went to retrieve it, Elizabeth saw the young wife of the prophet standing near the door. Here was an opportunity.

"May I speak with you a moment?" Elizabeth asked.

"Most certainly."

"Tell me—what's it like being the wife of a so-called prophet?"

"Well—I would say it has its moments."

"I mean, aren't you rather embarrassed to be in such a position?"

The young woman hesitated, and the shadow of a frown crossed her face. "Not at all. You see, I happen to believe in his mission."

"You mean to say you're as ignorant as all the rest of them?"

"If you want to say that, I suppose you may. We believe he really is a prophet—inspired of God."

Hannah came up beside her with the shawl. "I'm ready now."

Mrs. Smith said, “I hope you’ve enjoyed your visit—and that you’ll give a favorable report. We’re very different from what the world says of us.”

Elizabeth gave her a cold stare. “I shall feel it my duty to speak against you wherever I go. Good day, now. Come along, Hannah.”

She swept out the door, not caring to catch the look of astonishment on the young wife’s face. But out of the corner of her eye she saw Hannah wince.

3

Why would she say that? Emma, folding baby clothes later that week, kept thinking about it. The famous missionary lady, the female lecturer of whom they had all heard—elegantly dressed, a paragon of dignity. No one had been rude to her, no one had deliberately offended her. She had sat through two services, one a baptism, and she had talked with a number of people. And yet she had found nothing good to say about them. Nothing.

"I wouldn't give it another thought," Joseph had said. "Her head is stuffed full of her own importance. She can't look at anything with an open mind."

Emma sighed. It sounded reasonable. But why did this particular person, for all her closed-mindedness, have to have so much influence?

"It's the way of things," Elsa Johnson said. "You know that as well as I."

Emma, Joseph and the babies were living with the Johnsons now, in their New England colonial-style home some thirty-six miles south of Kirtland. Hiram, the settlement was called. Joseph had needed a quiet place to work on his revision of the Old and New Testaments. He'd moved the family to Hiram at the invitation of the Johnson family.

"It's a bit roomier than that cabin," Elsa had said.

Emma had to agree. They'd been in the log cabin most of the spring and summer. She'd watched it being built—Isaac Morley had put it up for them on his own land, near the communal group known as 'The Family.'

At the Johnson house they had two large rooms, one for themselves and one for the twins. The best part was that Joseph was no longer caught up in disputes among 'The Family'—matters that had taken up much of his time. And the endless parade of visitors through their crowded living quarters was a thing of the past.

"I can't tell you how good it is to be here," Emma told Mrs. Johnson. "This reminds me of my parents' house back in Pennsylvania, where I grew up. Harmony—that was the name of the town."

"That's a pretty name."

"A pretty place. Rolling hills, and soft grass, and the river so peaceful and quiet. There was a swamp area nearby—Ichabod Swamp, all full of birds and wild creatures."

"You must've had good parents," Elsa Johnson said.

Emma started to say something, then stopped. How could she tell this kind woman, her friend, that her father had disowned her? "I'm afraid they didn't get along with my husband."

"How could anyone not get along with Joseph?"

"I guess it was another case of closed-mindedness," Emma replied.

"How'd you come to meet him, anyway?"

She smoothed and folded a tiny blanket. "Well, he came out with his father—they'd been hired to look for a lost silver mine. Josiah Stowell, it was—he claimed to know where the mine was, and he'd hired workers to help him. Joseph and his father boarded with us for a while."

For a while. Long enough for her to know that he was unique, that there was no one quite like him in the world. But her father was adamant.

"No money-digger's gonna marry my daughter."

No use to explain that he was more than a money-digger or a glass-looker. Her father's mind was made up.

"He forbade the marriage. So we had to run away—we ran off together and got married the same day. We couldn't think of any other way to do it."

"It don't sound like there was one. You do what you have to do," Elsa said. "Where'd you live after that?"

"It's hard to count how many places. Let's see—first we were with Joseph's parents, right outside Palmyra. Then—"

"Wasn't that about the time he found the gold plates?"

"He was given them—yes. In September, it was. I even went with him to the hill and waited in the wagon."

"And you say you never saw them?"

Emma sighed. "No. He was only directed to show them to a few others. I wasn't one of them. But I did feel them—he had them covered with a cloth. I felt them through the cloth—I remember how the edges made a strange rustling sound. A metallic rustling."

"I don't know how I could stand not seeing them plates. My curiosity would've got the better of me for sure."

Emma smiled. "Well, I knew he had them. And I was convinced it was of God. I was content to wait."

"I have to see to my bread in a moment. What happened then?"

"Oh—news got out. The neighbors started bothering us—even threatened us. Joseph almost lost his life trying to protect them. Translating them was out of the question."

"So what did you do?"

"That's when we moved back to Harmony. By that time my father was ready to welcome us back. We made the trip in a wagon, with my brother Alva along to help. Joseph had the plates hidden in a bean barrel."

"You lived with your parents?"

"No. We had a separate little house, right near their big one."

"And that's when the translation began?"

"Yes. I tried to help.. But I was so busy—"

"I'd better see about that bread," Elsa said. "I won't be a moment."

Elsa Johnson went into the next room. Emma heard the heavy

clanking sound, the opening of the oven door in the brick fireplace. But her mind went racing back to the time in Harmony, when she had tried to assist in the translation. Burdened with housework, expecting a child...to act as a scribe was more than she could manage.

Fortunately there were other people who came to help.

Oliver. Oliver Cowdery. The young school teacher, boarding with the elder Smiths in Manchester, had heard the strange story of the ancient record. He appeared at the house of Joseph and Emma the following spring, convinced that he was divinely led to have a part in the translation. He became the scribe, writing down the words as Joseph translated them.

"The gift of tongues." David Whitmer's words spoke in her mind. "That's what it is, when you think of it. The ancient gift, carried a step further."

The Whitmer family had even taken Joseph, Emma, and Oliver into their home, the farmhouse between the lakes in Fayette, New York. There the translation was completed, and the church officially organized, according to divine commandment, on April 6 of 1830.

In that unsettled time, Emma had come to a decision. She would stop hoping for a home of her own, a place where they could be happy and safe together. Perhaps that was out of the question, considering the work and the mission they were embarked upon. Instead, she had decided that wherever they happened to be at the time would truly be their home.

It had made the wanderings easier. And there had been many, to be sure. Wagon trips, journeys on horseback—even hundreds of miles in a sleigh in the dead of winter.

There was only one thing she did long for—and sometimes that longing was so intense she felt she could not bear it. She desired a child of her own, a baby she would carry in her body and give birth to. A child that would live, born of the love between her and her husband.

Such a simple thing, granted to so many. But she was denied, left out—not exactly barren, for she had carried three babies to term. The past...dotted with graves. Near the house in Harmony, their first-born lay buried—Alvin, who had lived three hours. In Kirtland lay her twins Thaddeus and Louisa. Each had lived just a few hours. If it hadn't been for the Murdock twins, she didn't think she could have sustained the loss of her own.

A noise startled her. She turned from the pile of clean clothes. Nancy Marinda, the Johnson's eighteen-year-old daughter, stood in the doorway.

"One of them just woke up. I think it's Julia. Shall I bring her in?"

"Yes—thank you."

Nancy Marinda still seemed in awe of the babies—the first time she'd ever had anything to do with twins. It did take some getting used to. Emma remembered the shocked, dazed feeling when they told her she'd delivered twins, and the overwhelming grief when she knew both of them had died. Then, a miracle! Twin babies brought to her after all, to be nursed and held.

John Murdock's wife Julia had given birth at almost the same time and then had died, leaving her husband with three older children and the newborn twins. Logic and necessity dictated that Emma, with no children of her own, should take the little ones and raise them.

On the very day she received the Murdock twins, they had another surprise. Lucy Smith, Joseph's mother, and her group of New York Saints had arrived safely in Kirtland, after a hazardous journey out over Lake Erie. They'd had reports that the immigrants had perished, lost in a storm on the lake. But Mother Smith and her group proved to be very much alive, and found a joyous welcome.

Nancy Marinda came in carrying one of the babies. Emma reached out her arms.

"Oh, this isn't Julia—it's Joseph. Don't you know how to tell the difference?"

Nancy Marinda's face grew red. "Well, I—of course. I just didn't look."

Emma smiled. "This is fine. He usually wakes up first, then he wakes her. This way, I'll feed him first, and she can sleep a little longer."

She fed the boy, then Nancy Marinda held him while Emma nursed Julia. She sat in a maple rocker and drank water from a cup while she nursed the child. Her mother-in-law had said it was best to keep drinking water all the while she nursed. It seemed to work—there was plenty of milk for both children. Mother Smith should know, Emma reflected—she'd nursed nine of them.

As always, when she nursed, she felt the deep peace surrounding her, the special world in which there was just mother and child. At such times, it was hard to imagine that they would not have been safe if they'd stayed in the east. But it was true—God had directed them to Ohio for their own safety, among other reasons. She remembered the threats of mob violence in New York—the two times Joseph had been thrust in jail. They'd had to move twice in order to complete the translation of the sacred record in peace. She and the others had expected the persecutions to die down, once they had the Book of Mormon published and distributed, and the church organized. But the word of the Lord indicated otherwise.

"That ye might escape the power of the enemy, and be gathered unto me a righteous people...I gave unto you the commandment, that you should go to the Ohio, and there I will give unto you my law; and there you shall be endowed with power from on high..."

She could only marvel at the way the promise had been kept. She and Joseph had arrived in Kirtland by sleigh on February 1. On February 4, Joseph received a revelation instructing the elders to assemble together, and by the prayer of faith they should receive the law. Then, in several separate messages during that month, the law was given.

And it was beautiful, even more so than she had expected. They were instructed not to kill or steal or lie, to love 'thy wife' with all their heart and cleave to no one else, not to commit adultery or speak evil of one's neighbor, or do him any harm. They were to keep all the commandments and serve God, if they professed to love Him. They were to remember the poor, and consecrate all their property for the support of the poor.

"...inasmuch as ye impart of your substance unto the poor, ye will do it unto me..."

They were instructed not to be proud, but to keep their garments plain, their beauty the work of their own hands—not to be idle. But to her, the most wonderful thing was the promise of Zion, in a later revelation—the holy city, the New Jerusalem where the people would eventually gather. "...a land of peace, a city of refuge, a place of safety for the saints of the most high God."

Zion—the hope of the ages, the city set on a hill. It ran through all scripture and every Judeo-Christian sect, like a golden thread. Even the Shakers had a song about it. She began to sing as the baby looked at her with dark, solemn eyes.

> *"I want to eat of my Father's table the food that*
> *perisheth not,*
> *And drink of the waters pure and holy that flow from*
> *the city of God."*

Joseph had entered the room. "What's that?"

"One of the Shaker songs," she said.

"Oh, no." He winced in mock horror. "Spare me, please."

He'd been having trouble with one of the men who had converted from Shakerism. He collected his copy of the Bible and a handful of papers. He started into the next room where Sidney Rigdon was waiting. "I hope you don't put that one in the collection."

He was joking, she knew. She was supposed to be compiling a selection of hymns to be used in the worship services. She hadn't had much time to work on it lately, with the twins and the move.

"As a matter of fact, it's the first one," she said.

"Lord help us all." He went out the door.

She had no difficulty knowing when he was serious and when he wasn't. But there were some who had definite trouble with it—Brother Booth, for instance, who said he told too many jokes for a religious leader. But Joseph could not stop jesting and joking—it was part of his nature.

The room felt warm, like a day in summer. She thought of the past summer, when certain of the elders had received instructions to travel in pairs to the land of Missouri. There, it was promised, the place of the New Jerusalem would be revealed. Apparently Joseph had stopped joking long enough to designate the Independence area as the Center Place of Zion, and had even dedicated the site for the temple. She had remained in Ohio, in the Morley cabin with the twins.

Others had gone on to Missouri to settle, among them a group of the New York Saints, who had elected to stay together in a body. They had lived briefly at Thompson, Ohio, and then had been sent to colonize the land of Zion. They'd built their first houses there, and even dug the first grave—for Polly Knight, the wife of Joseph Knight, Sr. She had died shortly after the arrival in Missouri.

Emma held up the baby so that the soft cheek lay against hers. Polly's husband had kept them supplied with food in Pennsylvania all spring during the time of translation.

The Knights, like many others, had made sacrifices. Some, indeed, had given all they had. She wanted to weep as she thought of those who had sold their property in New York State—some of them selling at a loss and leaving farms, homes, even families—to follow the young prophet and the main body of the church to Ohio. Now, at the word of the Lord, they had journeyed on to Missouri.

And for what? A dream, a hope that the New Jerusalem would become a reality—a promise, in fact, with one condition: 'If ye seek it with all your hearts.' The city of light, set on the hill, and the return of the Lord Jesus—for they all believed in the second coming of Christ, the millennial reign of peace and justice upon the earth.

She began to sing, holding the child against her shoulder.

"Glorious things of thee are spoken,
Zion, city of our God—"

Noises outside, horses' hooves striking the ground in a gallop. Someone shouted, and the dogs started barking. Emma and Nancy Marinda looked at each other.

Nancy Marinda, the boy twin cradled in her arms, got up and crossed to the window. When she saw who it was, a blush spread over her face. "It's just Dan Perry. Can't imagine why he's in such a hurry."

"Most likely to see you," Emma said. "Go on now—I can manage."

Elsa hurried into the room, wiping her hands on her apron. Before Nancy Marinda could hand the baby to Elsa and go outside, Dan stood in the doorway.

4

"Come in, Dan," Elsa Johnson said. "The boys should be back in a little while—they just went to fetch some hay."

Dan glanced around. He saw the three women and the babies, and he shifted his feet, uneasy. "I didn't come to see the boys, ma'am."

"It must be Nancy Marinda, then. Here she is."

Why could women make him feel clumsy and out of place? He stepped into the room. "I—that is—I came to speak with Brother Joseph."

"He's busy just now," Emma said. "But he'll be stopping for something to eat soon. You're welcome to wait for him. Won't you sit down?"

He waited until Nancy Marinda and her mother sat down, then took the chair beside Emma. "Those twins are really growing. Even since Sunday, they look bigger."

"Speakin' of Sunday," Elsa Johnson said. "I'm surprised you even noticed the twins. We all saw you payin' special attention to that eastern lady's niece—that Hannah Manning."

Trust the sisters to get right to the heart of things. He tried to look stern. "Someone had to show her we was friendly."

"A right pretty little thing, too," Elsa Johnson said, "with that red hair and all."

Dan gave silent thanks for the fact that he didn't blush easily. "I guess she was, now that you mention it."

Nancy Marinda said, "'Bout the prettiest girl they've seen. That's what Luke and the others was saying."

"Well, I think it's splendid you were so hospitable to her," Emma said. "Maybe they'll realize we're not so bad."

"I don't think she thought we was bad at all," he said to her.

"Then she and her aunt seem to have a difference of opinion."

Dan looked into her dark eyes. "Most likely more than one, ma'am."

"What do you hear from your folks?" Elsa Johnson said,

Happy to change the subject. "Pa's put up a log cabin near the river, and they're busy gettin' ready for the winter. I thought I'd go out and help them, maybe stay out there."

"Well, you're young," Elsa Johnson said. "Not everybody can go up to Zion. It's a heap of travelin'. But with your parents there, maybe it's a good idea."

"I came to get the word of the Lord," Dan replied gravely. "It's a big step, and means a change in plans."

"We may all be out there before long," Emma said. Nancy Marinda looked sad, and Dan hoped that with all his smiles in her direction, he had not engaged her affections. A hard thing, to love unrequited.

The aroma of new-baked bread drifted to them. Elsa Johnson said, "If you stay a mite longer, you can have fresh bread and honey with us."

"That's right nice of you," he replied. "I'd probably best see Brother Smith and ride on back. There'll be a lot to do if I'm to leave before the bad weather sets in."

They could hear voices from an adjoining room, the sound of chair legs scraping on the wood floor. As they waited for Brother Smith and Sidney Rigdon to join them, Dan had time to reflect on the subject which had occupied his mind for five days.

The young lady. Hannah. He couldn't stop thinking about her. Love being a new experience for him, he felt overwhelmed by the suddenness and strength of it. Like being kicked by a horse, or slammed against the side of a wagon.

He'd ridden out to Mentor, where he heard she was staying. Her aunt and the Presbyterian minister had refused to allow him in. But he managed to find a back window, and with luck he found her too. They whispered together at the window—long enough for him to learn her destination and her home address. He remembered his parting words.

"I must—I will see you again."

And her reply. "I truly hope so."

He felt uncertain, as if he were treading on strange, new ground. Here he was, twenty-one, unskilled, with only a knowledge of farming and farm animals. His family said he had a gift, a way with animals. Was that enough to enable him to support a wife? And was it possible to win a sweetheart through clandestine meetings and whisperings through back windows?

He got to his feet as the men entered the room. He remembered in a vague way some story about the prophet himself eloping at the age of twenty-onc. Joscph was only in his mid-twenties now—maybe in affairs of the heart, he would be sympathetic.

Emma whispered something to her husband as the others began leaving the room. Then she followed them with the sleeping girl-twin in her arms. Dan found himself alone with his religious leader.

A smile lit Joseph's face. "I hear you wanted to see me."

Now that the moment had come, Dan hesitated. Perhaps his request was too trivial for the prophet to address. "Well, sir—some things have happened to me lately. You said I was to go on a mission to the east, but my partner wandered off somewhere and can't be found."

"Who was your partner?"

"Ezra Jones, sir. They say he went back to see about selling his farm."

"We'll find someone else—you can still fulfill your assignment."

Dan shifted his feet. "Wait, sir. There's something else. You see—well, I've been thinkin' some about getting married, and I figure I'll have to earn some money before I do. Now, my folks are gettin' ready for winter in Missouri, and they can use my help. I figure if I go out there, I can probably find some way of makin' a living. Taking care of horses, if nothing else."

"I see," Joseph said slowly. "I guess it makes sense, with your family already settled there."

Encouraged, Dan gestured eagerly. "And I figured—you see, some mail arrived for that missionary lady—Miss Manning—and they didn't know how to get it to her. Now, I could stop by the Shaker communities on the way to Missouri, and give it to her."

The prophet's smile faded. His eyes narrowed in a frown. "Just a moment. How do you know where to find her?"

Dan felt a sudden misgiving. "Well—uh—that is, her niece told me."

"Ah, yes—the niece. Does this young lady, by any chance, have anything to do with your notion of getting married?"

Dan felt the intent blue eyes on him and looked down. "Well—partly. That is—yes."

Joseph gave a sigh. When he spoke, his voice had a touch of sadness. "Then let me give you a little advice. If she's anything like her aunt, you can forget her here and now. She wouldn't make a good wife. In fact, I wouldn't wish her on my worst enemy."

"She's not!" Dan burst out. "I know she's not like that."

"I hope you're right. But, Daniel—don't get your hopes up. I hate to see you disappointed. That is—I know she has a pretty face, and a charming manner. But so do many others."

"I know, sir. It's just that I can't forget her."

Joseph raised his eyebrows. "You just met her. Now—go to your family, if you want. But don't do anything in haste—in fact, give it a good, long time. See what happens out there. I won't promise that if you go to work and do the things you're supposed to be doing, you'll forget something like that. But sometimes you do. And then you know it was probably for the best. Now—what else can I do for you?"

"I came to get the word of the Lord on the subject."

Joseph looked amused. "What? Whether to go to Missouri?"

Dan nodded, no longer certain. Joseph gazed at him a moment. "To tell the truth, Daniel—you don't need to get the Lord's word on every topic. Missouri seems like a good idea. But whether you visit the Shakers or not—and frankly, I think it's best if you don't—take care to preach along the way. And it's better if you don't go alone. Oliver and some of the others will be traveling up to Zion in just a few more weeks. Why don't you wait and go with them? It'd be safer."

Dan took a step toward the door. "I guess that would be wise, sir. Although—my mare and I—we've gone on long journeys before, and we've always come through all right."

"Do what you think best, then. Now—about Zion. When you get there, remember that the Lord's work is just beginning. Things are not what they should be—in fact, I fear that God isn't too pleased with some of what's happening there. I want you to be prepared, and aware—maybe you'll be able to help set things right."

Dan had no idea of what his leader was talking about. His mind was still on Hannah. "I'll truly try, sir. And don't worry about me—I'll be fine." They shook hands, and Dan thanked him.

"Don't you want something to eat? It's a long ride back to Kirtland."

Dan declined, anxious to be on his way. He hurried down the steps to where his sorrel mare stood waiting at the split-rail fence. He unloosed the reins, patted the mare on the neck, and mounted. Joseph stood in the doorway watching. Dan raised his hand in a gesture of farewell, then turned his horse's head toward the main road.

****

Later that afternoon Joseph walked through the fields to the road. He stood looking toward the northwest, to where the road wound into the deep woods and out of sight.

Thirty-six miles to the north lay the village of Kirtland, and if you followed the road further west, you would reach the nearest of the Shaker communities. Beyond that and far to the southwest stretched the land designated as Zion, the place of peace and safety. More than eight hundred miles of bad roads and hard traveling. He thought of young Perry, and a strange misgiving filled his mind. So late to be starting the journey alone—almost winter. Perry should wait and go with Oliver Cowdery, as he had suggested.

Dan had a stubborn streak, like most of the others. Once he got it in his head to do something, most likely he'd do it. Yet he was a good person, well-meaning—wanting to do the right thing. Joseph sighed, thinking of his people, the ones he'd hoped to mold into the perfect society, fit to inhabit the promised land. He'd urged the migration from New York State to Ohio, convinced it was the Lord's will. He and Emma had made the trip by sleigh in the dead of winter. And what had they found?

First there was the Hubble business, the young woman claiming to be a prophetess.

"That's right, Brother Joseph. She's comin' up with them revelations and proclamations faster'n you can turn around."

"And folks is believin' her, too. She looks right sincere about it, with her face going white and her eyes kinda bulging out."

When he met her, he was amazed at how frail she appeared—hardly more than a frightened girl. He recalled a similar situation in New York, and informed both her and his followers through a revelation of his own that "there is none other appointed unto you to receive commandments and revelations."

Then there were the 'strange notions' in the meetings.

"Why, if they aren't goin' into fits and trances, jest like them revival folks."

"In that one meeting, they was barkin' like dogs and carryin' on—one of 'em, Burr Riggs, why he sez he was aimin' to tree the devil."

He'd worked to put a stop to such antics, and had sent Parley Pratt and other elders out to preach against the manifestation of 'false spirits.' But his efforts to control the lives of his people proved more difficult than he'd anticipated.

"It seems like we're convertin' more folks than you can shake a stick at. Most of Rigdon's old congregation—they're all comin' in."

"They're flocking to us from all over—folks wantin' to be baptized for the strangest reasons you ever heard tell."

"A bunch of 'em heard about some miraculous healing, and came in that way."

"One man even joined because he heard some young Mormon girl predicted an earthquake in China. Doesn't that beat all?"

Too many people, coming in too fast—all eager to investigate and unite with the church. Patiently Joseph tried to educate them, to teach the things that would help and unify them. But old ways of thinking died hard.

He remembered trying to explain his new economic plan.

"Now, see—if everyone consecrates their land and goods to the Lord, then the bishop gives back only those things each person really needs, as his stewardship. Everything else is administered by the bishop. Then—don't you see? Those in need will have what they need, and those who had abundance will not have more than they need. Their surplus will be used to help someone else, and that way it will be fair."

"How can it be fair if one person gives a whole lot and another person gives nothing?"

"That ain't fair at all—especially if I'm gonna give up everything."

"But, don't you see?" Joseph said. "We'll be sharing equally, and all of us will have what we need."

"Need? I think we need a better explanation."

He had appointed a bishop, Edward Partridge, whose ability was equaled only by his patience. The concept of consecration didn't seem to be working well in either Missouri or Kirtland—there were too many inequalities. He thought of the 'Family'—the group he'd found trying to live communally. He had settled close to them, only to find that the endeavor had deteriorated into a series of petty squabblings. Far too often, he had to act as mediator.

"But, Brother Joseph—it was my own watch, hang it all! He just helped himself to it."

"It was community property. You was wearing what belonged to everybody. Ain't that right, Brother Joseph?"

"Community property, my eyeball! You went and stole it outright. Tell him, Brother Joseph."

When a group of Saints migrated from the area of Colesville, New York, they expressed the wish to remain together in a body. He settled them on land owned by Brothers Thayre and Copley, in Thompson. It didn't take long to realize that things weren't working out.

"We gave all we had and now them folks came in without anything. And they're taking more than we ever did."

"It ain't fair. They'll eat us out of anything we have." He'd sent the group of Colesville Saints on to colonize Missouri. Dan Perry's family had gone with them.

No sooner had he dealt with one situation when another one threatened to engulf them. In late August and the beginning of September, two articles by James Gordon Bennett appeared in the *Morning Courier and New York Enquirer.*

"Why, he's made us out to be a pack of fools!"

"What're folks gonna think now?"

Such publicity, hinting that they were ludicrous and—even worse—irreligious, didn't help matters any. Neither did visitors such as Elizabeth Brighton Manning, although she was not the first to denounce them. Now here was Ezra Booth, one of his own converts, saying that Joseph was too prone to jesting.

In spite of criticism and adverse publicity, he had his task set before him: to prepare his people, and any who would join with them, for the millennium. He sent elders out to preach in the surrounding areas, and dispatched missionaries to other religious and communal groups.

The Shakers. He recalled the excitement and interest he'd felt when he first heard about them. A group very much like his own, with the desire to live communally and as simply as the first Christians.

Upon examination, he encountered fundamental differences. Although their willingness to give up everything for the greater good of the group was commendable, it led to difficulties as far as individual liberty was concerned.

They believed indeed in the millennial reign of Christ—many of their songs had to do with the millennium. But they believed that Jesus had already returned in the person of Mother Ann Lee, one of their founders. And while they believed in order and neatness, they went so far as to forbid the mingling of the sexes or marriage among their followers.

"At this rate, there'll be no Shakers left," someone had remarked.

They lived for the most part as vegetarians, the eating of meat being discouraged in their communities.

He had sent missionaries to the Shakers, with directions from the Lord: "...they desire to know the truth in part, but not all, for they are not right before me, and must needs repent."

The forbidding of marriage was condemned, since marriage was 'ordained of God unto man.' It was permissible to eat meat, since human beings had been given stewardship over all things, 'but it is not given that one man should possess that which is above another; wherefore the world lieth in sin; and woe be unto man that sheddeth blood or that wasteth flesh and hath no need.'

They were told that the Son of Man would not come in the form of a woman, nor of a man traveling on the earth, and that the second coming would not occur until the inhabitants of Zion were assembled together in the appointed place.

Point by point, the Shaker beliefs were shot down. He sent the missionaries out, and waited.

To his disappointment, very few responded. It was as if the strict order and simplicity of their lives had too great a hold on their minds. Perhaps they were afraid to break away from their communal place and try to forge a more independent life among the 'world's people.'

He had almost given up on the United Society of Believers. One of the few that he'd baptized, a man he hoped would convince other Shakers, had turned out to be more of a burden than a help.

He took a deep breath, wishing he had been more forceful with young Perry. In a few days he would ride into Kirtland, find Perry and insist he not travel to Missouri alone.

To the west, the sun was setting in a bank of cloud. As he turned, he felt a chill wind on his face. Snow before long. Dried leaves scurried ahead of him as he walked back to the house.

5

Snow was falling as Dan rode into the Shaker community of North Union. He'd decided not to wait for the church conference, but had set out immediately with provisions for the journey and the packet of letters for Elizabeth Manning.

He reined in his mare by the side of a barn-like brick building. A young man about his age stood in the wide entrance holding a pitchfork.

Dan dismounted. The young man left the pitchfork leaning against the building and strode toward him. The man's clothes looked too small for him, the pant legs shorter than they should have been, the bottom of the jacket not long enough. He had dark hair that fell untidily over his forehead, thick dark eyebrows, and a wide mouth that looked irregular, as if he had some sort of scar on his upper lip.

"Good evening to you," Dan said. "Is there a place I could stable my horse for the night?"

"Right in here. Follow me."

Dan led the mare into the large barn and the stall that the young man indicated. Dan unsaddled her. “Name’s Pinky. She was sort of pink-colored when she was little.”

The other man nodded. “As good a name as any.”

Dan looked at him. “And your name is—”

“Nathaniel.”

“Well, now—I’m Dan Perry. I’m gonna be needing a bed for the night.”

“I can take you over to the main house, soon as you’re finished here. They’ll be gathering to eat soon.”

“That’s right nice of you.” Dan put the saddle over the side of the stall. He unstrapped the saddlebags and hoisted them over his shoulder. “I’ll go with you now.”

They made their way through the swirling snow. Dan wondered if his companion were warm enough in his thin jacket. “When do you have your meetings, Nathaniel? You know—the dancing and all?”

Nathaniel looked amused, his eyebrows going up. “Tomorrow—about mid-morning. You’ll see them gathering, and the ‘world’s people’ comin’ to watch. There’ll be the gifts of song, and the dancing.”

“And do you dance too?”

“If I’ve a mind to.”

Just outside the door, Dan paused. “By the way—have you seen two women travelers? One’s older, kind of ill-natured. The other’s young, very beautiful—reddish hair, a winning smile.”

Again Nathaniel looked amused. “I’m not supposed to notice such things."

"Oh, that's right—you—"

"However, I did see two visitors that fit that description. You'll most likely find them in the room where we gather to eat."

"Thank you—you've been most helpful."

Nathaniel swung open the large pine door. "You are Mormonite, are you not?"

"Yes—you can say that. We've been called many things, and we answer to all of them. The 'Church of Christ' is what we call ourselves."

To his consternation, he could not see Hannah among the wooden tables and benches. Nathaniel shrugged. "Maybe they retired early."

They sat side by side at the long table and ate the simple meal of soup, bread and apples. Nathaniel asked some polite questions about the Mormon beliefs, but Dan's thoughts were in too much of a turmoil to concentrate on proper answers.

"Yes, we have Sunday meetings—some on other days, too. We pray and sing hymns. And sermons. Once I heard our prophet Joseph speak for two hours."

She wasn't there. Perhaps he'd never see her again. This would've been his last chance—he'd have to rely on letters to win her attention. And he wasn't that good a writer.

"If some of us, for instance, decided to join up with the Mormonites, to live with them—would they be accepted?"

Dan bit into his apple. "Of course—You'd be welcomed. 'Specially if you had a useful trade and could earn a living."

"First I worked in the barn and the shops," Nathaniel said. "But now they have me adding accounts and learning about our dealings with the world. I think in time I shall be a trustee."

"What's that?"

"I'll help manage our business transactions, and I'll travel among the world's people with two other brethren. It's a position of great trust and responsibility."

Dan smiled and gestured with the half-eaten apple. "Well, good for you. A step up, eh?"

Nathaniel didn't smile. His dark eyebrows drew together, as if he were troubled. Dan waited for him to say something else. Just then a bell rang.

"That means we have to go to the next activity," Nathaniel explained.

"Which is?"

"For me, it's visiting with the sisters, in company with others of the brethren. But first we'll find you a place for the night."

Dan spent the night in a small dormitory room for travelers, with beds lined up against the wall. The room had two other occupants—a grizzled old man and a young boy who looked to be about thirteen. Dan didn't trust strangers. He used one of his saddlebags for a pillow, with his hunting knife close at hand. He knew that the taking of life was forbidden, but defending his own was another matter.

In the morning, he began looking for Hannah. After a meal of bread and butter in the common room, he went out to give his mare some oats. Nathaniel greeted him, dressed in blue breeches and a gray coat which seemed to fit him better than his working clothes.

"Mornin', Dan. I hope you slept well."

"Just fine, thank you. A lot better than a night in the open."

"If I be not mistaken, the ladies you are seeking have just come down to breakfast."

"Have they, now?" In his eagerness, his hands trembled; some of the oats spilled. "I'll go on over there."

When Dan entered the room, he spotted them at a table on the far right, Hannah with her back to the wall. He drew in his breath, afraid that everyone in the room would hear the pounding in his chest. She was wearing a cream-colored dress with yellow-orange flowers embroidered on the front—the colors of autumn, which made her auburn hair look even more beautiful.

As he stood wondering what to do next, she looked up and saw him. Her eyes widened, her lips parting in surprise; then she smiled. They looked at each other until Hannah's aunt turned and caught sight of him. Miss Manning leaned to speak to her niece, and not being a lip-reader, Dan had to imagine the words.

What's *he* doing here?

Nevertheless, he was here, and Elizabeth Manning would have to reckon with him—that is, if she wanted her mail. Now that he'd found them, he could wait. Smiling, he strolled out the door and leaned against the side of the building.

Groups of people were congregating in front of a larger edifice, obviously the meeting house, set further back and constructed of wood instead of the usual brick. As he watched, the doors opened and people started to make their way inside. When Hannah and her aunt crossed to enter it, Dan followed them in at a discreet distance.

He was so intent on finding a seat just behind them that it took a few moments before the novelty of the interior struck him. They were in a large assembly hall with wood paneling running up to the sills of the long, high windows. Wooden beams crossed the ceiling from the long front wall to the back. He saw white walls and ceiling, and dark blue woodwork. He sat blowing on his hands to warm them, admiring the spaciousness and clean look of the room. Other people crowded in, taking their places in the chairs set out for the visitors. He noticed the rows of pegs set into two peg boards about six feet from the floor—of course, to hang the chairs on.

Just then Hannah turned sideways and caught his eye. She smiled, her red curls dancing, and after that it was all he could do to look away from her, even when the two doors opened and the company of Shakers entered from opposite sides of the room.

They wore clothes of subdued colors, blue and gray, which contrasted strangely with Hannah's brightness. He watched as they marched in separate lines, the men in one and women in the other. They formed circles, then concentric circles, then two lines, one on the extreme right, the other on the left. Dan drew in his breath, struck by their unique appearance and synchronized movements as they stepped in time to a lively melody.

Not all of them were dancing. A small group of men and women stood against the side wall. They sang and kept time with their hands. He strained to pick up the words they were singing—something about a union bell, a harp and a little trumpet.

Hannah turned, and they exchanged glances. She smiled again, and he contrived to move his chair closer to her. With the performance before him, he began to experience a mood of delight and enchantment, knowing that the whole morning was enhanced by her being there.

Nathaniel swayed in the line of men, stamping and marching in step with the rest. The others had a look of sameness about them, perhaps because of the synchronized steps and similar clothing, but Nathaniel, with his scarred lip and unruly black hair, seemed to stand out. He looked different from the young man in the stable, transformed, with a set, resolute expression on his face.

They stood still, then broke into a weaving, circling dance with their arms curved in front of them. Dan had time to notice that there were at least five black faces among the dancers, and one among the singers.

"Who will bow and bend like a willow?
Who will turn and twist and reel
In the gain of simple freedom
in the bond of union holy?
Who will drink the wine of power,
Dropping down by the hour?
Mother's wine is freely given..."

Dan remembered about Mother Ann Lee and their belief that she was Christ in his second coming. That was strange in itself, he thought, but even more curious was the notion that they could shake off sin by dancing.

> *"I'll be reeling, turning, twisting,*
> *Shake out all the starch and stiffening."*

Other dances followed, and more songs. Dan's spirits sank at the knowledge that things were coming to an end, and he would have to say good-bye to Hannah again. In his consternation, he still had time to reflect on the childlike simplicity of both the Shaker melodies and words—they were like nursery rhymes, or old folk tunes. The whole performance seemed to have a magical, dream-like quality about it—pleasant and soothing, if you didn't think too deeply. He had just decided he could never be a Shaker—the celibacy requirement alone would stagger him—when the whole company began a final, spirited march.

> *"We will all go home with you,*
> *Home to worlds of glory,*
> *Where an eternal interview*
> *Awaits the pure and holy."*

He had to smile at the 'eternal interview'—he'd felt that way about some sermons he'd sat through.

> *"Bless the soul's connecting bond,*
> *Which the Cross ensureth.*
> *We may never meet in time,*
> *But our love endureth."*

As they marched out, the women through one door and men through the opposite one, he realized he didn't have much time. With the room still echoing from the music, he fumbled in his saddlebags for a slip of paper. He took a pencil which he kept alongside his knife, and scrawled quickly on the paper. Then he folded it. He rose from his chair before the ladies could stir.

"Good morning, Hannah—Miss Manning. What a surprise to see you here."

"Hello, Daniel," Hannah replied, smiling.

Elizabeth Manning didn't smile. "And what's so surprising, I might ask? Most people come to watch the Shakers, if they're in the vicinity."

"I'm sure they do," Dan said. "Quite a spectacle, wasn't it?"

"I'd like to know what you're doing here," the aunt said. "I thought you had your own deluded form of worship on Sunday."

He wasn't sure how to answer. "Well—I live nearby. Kirtland isn't that far away. And one of the first things our leaders did was to send missionaries to the Shaker communities."

"The blind leading the blind."

"Oh, Aunt Elizabeth." Hannah managed to smile even as she sighed.

Dan decided to ignore any insults as much as possible. "I'm on my way to Missouri. I'm aimin' to join up with my parents for the winter, and to give them what help I can—also, to build me a little homestead out there."

"Who'd want to go out on the edge of nowhere?" Elizabeth

Manning said. "Why, that's the end of civilization!"

"Oh, no," he assured them. "It's our place of refuge, where the New Jerusalem will stand."

Elizabeth Manning shook her head and compressed her mouth into a thin smile. "Such superstition. Mr. Perry, you look more intelligent than that. But then, so does your so-called prophet. Looks are deceiving."

"Sometimes they are," Dan said. Hannah glanced at him with an apologetic smile.

Elizabeth Manning stood up. "Now, if you'll excuse us—Come, Hannah."

"Miss Manning, I have some mail for you," Dan said quickly. She looked at him. He tried to prolong the moment, now that he had her attention. He explained how he had carried it from Kirtland in the hope that they would soon reach North Union.

"Indeed," the aunt said. "Well—where is it?"

He slowly unfastened the saddlebag and drew out the bundle of mail tied with a ribbon. He handed it to her with a flourish. At the same time he pushed the folded paper into Hannah's hand. Hannah's fingers tightened on it; she drew it behind her.

To his surprise, Elizabeth Manning now thanked him. "Well, that's very nice of you, young man—I appreciate it." She was looking at the envelopes. "Yes—this one's from my editor, and this—from my brother. I knew I should've stayed longer in Kirtland Mills."

"I'm sure you'd be welcome there if you cared to return." Out of the corner of his eye he saw Hannah smooth out the paper and glance at it.

“It’s out of the question,” Elizabeth Manning said. “I can do nothing among the Mormonites except to observe them and report what I see. Unfortunately everything I see is superstition and ignorance—a vast delusion.”

“Some of our people may be as you describe. But for the most part, we’re sober and industrious—the very ones to build a community based on Christian teachings.” Dan looked at Elizabeth, but his mind was on the note he’d slipped to Hannah.

Meet me—horse barn—2 PM

“That doesn’t make you any less deluded.” Elizabeth Manning’s voice sounded less stern, a bit chiding. “Following a man who claims to have direct revelation from God.”

Dan made no reply. As the women turned to leave, Hannah gave him a quick. fleeting smile.

He lived with the memory of that smile until the early afternoon. At twenty minutes of two he entered the horse barn. He brushed and patted the mare, torn between the fear that Hannah would mistake the cow barn for the horse barn, and the anxiety that her aunt would get wind of things and forbid her to see him. Or worse, that auntie would turn up as well. His mouth dry, he whispered a prayer. If Hannah came alone, there’d be time to tell her what he wanted to say. Then another fear struck him—perhaps she would just laugh at him and leave for good.

A shadow appeared at the door. Hannah stood, looking uncertain. All thoughts of organized speech left his mind.

“So there you are.” She stepped toward him, and her shoes sank into the straw. Wisps of straw clung to the hem of her dress. “I wasn’t sure—”

“Thank you for coming to meet me.” He hoped this was a good beginning. “It’s such a joy to see you again.”

“It’s nice to see you, too. I was afraid I’d be late—I had to wait till my aunt took her afternoon nap. First she had to read all her mail, and then she re-read it. But finally she fell asleep.”

“And shc thinks you’rc napping too?”

“I had to sneak out.”

Dan swallowed. “I appreciate your effort all the more. Hannah—”

“What did you think of the singing and dancing?”

“Quite a spectacle.”

“I liked it when that one young woman was singing alone—how she swayed in rhythm and lifted up her hands. It was like a prayer.”

“Yes—the meetings are very interesting. So are their beliefs. The thing that disturbs me the most is the forbidding of marriage. Why, marriage is ordained of God—it’s a sacrament.”

She nodded and drew her cloak close around her shoulders. “I’ve heard all the rumors about them—how, instead of marriage, they practice all sorts of unspeakable things. But I don’t believe it.”

“They’ve been a persecuted people—much like my own. Public opinion has been hard against them.”

She smiled. “And has it been so hard against you?”

This was not what he had planned to talk about. Nevertheless, he tried to answer. “Yes, we’ve endured hardship and persecution, and I daresay we'll see more. We've traveled to Ohio thinking to escape the troubles in New York State. Our prophet Joseph has been jailed at least twice, and our meetings have been disrupted. But when we finally get to our promised land, maybe we'll be safe."

She nodded, as if she understood some of it. He said quickly, "Hannah—there's not much time, and in spite of what I said about trials, I feel I must speak to you. You see—that is, I love you, and if you would only say I had a chance of marryin' you, I'd be the happiest man alive."

She opened her mouth to speak, but he went on. "See, if these were normal times, I could come courtin' you, and bring you gifts and such like. But I'm on my way to Missouri with plans to claim an inheritance, and once I get a house built, I'd be pleased if I could send for you. More than that, I'd come back and fetch you myself."

She said, "Well—that is, I feel honored, Daniel, that you should ask such a thing. But I'm not a member of your faith."

He gestured—he still held the brush he'd used for the horse.
"That doesn't matter—not to me. It says in the New Testament: 'The unbelieving wife is sanctified by the believing husband.'"

"But I'm not exactly unbelieving. I was baptized when I was a baby."

He smiled. "Before you reached the age of reason and could decide for yourself. Like I said, it doesn't matter to me, if you're content."

"But I'm not content. I'm searching for truth in religion like most other folks. And I think my aunt's view of things is very rigid."

"Well—that's a splendid start. So—what's your answer? Will you wait till I get established, and let me come back for you?"

"Sometimes I think I'd do anything to get away from my aunt."

"Then come with me now! We'll ride back to Kirtland and be married there. Then we'll go to Missouri together." He spoke with passion, but at the same time he wondered how to get both of them to Missouri on his meager resources.

"Dan, wait. I want to be so sure it's right. I—I do like you—don't think otherwise. But if I married you, I'd want to be of your faith. I think I should go home and think about it, and pray for guidance."

He considered a moment, then nodded. "I guess that's best. I know the truth will be shown to you, if you ask with real intent—that's the promise. May I write to you? And you'll write to me?"

"Of course. And I'd read the Book of Mormon, but my aunt took it away."

"I'll get you another. In fact, I'll give you my own. Don't tell her you have it." He hauled it out of the saddlebag.

"Don't worry. I'll keep it safe. I'd better go now, before she wakes up and misses me."

"Wait." He put both arms around her and drew her close to him. She made no resistance as he kissed her. Her lips were softer than he'd imagined, and they tasted of apples and honey. "Don't forget that I love you."

Then she was kissing him back; he felt her arms going around his neck. She whispered, "I think I love you too."

The feeling of her nestling against him gave him new courage. He thought of begging her to come with him again, but the voice of reason prevailed. He summoned his discipline as an ordained minister. "Let's have a prayer together, and then we'll say good-bye."

She agreed. He held her hand and prayed aloud that the spirit of truth would guide her in her search for the church of Christ, that she would be protected and comforted by that same spirit. He then entrusted her to the care of Almighty God, "until we do meet again."

They stood together in silence. The mare stamped her foot and gave a low whinny.

"Good-bye, Daniel."

"Good-bye, my own dear. God go with you."

He watched as she turned away. He wanted to treasure up every gesture, every look. She pulled up the hood of her cloak, covering her lovely hair. One last smile, and she was gone.

He stood trembling, marveling at all that had happened. He saddled the mare and hoisted up the saddlebags. As he was putting the bridle on her, Nathaniel appeared from an adjoining stall. Nathaniel's face looked redder than usual; he was breathing fast. Hard-working fellow, Dan thought.

"Leaving?"

"That's right. Thanks for all your help." Dan led the mare out into the sunlight.

"Good luck out in Missouri," Nathaniel said.

"Thanks." Dan gathered the reins and swung up into the saddle. He tried to remember when he'd told Nathaniel about Missouri.

"Say, Dan?"

“What?” Dan turned to look at him.

“Oh, nothing. Never mind. God speed.”

Dan rode away thinking that perhaps she was watching him from some window or doorway. He took the road to the southwest. His mind still reeled with the events of the day. With any luck, she would be his wife. The hope of winning her, of being united with her again, filled him with overwhelming joy, and the music of the Shaker song danced in his memory.

‘We may never meet in time,
But our love endureth.’

6

Nathaniel knew he didn't belong in the horse barn that afternoon. Like the other Believers, he was expected to spend the Sabbath in his room or close to it, meditating and praying. But he'd gone out there on the pretext of checking on the animals.

He'd had no intention of eavesdropping on Dan and Hannah. Caught unawares by their meeting, he found himself trapped in the adjoining stall, unable to move without their detecting him. As he stood wondering what to do, he'd heard every word.

He wasn't sure at what point he realized that his elders and teachers had lied to him. He'd known for some time that he wanted to leave the community, but he'd ascribed it to some moral failing in himself. Now he knew otherwise.

Maybe it was the ease with which the young couple addressed each other, as if it were the most natural thing in the world. Shaker brothers and sisters were forbidden to speak to each other without the permission of the elders, unless a third party was present. Or perhaps it was when Dan said, "Marriage is a sacrament." When he heard the words, spoken with such assurance, Nathaniel knew they were true.

If that was the case, then maybe other statements of the Mormonite elders were true. Nathaniel remembered the three missionaries who'd visited them last March, and the stormy debate which had resulted in the Mormonites being expelled from the community. He'd memorized their names—Parley Pratt and Sidney Rigdon. The other was a Shaker defector—Lemon Copley. Nathaniel even recalled the issues under discussion—marriage and the nature of the messiahship.

He'd been told that the Believers were the only ones who could have a pure relationship with God, or with each other. Yet here was young Dan, professing his affections with such sincere tenderness that the very air trembled with it. But what really shook him to the core was the prayer, uttered aloud. Vocal prayer had no place in Shaker tradition. Hearing such a thing for the first time, he felt as if a fire had been kindled in his soul.

He would go to Kirtland for further instruction—to Joseph Smith himself, if need be. He emerged from the stall. He was breathing hard, his face soaked with perspiration. He'd wanted to ask Dan how to find the Mormonite leader. But he hesitated, fearful of being overheard. While he was ready to leave the community, he needed a bit more time. The one he wanted to take with him was not as ready as he.

He busied himself about the horse barn. He checked the bridles and the other gear, and saw that the animals had food. Being careful not to do any major task, forbidden on the Sabbath day, he nevertheless managed to straighten and tidy things in the orderly way he'd been taught.

As he worked, his mind went back to the time when he was nine years old and had a real mother and father. 'Nat,' they'd called him; his father had rumpled his hair and his mother had pressed him close to her. He remembered how she'd smelled of violets and crushed ferns.

He didn't like to remember how he'd returned home from checking his traps in the woods, only to find their cabin in ruins, his parents and baby sister burned to death. Even his pet dog had disappeared.

"Iroquois, most likely," the nearest neighbor said. "They got all your stock, too."

They brought him to North Union, to be educated by the Shakers and taught a trade. Here he was no longer Nat, but Nathaniel, since nicknames were not allowed among the Believers. He tried to adapt to all the new rules, but he kept forgetting. After several severe reprimands, he learned not to call attention to himself. In time they came to regard him as a proper member of the community. But if it were not for Amanda, he didn't think he could have borne it.

Amanda had arrived at the same time, orphaned by typhoid fever. He'd regarded her with fascination as they grew up; he attended school with the boys in the winter months, while she had her schooling with the other girls in the summer. It was only when their education ended and they were considered mature enough to be adult

Shakers, she at fourteen and he at sixteen, that he knew he loved her.

He was glad now that he had not made a great effort to associate with her—the elders would've taken pains to separate them. Instead, just recently they had assigned her as the one to make up his bed in the morning and care for his clothes, which included mending them and seeing that he had new ones when he needed them. As one in training to be a trustee, he had greater freedom to move about and converse with people than most members of the society. Still, it was best to be careful.

He knew that they were free to leave the community if they wished. But if his feelings were suspected, he would be 'labored with' and told that once he went to the 'world's people,' he could never be saved. He believed that he could withstand such treatment, but he feared for Amanda; she was so delicate and frail-looking.

As he started for the door, his eye fell on the admonition posted on the wall of the barn:

'A man of kindness, to his beast is kind,
Brutal actions show a brutal mind.
...God's omniscient eye
Beholds thy cruelty. He hears his cry.
He was destined thy servant and thy drudge,
But know this: his creator is thy judge.'

One of the community rules stated that it was forbidden to give an animal the same proper name as one would give a person. Another forbade any Believer to play with a cat or a dog. Nathaniel tried to comply, but the barn kittens were so playful. Sometimes when no one was looking, he tossed straws and watched as the kittens pounced.

Time for the evening meal. He made sure the barn was secure, then retired to his room for the required interval before meal time. He marched to the dining hall with the others, then knelt—always with the right knee first—in silent grace. He ate in silence the meal of johnnycake with tiny pieces of meat, and milk porridge. When he'd brought Dan in to eat the night before, he had not bothered with the kneeling since he'd been working late, and Dan was a guest. A trustee could get away with all sorts of things.

When the first bell rang in the morning, he threw back the covers. He knelt in silent prayer with his three roommates. Within fifteen minutes they'd put on their working clothes and stripped the sheets and blankets from their cots. Nathaniel laid his bedclothes neatly over the pillows on two chairs at the foot of his bed. Then he left for his chores just as the sisters were entering to make the beds and put the room in order.

Nathaniel had to marvel at how much work they did before breakfast. When the breakfast bell finally sounded, the chamber work had been finished, fires started in the dwelling rooms and shops, the animals fed, cows milked, and arrangements completed for the day's industry. As he tramped from the horse barn over to the cow barn, his gaze fell on the fields, blanketed now by snow, where they grew rye, oats, barley, corn, flax, turnips, and potatoes. Further on stood the precious orchards which produced apples, pears, cherries, peaches, plums and quinces.

He went into the cow barn which housed the milch cows, the working oxen, the young cattle, hogs and some of the sheep. Just as he'd expected, Amanda sat in the last stall milking the one-horned cow.

"Thee came alone," he observed.

She shook her head and smiled. "Nay. Sister Mary Ann is with me."

"Oh. So I see."

The aforementioned sister, a little, scrawny woman, was pouring a saucer of milk for the cats who were lined up waiting. Nathaniel counted six of them, and two half-grown kittens.

"I've been meaning to speak to thee." Amanda wiped her forehead and pushed her white bonnet back. Under it, her hair was the color of dried pine needles.

"And I with thee."

"Brother Nathaniel, thee has need of new clothes. Thee has grown tall, and I must make some for thee."

He looked closely at her. "That would please me."

She brushed a stray wisp of hair back from her forehead. "'Tis not about pleasing thee. 'Tis out of necessity that I do speak. Now, what have thee to say to me?"

"Sister Mary Ann," he said. "I see we have need of another milking pail. Will thee be good enough to go up to the kitchen and fetch one?"

"But—" Mary Ann glanced at him, then looked over at Amanda.

"Don't worry," Nathaniel said. "I'll be here to look after our young sister."

Mary Ann left, wiping her hands on her apron. Nathaniel smiled at Amanda and moved close to where she sat. He knelt beside her the way they did before and after meals. But his thoughts had nothing to do with food.

"Dear sister." His eyes sought hers. "Thee knows it has been three weeks since I first spoke to thee and told thee my feelings. Thee has had plenty of time for reflection. I had looked for some word, some sign that I didn't hope in vain. And now I'm more sure than ever that I must leave and go to the world's people. My way lies there; I know it. It's as if I'm being called to go to them—to one group in particular."

"I have thought." She kept her eyes on the milk pail.

"And what does thee think?"

She turned to face him. "If we left, where would we go?"

"There's a place east of here—Kirtland. We can be married there, and I know of people who will help us."

"The world's people?"

"They're called 'The Church of Christ.'"

"Mormonites?" She drew in her breath, and her eyes widened.

He said, "I trust them. There's a man named Parley Pratt, and another—Sidney Rigdon—"

"But how will we live?"

"We'll do what the world's people do. Does thee know how many trades I've learned? Look at me. Thee sees a joiner, cooper, wagon maker, mason, and carpenter, not to mention a caretaker of animals. Also a trustee—I could work doing accounts for any farm or business."

Her mouth formed a smile, but her upper lip trembled. "I'm ready to go with thee, then."

He clasped her hand, an act strictly forbidden. "Thee will not be sorry. There may not be much time—we may have to leave quickly, once our intentions are known."

"Oh, dear brother—I hope that what we do is right."

"I've become convinced just recently that marriage between man and woman is a sacrament—something that pleases God. In fact, I know now that it's a gift from him."

"Thee does talk strangely. But thee was always quicker and more clever than most of us."

"Thinks thee so?"

Just as he put her hand to his lips, Sister Mary Ann appeared with the extra pail. Mary Ann gave a little cry and thrust her hands to her face. The pail clattered at her feet.

It took all of Nathaniel's ingenuity to maintain control. "Pick up the pail, Sister. Thee needn't throw it."

"This is how thee takes care of our young sister?"

"I intend to take even better care of her in the future," he replied. At the same time his mind was racing; trustee or not, he'd made a serious mistake.

Mary Ann backed away and stared at him. "I think Brother Issachar should be told immediately."

"Stay, sister." Nathaniel moved to block her leaving the stall. "I could say thee did not see what thee claimed."

Mary Ann gasped. "It would be a lie!"

"Then I shall tell him the truth. I shall tell him that thee feeds the cats precious milk every morning—milk that could be sold to the world's people. And by doing this, thee keeps the little beasts from their work of catching vermin."

Mary Ann had turned white. "I—I will say nothing."

"Good. Give us at least a week. Then thee can tell the elders and eldresses anything thee chooses." He looked at Amanda. "Good-bye, dear sister. I'll see thee in a while."

That evening, instead of a singing meeting where the songs were practiced, they had what was known as a 'quick meeting' or 'Shaker high.' When they had all assembled, Elder Issachar stepped forward and looked around at them. Nathaniel had the uneasy feeling that the gaze was particularly directed at him. Issachar began by remarking that every good Believer was known by the variety of his or her gifts. Then he stamped his feet and shouted, "Shake off the flesh!"

Immediately those around Nathaniel were stamping and trembling. Issachar shouted, "Sweep out the devil! Sweep out every carnal desire!"

With imaginary brooms the company swept and stamped. The brothers shouted, the sisters exclaimed in softer tones. One sister's voice rose in a high babble as she exercised the gift of tongues. Others joined her.

Suddenly there was a shout from the rear. "The gift! The turning gift!"

Nathaniel strained to see. The ranks parted, and to his dismay, Amanda rushed forward. She turned on her toes, whirling, her hands curving as she twirled, always with the right hand higher than the left as dictated by their rules. He tried not to show his concern as he watched, but inwardly he wondered at her calling such attention to herself just at that time, in light of their intentions.

At first he thought she was simply pretending, play-acting. Then he noticed the unnatural, set expression on her face, as if she were possessed—her eyes blank, staring, her mouth contorted, the corners of her lips twitching a little. She spun faster and faster while the others shouted around her. Then she sank to the floor in a heap. Nathaniel felt something sinking in his own chest. Amanda lay on her side with her legs drawn up to her chest. Her body gave a series of convulsive jerks. Why now, he wondered? Had something gone wrong?

He felt piercing eyes on him. Mary Ann stood staring at him, her face pale and strained, her eyes narrowed in anguish. He knew that they were supposed to confess any sins before they participated in the meetings, especially the sin of touching someone of the opposite sex. Now he realized that Mary Ann could not keep silent much longer. He'd put too great a burden on her. He had to act quickly. He knew a wagon-load of butter and fresh milk was due to leave in two days. He would be on that wagon in the clothes he stood up in, and so would

Amanda, disguised under a cloak of burlap.

He couldn't sleep for thinking of it. He went over every last detail in his mind. Meticulous and orderly as his training had been, he could not imagine anything he'd forgotten. He moved through chores and duties like one in a trance, acting automatically. He deviated from his routine only to check on Amanda at the milking.

"Tomorrow morning, after breakfast," he told her. "Be in the horse barn. I'll have a cloak for thee."

She looked exhausted, pale after last night's exertion. Her eyes did not meet his. "I will do as thee says, dear brother."

"And soon I will be more than your brother."

To his satisfaction, everything went like clock-work, indeed as if some higher Power were in control. Rising with the bell, he did his morning chores. As he worked, he thought how he had served the community to the best of his ability during his few years of adulthood. He readied the wagon and harnessed the team of horses, then spoke briefly to Brother Jan, the driver.

"There'll be a third person with us. Leave the double doors open."

"As thee wishes."

His heart was doing funny things in his chest as the appointed time drew near. His mouth felt dry; the seconds passed. The lead horse stamped his foot on the ground. A slight figure appeared from the shadows of the barn. Nathaniel threw the improvised cloak over her and helped her onto the wagon seat. He took his place in the middle. Brother Jan looked startled, but didn't question his authority.

They left the settlement. Nathaniel thought he saw Elder Issachar walk out of the main building and look around. Nathaniel smiled to himself. Too late now.

Later, after he'd told Jan their plans, he held Amanda in his arms and tried to reassure her. "See behind us, dear, to the west? No clouds at all. No trouble traveling today."

It meant that Dan, already far to the west, would have clear roads for his journey.

Amanda said very little; she trembled, as if she sat in a chill wind. He took off his coat and put it around her, but still she shivered. For his own part, he felt warm, a bit feverish. When he finally got up enough courage to kiss her, her lips were as cold as Lake Erie.

****

"Is that all?" Joseph asked. He glanced over at Sidney Rigdon who sat at their host's writing desk. They both looked at Brother Owen Crawford, who'd ridden in from Kirtland with a message from the new bishop.

"There's one other thing." Brother Crawford stood clawing nervously at his beard with one hand. He ran the other through his shock of graying hair.

"What is it?" Joseph asked. "Take your time. Sit down, if you like." He felt both touched and amused by the man's nervousness. Everyone knew that Owen Crawford was an excellent farmer, with a good-sized farm west of Kirtland; there was no reason he should be ill-at-ease in the presence of his prophet.

With the defection of Ezra Booth, both Joseph and Sidney were endeavoring to spend more time with the ordinary people, talking with them and listening to their concerns. In fact, their current preaching series, in the towns around Kirtland, was an effort to repair the damage done by Booth's public apostasy.

Brother Crawford drew a deep breath and began. "Well, sir—what do you know about the Shakers?"

Sidney snorted, and Joseph gave a little laugh. "The Shaking Quakers? The United Society? More than I care to know."

Sidney said, "I think they're some of the strangest people we've ever met. We went on a mission to the nearest settlement, you know—the one near Cleveland."

"That's right," Joseph said. "Last March. According to Parley Pratt, they utterly refused to hear or obey the gospel."

"Well," Crawford said. "Something rather strange has happened."

Joseph said, "If it has to do with the Shakers, I'm not surprised."

Crawford nodded. "Well—about a month ago, this young couple showed up at my door. They was wearing Shaker clothes, and she had some sort of burlap cloak. She was a pretty little thing, but she didn't look well. She kept trembling, even though we had a good, hot fire."

"Sounds like she was ill," Joseph remarked. "Go on."

"The young man did most of the talking. He said he was looking for someone to marry them. He mentioned both of you by name, and Brother Pratt, which I found a bit surprising. He seemed to know a lot more than I would've figured."

"So, did you marry them?"

"I fed 'em first, and got 'em comfortable. I stepped into the next room to get my Bible. Just as I started back, I heard this outburst from her. She was saying how everything was all wrong: the food was too rich, the colors—get this—the colors were not right, and she didn't want to be married. He began to plead with her—he said he'd build her a house with everything painted in Shaker colors—the bed green, the floors reddish-yellow with the proper rugs and so forth. She said she didn't want to be his wife, that carnal desire was wrong and she couldn't bear for him to touch her. He was almost crying then, the poor young fellow—he said that if she married him, he'd never lay a hand on her, but they would live as brother and sister, and he'd take care of her.

"Well, at that point, I wasn't about to marry them, so I said it'd wait till morning. Then I put 'em to bed in separate parts of the house. I talked to him some, before he went to bed. I said it was better not to marry her, if she felt that way.

"Well, the next morning, soon as she was up, she began talking about going back to the Shaker community. He begged and cajoled—I never heard anyone take on so. He swore up and down how he loved her, and how he'd do anything for her. He didn't even care that I was listening.

"Finally I asked if I could talk with her in private. He agreed and stepped outside. I tried to get her to say how she really felt, which wasn't hard. She felt desperately lost, like a fish out of water. All she knew were Shaker ways, and all she wanted was to go back and be with them again. Did she care for young Nathaniel? She did, but she felt she wasn't strong enough to do as he wished."

Joseph frowned. "They even have a song—'like branches in the bloom, or like a fragrant flower.' It has to do with their own fragility."

Sidney looked at him. "Since when do you know Shaker songs?"

"Oh—Emma knows several. She picks up all kinds of songs."

Sidney said, "So what happened with—Nathaniel, you say his name was?"

"Well, I went outside and talked with him privately. I said they could have as much time as they liked—they could stay the winter with me, if they wanted. But if she still felt as she did, the kindest thing would be to take her back to the Shakers.

"So they tarried with me a few days. Nathaniel helped around the barn and such—more than earned his keep. Then she began having hallucinations and strange falling fits—visions about being lost forever. Damned, if you will. We tried to reason with her, but it was like talking to a wall. Finally Nathaniel said he'd take her back. I offered to go with them, but he said no; he'd brought her out, and he'd see that she got safely back."

"So they left," Joseph said.

"I even lent them a horse."

Joseph smiled. "I hope it wasn't your best horse."

"Wait till you hear. He came back."

"No," Joseph said.

"He did. Alone. I was as amazed as anybody. He brought the horse back, thanked me, and asked if he could work for me over the winter."

"I'll be busted," Sidney said.

"He's quite a worker, too. Not much to look at. He's got this kind of scar on his mouth—says a mule kicked him when the Shakers first took him in."

"So, wait a minute," Sidney said. "He just took her back—like that?"

Crawford scratched his beard and shrugged. "I guess he knew what to do. He was kind of subdued-like, when he first came back. He said he felt the way he did when he'd lost his first family."

"He's still with you?" Joseph asked.

"Like I was saying, he can do twice as much work before breakfast as any man I ever saw. And so handy—that place has never been in better repair."

"I'd like to meet him," Joseph said.

"I'm sure you'll have a chance. He's been readin' the Book of Mormon—he says the Shakers taught him to read, but he was never allowed to read anything about philosophy or religion. And—what else can I say? He seems to take pleasure in the simplest things. Like rompin' with the animals—he's out there throwing sticks for the dogs most every morning. And when I left, he was just carving a little flute out of willow wood. Says the Shakers only had imaginary instruments, but he was going to have a real one and teach himself to play it. Knowing him, I believe he will."

"You think he'll actually become one of us?" Sidney asked.

"Well, I wondered about that," Crawford said. "I studied about how to teach him. But he absorbed more in one afternoon than most folks do in a whole week of sermons. I wouldn't be surprised if he asked for baptism at our next meeting."

"Will wonders never cease?" Sidney asked.

Joseph said, "I hope he recovers from this disastrous experience with the Shaker girl."

"Well, like he says—she was the only one he wanted. He doesn't figure he'll ever get married now."

"Not for a while," Sidney said. "But I know some young ladies around Kirtland who might change his mind."

"To be sure," Joseph remarked. "Just give him time. Why, every time I see a pretty woman, I have to pray for grace."

All three laughed. Then Brother Crawford took his leave, and Joseph and Sidney resumed work on that evening's preaching service.

7

Nathaniel Givens gave his name for baptism at the end of February. Brother Crawford had just heard about a marvelous vision shared by Joseph Smith and Sidney Rigdon in Hiram, in which the three glories, or degrees of the afterlife, were opened to their view. Brother Crawford tried to explain it to him, and quoted first the passage in First Corinthians:

"'There is one glory of the sun, and another glory of the moon, and another glory of the stars; for one star differeth from another star in glory. So also is the resurrection of the dead.'"

Nathaniel thought that sounded a lot better than eternal bliss if you were a Shaker, and damnation if you were not.

He was baptized with a company of others in Kirtland. A week later he was called to the priesthood and ordained to the office of deacon.

As he walked in the fields and worked around the farm, he felt a quiet peace, a sense of completion and oneness he had never known.

It was as if the elements in his being, the spiritual and physical, were no longer at war, but reconciled and directed toward some higher goal. For him, the fields became graced by the presence of God, the woods of towering oak and pine a cathedral. At certain moments he thought of Amanda, and the greater life she'd been unable to receive. He wondered if there were something more he could've done for her.

He prayed that she would be safe and sheltered from harm, that she would no longer be afraid. Then he closed the door on that chapter of his life. He began to feel an overwhelming desire to consecrate his gifts, to use them in some supreme effort as an expression of his love for God.

He had no money, nor did he have the gifts of oratory or exhortation or expounding, the way others had. He had only the skills of a builder—wagon-maker, mason, worker in wood. He knew most every kind of wood—oak, maple, poplar, pine, birch—and how it should be worked and cared for. What kind of gifts were these, and how could they be used for the glory of God?

He began doing repair work and odd jobs for people around town. One afternoon he went into a public house to meet with a man who wanted to hire him. While he waited, he listened to the voices around him.

"Why, land's sakes, everyone knows there's gonna be trouble about that Law of Consecration business."

"Folks is gettin' good and mad. It just ain't fair, is what it is."

"Some are sayin' it's just a trick to git their property. One of them Johnson boys, he thinks Smith is out to git that house away from his parents."

"That place in Hiram?"

"Yeah—where they been stayin'. It's a nice house. Why, Eli Johnson—he even says Smith has been makin' eyes at his younger sister."

"If that don't beat all."

"Trouble's gonna come of it. You wait and see. Eli ain't one to take it lyin' down. You can bet he's got a bunch of others all stirred up, too."

Nathaniel transacted his business and hurried back to the farm, deeply troubled. No one had ever talked that way in the Shaker community.

"I wouldn't worry none," Crawford assured him. "Folks talk all the time against the church leaders—some ain't happy no matter what they do. It's all talk. They won't do a thing."

"But—some years ago, they set fire to Union Village. These were outsiders, and it started with talk—they hated the Shakers. They burned the buildings, destroyed the crops—the other Believers had to share with them so they could survive the winter."

"Well, that was then. I don't think anything like that's gonna happen now."

****

Measles. The twins had fallen sick, first one, then the other. Both parents, near exhaustion, had soothed the babies through a series of sleepless nights. Concerned as he was for the children, Joseph worried about Emma. He knew how hard she worked. Her life seemed more harsh than he would've wished for her—the succession of lost babies, and now these two ill.

He sat near the dying fire with the sickest twin in his arms—the boy Joseph. He'd sent Emma off to bed in the next room for a few hours rest. Beside her, Julia slept at last.

After a while the boy slipped into a fitful sleep, and he heard Emma's voice telling him to lie down on the trundle bed. He carried the child to the bed. Grateful for the silence, he lay down beside the boy and fell asleep.

He woke to lights and noise. Emma screaming "Murder!" Both children crying. Joseph felt hands in his hair, hands on his clothes and limbs. A mob of men carried him out the door.

The rush of cold air hit him. Terrified, he struggled. He got one leg free and kicked at the nearest man. There was the sound of a body falling heavily on the outside steps. Then someone else rushed in and grabbed his leg.

"By God, we'll kill you if you don't hold still!"

They carried him around the corner of the house. The one who'd been kicked thrust a blood-soaked hand into Joseph's face.

"God damn ye, I'll fix ye!"

Joseph knew then his kick had struck home. He felt fingers tightening around his throat. Unable to throw them off, he blacked out.

When he regained consciousness, they'd borne him a good

distance from the house. Someone had fashioned a lantern out of a gallon can, and the flickering light cast a strange glow on their faces. Then he saw Sidney Rigdon being dragged by the heels. Joseph thought he was dead; he was too old to survive such treatment.

Joseph tried to speak. “You’ll have mercy and spare my life, I hope.”

One of them swore at him, and two others tried to answer at the same time. “Call on yer God fer help!” “We’ll show ye no mercy!”

Men appeared from every direction. One ran from the orchard with a plank. Joseph knew now they intended to kill him and carry him off on the plank. They turned and took him into the meadow, away from where he’d seen the body of Sidney Rigdon.

“Simonds,” one of them said. “Pull up his drawers; he’ll take cold.”

“Ain’t ya gonna kill ’em?”

“Yeah. When do we kill ’em?”

A group of them gathered a few yards away. Someone shouted, “Simonds! Simonds, come here!”

“Don’t let him touch the ground.” Simonds went to join them. “He’ll get a spring on you.”

They waited while the group conferred. Joseph assumed they were debating whether to kill him or not. When they returned, he caught hints of their intentions.

“Pound and scratch ’em good!”

“Tear off his shirt! Now his drawers!”

“Simonds! Simonds, where’s the tar bucket?”

"I don't know where 'tis. Eli's left it."

They brought the bucket of tar. Someone yelled with an oath, "Let's tar up his mouth!"

He saw the tar-paddle coming at his mouth. He twisted his head away.

"Damn ye!" one of them shouted. "Hold up yer head and let us give ye some tar!"

He felt the sticky tar going over him. They held his head, and someone tried to force a vial into his mouth. He felt it break in his teeth.

"Get the feathers! Where's the pillow?"

Then someone was clawing him with his nails like a mad cat. "God damn ye, that's the way the Holy Ghost falls on folks!"

With shouts and oaths they disappeared into the night. Joseph tried to get up and fell back again. He pulled the tar away from his nose and mouth so he could breathe freely. He struggled to his feet. Two lights twinkled far off. He made for one, and found it was the Johnson house.

He knocked at the door. Emma saw him first, and fainted. He realized then that the tar made him look as if he were covered with blood. He called for a blanket.

Brother Poorman ran up as he stood waiting. "I'm afraid I've killed him!"

They threw Joseph a blanket; he wrapped it around himself and stepped inside.

"Killed who?" someone asked. During the attack, most of the

sisters in the neighborhood had crowded into the Johnson house.

"Poor Father Johnson," Poorman replied.

Barricaded in his house by the mobbers, Father Johnson had threatened to blast a hole in the door with his shotgun. At that, the mob had fled. The old man had seized a club and chased after the men who had Sidney Rigdon. He managed to wallop one of them. He was about to hit another when the mobbers left Rigdon and turned on him. They chased him back toward his house, where he met Brother Poorman coming out of the cornfield. In the dark, each thought the other was one of the mobbers. Poorman felled Johnson with a severe blow on the left shoulder.

Father Johnson soon appeared at the house. He quickly resolved the misunderstanding with Brother Poorman.

Joseph's friends spent the night scraping and removing the tar from him. By morning he was able to get into his clothes and preach the usual Sunday sermon to the local congregation, his face scarred and bruised. The mobbers even attended the service, to see if he would speak. He not only preached, but baptized three people that afternoon.

Joseph spoke with a slight sibilant lisp afterward, due to his broken tooth. Sidney Rigdon, delirious for days from having his head dragged over the frozen ground, fled to Kirtland, then out to Chardon, to get away from the mob. The mobbers, an inter-denominational group headed by Simonds Ryder, a Campbellite preacher, continued to harass the Johnson household.

The icy blast of air proved to be too much for the little twin

Joseph, who caught a severe cold on top of the measles and died the following Friday.

****

It wasn't long before everyone in Kirtland knew what had happened. Nathaniel, repairing the roof of the public house, heard other details.

"They say ol' Rigdon didn't put up any fuss at all. But Joseph—why, he kicked and fought like a wild man."

"I heard tell they had Dr. Dennison waitin' to castrate 'em. But the doc refused. He told 'em all to go home and take their whiskey with 'em."

"So the doc wouldn't do it?"

"Y'know what else I heard? Ol' Joe was afraid to show his face in Kirtland. Yes, sir. He and a bunch of 'em started for Missouri, and they went way around by way of Warren, so they wouldn't have to come through here."

"Who can blame 'em? One taste of tar lasts a long time."

Nathaniel turned away, sick at heart. All he wanted was to meet the prophet, and now he'd probably never get the chance.

"Sure you will," Crawford told him. "Things'll settle down. Those boys'll find something else to do. You'll see."

8

Independence
May 1832

My dearest Hannah,

I do not Know if you have received my earlier letters. It may be that they never reached you, for I have yet to hear from you. I hope that you are Well.

In my first Letter I told you about arriving just before Christmas, and finding my mother and Father living with seventeen other People in one tiny log house! I made the twentieth person, and went to work with a Will. We had the frozen ground for a floor, and our food was mostly Corn bread and beef. But our prayer meetings were full of hope, and the Lord blessed us with an outpouring of his Spirit. Even little children Prayed and prophesied.

We are working to build more log homes and have cleared land and planted crops. But things are harder than I thought they would be—all our Supplies must be brought in from a distance, so we are used to making do without a lot of Things we once thought were necessary. There is talk of some mills being built, and a store, and soon we will have a newspaper from our own Press—W. W. Phelps & Co. The first issue of the "Evening and Morning Star" should come out in a few Weeks.

We do have schools whenever and anywhere we can. For the most part I work in the Fields, but just last week I sat on a log and taught a bunch of children, all lined up on a log facing me!

Last month we Rejoiced to see our prophet Joseph Smith once again. He traveled to Missouri with some of the other Leaders, and they had a conference in which he was presented to us as the President of the High Priesthood. In terms that you can understand, it simply Means that he is the Presiding officer, or "church president."

There is a rough element out here, men who do not seen to be happy unless they are either fighting or have the prospect of a good Brawl ahead of them. They do not like us "mormons" much, and we try to keep out of their way. Maybe in Time they will come to appreciate our civilizing influence.

It may be some months before I can get a cabin Built and land cleared for us. Right now I am working to help my parents, and others in Need. I ask that you wait for me—write and tell me how your search for Religion is going. It will only be a little while, and that I might soon come for you is the fond Prayer and hope of your devoted Friend,

Daniel Perry

Hannah read the letter through twice, then folded it carefully and put it in the box under her bed. In it she kept her special treasures—the book Daniel had given her, and her favorite piece of jewelry from her mother, a necklace consisting of a small silver cross with equal arms and a dove suspended from it. "The Huguenot cross," her mother had called it.

Early September. The letter had taken all summer to reach her. Surely he'd put the cabin up by this time—maybe the next letter would say he was on his way to fetch her. Then she began to wonder where his earlier letters had gone. Usually her father picked up the mail; she'd just happened to be near the post office that morning.

When her father and brother came home from the fields, she put the supper of bread and stew before them. She waited until her father had finished eating.

"Papa, I've been expecting some letters from a friend in Missouri. I should've heard by this time. Do you know anything about them?"

Her brother, thirteen-year-old Russell, looked troubled, and his dark eyebrows drew together. Their father wiped his mouth. "If it's that Mormonite fellow, you can forget about him. Your aunt said you're not to receive anything from him. In fact, she took the first one and burned it."

"I should've known." She tried to conceal her anger with a shrug. "Well, it's my mail, and I think I have a right to read it before it gets burnt."

"Now, Hannah." Her father's gray mustache and side whiskers quivered. "With your mother gone, God knows I'm trying to do my best for you. If Elizabeth says you shouldn't hear from this fellow, she ought to know what she's talking about. She says he's deluded, ignorant, and dangerous."

Tears stung her eyes. "If you ask me, *she's* the one who's deluded. Her mind is so closed, she wouldn't even recognize Christ if she stumbled over him."

Russell laughed. Papa Manning looked stern. "Now, Puss—none of that. Elizabeth is an authority on religious matters. If she says something is a delusion, how can you argue with her? I sure can't."

"At least I should be given a choice," Hannah said.

"She told me the same thing she'll tell you—your Huguenot ancestors came to this country seeking religious freedom. And they certainly didn't go through all the persecution and hardship so you could run off after a bunch of ignorant lunatics. What would your mother say?"

He began to blink and sniffle the way he always did when he thought of his dead wife. Hannah went to poke up the fire, and Russell grasped the ladle of the stew pot. "More stew, Papa?"

Hannah straightened up from the fire. "'Seeking religious freedom,' did you say? Then they would approve of my going to the missionaries and just hearing what they have to say."

Russell looked up from his bowl of stew. "As a matter of fact, they're having meetings next week. Over at the Ordwell farm—I just heard."

Hannah clasped her hands together. She tried not to sound too eager. "Couldn't we go, Papa? Just to listen? I know it would do a world of good for both Rusty and me—give us something to think about besides Mother."

Their father sat a moment. He frowned, and his gray eyebrows drew together. Finally he sighed. "Oh, Puss—do what you like. Just don't let Elizabeth hear about it."

Hannah couldn't resist darting a triumphant glance at Russell. The boy smiled, his eyes a-light, and she knew he was already looking forward to the entertainment and the relief from grieving.

Hannah had never been too interested in religion. Her aunt's rigid thinking appalled her. She'd resolved not to become anything like Aunt Elizabeth, even if it meant being completely irreligious. Now, with the loss of her mother, she felt the need to play the part of both maternal and spiritual guide to her brother. When he asked, she tried to explain about the Huguenots.

"For some reason, the Protestants had a terrible time in France. Their leaders were ambushed and killed. There was something called the St. Bartholomew's Day Massacre—"

"I heard about that. Mother told me once."

"Did she? What did she say?"

He looked blank. "I—I sort of forgot."

"Then I'll tell you again. It was a terrible slaughter, beginning in Paris. Finally Henry IV issued an edict of toleration—the Edict of Nantes. They were safe for a while. When that was revoked by Louis XIV, a whole population had to flee for their lives. That's how Papa's ancestors ended up in England."

"Why England?" The boy ran his hand through his unruly shock of auburn hair. At the awkward age between childhood and adolescence, he could never get his hair to stay out of his eyes.

"They went to any nation that would take them in. Our original name was 'Manet' before it was anglicized."

He smiled and gestured with hands grown too large in proportion to his body. "I should've been Russell Manet!"

"But Mother kept her French name—Beaucourt. Her family left later. They came directly to America—to Richmond, Virginia."

"But, why?" Russell asked. "I mean—couldn't they just be let alone? Why did anyone have to flee anywhere, just because of their religion?"

Hannah tried to think what Daniel would say. "Well—I don't know. Maybe the new ideas were just too different."

Russell frowned. His eyes narrowed as he thought. "Do you suppose there'll ever be a place where people could go and just be different? And no one would bother them?"

She smiled. "Mother told me about the Huguenot 'cities of refuge.' But they were only protected for a little while." Then she stopped as Daniel's words danced in her mind: 'Our promised land...a place of refuge.' "My gracious—that's what the Mormonites believe! They think there'll be such a place."

His eyes widened. "How do you know?"

"My friend—he said it would be a—a 'New Jerusalem.' A community based on Christian teachings."

"That I'd like to see. Who's going to build it?"

"They think they are."

With their father's permission, they walked through the fields to the first meeting at the Ordwell farmhouse. They entered to find the main room filled with their Allegheny County neighbors.

Hannah watched intently as the spokesman, the younger of the two missionaries, rose from his chair. In contrast to her clumsy young brother, he seemed to move with grace and purpose. He held their full attention as he related the story of the young Joseph Smith finding and translating the ancient plates which contained the record of the Book of Mormon. He quoted passages from the book and concluded by proclaiming it an additional witness of the divinity of Christ.

"He's a tolerable good speaker," Russell said on the way home. "It'd please me if I could talk like that—so certain and unafraid-like."

"Maybe someday you will."

Twice more they walked over to hear the young preacher. If Hannah heard his name, she did not remember it.

"Orson...something," her brother said. "I think that's what they said."

In the last presentation, the missionary described the area around Independence as the land of promise, where the temple of the Lord would stand in the last days, when "'they shall not hurt nor destroy in all my holy mountain; for the earth shall be full of the knowledge of the Lord, as the waters cover the sea.'"

He concluded with more of Isaiah, his expression ecstatic as he lifted his hands. "'Cry out and shout, thou inhabitant of Zion, for great is the Holy One of Israel in the midst of thee.'"

Hannah and Russell stood outside in front of the farmhouse. "Well, Rusty, there's your city—your place of refuge. Zion."

"I don't know about you," he said. "But I feel like gettin' baptized."

Hannah felt a momentary surge of alarm—after all, she was responsible for whatever happened to Russell. Her father and aunt would hold her accountable. Then she thought of Daniel—she had found the confirmation she was seeking.

"Frankly, I've never been that excited about religion. I thought it was a bunch of pretty stories. But for the first time, I feel that this is real—everything he said is true."

"What are we waiting for?"

They stood looking at each other as their neighbors filed out of the front door. Hannah spoke slowly.

"Maybe we need to go home and think about it. We should probably ask Papa's permission."

"And you think he'll give it? Aunt Elizabeth will tar and feather him! Tell me—" His large hands sliced the air in an impatient gesture. "You think our ancestors asked permission before they followed their conscience? Who do you think they asked? Louis XIV?"

"Perhaps they were braver than we are," she said.

"I don't think so. More stubborn, maybe."

In the end both of them gave their names for baptism. The service took place that afternoon by the Ordwells' creek, and even though the water was spring-fed, neither of them felt chilled. Hannah stepped on shore holding her brother's hand. She hoped they had inherited both courage and steadfastness.

On the way home, Hannah told Russell about her engagement to Dan Perry, and how he was coming for her as soon as he put up a cabin.

"Why don't you just go there?" he asked. "I wouldn't wait."

"You mean—run away? Leave you and Papa—wouldn't you worry?"

"I'd know you were going to Zion. In fact, I'd go with you if you let me. I could help with that cabin."

Their resolves melted away with their father's anger. In vain Hannah tried to soothe him.

"Papa, I've never felt such peace before. I know what we did was right."

"A whim of the moment! Mass hypnotism—that's what it is! I was talkin' to ol' Grandpa Ordwell himself. He said it was all he could do to keep himself out of that water. He said the urge was irresistible."

"I felt it was a logical decision," Hannah said. "I've been struggling with it for some time."

"She has, too," Russell said. "She told me—ever since she went west with Aunt Elizabeth."

"Well, you're gonna have to keep struggling," their father said. "Especially when Elizabeth hears what you've done."

"Let's not tell her right away," Russell suggested. "It seems so peaceful without her knowing."

Before the missionaries left the area, Hannah had a letter ready for them to carry west.

Dear Daniel,

I have received your letter of last May, for which I thank you. Anything you sent before has been destroyed by my aunt, but I am careful now to visit the post office myself at least twice a week.

You ask if I am well. My father and brother and I are in good health. Our mother fell ill early last spring with some intestinal ailment. No one could save her. She passed from this life a week later.

I have some good news. My brother Rusty and I have both obeyed the gospel and were baptized. I know you will rejoice to hear this. It has given us great peace and comfort, and we no longer miss our mother as much.

Our father did not understand at first and was upset, mostly because of things my aunt had said about our religion. But he accepted our decision until Aunt Elizabeth stirred him up again. Now she is threatening to come live with us, where I suppose she can harangue us on a regular basis. If she does move in with us—and she usually gets her way—then I do not think I am needed here any longer. She will keep the house in her own way and cook for my father.

It will be difficult for my brother and me once she does move in—we are so used to talking together and reading the scriptures out loud. But we are trying to put our trust in the Lord.

We have a plan, if you are willing. If we have not heard from you by springtime, Rusty and I plan to start traveling west. We have talked about it many times—the journey to the promised land. He will help Papa with the spring plowing and planting, and then we will start. He hopes to return in time to help with the harvest.

I hope things are well with you. I hope that soon we shall be together, united by more than gospel bonds.

Always your friend,

Hannah Beaucourt Manning

****

Nathaniel sat in the public house drinking cider that had aged long enough to have a kick to it.

"Why, hello, Nat." A voice spoke close to his ear. He looked up to see a bearded man clad in buckskin pants and jacket.

"You most likely don't remember me," the stranger said. "I did some work on the Gilbert and Whitney store last spring. Thompson's the name."

"Oh, yes." Nathaniel tried to remember. "Here—have some cider."

"Don't mind if I do." The man took the earthenware pitcher and poured cider into an empty mug. He drank. "Man, that stuff packs a wallop."

"It warms you right up, after all the cold weather we been havin'."

"Talk about cold," Thompson said. "We just came in from Cincinnati, my partner and I. Been preachin' down around northern Kentucky and thereabouts."

Nathaniel wiped his sleeve across his mouth. "That's where they sent you, eh?"

"'Twas God that sent us. My partner and I, we went into the woods to pray, and we both had the impression we should head for Cincinnati. So that's where we went. But now—" He took another pull at the cider mug. "What's been happenin' around here?"

"Well, let's see." Nathaniel tried to think.

"I hear there was a stagecoach accident on the way back from Independence, and the bishop jumped out of the coach and broke his leg."

"You've been away a long time," Nathaniel said. "That was way last spring. Joseph Smith and Rigdon and the bishop, they was all traveling together. After it happened, the prophet sent Rigdon home to Kirtland while he stayed there with Bishop Whitney in Greenville."

Thompson frowned. "That little town in Indiana?"

"Yeah. Took about four weeks before the bishop was able to be moved."

"They got back all right?"

"Oh, yeah. Let's see—what else? Jesse Gause has gone missing."

Thompson set the cider mug down with a heavy 'clunk.' "Is that right? The second counselor to the prophet?"

"Yes," Nathaniel said. "Well, not any more. That is—he started off with Zebedee Coltrin in August on a mission to the east. Brother Coltrin got sick and headed home. Gause hasn't been seen since. In fact, they officially expelled him from the church a few days ago."

"Who'll take his place?"

"That's not been decided. Folks think it might be F. G. Williams."

"Hm. Strange—I mean, about Jesse," Thompson said.

"Yes. He was a Shaker—from North Union, like me. I hear he stopped there and tried to get his wife to quit the Shakers and come with him. But she refused."

Thompson nodded and looked at the table top. "Too bad. That must've been a disappointment."

Nathaniel managed to keep his voice steady. "I reckon folks get over these things."

"Still—he was a good man."

Nathaniel tried to think of other news. "A whole bunch of new people came in. When the prophet was away in Indiana, around in October, a man by the name of Patten came down from Michigan. Elder David Patten. Well, he had to wait for Brother Smith to return, so he went and harvested the prophet's entire potato crop, for something to do."

"I'll be derned," the other said.

"Brother Joseph went out to New York about this time, and when he came back, his son had just been born. That was the first week in November, as I recall."

"A son! That's good news. Let's drink to that."

They both raised their cider mugs, and Nathaniel said, "They're calling him Joseph Smith III. They say he favors his mother. And about this same time, a bunch of other folks moved to Kirtland from somewhere in New York. Mendon, I believe. Three of them—Brother Brigham Young, his brother and another one of his relatives—Heber

Kimball—went out and found the prophet chopping wood behind his home. I don't know what they thought, to find a prophet chopping wood like any of us. But I guess they figured it was all right."

Thompson looked at his empty mug. "Well, 'course it's all right. What sort of man is this Brother Young?"

"He's not too tall, but he's compact-like. Broad shoulders, kind of sandy hair. He does all kinds of carpentry—I understand he's a painter and glazier."

"That's more good news. Folks are comin' to us from all over. Anything else?"

Nathaniel grasped the handle of the pitcher. "More cider? There's talk of building a—well, I guess it's to be a new meeting house. The rumor is—let's see if I can remember. We're supposed to establish a house of prayer, of faith and learning, and a bunch of other things. In other words, a house dedicated to God."

Thompson raised his eyebrows. "Any idea what it's supposed to look like?"

Nathaniel smiled. "I don't think they've got that far. I just heard about it for the first time a couple of days ago."

"It sounds like a useful project. Well-timed, too."

"How do you mean?" Nathaniel asked.

Thompson gestured and tried to explain. "Well, if you get enough people building something, then they won't be squabbling and arguing as much."

Nathaniel said, "Since Christmas Day, it's been too cold to argue. Any news from south of here?"

"Not much. I want to get the latest copy of the *Star* and find out what's happening in Missouri."

Nathaniel stood up. "I think I saw one over at the store. I'll go with you."

Nathaniel paid for the pitcher of cider and they prepared to step out into the cold.

9

Parley Pratt stood talking with Dan after the Sunday morning prayer service.

"You must remember, my young friend—we're settin' on a powder keg here."

Dan gave Elder Pratt a long look, to make sure he wasn't joking. The leader smiled, but his eyes, set wide apart under busy eyebrows, were stern. Dan swallowed.

"In what way, sir?"

"Those other settlers are more upset than you can imagine. In the first place, there would've been plenty of room for all of us. But the government moved all the Indians in and established the border between us and Indian territory. So of course they resent us—we're takin' up land they could've had."

Dan shifted his feet in the damp dirt of the road. "But surely there's enough—"

"And our talk of promised land and inheritance doesn't make 'em like us any better. They watch us trying to make a permanent community out of land that's free and wild, and they see all the impoverished Saints comin' in lookin' for a free meal—what do you think goes through their minds?"

Dan shrugged, amused. "From what I can figure, not too much. When the next fight's gonna be, and the next snort of whiskey."

Pratt raised his eyebrows. "That's where you're wrong. With all our talk of angels and healings, they think we're fanatics. Or worse—lunatics."

Dan smiled. "But we're not. At least, most of us are sane."

"Well, Dan—we'd like them to think that. Now—I know you mean well, and you're sincere about what you said in the meeting. But, son. Those are the kind of words that'll bring the whole county down on us."

Dan's smile faded. "But, Brother Pratt—you know slavery is wrong. It's obscene—a terrible sin. For one human being to own another—"

"Son, I know that as well as you. But you're talking like a—a dyed-in-the-wool abolitionist. Do you know how that's gonna sound to those slave-owners? They're already riled up as it is."

Dan tried to suppress his agitation, but his voice trembled. "So we're here to establish the perfect community, and we're supposed to pretend this monstrous evil doesn't exist—or that it's all right? We should just turn a blind eye?"

Pratt put a hand on his shoulder. "Son, I don't know why the Lord chose Missouri. Seems to me he could've picked a better climate, for one thing. But for whatever reason, we're in here. And we can't set all the wrongs right in one summer. Why, the prophet even said, 'The whole world lieth in sin, and groaneth under darkness and under the bondage of sin.' Slavery isn't the only thing that's wrong."

Dan took a deep breath and let it out. He looked down at the ruts in the road. Pratt went on.

"I know how you feel. And I'm not asking you to turn away from human suffering. We're called to help in any way we can. But our first task is to set up a community—establish it and live in it. Everything else has got to be secondary."

"Even slavery?" Dan spoke in a tone of wonder.

Pratt nodded. "Even the worst thing you can imagine. I believe the issue of slavery will be decided once and for all in just a short time, and what we do here will have very little to do with it."

Startled, Dan looked up. "What d'you mean?"

"The prophet had a revelation last Christmas Day—he predicted a war beginning at South Carolina, where slaves would rise up against their masters. A most terrible conflict."

"Oh." Dan stared at Brother Pratt, at a loss for words. Brother Pratt pressed his thin lips together.

"So, you see, son—all I can say is that we have to try and live in peace with these people. We are all in God's hands—he won't allow wicked institutions to last forever. Try to watch what you say—don't add fuel to their hatred of us."

Dan managed to nod. "I will, sir."

"Go and build your house. I understand you have someone waitin' for you in the east."

"That's right—in Pennsylvania."

Pratt smiled. "Well, what are you waitin' for? Go and fetch her."

"You reckon it's safe? I mean—to bring her out here—"

"Son, nowhere's really safe, unless you're dead. Life is a risk. Just don't mention 'slavery' or 'abolition' for awhile."

That very night, a Mormon cabin was set afire and the family forced to flee to a neighbor's. A few days later, he wrote to Hannah.

My Dearest one,

I have started Work on a small Log house for us, close to where my parents Live. I must stop and Help get the crops in the Ground, but I have assurance that other Hands will help me raise the house when the Planting is done.

It would be Wise for you and Rusty to journey as far as Kirtland, I think, and I will come and Meet you there. This is terrible wild country, though it be Beautiful. There are men here just itching for a fight, as I have told you Before. I would not like you and your young brother to meet them on a Dark night, or any night for that matter, without me to Protect you.

I am enclosing the sum of six dollars, which I Have saved. I have Collected some of it by doing Work on two farms Nearby. I wish I had more to Send, but this will Help you get to Kirtland, where you will Stop and wait for me.

Keep yourself Well and safe; use wisdom in your Travels. That I might see you again is the Fond desire of my heart.

Daniel Perry

After he sent the letter, he met a group of five Missourians on the road.

"Another blasted Mormon," remarked a grizzled man in front.

"We oughta run the whole pack of 'em out," growled a voice from the rear.

"How'd you like that, son? We'd take you and your angels and gold plates, and chase you clean outa the county!"

Dan thought of Brother Pratt's words and said nothing. He stood aside for them to pass.

"This one don't talk. Let's use 'em up now. He can call on the angel Moroni for help."

Dan raised his head to face the speaker. The man had a lean, clean-shaven face and eyes that appeared strangely empty—half-closed slits without a glimmer of life or interest. For a few seconds they looked at each other, and Dan felt as if he were gazing into the face of evil itself. His heart pounded, and the last image of Hannah's face flashed through his mind.

The grizzled one shrugged. "Don't waste yer time. There's a way to git rid of all the vermin at once, and this ain't it."

They strode past. One of them muttered, "Abolitionist!"

Dan made no move, his eyes fixed on the ground. After that encounter, he made a point of riding his mare on every errand. He stood a better chance of getting away if he were on horseback.

****

Elizabeth Manning leaned up against the fireplace, her arms folded as she watched her brother. Calvin Manning sat looking at the letter before him on the table.

"I can't believe it." He sighed and rubbed his bushy gray eyebrows with a callused hand. "Her, planning to run off out west. And Rusty, too!"

Elizabeth gave him what she hoped was a severe look. "I told you she was devious. Both of them. I tried to warn you."

"I don't know why he'd send her six dollars," he said. "She has all her mother's jewelry—enough to take her anywhere."

Elizabeth pulled out the chair across from him and sat down. She arranged her skirts. "The point is—what do we do now? I kept the letter for a week, thinking if she hadn't heard, she wouldn't do anything. But you know he'll write again. He may even try to come out and get her."

Manning shook his head. "It beats me—I don't know. I can't lock up both of 'em. Maybe if I hid that jewelry, she wouldn't have the means to go out there."

"That's it." Elizabeth's mouth tightened. She summoned her most decisive voice. "We keep the six dollars, burn the letter, and hide the jewelry. She won't be able to do a thing. God knows you can't reason with her."

Manning sighed again. "All right—I'll go up to her room. Best to do it now, when they're off at meeting."

"You should never have allowed them to go over there in the first place. Both of them baptized after three meetings!" She rose from her chair and picked up the letter. She thrust the money in the pocket of her skirt.

She threw the letter into the fireplace and used the poker to push it into the flames. When she looked up, Manning was standing at the foot of the stairs, a piece of paper in his hands.

"They're gone," he said.

"What?"

"The jewelry's gone. She left this—this—" He gestured. Elizabeth snatched the note and read it aloud.

"'Dear Papa,

By the time you read this, Rusty and I will be on our way to the west. I am going to Missouri, to be married to Daniel Perry. He is a good man and we love each other. Rusty will return to help with the harvest.'"

There was more—a thank you, a reassurance of her love, a promise that she would try to be wise and do the right thing. She said he was not to worry about them; she would send a letter when she had reached her destination.

"Well, Elizabeth," he said after a pause. "It's the way of things. You raise a daughter, she marries, and if they go West, you never see her again. Oh—what would Jeanette say if she were here?"

"For heaven's sake, Calvin!" She wished she could reach over and shake the weakness out of him. "Jeanette's dead, and you have to do something! You must act now—this instant! Find them before they get any further."

He raised his hands in a helpless gesture. "I—I'll do my best. I suppose—well, that is—I'll go over to the Ordwells' first."

But no one knew what route the young people had taken, or how they planned to travel.

"The river, most likely," Elizabeth said. "Try to reach the landing before they do."

Manning and one of the neighbors rode off into the night. Elizabeth busied herself cleaning the hearth, furious at the two youngsters for being so stupid and stubborn. Calvin had never been firm enough with them, and as for Jeanette—her discipline had been a joke. Calvin would soon have them in hand, and then she'd give them a piece of her mind they'd never forget.

She poked in the ashes and planned what she was going to tell them. The poker found a piece of the letter which had not burned. The words stood out, mocking her.

'Kirtland, where you will Stop and wait'

10

Kirtland Mills, Geauga County. Little settlement outside Cleveland, just south of Mentor and east of the Shaker community. To the north stretched Lake Erie; the Chagrin River flowed closer to the town. With its farms and businesses, it offered an ideal gathering place for people who would eventually make their homes in the land of Zion.

Joseph Smith, settled in rooms attached to the Whitney store, thought of the few acres of farmland he now had—well-run, thanks to people like Nathaniel Givens. He glanced out the window just in time to see Nat swing past on some errand, hammer in hand. He thought briefly of Nat and his strange Shaker upbringing. So far the young man seemed to be doing well, though he'd shown no inclination to marry or even to associate with women.

Joseph sighed. Brother Nat needed more time than most. At least he was loyal, and extremely eager to begin work on the House of the Lord, whose dimensions had just been given in a revelation on June 1.

Joseph turned his attention to the papers before him on the desk. The words stared up at him.

'...fifty and five feet in width, and let it be sixty-five feet in length, and in the inner court thereof...'

After months of high expectation, the details were beginning to fall into place. It would be a large structure, built 'not after the manner of the world,' with the lower part of the inner court dedicated 'for your sacrament offering, and for your preaching, and your fasting, and your praying, and the offering up your most holy desires unto me...'

Joseph allowed himself a moment to savor the fact that things were going better than he had hoped. First, the plans for the House of the Lord. The School of the Prophets organized, the two counselors to the President of the High Priesthood ordained. Emma content, in her own place at last. The children Julia and Joseph both doing well. His uncle John Smith, the only one of his father's family to join the church, now settled on a farm in Kirtland with his wife and family. Brigham Young hired to lay the floor of their cabin—probably at work this very minute. Even Sidney Rigdon in better health, although Joseph still worried about him. Sidney's injuries during the tar-and-feather assault of the year before had left their mark. The man acted argumentative, more opinionated—less tolerant, somehow—maybe a factor of aging. Made things difficult, since he was now a member of the First Presidency along with F. G. Williams.

He thought of other troubles, brought under control at last. The excommunication of Philastus Hurlbut for unchristian conduct toward women. And before that, the spirit of insubordination among the leaders in Zion. They'd sent angry letters of protest, determined to handle matters in their own way. He'd replied with letters of his own, warning them that the judgments of God awaited them if they didn't repent. A council of twelve high priests had appointed Orson Hyde and Joseph's brother Hyrum to draft a letter of admonition.

Now, after letters of contrition and explanation from the elders in Zion, it seemed that things were harmonious at last—except for one issue. He'd learned that Sidney Gilbert, the store owner, had withheld credit from some of the impoverished families who had asked for assistance.

He looked up as Nathaniel entered the room.

"Begging your pardon, Brother Smith—I've finished the work you asked me to do. You won't have any more trouble with that door—if you do, I'll be mighty surprised. I'll be going home now."

"Thank you, Nat. By the way—if you knew of certain poor Saints who had nothing to sustain them, what would you do?"

"Why, sir, I—" Nat frowned, and his scarred mouth worked as he thought. "I'd give 'em what I had—I'd share with them the way the Shakers did. We had no poor among us—that is, we didn't have much, but everyone had enough to eat, and clothes to wear."

Joseph smiled. "I'm thinking you've caught a bigger vision than some men in high places. Go on your way, now. "

Nat went away shaking his head. A good man, Joseph thought. It might be well to forget the negative things and reflect on the reasons for rejoicing—and there were many. For every person who was causing trouble, he could find at least a dozen like Nathaniel—industrious, humble, kind-hearted. He could imagine the Lord saying, "For such as these, I gave my life."

In addition to the other good happenings, he and Sidney had finally completed the first phase of their work on the New Testament. Eventually he hoped to publish it in one volume along with the Book of Mormon—a project planned for W. W. Phelps & Co.

He set to work on the papers before him, which included a plan for the city of Zion. But as he turned his attention to the affairs in Missouri, he felt a strange uneasiness, like a shadow spreading in the room.

****

Nathaniel sat in the public house, a mug of cider in his hand. Spread out on the table lay *The Evening and the Morning Star*. The late afternoon light cast golden pools on the paper as he strained to read.

'The great day is hastening when the whole house of Israel will be gathered home from their long dispersion, to Zion and Jerusalem.'

"Hello, Nat." Brother Crawford stood beside him. "Thought I'd find you in here. Cider again, eh?"

Nathaniel smiled. "Want some?"

"No, thanks. My land, if the prophet knew how much you liked yer cider, he'd add that to the list of things we're not supposed to drink."

"Oh—the Word of Wisdom?"

Crawford pulled out the chair across from Nathaniel. "Some folks say we should even make it a test of membership. The men give up their hard drinks, and the women give up their tea and coffee."

Nathaniel, who had done without a great many things, raised his eyebrows as he looked at his friend. "It probably wouldn't hurt 'em none."

"What're you reading?"

"Just the *Star.* It says here about the Jews, how they'll soon be gathering to their homeland."

Crawford reached over and turned back the edge of the newspaper. "February. A little out of date."

"I do my reading when I find the time," Nathaniel said.

"Wouldn't you like to know what's happenin' in Missouri right now? 'Course we wouldn't hear anyway, for some weeks."

"We'd have to wait for the next paper." Nathaniel took a swig of cider. "Sure you don't want some?" He set the mug down. "I figure it's just the usual everyday things. Chores. Finishing up the planting, gettin' ready for the warm weather. Having prayer meetings and such-like. Maybe puttin' up a log house or two." He thought briefly of Dan and hoped that things were going well for him. "Probably just the same as around here."

Crawford ran his fingers through his shock of graying hair. In the sunlight his face looked rough and tanned. "'Cept they ain't buildin' no House of the Lord."

"I imagine they'll help. That committee sent 'round to every congregation for money, and they need it by September."

Crawford put both elbows on the table and leaned forward. "They expect most of it to come from around here. Why, they had that special service just last week, and all they did was solicit funds."

"Well, think about it," Nathaniel said. "You don't put up a building that large for nothing."

One of the men waiting at the counter turned around. His Adam's apple quivered as he spoke. "You talkin' about that meeting house? I hear Brother John Tanner already gave three thousand dollars to the bishop for storehouse supplies. And he's fixin' to sell his farm and sawmill and gristmill back in New York so's he can give some more."

"Some folks is really dedicated," someone else said. "But that ain't even a small part of what they'll need."

Crawford said, "Were you there when they came back with the first load of stone from the quarry? Hyrum Smith and old Reynolds Calhoun, why, they just lit in and began diggin' foundation trenches right away. They didn't even stop to get their second wind."

"The only thing'll stop 'em is money," the first man at the counter said. "Or the lack of it."

Someone else said, "And who's gonna work without pay? Why, I hear they expect us to give one day in seven to the construction."

"Is that so?" Nathaniel said. "It'll go fast, then. And some will do more, if they can."

"Like ol' Nat, here." Brother Crawford chuckled. "He'll work till he ain't got a breath left in his body."

"So will you, and you know it," Nathaniel retorted. "How else will we get the blessings that've been promised?"

"That's the spirit," one of the others said. "Maybe we'll even come down and watch you work."

****

Dan rode into the town of Independence early that day to have his ax sharpened and a new handle put on. As he explained to the clerk at the store, he finally had time to work on his own cabin.

"I been puttin' up all these buildings for other folks—sheds and such. It's high time I built a house for me."

The clerk had small eyes that squinted against the light and made him look sleepy. He ran a hand through his salt-and-pepper beard. "Let's hope it don't get burned down as soon as you get it built."

Dan shifted his feet, anxious to be on his way. If he got started early enough, he could finish trimming out the logs and they could raise the cabin that next week. "I'm not worried. I think we're safe. We're away from the main part of things—off by ourselves, there on the river bank."

"I don't think anywhere's safe, the way that Reverend Pixley feller's been stirring people up about false prophets. Say, you didn't see a big crowd of folks hangin' around outside, did you?"

"No—things looked pretty quiet. And don't call him 'reverend.' He's a lying trouble-maker—full of the devil."

"Don't say that too loud," the clerk said.

"Why not?" Dan drew out his money and laid it on the counter.

He looked around as footsteps clattered on the wooden porch.

The front door burst open. A thin young man rushed in, red-faced, his shock of black hair down over his forehead. Dan had just enough time to see that the newcomer towered over him by at least four inches.

"Something's afoot, and I don't like it. All of 'em crowdin' in there like that. It sure ain't no church service."

"Now, Brother Benjamin—why doncha take a deep breath and tell us what yer talkin' about?" the clerk said.

"A whole bunch of them—meetin' down at the courthouse. Never saw so many all together."

The clerk scratched at his beard. "So that's where they all went."

Benjamin glanced toward the front window. "It's that business in the paper—that article about free people of color."

"Warn't nothing wrong with it," Dan replied. "I hear he wrote another one, just to calm things down."

Benjamin put a bony hand on the counter. "Well, it really got 'em riled up. One of 'em told me they won't be happy till they run us out of here."

The clerk counted the money Dan had left. "I guess you heard about that manifesto."

"What?" Dan stood the ax on its head and leaned it against the counter.

"They been passin' it around. Brother Gilbert happened to see a copy. It says they don't want any more Mormons in Jackson County. And they want us to close our press and storehouse, even our shops."

Dan felt outrage rushing over him. "That's ridiculous! They have no right to demand such a thing."

The clerk said, "Well, those who don't want to do it are supposed to ask those brethren with the gift of prophecy about what's gonna happen to them."

Benjamin shook his head. "I didn't figure things was that bad."

"I reckon we ain't seen nothing yet." The clerk gave Dan a thin, crooked smile, and one side of his mouth twitched. "Still want to put up a cabin?"

A sudden shout echoed from outside. A horse neighed.

"What's that noise?" Benjamin asked.

Dan gripped his ax. He'd left his mare in the livery stable instead of tying her up outside. "Let's go over to the courthouse and see what they're up to."

The clerk frowned. "Like as not, Brother Gilbert's over there already. Why doncha wait till he gets back?"

Dan glanced at Benjamin. "I'm not in the habit of waiting." He shouldered the ax as they strode toward the front of the store.

The clerk's voice followed them. "Please, boys—be careful. If they're in an ugly mood, stay clear of 'em."

"Bunch of rattlesnakes," Dan muttered. He kicked open the door and they went outside. The sun hit them as they moved away from the shadow of the buildings.

"Heat's coming on," Benjamin said.

Dan grunted. He felt drops of perspiration on his forehead. A slight breeze stirred in the trees behind the printing office.

"Brother Phelps is in there workin'," Benjamin said. "He's got his coat off."

"Can't say I blame him—day like this."

Dan felt Benjamin's hand on his arm. He tensed; they both stopped. A man came running out of the courthouse. His shoes made a clatter on the floorboards. Two more followed, then a whole stream of them. Their feet pounded on the dirt outside. They were yelling, some whooping like Indians. In a flash Dan realized that the crowd was heading straight for them.

"Get back."

They drew back against the bricks just in time. The crowd thundered past. The main body surged ahead, with groups of stragglers to the sides and rear. Clouds of dust rose from their feet.

"Beats me where they think they're going," Dan said.

"Be still! What're they shouting?"

A knot of stragglers sped past them. Above the din, a voice yelled, "I'd like to see what they print next month!"

"The printing office," Dan said.

"My God! You're right," Benjamin whispered.

The mob descended on the office of the *Star*. Glass splintered. Dan heard shouts and oaths, the thud of machinery hitting the floor. Those who couldn't crowd into the building rampaged around the outside and began smashing everything they could find.

"We can't let 'em do this," Dan said.

"Who's gonna stop 'em? There's at least three hundred pukes out there!"

Screams echoed from inside, the high-pitched shriek of a woman. A child wailed. Dan couldn't tell how many seconds elapsed before men emerged carrying chairs and tables from the shop.

They threw the furniture in the street. Dust thickened the air; Dan felt a dryness in his throat. He could see Saints milling around as well as mobbers; he recognized the family that lived in the building. The young wife and two daughters huddled together and cried out as their belongings cascaded into the street.

"I can't stand it," Dan said.

"You've got to." Benjamin's hand gripped his wrist.

More glass shattered. The crowd was roaring now, all individual voices lost in the noise. The press crashed to the ground from the second-floor window. A rain of books and papers followed.

"So much for the Book of Commandments," Benjamin muttered.

Little bits of metal flew through the air. Then Dan realized it was the type from the press. The pieces hit the ground, and the mob trampled them into the dust.

Some of the men moved on to the stores and started dumping goods out into the street. They brought out bolts of cloth from the Gilbert and Whitney store and flung them. The bolts unrolled and fluttered like bright banners on the town square.

Dan saw Phelps in his shirtsleeves rushing to gather up papers. One of the mobbers, a man in overalls and a tattered shirt, ran at Phelps and tripped him. The papers fell from his hands as he tumbled to the ground.

Dan felt anger flooding over him, helpless outrage as he thought of all their work and effort, now smashed in the street. It was as if they had taken part of his own life—his cabin, about to be built, his dream of a life with Hannah—and thrown it out with the press and furnishings. He gripped the ax. "I'm going out there."

Benjamin's grip felt stronger than Dan had expected. "Listen to me, brother. We're supposed to be men of peace."

Through the dust they saw Brother Gilbert trying to talk to the mob. He stood in the doorway of his store and gestured wildly.

"Let me go," Dan insisted.

"It's no good, Daniel. We can't fight them now. They'll kill us."

They began to scuffle together, Dan determined, enraged, Benjamin firm. They grappled for the ax handle, Dan with his back up against the wall of the building. He saw the two girls and their mother fleeing toward the woods beyond the shops. Benjamin got hold of the ax and clobbered him with the handle. He felt the blow on the side of his face. He staggered back against the wall. The back of his head hit the bricks. He felt darkness closing over him.

When he regained consciousness, he heard shouts. "Bishop Partridge!" "Let's go after the bishop!"

He opened his eyes. Benjamin leaned over him. "I'm sorry, Daniel. I couldn't let you go out there."

"What—what else do we do?"

"Well—we appeal to the authorities. The law's on our side. Let's find Brother Partridge or Brother Pratt—they'll know what to do."

"I mean—right now. There has to be something—"

"Let's help those who need it. Save your energy for our own

people. Most of the crowd's gone off."

They found Phelps on the ground crawling after papers. They helped him to his feet. He looked dazed, his face pale. His voice trembled as he looked at them. "*'The blood of Ephraim.'*"

"What?" Dan tried to brush the dust from the older man's shirt.

"That's as far as we got. Those are the last words that were printed." Phelps shook his head.

Dan and Benjamin began gathering up pages from the road. Some were the scattered Book of Commandments. Others were copies of the *Star*. Phelps said, "The first newspaper this far west. You think they would've liked it."

"Snakes can't read," Dan remarked.

"That way of thinking isn't going to help us none," Benjamin said.

Dan caught sight of something moving amid the bolts of cloth. He rushed over to the square. The store clerk lay on the grass, his gray beard streaked with blood. Dan knelt beside him.

"Come on. Let's get you up."

The man grimaced. Blood came from a cut on his lip. He looked at Dan and raised his hand. "I'll be all right. I'm tough—walked all the way from Ohio on foot. They can't kill me."

"We've got to get you out of here."

He shook his head. "My son's gone for help. You get out of here, now. Go look to your family."

Shouts echoed from the road, the mob returning. Dan felt a cold, hard fear churning in the pit of his stomach.

"We got 'em!" someone shouted. "The ol' bishop hisself!"

"Where's the tar bucket?"

Dan ran back to where he'd left Benjamin. Phelps and two other men were picking up bits of paper. Dan looked for Benjamin in the crowd, but he had disappeared. When Dan tried to retrace his steps to the square, a crowd of Missourians blocked the way.

Screams pierced the air. He knew something terrible was happening to Bishop Whitney—maybe they were killing him. Fear shot through him; he felt as panicky as a cornered wild animal. He tried to think what to do.

First, his ax. He ran back to the side of the building and snatched it up. He started for the stable. Missourians were everywhere; he saw six of them crowding around Phelps. Then they were beating Phelps; the man sank to his knees. Another man lay sprawled on the threshold of the printing office.

Dan turned and raced between the shop buildings. Panting. Nostrils clogged with dust. He circled around and approached the stable from the rear. Pinky gave a little whicker as Dan's boots crunched in the straw.

"Quiet, girl." He unloosed the reins and led her outside. He strapped the ax to the saddle and mounted.

They cantered through the cornfields on the outskirts of town. His home lay on the other side, by the river. He rode south and hit a rutted road running past woods and farmlands. The mare faltered. Dan reined her in, thinking she'd gone lame.

They sprang up from the bushes, five men in work clothes and boots. Pinky reared. They grabbed the reins. Before he could get his hands on his only weapon, they dragged him to the ground.

"Another Mormon! They're worse than vermin!"

"And look here! A fancy new ax!"

Dan tried to fight. He felt kicks in his groin and abdomen, a blow to his knee. He crumpled and fell into the weeds.

"Too bad we don't have any tar. We could tar this one up just fine."

"Leave him be. He ain't good for nothing now."

Dan opened his eyes to see the same lean-faced man he'd encountered before. The man grinned down at him.

"Whatsa matter, sonny? No fight left in you?"

Dan said nothing. The man kicked him in the side. Dan grunted and closed his eyes. He waited for the next blow. He could hear something happening with the men and the horse, someone shouting, "She's a prize. She'll fetch a good price."

He heard their voices going further away. He lay still, afraid to move. When he opened his eyes, the men had gone, along with his mare and his ax.

Sick about the mare. His own, raised from a tiny filly. He tried to get up. Half his body felt crushed. The main trouble was his left knee. It hurt with each step. He found a tree limb along the road and tore branches from it until it formed a crude walking stick. His hip began to ache worse than the knee. He wondered then how he was going to walk the fifteen or so miles to his parents' house.

He couldn't. He would head for Bishop Partridge's house and rest there that night. Then they would help him get home.

He turned off to the road that led to the bishop's house and stopped to rest. He leaned against a tree, numb with shock, unable to believe what had just happened. A noise behind him. He turned to look.

Two men were walking, their feet raising dust from the road. One, a young man, carried a hat, with a vest and coat draped over his arm. The second wore only a shirt and pantaloons; he was covered with tar and feathers. Blood oozed from a wound on his forehead. It took Dan some seconds to recognize Bishop Partridge.

"Oh, Brother Partridge." He limped toward them. "I'm so sorry; I—"

"There's nothing to be sorry for," the bishop said. "We haven't injured anyone. If I have to suffer for my religion, it's no more than others have done."

"They dragged him from his house," the clothes-bearer said. "About fifty of 'em. Frightened his family out of their wits. And his wife with a newborn child."

"What happened to you?" the bishop asked.

Dan said a few words about the beating, and losing his horse to the mob. He felt ashamed; his troubles seemed light in comparison to what he was hearing.

"Brother Allen got tarred and feathered too," the young man said. "They gave him the choice of leaving the county or denying the Book of Mormon. He refused both."

"Come on, Brother Dan," the bishop said. "We'll take care of you."

Dan tried to follow them, but he had to lean on the tree branch. They pulled ahead of him. The house in sight, he stopped to rest again. He feared his leg would give out before he could walk the last eighth of a mile.

He saw the bishop's two young daughters meeting their father in the doorway. Both were crying; they threw their arms around him. Dan could see their shoulders shaking as their father tried to comfort them.

Hard on children, Dan thought. Not fair. How could they possibly understand about the cruelty of adults? He joined others that evening as they scraped the tar and feathers off the bishop. The task proved more difficult because acid had been mixed with the tar and was eating into his flesh.

"Nevertheless, I'm proud to have been persecuted for the truth."

Just after dark, two families came in saying they no longer felt safe in their own homes. People made up beds for them on the floor.

Dan rested with the Saints and neighbors. He thought with wonder of the young man who had ridden out so bravely that morning to sharpen an ax and begin his cabin. Later he lay on the floor in a blanket. It seemed that the young man had gone forever, and in his place lay some bruised, bewildered stranger.

When Dan finally got a ride back to his parents' house, a surprise awaited him. His mare had returned ahead of him.

"You had us all worried," his father said. "She came trotting in late Saturday, as saucy as you please. She had everything—saddle, bridle. You were the only thing missing."

He'd lost the ax, but he was so happy to get the mare back that he didn't care. "I never thought to see her again."

Too sore to ride or do much else, he spent his time currying the mare. His father said, "I'd like to see the day when you set as much store by a woman as you do that horse."

That evening, Brother Bradford rode in with alarming news. He had to stop and catch his breath before he could speak.

"The mob—rounded up all the leaders they could find—the bishop and John Whitmer—about five or six others."

"When was this?" Dan asked.

"Tuesday. They said they'd kill us all if we didn't agree to leave the county."

"Leave?" Dan's mother gasped.

"They was armed to the teeth, and they had this red flag. Someone said it was a sign of blood. Whatever it was, they meant business. They said they was gonna beat our leaders to death and set their slaves to destroy our houses and crops."

Dan's mother began to sob. His father put an arm around her shoulders. His gray eyebrows rushed together in a frown. Bradford went on.

"The leaders offered their own lives if our people could stay here in peace. The mob refused."

"So where does that leave us?" Dan asked.

Bradford drew a deep breath. "Half our people have to be out of here by January. The rest must leave by April."

"This is certain?" Dan's father said.

"They signed. Our leaders all promised, and they signed their names—they had to. The newspaper and the Gilbert and Whitney store must close, and no more Mormons can come into the area."

Dan thought of Hannah, now somewhere between Pennsylvania and Kirtland. He'd heard no news to the contrary. He gave silent thanks that he'd directed her to Kirtland first.

His father went with Bradford to alert the rest of the Colesville Saints. Dan, unable to walk more than a few yards without pain, stayed with his mother.

"Don't worry, Mama," he said. "You heard the man. We've got till the first of the year—maybe even longer."

11

Hannah sat in the high-backed rocker beside the bed. She rocked gently as she read to herself. She'd been reading aloud for the past half an hour, but now Russell was asleep.

She sighed and looked over at him. He slept with his mouth open, taking shallow breaths, his face pale in its nest of red-gold hair. Perhaps she should've left home without him. A lot of help he'd been so far.

First, his insistence on traveling overland instead of taking the river boat. They could've been halfway to Missouri by this time. Then, just as they got off the stage at Canton, his terse announcement: "I'm not well."

"What do you mean? What's the matter?"

"I feel strange—like I want to lie down and puke at the same time."

He sat on the step while she arranged for a room in the inn. She rented the last available one, which happened to be on the second floor. Then she had to get her brother up the stairs before the innkeeper suspected anything was wrong. If he thought Russell had some contagious disease, he would most likely ask them to leave.

She got him to bed and asked at the general store for the nearest doctor. The physician, a portly, red-faced gentleman, came to the inn to examine Russell. He turned, and Hannah could smell the liquor on his breath.

"Well, miss—see that he stays in bed and gets plenty of rest. Travel is out of the question."

"But—what is it?" she asked.

"Grippe. Saw two other cases of it this afternoon. I'll leave something to help him sleep. Try to get him to drink—he won't want to eat for a couple of days."

So Hannah nursed him, watching over him anxiously until the fever broke. When he was able to eat again, she began helping in the kitchen of the inn in an effort to cut their expenses. Russell stayed in bed, as weak as a kitten.

"Read to me," he begged one afternoon when she returned from the kitchen.

That's when they discovered the Book of Mormon was missing.

"Oh, no—I'm so sorry," he said. "I put it down beside me on the skiff—when we crossed the river. I must've forgotten to take it up again."

"Well, it's gone now. You dolt. Why'd you have it out anyway?"

He looked devastated. "I was going to read some of it that night."

Remorse flooded over her. "Oh, Rusty, I didn't mean it. Please forgive me. To speak to you like that—how could there be a worse sin?"

He swallowed. "Our book's probably on its way to St. Louis by this time. That man who hired the skiff when we got out—remember? He said he wanted to catch a boat at Steubenville."

"The book may get to Zion before we do."

"I'm sorry to be such a trouble," he said.

"Now, let's stop talking that way. We'll make the best of things—see if we don't."

They borrowed a Bible from the inn-keeper and she read to him from the New Testament. The words served to calm him, and his sleep became peaceful, less broken.

She found a Mormonite family in town. One of the elders came to lay hands on Russell and offer a prayer for his healing. The family would have taken them in, but they decided that moving him across town would not be wise. Instead, they brought dishes of food and savory broth.

Now, as Hannah sat watching, Russell stirred. He opened one eye.

"How long have we been here?"

"I reckon three weeks. It's the beginning of August already."

"I'll soon be up and about," he said.

"There's no hurry. We're well taken care of. You'll be another four days at least, just gettin' on your feet."

"It was a powerful sickness."

She told him how the local family of Saints had urged them to go to Kirtland, where they would find help for the trip to Missouri.

"Kirtland's not far now."

"I reckon that seems like the wisest course."

But as Russell began to recover. Hannah fell ill. By the end of that week, she felt too faint to get out of bed. Russell, still weak from the illness, tried to take care of her. Without the local family to bring them food and moral support, they would have had a terrible struggle. As it was, things were not easy.

"One sick person taking care of another."

"Don't fret, Hannah," he said. "It's my turn to do for you now. Remember—like you said, we're both in the hands of God."

But Hannah did fret; she'd never been one to take things calmly. She looked at Russell from the mound of blankets and thought how nothing could be worse than the two of them falling so ill on the way to the promised land.

****

Oliver Cowdery, the first to bring the news to Kirtland, would never forget Joseph's reaction.

"They tarred and feathered Brother Partridge and Brother Allen, threatened women and children, beat and abused anyone they could find—"

Oliver paused. Joseph was weeping, burying his face in his hands. "Oh, my brethren!" he exclaimed between sobs. "If only I had been there to share your fate!"

Oliver waited, then said, "What they did in terms of property damage is beyond belief. Fences, crops, livestock, houses, furniture—Parley thinks the damage is more than six thousand dollars."

"My brethren! Oh, my God—what shall I do in such a trial as this?"

Oliver felt his own eyes growing moist. He went on with the rest of it—the agreement to leave the Jackson County.

Joseph raised his head, his face tear-streaked. After a while he said, "And will they be allowed to leave in peace?"

"The Missourians have pledged as much—for what it's worth. But any of our people moving into the county must know that their stay is temporary—as the signed statement reads, 'until a new location is agreed on for the society.'"

Joseph nodded and brushed his hand across his eyes. "That gives us a little time. We'll go directly to the governor, if need be."

"The lieutenant-governor was right there, the day the mob took action. Lilburn W. Boggs, himself. He did nothing to stop them. In fact, he remarked, 'You now know what our Jackson boys can do, and you must leave the country.'"

Joseph sighed. "Well, we'll see about that."

Oliver felt such weariness that everything seemed jumbled together in his mind. He'd eaten very little since his flight from Independence. From all he'd heard, he felt lucky to have escaped with his life. His health—an added burden. That made four. First, the death of his brother Erastus in June, at the early age of thirty-seven. In addition to his own sorrow, he carried a feeling of heaviness for Erastus' two young daughters, his nieces.

Second, his own wife, Elizabeth Ann—his bride of seven months, whom he'd left with her parents in Missouri. He thought he'd done the safest thing, to leave her. But where was she now, and what was happening to all of them?

Third, his shattered dream of Zion, the community which had looked to him as leader. He shook his head, wanting to weep as he thought of it.

In the course of dispatching Orson Hyde and John Gould to counsel the Missouri Saints, Joseph informed Oliver that the church needed him in Kirtland.

"But—but my wife! She's waiting for me to come back."

"She can come here when it's safe to travel. She'll be all right. And so will you. You can live with us for a while—in a few weeks I want you to start for New York and purchase another press."

They announced the plight of the Missouri Saints at a public meeting. Oliver knew that most of the people assembled had relatives or friends in the Independence area. People rose to pray on behalf of the families in the promised land, tears coursing down their faces, their fingers clutching the hands of those seated next to them. From where he sat, Oliver saw a young man turn pale and put his hands to his face, as if he'd suffered a physical blow.

"Who's that?" he whispered to Joseph.

"Brother Nat Givens—he's come to us from the Shaker faith."

Oliver found himself wondering who an ex-Shaker, newly converted, would know in Missouri.

****

The young man stood on the brow of the hill overlooking the river. Of medium height, he had a wiry, thin build, the right size for slipping through woods undetected. His black hair hung shaggy about his ears, and the first traces of beard outlined his jaw.

He pushed back a low-lying oak branch. He could see the landing at Gallipolis, and the lovely curve the river made as it approached the town. A river boat was just pulling away from the dock, heading down river. He watched as the paddle wheel churned the water to a white froth.

The shadows were lengthening. His mother would be looking for him. Her voice rang in his mind. "Gabriel? Haven't you filled that wood box yet?"

He sighed. He'd spent the afternoon reading, and he was not sorry. The trouble was, they all knew how he loved to read and study. It only fueled their determination that he should enter the priesthood. And he felt equally determined that his calling lay somewhere else.

Anywhere else. As he looked at the brightly colored parasols sported by the ladies on the boat, he knew the life of a celibate soul-winner was not for him. He considered himself a healer, but of bodies, not souls.

He had immersed himself in the medical books of his friend and neighbor Dr. Beauchamps. He also knew the healing herbs from his mother's kitchen. In fact, even though he'd not turned sixteen, he had a reputation for healing animals—pets and injured wild creatures. He thought of the young crow whose broken wing he had set. Carefully, humbly, he'd performed the maneuver, with the feeling that a force outside himself was working with him.

The crow had recovered, and now, as far as he knew, it flew with the other crows about the town and through the fields. Every time he heard the chorus of caws, he wondered if his crow was among them. Perhaps watching him secretly, even now.

Anyone watching him would know how he—eager to read anything—had fetched the book from the trash heap where the gentleman from the river boat had thrown it. The Book of Mormon. How it got there didn't concern him. It was his now, and he'd spent the afternoon reading it.

He hid the book in a hollow tree—they'd only make a fuss about it at home. Then he made his way back toward town. He thought of what he'd read—Nephi and his brothers, and the sea voyage to a promised land. His own ancestors had been lured to America in the hope of finding such a place. But their expectations had turned to bitter disappointment, and they'd had to struggle for their very existence in the wilderness. Now there were only a few of the original French families left, among them the Beauchamps and his own, the Romains.

Romain. The very name meant Roman, as in Roman Catholic. While he'd dutifully gone along with the liturgies of his church, he'd always felt that something was lacking—as if he were offering ritual obeisance to some pagan god. Now here was the Book of Mormon, with its message that God was supremely real and could be approached at any time, without the intervention of saints or lesser beings. If the book were to be believed, then God was everywhere, ever-present in the world, and needed no incense and rituals to attract his attention.

Already Gabriel's curiosity was racing. Intrigued by the depiction of the Christian religion in such forthright, direct language, he imagined himself going north and finding one of the witnesses who claimed to have seen the plates—he'd heard there were followers of this particular sect up around Kirtland. Maybe he could even talk with Joseph Smith himself.

His sister Marie-Françoise, fourteen months his junior, stood waiting by the dogwood tree. Her hair, dark like his own, hung in strands close about her ears and then cascaded to her shoulders. Small-featured, she had gray eyes set far apart, and beautiful dark eyebrows.

"Up on Mound Hill again," she said. "Right?"

He smiled and strode toward her. Wherever he went—even if he should be convinced that he should go and study for the priesthood—it would be hard to leave her. Of his three sisters, she was his favorite, and closest to him in age.

He gave her a teasing look. "What's it to you?"

"I thought I'd warn you, though you probably don't deserve it. *Maman* is beside herself, waiting for you to get home. Father Ronsard's coming to dinner tonight. They want to talk about sending you away to seminary."

"Thanks for the warning," he said lightly. "I'll try to look properly pious."

"I think they're serious this time. I heard them talking."

"*Eh bien.*" He tweaked her ear. "When I'm ready to go to seminary or anywhere else, I'll go. But not before."

"I hope you don't have to leave right away, Gabriel. I suppose I would miss you."

"Not as much as I'd miss you. So don't worry. It's only talk."

He gave her a brave, defiant smile. But as they went up the porch steps, he felt as if the muddy river waters were closing over his head.

****

October...Nathaniel's birth-month, his favorite time. From where he sat in the meeting, he could see the maples and other hardwoods ablaze with reds and yellows, as if lit by an inner fire.

He stifled a yawn and wished he were out there in the crisp, autumn air. They'd already heard two hours of Sidney Rigdon. The old man was slow to wind down. Nathaniel had heard rumors that the severe beating, along with the tarring and feathering, had affected his mind. A tragedy, if it were true. For no one had more impressive oratorical gifts than Brother Sidney.

And no one was more eloquent in pleading the cause of the newly-begun House of the Lord. Nathaniel could hardly wait for the outer structure to be in place so that his own contribution as skilled carver and wood-worker could begin. Meanwhile he helped haul stone from the quarry, and worked wherever he was needed.

A flash of color drew his eye. One of the sisters in the first row had thrown back the hood of her cloak to reveal hair of bright auburn. A memory stirred in him. Where had he seen hair that color?

Then he knew, and a sudden pang shot through him. Could it be? No—she was supposed to be in Missouri with Dan; surely they were together by this time. He watched, perplexed, and when she turned to whisper to the person next to her, she saw that it was indeed Hannah.

He waited while the last hymn was sung. Even before the benediction had finished, he was edging his way forward. When she rose from her seat, he was standing beside her. Women's voices buzzed around them.

Nathaniel tried twice to speak, then managed to say, "Excuse me, Sister Hannah—you don't know me, but—but I saw you once at North Union."

Her eyes widened. "The Shaker settlement?"

"Yes—you see, that is—I talked some with Dan. I thought you'd be out in Missouri by now."

"You know Daniel?"

"Yes—I mean, not very well. But I knew he was on his way–"

"Rusty!" she cried. "Here's someone who knows Daniel!"

A young fellow, hardly more than a boy, leaned forward. Hannah introduced him as her brother.

Nathaniel took his hand. "Pleased to meet you. I'm Brother Givens. Is Dan here?"

A shadow crossed her face. "Why, no. He's in Missouri, and we're on our way to join him."

"And he's all right? He's not—"

"As far as we know, he's fine," Hannah said. "It's been a while since we've heard. But I know he's expecting us—he should have a cabin waiting for us by this time."

It took Nathaniel some moments to realize that they had been in Kirtland less than two days and knew very little of the Missouri troubles. He took her aside from the crowd and explained what he knew.

She blinked. "Oh, dear. He said nothing of this."

"It all happened so fast," Nathaniel said. "Our leaders—"

"Oh, my Lord—what shall we do now?"

"Our leaders are trying to appeal to the governor of the state. Brothers Hyde and Gould went out there to help them."

"Oh—we have to get out there." Her chestnut eyebrows drew together. She twisted the end of her cloak. "I have to find him. I'd best reach him before the year's end."

"Now—stay calm," Nathaniel said. "Think a moment. You might do better staying here for a while." She turned determined eyes upon him, and he finished weakly. "I mean, just till things settle down and we know it's safe."

"Oh, no. We have to get there." She drew in her lower lip and frowned. "Oh, how can we manage it?"

He said, "Let me make some inquiries. I know most of the townspeople—I'll see if there's anyone going up to Zion anyway soon. Where are you staying?"

"We're boarding with Sister Kimball."

"I'll come around in a day or so. Sooner, if I can."

For the first time she smiled. “Thank you. You’re very kind.”

As he turned away, Nathaniel could think of nothing more important than her getting to Missouri for a safe reunion with Daniel Perry. Strange—since Amanda, he hadn’t figured on caring about anything that much again. He sought out the information she needed, spurred on by the memory of her blue eyes. He wished he could bring a look of happiness to them, instead of anxiety and despair. True to his word, he made his way to the Kimballs’ front parlor the next afternoon.

Sister Kimball went to fetch her, and soon both Hannah and her brother hurried in to meet him. Nathaniel felt awkward in the homespun suit he’d worn for the occasion, not used to ladies’ parlors and fancy adornments. Sister Kimball didn’t help matters any.

“Land’s sakes, I’m so used to you in your work clothes, carting stone for the building. To see you all dressed up takes some getting used to.”

Nathaniel reddened; he’d simply wanted to appear presentable, and this was all he had. When Sister Kimball left, he took a step toward Hannah.

“As far as I can determine, there’s no one planning to go up to Zion in the next few weeks.”

“No?” Her well-defined eyebrows drew together.

“But a party did leave yesterday—two families with wagons, headed toward New Portage. With luck, we might be able to catch up to them—be safer that way.”

“I’d like that,” she said. “We could be ready very soon.”

"Like tomorrow morning?" he asked.

"Tomorrow? Yes—of course. Couldn't we, Rusty? This afternoon, if necessary."

Rusty nodded, but he looked dubious.

"Tomorrow's best," Nathaniel said. "That way, I can finish up some work, and get someone to take my place in the quarry."

"You?" She stared at him, and he knew she didn't understand.

"I'm aimin' to go with you. I want to see that you get there."

"Oh." A frown crossed her face. "But it's trouble for you—taking you away from the House of the Lord–"

He smiled. "There's plenty to carry on the work. My part will come later, when the woodworking begins." Misgiving hit him; perhaps she didn't want his help at all. He moistened his lips and went on.

"I feel it's something I owe to Dan—to see that you get there safely. He once did a great thing for me—I doubt that he ever knew it."

A smile lit her face, and she murmured her thanks. He added his last reason. "Besides, I have a longing to see the place."

"I'm hankerin' to see it too," Rusty said.

They made plans for the departure, and he agreed to come by for them in the morning. Then, before he had time to wonder at declaring himself the leader of an expedition, he left the house.

12

Before the journey, they took stock of their resources. Hannah had six pieces left of her mother's jewelry. Nathaniel had the little money he'd saved over the last four months. In his leather knapsack he carried a supply of dried apples and raisins, a loaf of bread and some cheese, walnuts, and fresh apples from Brother Crawford's orchard. He also had a change of clothes and some carpenter's tools.

"Ready?" he asked.

"We have everything." Hannah drew her cloak around her.

"The stage leaves at noon." His eye fell on the two valises. "Uh—what are those?"

Hannah gave him a quick glance. "My things. Everything we'll need when we get to Missouri."

He lifted one. "What's in it—stone from the quarry?"

Russell laughed, but Hannah flushed with anger. "Don't be ridiculous. It's clothes, and—and everything a lady needs."

He set it down. "That may very well be. But, Sister Hannah—

where we're going—that is, it might be muddy, even stormy. We may have to walk long distances. The less we have to carry, the better."

"Oh, we'll manage. Rusty will carry one, and I'll take the other."

"I'm only saying that if we can travel lighter, it might not be a bad idea."

She would not be dissuaded. Nathaniel shrugged. "Come on, then."

He led the way down the path, determined not to pick up a valise. Rusty struggled with the heaviest one, and Hannah carried the other. Halfway to the public house, Nathaniel relented and took the valise from her. She flashed him a smile. What had he got himself into? He set the bag on the wooden steps.

The stage came in twenty minutes later. Nathaniel helped stow the baggage. He elected to ride up with the driver. Rusty could attend to Hannah's needs inside the carriage. Then she could be as high and mighty as she pleased. Did Dan Perry have any idea what was about to appear on his doorstep?

Once they were on their way, Nathaniel gave himself up to the rhythm of the journey, the jouncing of the coach and the pounding hoof beats. The wind brushed against his face, full of the scent of pine needles and damp earth, and he felt better. After all, it was his chance to actually see the land of Zion, and he wasn't about to let a contrary woman spoil it.

At the next stop, he felt restored enough to take a place inside the coach. Hannah gave him a brief smile, then turned to look out the window. Nathaniel tightened his lips, feeling slighted. Something ached in his chest as he watched her. He had never seen such a beautiful woman, nor had he realized one could have such an effect on him. It wasn't fair, that she should look so lovely and full of promise, but inside be vain and selfish.

When they halted at noon, they found the stage stop crowded with people. Two children clung to their mother's skirts, and a trio of well-dressed gentlemen loitered in the doorway.

Nathaniel said, "Now, watch the driver. When he heads back this way, be sure you're in your seats. Otherwise someone else might take your place."

"What do you think—we've never traveled before?" she asked.

"He's only advising us, Hannah," Rusty said. "We'd be in trouble—delayed—if we didn't know."

Nathaniel stepped off first. He held his arm out to her, to help hand her down. She ignored it and jumped down. Rusty followed. "I'd say it's time to eat."

"Yes—I'm hungry. But there's such a crowd," she said.

"Oh, you want some food?" Nathaniel asked. "Come this way, then."

Hannah frowned, then followed him. He led them across the road to a large maple, its branches hung with red leaves. He found a level piece of ground and spread out his greatcoat.

"Sit, your majesty."

She eyed him, then sat down, arranging her skirts. Rusty knelt beside her and looked at Nathaniel.

"Do you want me to run across and buy something?"

"Not necessary." Nathaniel fished around in his knapsack and brought out a loaf of bread, cheese, and a small cutting board. From his belt he produced a woodsman's knife. They watched as he cut bread and cheese, then handed it to them.

Hannah took it with a surprised, gratified look.

"You're welcome," he said to her.

She gave her head a little shake. "Oh, yes—of course. Thank you."

He paused. "How about a smile with that? 'Thank you, Brother Nathaniel.'"

She repeated it softly, as if unwilling, but her lips curved in a smile. Rusty parroted her, drawing out the words in the imitation of backwoods speech. They all laughed.

"That will do," Nathaniel said. Hannah raised the bread to her mouth. As she was about to take the first bite, Nathaniel said, "The one we should really thank is our heavenly Father. Will you return thanks over the food, Rusty?"

They bowed their heads while Rusty mumbled a brief prayer. Then they ate.

"This bread is delicious," Hannah said.

"I'm glad you think so, sister," Nathaniel said. "I baked it myself."

Her eyes widened. "Well—I must say, it's very good."

"Surprised, are you? I learned to do many things in the Shaker community, and bakery work was one of them."

"It has an unusual taste," Rusty said. "Sweet."

"Almost like apples," Hannah said.

Nathaniel nodded. "Cider."

"You put cider in the dough?" she asked.

"Why not? Cider and honey. Enough of that will sweeten anyone's disposition."

She appeared not to notice this last comment and finished her bit of bread. She licked the ends of her fingers like a fastidious cat. Nathaniel watched, fascinated. Rusty broke the silence.

"I'm going to run over and get some water."

"As you wish," Nathaniel said. The boy left, his feet sending up tiny puffs of dust from the road. Nathaniel's throat tightened as he realized he and Hannah were alone. "Be you thirsty?"

"A bit."

He unstrapped a canteen from his belt, uncorked it and handed it to her.

"Cider?" she asked, smiling.

"Pure spring water. The best there is—from Brother Crawford's well."

She paused before she drank. "Thank you—Brother Nathaniel."

He tried not to smile. "That's getting better." He wrapped the remaining bread and cheese in cheesecloth and cleaned his knife on his jacket sleeve. He took one of the apples and rubbed it on the same sleeve. Then he quartered and cored it. She took the slice he offered and nibbled daintily.

They walked over to the coach. "It was good not to bounce around for a while," she said.

He looked at her. “We’re lucky, so far. We may not have this good a rig further west.”

All nine seats in the interior filled up as the driver took his place. Nathaniel saw that the two Mannings had their places inside, then climbed up with the driver.

“It’s a smart chance most of those folks’ll get off at New Portage,” the driver said.

At every stop, Nathaniel inquired if anyone had seen a bunch of people passing through in two wagons.

“Heading toward Independence,” he explained to one station master.

“That’s a far piece. They have a hoss with funny piebald spots, looked ready for the bone pile?”

“I couldn’t say. Maybe.”

“Two rigs went through here together, the sorriest bunch you ever saw. Mormonites, headin’ for the Indiana border. That last wagon—you never saw such a rickety get-up. Looked like one more hill would jest about finish it.”

“How long ago?” Nathaniel asked.

“Two days. Why—you ain’t interested in Mormonites, are you?”

Nathaniel thanked him and went to find Rusty and Hannah.

“Two days ahead of us. If we ride all night, we’ll have a good chance of catching ’em.”

Hannah said, “What do you mean—all night? I’m tired, and I want to sleep in a bed.”

Nathaniel met her gaze. “Suit yourself. We can catch up with ’em early, or try to find 'em later. But if we give up our places on the stage, we may have trouble finding seats on the next one."

"And this is a good one," Rusty said. "They're bringing in fresh horses now."

"And I don't know where you'd find a bed," Nathaniel said. "This isn't an inn. You have your choice of the floor, I guess, or else the woods—might not be too bad."

She turned away, and he saw that she was trying not to cry.

"Don't worry none," he said. "I hear you can sleep real good on one of these big rigs."

She sniffed. "I just never did it before."

She looked more frightened than adamant. Nathaniel felt a curious pity for her, a desire to protect her. "Let's have something to eat," he said.

They found a small table inside, close to the fire. Nathaniel bought cider, and they ate more bread and cheese. He cracked walnuts with the end of his hammer and spread them out on the table top. He watched Hannah, concerned that she looked pale and subdued. Tired, most certainly. He handed her bits of apple and walnuts. She ate listlessly.

"Try some cider," he urged. "It does wonders."

When they climbed back on board, only three others joined them—a stocky, well-fed man who took up two places, a thin, sad-looking woman and a boy. Rusty sat opposite Hannah, in the middle seat.

"You'd be more comfortable with your back to the driver,"

Nathaniel told her. "Here—on the end."

She sighed, then followed his advice. He took the seat next to her. As the stage gathered speed, he looked out at the woods and fields rolling by in the twilight. From the crest of a hill, a light glimmered in a lone farmhouse.

Hannah's hands moved nervously, and she gave little sniffs. Nathaniel began to speak in a low, soothing voice, just loud enough for her to hear.

"I always liked this time—when candles are first lit. When I lived with the Shakers, I remember coming home from the horse barn, through the apple orchard, and there'd be just enough light to see by, maybe an afterglow, all red-like, just over the hills to the west. And then I'd see the lights starting to flicker in the main house, just a little flicker at first..."

She made no sound. He felt her head settle on his shoulder; he held his breath. She slept.

Some time later, he awoke to find his own head resting on hers. How had that happened? In the darkness he arranged his greatcoat over them. Fearful of waking her, he leaned his cheek back down against her hair. Maybe she was beginning to trust him a little, like a skittish horse gentled down at last.

In Dayton they had to transfer to a smaller stage, with four horses instead of six. Nathaniel sat opposite Hannah, facing the front. He didn't know why, but it gave him pleasure just to look at her. He'd discovered that the majority of women in that part of the world, even the young ones, did not possess great beauty. Most of those at

Kirtland already had tight-lipped, resigned expressions like their mothers. But Hannah had full, curving lips, well-formed features, and an alert, intent look, as if she were open to the fullest possibilities of life.

As he watched her, he searched for the quality that made her so beautiful. Not just the brightness of her hair, or her blue eyes. A combination of everything, surely. To him, she was the embodiment of perfection.

Then his heart gave a leap. She was staring back at him, smiling, the corners of her eyes crinkling a little. She looked ready to burst into laughter. Chagrined, he shifted his glance.

He knew then—he loved her, and this time he sensed he would never stop caring for her. His destiny—to love women who could not return his feelings. Here she was, promised to another man, loving him enough to search him out over hundreds of miles of wilderness. And he, Nathaniel, had sworn to help her do it.

She mustn't know. It wouldn't do for her to suspect, even for a moment. He tightened his lips and pretended to be busy with the strap of his knapsack. The stage hit a bump and lurched sideways. The jolt flung everyone to the right side of the vehicle.

One of the women screamed. Hannah looked around, wide-eyed. Nathaniel reached across and took her hand.

"You're all right. It didn't go over."

A horse neighed. They could hear the driver commenting profanely. Nathaniel thrust open the door and jumped out.

"There's ladies present!" he yelled.

"I don't give a royal fiddler's behind—the blasted wheel's done come off!"

Nathaniel held open the door and began helping the passengers out. "Come on, lad," he said to a thin-faced boy whose front teeth protruded like a ferret's. "Off you get, now. Wake up, Rusty."

He helped Hannah to the ground, not daring to meet her eyes. What if she suspected already? He wondered about the best way of handling it. For once, the contents of his knapsack could not serve him.

They came in handy, however, with the repair of the wheel. With everyone out of the coach, Nathaniel and Rusty helped fetch the wheel and put it back on the shaft.

"She's good and tight now," Nathaniel said at last.

"It's them dratted rutty roads," the driver said.

"It's starting to rain," one of the women wailed.

"Blamed if it ain't," the driver said. "That's all we need—confounded mud ahead."

"I think we should look at the other wheels, too," Nathaniel said.

"That's the first dad-blamed sensible thing anyone's said for ten miles."

Nathaniel decided that it would be better for him if he began treating Hannah with less familiarity. Since he'd encouraged a friendly attitude on her part, this presented a difficulty. As they were straightening things up and putting tools away, Hannah moved over to him. He felt her nearness even though he couldn't see her, and a funny, prickly sensation tingled at the back of his neck.

"Please, Nathaniel—could I have some cheese for the boy and his mother? They haven't eaten since yesterday."

He wondered that he'd once thought her proud and selfish. "Of course." He reached in his pack for the food. "It might be better if you called me 'Brother Givens.'"

Her eyes met his, and she blinked, then smiled. "Well—how ridiculous! What's wrong with your first name? I know—I'll call you 'Nat.' Or Natty."

He swallowed, wishing he'd said nothing. She took the cheese, along with the little bread board and knife.

"Give them some bread, too," he said.

Her eyes danced. "Thank you, Natty."

He gnawed his upper lip as he watched her walk back to the group of passengers. How did you get someone like her to do what you thought best? Obviously, you didn't.

To be sure, the last thing he wanted was to distance himself from her. He tried not to think how difficult it would be at the end, when he finally parted from her for good. A man accepted such things and kept going.

The rain splattered against the side of the carriage. Nathaniel felt it in his hair; he shook his head. Everyone climbed back into the coach. Nathaniel resumed his seat. He watched the water streaking the oilskin window. When he looked down, he saw the hem of Hannah's gown stained with mud.

She didn't seem to notice. She was looking out the window, her lips parted, her gaze dreamy and wistful. She's thinking of Dan, he told himself, and a wave of despair washed over him.

****

"In the first place, it wasn't like you think," Parley Pratt said to the youthful interviewer. "I mean, we all thought the hostilities would die down. There was no reason to think otherwise. We figured, give those old boys about three months or so, and most likely we could begin to set things right.

"Now—you're asking about that manifesto. Sure we all signed it—the Whitmers and Phelps and the rest of them, but it was under duress, and I don't figure that counts in any man's book.

"Well, we gave 'em time to cool down, but no one really believed we'd have to get out of Jackson County. Why, even the prophet was sayin' it was all right to keep goin' in there and settlin'—it was our inheritance, our promised land.

"It's true—I hate to admit it. There was young fellers braggin', sayin' the gentiles was gonna end up sellin' us their land. Dan Perry and some of those others. And you can be sure that didn't go down too well. Oh, I tried to git 'em to shut up, but it was like talkin' to a mule.

"So what did we do? That's a good question. Well, first, William Phelps and Orson Hyde, they went over to Jefferson City with a petition for Governor Dunklin himself. He didn't hold out much hope. He finally sent word that he was sympathetic and all, but we'd have to bring suit for damages against the mob in the circuit court.

"Now, the prophet had advised us to seek legal help, so we went and employed counselors to help us. Let's see if I can remember—Doniphon, Atchison, Reese and Wood from Liberty County. Hired for the sum of one thousand dollars.

"What do you mean—was that a lot? Of course it was. They said it was necessary because taking our case would deprive them of other business in those parts, since feelings were still running pretty strong. So we paid 'em what they wanted. Edward Partridge and Phelps signed a note, and it was endorsed by Gilbert and Whitney.

"Well, as soon as word got out to the settlers that we'd hired these lawyers, they knew we were planning to hold our ground and try to get redress. The news spread like lightning. Then the wave of attacks began. First, about the end of October, a mob—about fifty people—attacked ten cabins west of the Big Blue River. They broke down doors, tore off roofs, smashed furniture. They even threw stones at the men and drove the women and children into the woods. They spent the whole night shivering in the cold.

"The next thing we knew, they were wrestling down and beating our men in the streets while the women and children cowered in thickets. Then a bunch of them went over to David Bennett's home—now both the man and his wife were terribly ill. I'll be darned if that mob didn't break in, drag them from their beds, and beat him to death with his own gun. His wife and children fled into the woods.

"About this time we began to realize that legal redress might take a while. And—justice or no justice—it was time for action."

13

Gabriel finished the Book of Mormon in the warmth of the blacksmith shop. Just as he closed the book, his brother Étienne called for more wood.

"Coming." He set the book on the bench and tramped out into the cold. He hoisted split logs from the pile, annoyed at being interrupted even though he'd come to the end. He liked time to think about what he'd read, to ponder the meaning of it.

Étienne, oldest and tallest of the five Romain children, had taken over the blacksmith shop at their father's death. Gabriel trudged back inside with the armful of wood. In the flickering light, he saw that the book had vanished.

"Another load, and it should be enough," Étienne said.

"Did you see a book on the settle?"

"I did. What are you reading such trash for?"

"I read anything I can find. And maybe I don't think it's trash."

Étienne gave him a critical look. "You're so lucky. You don't have to be a blacksmith. You're going to be a priest."

Gabriel met his brother's gaze. "Maybe I'd rather be something else."

"Like what? A Mormonite?"

"No. A—a healer, like Dr. Beauchamps."

Étienne gave a brief laugh. "Don't be crazy. Dr. Beauchamps is *fou.* Everyone knows it. But *Père* Ronsard--look how he's respected. People treat him like he's God and knows everything. He speaks, and they can't wait to do what he says. That's how they'll treat you."

"*Eh bien.* Where's my book?"

"You don't want it. It's what heretics read. Huguenots. You shouldn't be wasting your time like that."

Gabriel sighed. "If you don't need me anymore, I'll go on home."

His brother turned and strode into the next room. Gabriel heard the sound of the hammer striking against steel. He pulled his coat around him and went out the door.

He didn't hurry as he walked through the area of stores and offices. Strange, how the little remnant of French Catholics had managed to isolate themselves from the rest of the town. *Père* Ronsard did indeed tell them what to do, even what they should or should not read, and like faithful sheep, they obeyed. Sometimes Gabriel believed that he and Dr. Beauchamps were the only ones with a less parochial view of things.

Thanks to the doctor, he knew there was far more to life than what Father Ronsard proclaimed. He wondered if the good father had any idea of the books in Dr. Beauchamps' study—writings by Voltaire,

Martin Luther, and even George Fox, the founder of Quakerism.

Gabriel also knew there was more happening in the town than met the eye. Situated on the northern shore of the Ohio River, Gallipolis and the neighboring towns seethed with abolitionist sentiment. He knew the local places where escaped slaves could be given food and a night's shelter before they went north. He'd seen the haunted faces of the women, the frightened children, some of them too hungry and ill even to cry. He'd seen the men, their manner ill at ease, their expressions full of suspicion. Sometimes Gabriel wondered that they could trust anyone at all, after the things that had happened to them.

He had remained with his family longer than most males his age so that he could help people find their way to freedom. He could come and go without attracting the attention of those who sought fugitive slaves. For who would suspect the younger son of a deceased blacksmith, a youth who intended, at some future date, to become a priest?

Now he had an uneasy feeling—perhaps this particular phase of his life was at an end. Once his brother told his mother about his heretical adventures with the printed word, she would no doubt inform the priest and they would pack him off to seminary before he knew it. Not even Dr. Beauchamps would be able to plead his cause. And, although there was a time when he might not have protested, he knew now that the priesthood was out of the question.

In his last few days of reading the forbidden book, even in that last hour, he'd encountered something he had not believed possible—the sense of the actual presence of Jesus Christ. He could not explain it; he certainly had not willed it. But he could not deny that it had happened—he felt the reality of it even as he walked down the main street and pulled his coat collar up to shield him from the wind.

For that reason alone, he could not go down the path they had planned for him. If the very spirit and presence of Christ could be found in a heretical book, then the Church—by insisting that it alone was right—proclaimed a lie. And if one lie existed, most likely there were others.

All this was not easy for him. His upbringing formed a vital part of him, and as he struggled with truth and falsehood, with things of God and things man-made, perspiration broke out on his forehead. The presence surrounded him, going before him like a pillar of spiritual light; he felt warmed, consumed, on fire with it. He seemed to see his front porch and steps through a dream-like haze. He felt light-headed, physically drained, as if he had fallen in love for the first time.

"Gabriel—what's the matter?" Marie-Françoise stepped outside and closed the door behind her. "Are you ill?"

"Oh, no. I've been—well, just reading and thinking."

"Oh—*mon pauvre cheri*."

"I'm not your *cheri*, and you know it."

She gave him a hurt look. "Well, you don't have to be so grumpy."

"I'm sorry. I—Marie, I may have to go away for a while."

"I know. *Maman* and Father Ronsard have been talking all morning. She's getting your clothes together."

He swallowed. So soon—he was hoping they'd wait till spring. "I'm not going to seminary."

"You'd better tell them. I wish you didn't have to leave. But when you're a priest, Gabriel—I'll come and stay with you, and keep house."

He tried to keep his voice steady. "I'm not going to be a priest."

She paused. "They all expect it. But I wouldn't want to, either."

He reached out and put a hand on her shoulder. She turned to open the door. They went inside.

Their mother, dark and slender, short like her children, moved toward them from the hearth. She had the same fine features and gray eyes as Marie. Unlike Marie, she wore her hair in a severe bun at the back of her neck. The style, coupled with her black dress, gave her an austere, pale look. Gabriel knew she liked to play the part of a French aristocrat. With her thin face, she appeared more faded and weary than aristocratic.

"Gabriel, you must pack. Father Ronsard wants to take you with him in the morning."

"I see." He had one last chance. "*Maman*, if it's all the same to you, I don't think I have the temperament to be like *Père* Ronsard."

"So—you have your own temperament. That's understandable."

"That is—would you consider sending me to medical school instead? I've read most of the books in Dr. Beauchamps' library."

"Don't be ridiculous. Everything is all arranged."

"But, *maman*—why not? Why can't I choose what I want to do?"

She frowned and folded her hands together. "Because you don't even know what you want. You're too young. You have a great opportunity, and you're taking it lightly. If you had any sense at all, you wouldn't even speak this way."

"Please, *maman*--"

Her jaw quivered. "We've waited long enough. You're wasting time. You will go to your room, Gabriel, and pack what you need. You leave in the morning."

Still he waited. "And if I choose not to?"

She looked at Marie-Françoise. "Will you leave us for a moment?"

The girl nodded and went into the next room. Their mother put her fingers to her lips and gave a little cough.

"Gabriel—I've never told you this. I always hoped it wouldn't be necessary. There's a special reason, as you've probably suspected. That is—long ago, back in Paris, a—a child died because of me."

He gave an intake of breath. She looked at him. "I was taking care of a baby for a little seamstress who lived in the next street, and—and one day the little one just wouldn't stop crying. I picked him up and shook him—just a little—and after that he stopped breathing."

Gabriel waited, not sure what to say. She sighed and went on. "Nothing—there was nothing anyone could do. No one knew what I had done—but I felt responsible. I caused the death of that child."

"But you don't know," Gabriel said. "Maybe he was ill—he would've died anyway."

She didn't seem to hear. "All this time I've felt haunted by it. Then it came to me—if I gave a child to God, offered him as a special servant, then maybe I would be forgiven."

"I see. So you thought you would give *me*—"

"You were the one—the quickest, the most intelligent of all my children."

He took a step toward her. "Tell me, *maman*. Aren't there other ways? Say—a healer, or one who points the way to freedom. Isn't that serving?"

"Not the same way a priest does—where he gives up everything to God and the Church."

His mouth felt dry. "I—I understand. I'm to be a—some sort of sacrificial lamb, so that you can feel better about this thing that happened."

She nodded and dabbed at her eyes with a handkerchief. "Oh, Gabriel—it's such a comfort to tell someone at last."

"Why don't you just tell Father Ronsard and have him say a special mass or something? Let him know the whole story."

Her voice broke. "I've told him a little. He seems to think your choosing a vocation is an excellent thing."

"All right." He shrugged, then let his breath out. "I'll go upstairs now."

"Thank you, Gabriel. *Merci*. Your clean clothes are in your bureau."

In his room, he gathered a few items, then folded them in a blanket. He rolled up the blanket and fastened it with a leather strap at each end. He sat on the bed and looked at the wooden floorboards for a long time, then at his shoes—they were new, ready for a journey.

Then he stood up, put on an extra pair of socks, and found his woolen sweater that he used for the coldest days. He was pulling it on when he heard the knock at the door.

"Entrez."

Marie-Françoise opened the door and hurried in. She gave him an anxious, open-mouthed look. "Tell me—what did she say to you, to convince you?"

"Convince me of what?"

"Oh, Gabriel—you know. Why do you tease me now?"

"Because maybe it's the only thing I can do."

Her eyebrows slanted in a frown. She looked at the rolled blanket. "Is that all you're taking? What about the trunk? *Maman* said you could have it."

He mumbled something about packing later.

"*Maman* says you're to come to dinner now. Étienne just got home."

Gabriel picked up the blanket and walked toward the door. Then he stopped. "Marie—promise me something. I'm going out later tonight."

"Do you think they'll be coming across in this weather—so cold and windy?"

"You can't tell. There might be someone needing help. It's best to look. Promise—if anything should happen to me..."

"What?"

"Tell *maman*—say that she has given me to God, and I have pledged myself to serve him. But it has to be in my own way, and according to my own abilities."

She was still frowning. "I—I will. I'll tell her."

"Later on—when I've gone."

"I promise."

He stowed the blanket-roll behind the coat rack and followed Marie in to dinner.

In the months afterward, whenever he thought of his family he remembered that meal, with his mother sitting so straight at her end of the table. Her face looked drawn and strained, her mouth red against the pallor of her skin. She acted indifferent, withdrawn, as if nothing unusual had occurred between them. Gabriel watched her, and a little ache began in his chest. Étienne, in his father's place, cut the crusty bread and served it.

Toward midnight Gabriel left the keeping room and went into the parlor. No one else seemed to notice; they were accustomed to his night excursions. He opened the door, then reached for the rolled blanket. He grabbed his coat and walked out onto the porch.

He stood in the moonlight to fasten his coat and put his arms through the straps of the blanket-roll. Then, fearful that someone would suspect his intentions and call him back, he set out for the river. He felt too cold to sense regret, or even uncertainty. He would write to Marie later, once he got to where he was going. He reached the river on the other side of town and followed it north.

He came to a halt. A sound coming from the river bank—a moaning. The wind? He crouched low and crept through the dried ferns.

Two logs jutted out from the bank. The man lay sprawled across them, one leg in the river. Gabriel had to step into the water to lift him up and drag him to shore. Gabriel set him down in the ferns. The man shivered. Gabriel could hear his teeth chattering. His clothes were soaked, and his right arm, swollen below the elbow, dangled useless.

Broken? Gabriel put his fingers around the arm, felt the break in the larger bone. Were the edges aligned? To move him any distance would worsen the injury.

Gabriel found a stout stick and splinted the arm. He fastened it with one of his leather straps. Then he shook out the blanket and crammed his few belongings into his coat pockets. Even with the blanket over him, the man kept trembling.

No time to lose. Gabriel tried to hoist him to his feet. "You're safe—you're on the Ohio shore. But you must walk. Please—try to walk now."

The man made a sound in his throat and took a step. Gabriel put his arm under the man's uninjured arm and around his back, then led him toward town.

They kept to the shadows, their way lighted by the Hunter's Moon. Finally they reached Dr. Beauchamps' back step. The injured man staggered; it felt as if he'd gained weight on the journey. His own strength exhausted, Gabriel knocked at the door.

Dr. Beauchamps opened it. "*Mon Dieu!* What have we here?"

"His arm's broke." Gabriel was breathing fast. "And he's half-frozen. It was too far to the safe house—I thought he should come here."

The doctor's eyes shone in the moonlight, and the wrinkles stood out on his forehead. "Let's get him in."

Together they brought the man to a cot beside the wall. The doctor lit another candle from the one sputtering on the desk. "I was just about to go to bed." He ran his hand through his bushy gray side whiskers. "Another moment, and both candle and fire would be out."

"I didn't know what else to do. I tried to set the arm."

"Let's have a look." The doctor poured water into a basin, then washed and dried his hands. "Looks like he swum the river. Lift him up, now."

Gabriel raised him to a sitting position. They removed the blanket and the ragged, damp shirt.

"Look, here," the doctor said. "Lashes all up and down his back. These are fresh."

Gabriel looked at the long welts criss-crossing each other, the two fresh ones oozing.

"I have a salve for those. Let's see the arm." The doctor unwrapped the leather strap and looked briefly at the make-shift splint. Then he examined the arm with a grasp less gentle than Gabriel had used. The man's eyes flew open, and he cried out.

"Sorry," the doctor said. "We're almost done. It's fractured, but it's in a good position. We won't need to send for the bone-setter. See this bruise? Something hit him pretty hard."

"Will he be all right?"

"I don't know. We'll put a good splint on it. He looks strong—he may heal up and be fit as a fiddle."

"Can't we be sure?"

The doctor looked at Gabriel before he spoke. "He's got a chance, if we can keep him quiet and warm. What's this?"

He pulled a soggy, folded paper from the shirt pocket. He peeled it open and held it closer to the candle. "I'll be dad-blamed." He handed it to Gabriel.

Gabriel squinted to make out the first few words. "It says his name's Ebenezer."

The man made a sound, as if to speak. Gabriel met the doctor's eyes. "These are his freedom papers. His master set him free."

"'Course that doesn't mean anything," the doctor said. "The traders could just catch him and sell him again. He's lucky he got across the river. Must've been quite a struggle, with that arm the way it is."

"He's sure spent now."

They washed the dirt from him, and the doctor found some dry clothes. "Looks like he's about my height."

Ebenezer slept, covered by the blanket. Gabriel now had time to look at him. A young man—maybe around twenty-three. The face—not pallid like his own, but a warm, copper color. Thick black eyebrows and long, curly hair. His nose flat and broad, his mouth wide. His eyelids, unusually long, fluttered as he took a deep breath. Gabriel thought of the injury, the unhealed welts on his back, and felt a sorrow too deep for words.

"Don't look so troubled," the doctor said. "He's safe enough here."

"I know. I–"

"If you're going to do this kind of work, Gabriel, you can't let sympathy get in the way. It clouds your judgment—and that's no good to anybody."

"This is what I want to do."

"Well, then. We'll splint that arm, and get some more blankets on him. And he'll need rest—a day or two, maybe more. I have to be away tomorrow."

"I'll stay with him," Gabriel said.

"You?"

"I'll take care of him—I don't intend to leave your house. You see—I was on my way out of here when I found him."

The doctor gave him a stern look. "You don't mean it."

"They're fixing to send me off tomorrow—to seminary. I can't do it. I mean—for a long time I've felt that I belong somewhere else. Now I'm certain of it."

In the dim light, the doctor's face looked gentler. "Well, I'll be blamed. But—running off in the night. It seems like a reckless way of settling it. Just where do you figure on going?"

"Somewhere north. I'm not sure, exactly." He shrugged and stared at the candle. "I'll know when I get there."

"I expect you will."

He turned quickly. "Don't say a word—not to my family—my brother. Even Marie. I reckon we'll hide till Ebenezer here's well enough to travel. We'll head for the safe house and rest there. Then I'll go north with him."

The doctor took a deep breath, then shook his head. “My lips are sealed. But—I figure there’re things I can do to help.” He scratched at his side whiskers. “I‘d say you’ll need a knapsack—maybe two—and a bit of food. Let’s see to our patient, here.”

The doctor fetched two pine boards and put them on either side of the arm. Ebenezer didn’t move, nor did he make a sound until Gabriel held up the arm. Then he gave a groan. The doctor wrapped stout rope around the arm and boards.

“Now—don’t answer that door, no matter who it is. Keep it locked till I get back tomorrow night.”

The doctor retired to his own room. Gabriel blew out the candle and wrapped himself in a blanket. He stretched out beside the cot and slept. He awakened to light—the sun on his face. He blinked. Ebenezer was leaning over the edge of the cot, staring at him.

Gabriel raised his head. “Uh—good morning.”

“Morning. Why you sleeping on the floor?”

“This was the best place I could find. I had a heavy blanket, so I wasn't cold. How do you feel?”

“I got a powerful misery in my arm.”

Gabriel got to his feet. “I’m not surprised. You’re hurt bad, Ebenezer.”

He looked puzzled. “Don’t call me that.”

Gabriel looked at him. “But it’s your name—it’s on your freedom papers.”

“Only the master say that. The others call me ‘Ebner,’ or ‘Eb.’”

Gabriel nodded. “Eb it is, then. Are you hungry?”

"I can eat."

"I'll see what the doctor has in his pantry."

Eb's eyes narrowed. "Gabriel."

"How'd you know my name?"

"I heard you and the other man—last night. But, man—you a scrawny little thing. And I'm big. How'd you get me here?"

Gabriel smiled. "You're not that big. And I'm stronger than you might think. But you walked—don't you remember? I got you on your feet, and you did the rest."

"I don't remember nothing. I thought I was drowned for sure."

"Do you remember how you broke your arm?"

Eb put his left hand over the splint. "The beating. It seem like I just couldn't take another one. I pulled the whip from his hand—"

"Your master?"

"No. My master, he dead. Gave me the papers before he died. This the overseer—meanest man I ever met."

Gabriel nodded. "So you grabbed the whip—"

"Blamed if he didn't hit me with a board. I dropped the whip and lit out like crazy."

"You rest now." Gabriel headed for the doctor's living quarters.

Dr. Beauchamps' coat rack was empty; he'd already left. Gabriel found a pot of coffee, which he set back on the hearth to warm. Then he collected cheese, ham, and pieces of bread which he sliced from a loaf in the pantry. He also found a burlap sack which he planned to use for a sling.

He draped the burlap over his shoulder and carried plates, bread, knife and food back to the study. He set a plate beside Eb. Then he sat cross-legged on the floor to eat his own breakfast.

"That do look good. Seems like days since I ate. What's this?"

"*Jambon,*" Gabriel said, his mouth full.

"Looks like ham to me."

He gestured and swallowed. "It is."

"Then why didn't you say so? You said something else."

"I said it in French."

"French!" Eb's eyebrows went up. "Is that what you are?"

Gabriel explained how his people had come to America to live in a colony, but things had gone terribly wrong and they had almost starved.

"Lord Almighty! I heard there was French folks here, but I never thought I'd run into one."

"There's not many left now. They all went other places—the ones that survived."

"By gum." Eb gave him a grave look. "I'm sure glad there was one around last night."

"Oh." Gabriel shrugged, unsure how to reply.

"So you rescue folks regular-like?"

"Mainly I show them the way north—lead them to the safe house. You're the first I found with an arm broke."

Eb finished the ham and cheese. "Like you told the man—you want to go north with me?"

"Well, you can't manage very well by yourself. And I'm going that way anyway."

"I see." Eb finished the last crumbs of bread.

"Want some more?"

"I'm fine for now. I'm not all that hungry."

"It's the arm," Gabriel said. "I wish I could give you something for the pain. The doc might have some whiskey."

"Where up north?"

"If we get to Lake Erie, there's a place I'd like to find. But I have no idea—See, I figure I can work as a blacksmith most anywhere—that's what my father did."

"A smithy, huh?"

"I can teach you, too. It's not that hard. What were you figuring on doing?"

Eb gave a sigh and looked out the window. "What I want most is to get my wife out of Virginia."

"You married?" Again Gabriel felt the stab of sorrow.

"I didn't reckon on leaving her like this."

"But if you know where she is—*eh bien,* we can fetch her! We'll go to work and buy her freedom."

"Don't talk crazy. And stop flipping your hands around like that."

"But we can. What's the matter? Was I speaking French again? Oh, blame it—the coffee!"

Gabriel ran in to the hearth, where the coffee was beginning to boil. He poured it into two cups and took them into the study.

"It's thick. Dr. B. likes it about like river mud."

"It'll do fine."

They sipped the coffee in silence. Finally Eb said, "When do we leave?"

"Think you can travel? We'll move at night, hide out during the day till we get north a little. You get some rest now. The first thing I'm gonna do is make you a sling—you can't move that arm."

"No?"

"You have to keep it as quiet as possible—it'll heal faster."

"That's good. You be hopping around and moving your arms enough for both of us."

Gabriel washed up the few dishes. He fashioned a sling out of the burlap bag. He thought of waking Eb and trying it on for size, but resisted the temptation. Then, in the late afternoon, uneasiness gripped him.

What was it the doctor had said? Something about recklessness, a better way to settle things? Suddenly Gabriel felt a chill at the back of his neck. The doctor's loyalty was to his family, not him. Panic set in; he went and awakened Eb.

"We have to leave."

"All right—if you say so."

"Let's just put this on." Gabriel slid the burlap under the arm and tied it around Eb's neck.

Eb looked at it, then blinked. "It's not dark yet."

"We'll hide in the woods. Just trust me. We're going to a Quaker farmhouse—it's some distance. But once we're there, you can rest two days if you want to."

"Is it traders you're feared of?"

"Right now, it's my family. I'll tell you on the way."

They stopped for food at the nearest safe house. At dusk, they started out again. Eb traveled better than Gabriel had expected; aside from the arm, he seemed strong and accustomed to strenuous work.

"It don't hurt as much when I'm walking."

Toward dawn they reached the farmhouse and found a place to rest. The Quaker family had a concoction which soothed Eb and allowed him to sleep free of pain. Gabriel, stretched out beside him on the bed, mused on the fact that they were both on the way to freedom.

Just outside Canton, they heard that Mormonite missionaries were in town.

"That's the group I'm looking for," Gabriel said. "Let's go hear them."

"I don't know. Brigham Young, did you say? What kind of name is that? It ain't even in the Bible."

"It's all right. Trust me."

They walked up the main street of the town in the early evening and took their places at the advertised preaching service.

14

Nathaniel and the two Mannings trailed the Zion-bound wagons to a point just short of the Illinois border, beyond the town of Clinton. Now, fully expecting to overtake them, he scanned the woods from his seat beside the driver.

A storm had come through in the early morning. Trees lay by the road's edge. Then the horses stopped. A downed tree blocked the road.

"Can't hitch the team to it?" Nathaniel asked the driver. "Haul it to the side?"

"Too big. There's another down beside it, big as this 'un."

Nathaniel chewed his lower lip as the others climbed out of the coach. The wagons had to be dead ahead—on the other side of the fallen trees.

"We'll have to go back, get help," the driver said. "You wanna git back in?"

Nathaniel shook his head. "We're gonna take our chances. Rusty!

Haul down the luggage."

The boy brought down the two valises. Nathaniel reached for the largest one. Hannah gave him a questioning look.

"We're so close I can almost smell their bacon," he told her. "We're gonna walk a bit—think you're up to it?"

Her eyes flashed. "Of course."

"Come on, then." He pushed ahead. Rusty struggled with the smaller valise. They climbed up over the tree trunks.

"Best to stay on the side of the road, away from the ruts," Nathaniel said.

The valise grew heavy. His shoulder began to ache. He was breathing hard, the perspiration rolling down his forehead. He strained to see through the trees. Then he felt Hannah touch his arm.

"Put it down," she said.

"What?"

"The valise. It's too heavy—too much. I've been thinking—from what I've seen, I won't need half these things."

He set it down. She opened both of them and repacked the things she wanted in the smaller one. Nathaniel tried not to stare at the quantity of dresses left in the large valise.

"There," she said. "Let's go."

Nathaniel nodded, and they walked on. He imagined some rough scout from the Indian lands finding the bundle of fancy ladies' clothes in the woods.

In another three miles they came upon the wagons. The occupants looked weary, even the children, their faces creased with dirt from the road. They welcomed the three newcomers with joy.

"Goin' up to Zion? We'd be pleased to travel with you," Nathaniel said.

First, he and Rusty set to work repairing the wheel of the second wagon. The party had two strong men, but their skills did not include working in wood or making simple repairs. As their journey continued, Nathaniel began to wonder what they did include. They were all Easterners, and the tasks of surviving in the wilderness came hard to them.

A married couple owned the first team and wagon—Lem and Diana Wheeler. They were big, blond people with two young children to match—a boy of three and a girl who said she was five.

"This many." She held up sticky fingers.

Her brother stuck his finger in his nose as they watched Nathaniel tighten the wheel.

"What be your names?" he asked.

The girl spoke again. "I be Adah, and him's Jacob."

The second wagon had the Beckett clan—Timothy and Pandora, husband and wife. They were both dark-haired, of medium height. Traveling with them was Timothy's aged mother and his sister Aletha, a scrawny little woman whose mouth seemed set in a perpetual frown.

Nathaniel learned that Timothy Beckett was an artisan—a clock maker—and Lem Wheeler had worked as a miller. Anything else seemed beyond them. In a matter of days, Nathaniel found himself the nominal head of the expedition. The rest looked to him for direction.

"If you're not having prayer every evening, then we'd better start," he informed them.

He presided over the brief prayer services after the evening meal. He felt Hannah's eyes on him as he spoke, and a heady feeling of elation ran through him.

Another pair of eyes followed him too—those of Aletha Beckett. When she learned Nathaniel was unmarried, she began to act as if his appearance was an answer to prayer. Nathaniel, caught between his love for Hannah and his desire not to disappoint anyone else, tried to put as much distance from the women as he could.

While he concentrated on the duties of leadership, the other women began picking on Hannah. As if jealous of her beauty, they demanded that she do the most menial tasks they could find. By the time Nathaniel realized what was happening, the pattern had been established.

"Why—where's Hannah?" he asked as they assembled for prayers.

"I expect she's down at the crick washin' the children's clothes," Diana said.

"At this time of night?"

"She coulda done it earlier, but she hadn't finished her other work."

Furious, Nathaniel said, "What do you think she is—some kind of servant?"

"She's expected to work like anyone else."

His eyes flicked over the group. "Where's Rusty?"

"I expect he's with her," Aletha said. "The lady with the log house waitin' for her needs help."

Nathaniel left them and strode down to the creek's edge. He met Rusty on the path with a basket of wet clothes.

"How long has this been going on?"

"What?" Rusty asked. "The washin'? She's about done."

"No—all this work."

Rusty looked puzzled. "I don't know—maybe a few days."

"Why didn't you tell me?"

"Well—I figure she thought it was how things should be."

Nathaniel found Hannah kneeling by the shore. "You're finished. Rinse them and get up."

She straightened up. "You're right, Nathaniel. This was the last of it."

He helped her wring out the clothes and sent Rusty back to camp with the basket. Hannah put her hand up to brush her hair from her face. He saw how her fingernails, once perfect, were broken and uneven, her fingers red. But her face was still beautiful, with its wholesome, open look. Being close to her, alone in this twilit place, made his heart do strange things.

"It's dangerous for you to be alone down here in the dark."

A faint smile lit her features. "I'll be all right."

He drew in his breath. "Hannah—I don't like to see you working so hard."

"Well—I expected we'd have to make ourselves useful."

"But—you're doing more than your share—I didn't realize—"

She looked at him, her eyebrows up. "Nathaniel—it's all right. I'm strong, and—don't you see? Don't you understand about the women? It's so hard for them. Both those wives are exhausted—they're to be mothers soon. Diana has her hands full with the children. And Pandora—she's lost three babies already. She's not strong."

He blinked, wordless. She said, "I must do what I can. Nathaniel—" She shook her head.

He remembered the group assembled for prayers. They would wonder why he lingered so long with a woman betrothed to someone else. He gave a little cough.

"We'd best go back now."

****

Missouri stretched on all sides of them, a sea of meadows. So this is the land of Zion, Hannah thought as she walked beside the first wagon. They had left the forests behind and found a wide, rolling prairie whose grasses rippled like waves in the wind. The newness of it fascinated her—a dramatic change from the eastern woodlands.

An amazing variety of trees grew by the stream beds. Besides the usual oaks and maples, there were hickory, elm and black walnut. Nathaniel had pointed out cherry, honey locust, wild plums, grapes, and persimmons. The hogs, cattle and horses which they saw seemed to have an abundance to eat. Deer bounded over the prairie, their white tails held high. Once they spotted buffalo, five shaggy animals grazing in a close group.

She had never seen so many birds—flocks of turkeys making their strange, wild cries, the waters full of geese and swans. She thought of all the rivers they'd crossed, either fording or by ferry. The names formed a litany in her mind—the Mud, the Miami, the Wabash, the Illinois, the mighty Mississippi, the Salt, the Chariton and Missouri. Now—Nathaniel assured them—they'd almost reached their destination.

Hard to believe. She smiled—what had she expected? Castle walls, ramparts with sunlit flags flying, trumpets blaring—there was not the slightest sign of civilization. One lone cabin in the last ten miles.

The high grass swished as she passed, and she became aware of a sweet scent in the air, like rich, damp soil. She felt a surge of joy—this would be her home, this lush, pristine land, fertile and lovely. Then Nathaniel was walking beside her—she sensed him, a bright presence on her right.

He glanced at her and smiled. "This puts me in mind of a song the Shakers sang." He began to sing in a low baritone.

> *" 'Tis a gift to be simple,*
> *'Tis a gift to be free."*

When he finished the phrase, 'the valley of love and delight,' he stopped. "I—wasn't one of their best singers."

"But you do very well." In an effort to reassure him, she took his hand in hers. He stopped. A shocked, pained expression went over his face.

She withdrew her hand. "What is it, Nathaniel? Every once in a while—like now—you act so strange. I thought we were friends."

He paused before he spoke, and one corner of his mouth twitched. "I be more of a friend to you than you can possibly know."

She looked into his eyes, puzzled. "You mean—"

"I mean you're promised to someone else, and I cannot bear to leave you."

She struggled to understand. "Well, yes, but—"

"How do you think I feel? I've brought you all this way, and soon I must go back and never see you again."

"But you knew that—I mean, you knew about Daniel."

He looked straight ahead and spoke in a muted voice. "I didn't think to fall in love with you. But it was impossible not to. I couldn't stop it."

She felt like trembling as the words washed over her. She wondered what to do. "Nathaniel—I don't know what to say."

"Don't say anything. It's not something you need worry about. I—wasn't going to tell you—I'd hoped to keep it from you."

"Well, I'm glad you didn't. It's best that I know. It explains some things—Nathaniel, I'll always be grateful to you, for taking care of us the way you have."

Moisture glistened at the corners of his eyes. "Don't. There's no need."

"No. Wait—I value your friendship. I would like us always to be friends—after all, we're brother and sister in Christ."

He gave a terse laugh. "Husbands don't like their wives to have friends like me. At least, I wouldn't."

She'd handled it badly. What did well-bred ladies do? Her mother had never mentioned it. Nathaniel moved up to the front of the wagon and clicked to the horses. Hoof beats sounded off to the left. He turned.

She followed his gaze. Just over the rise she saw a cloud of dust. As it grew larger, she made out figures—five, six, no—nine riders galloping toward them over the prairie. Nathaniel grabbed the reins of the lead horse and brought the wagon to a stop.

Rusty walked up behind them from the second wagon. He held the little boy Jacob by the hand. "What do they want?"

Nathaniel squinted in the sunlight. "Don't know. I'm not sure they mean us any good." He stepped back to the side of the wagon. He reached over the side and brought down his knapsack and greatcoat.

"Here." He handed the coat to Hannah. "Put this over your shoulders. And pull your cloak up over you. Cover your hair—your face, too."

"What?" She stared at him.

"Do it. Quickly, now." His voice sounded more forceful than she'd ever heard it. She shrugged, but her fingers shook as she pulled both cloak and coat around her.

"What do we do?" Lem asked from the wagon seat. Diana and the little girl, roused from their naps, looked over the side of the wagon.

"Let's see what they want," Nathaniel said.

"We sure can't outrun them," Timothy said from the second

wagon.

A horse neighed from the group of riders. Someone shouted. The lead horse on the first wagon reared up in terror. Nathaniel grabbed the reins and brought him to a halt.

"All we need is horses bolting," Lem said.

The men rode up to them. One, lanky and bearded, looked down on them. "Mormonites, ain't ye?"

"We are, yes," Nathaniel said. "We don't mean any trouble."

"We're peaceful," Lem said.

"I reckon ye've come here to settle," a stocky, red-faced man said.

"That's our intention," Lem said.

"Well, we got other plans for you," the red-faced man said. "Come on—out! All of you!"

He hit the side of the wagon. Pandora screamed. One of the horsemen cracked a whip, and at first Hannah thought it was gunfire.

"Hannah—here." Diana handed Adah down over the side of the wagon. The little girl began to cry. Hannah held her close and smoothed back the damp, blond hair.

"Hush, honey. You're all right."

Lem jumped to the ground and helped Diana down.

"Please," Timothy was saying. "My mother—she's not well. And my wife—"

The whip cracked again. The lanky man spoke. "Shut up and get down. You shoulda thought of that before ye came in here. We've had enough of your kind."

"Stand back," another one said. Aletha gave a shriek. Pandora broke into sobs. Hannah moved away from the wagons. The others followed, except for Nathaniel. He stood holding the reins of the lead horse.

"I said 'Move!'" The lanky one dismounted.

Nathaniel stood his ground. "We have supplies and things we need."

A rough, grizzled horseman approached him and sneered. "Oh, you do, do ye?"

"I'll be derned," someone said. "An uppity one."

"Let's show 'em." Four others dismounted. The grizzled man held the reins of their horses as they surrounded Nathaniel.

Aletha screamed again. Hannah took a step toward him. "Nathaniel!"

"No, you don't." A horseman blocked her path. "Ye can watch if ye've a mind to. But you're goin' that way. See them trees? The river's down there."

"Go!" Nathaniel shouted. "Do as they say—start walking!"

The group began to move in a northerly direction. Hannah kept turning to look. She saw men unhitching the teams, then boarding the wagons. They ripped open the bags of wheat and corn, and spilled them out on the prairie. One of them smashed the precious grain-grinder against the side of the wagon.

Three men wrestled Nathaniel to the ground. He kicked and struggled.

"Tie his hands," a man said. "Now—get him up. Tie the end to the wagon."

"Let's see if he renounces his religion the way the last one did."

They stood back, and one of them raised the whip. Ten times the lash flew over Nathaniel's back. He made no sound. Finally he slumped against the side of the wagon.

"This one ain't no fun. You could hear the last one hollerin' clear to St. Louis."

Two of them rode away with the teams. Hannah watched open-mouthed as the horses disappeared over the rise.

"Set the wagons on fire," the grizzled man said.

"Naw. There's nothing left to burn. We'll fetch 'em later."

"Hey, lookee here," someone said from the back of the second wagon. "Fancy ladies' stuff. Jewels." The rest rushed back and crowded around him.

"Quick. Take the boy," Rusty said. Hannah grabbed Jacob's hand. Rusty ran back to Nathaniel. Rusty reached to his belt for his knife, unsheathed it and cut Nathaniel loose from the wagon.

"On your feet." Rusty stopped to grab Nathaniel's knapsack from the high grass. Then they both hurried toward Hannah. She saw that Nathaniel was limping, his hands still tied together. When he reached her, his breath made a strange, gurgling sound in his throat. Drops of blood fell on the ground as he shook his head. He did not look at her.

"Keep walking." Rusty took his knife and cut the rope from Nathaniel's wrists.

"That's right!" The lanky, bearded man had swung up behind them. "Blasted Mormonites! You ain't stoppin' till you're clean outa the county."

The whip cracked as the other horsemen joined him. Jacob began to cry. Rusty picked him up. Hannah hugged Adah closer and felt the child's arms tighten around her neck. Ahead of them, Timothy walked with Pandora leaning against him. Aletha and old Mother Beckett followed them, the ancient lady tottering with uncertain steps. Diana, the children's mother, walked beside her husband.

Hannah knew the women would have to rest soon. She and Rusty could not carry the children indefinitely. She worried about Nathaniel—to judge from his labored breathing, someone should be carrying him. Once he turned to look at their tormentors. She saw that the back of his shirt was soaked with blood. Her heart ached for him—for them all. They had no food, no supplies. What would become of them now?

Her clothes—everything she had was gone. Strange—of all her jewelry, she'd chosen to wear the only thing that mattered to her.

"I still have it," she told Rusty.

"What?"

"The Huguenot cross."

He gave more of a wince then a smile. "I was just thinkin' of them. It's like what they had to go through."

Nathaniel spoke for the first time. "Save your strength for walking. We're gonna need it."

Hannah met his eyes. "How do you feel?"

"Never mind me. I'll survive."

Rusty said, "I keep thinkin' we missed something. There's a war, and nobody told us."

"Oh, we knew," Nathaniel said. "This is the frontier, after all. Things are unsettled. But I thought I could get us through."

"Don't blame yourself," Hannah said. "You did splendidly."

Ahead of them, Pandora gave a moan and crumpled to the ground. Everyone stopped.

"No, you don't!" The whip cracked. "Get movin'!"

Nathaniel stooped and gathered up Pandora in his arms. "See to your mother," he said to Timothy.

The old lady could no longer walk. "Go on," she begged. "Leave me. I've seen the promised land. I don't need anything more."

Timothy put his arm around her. Together he and Aletha supported her, one on each side.

"Come, on, Ma." His voice broke. Aletha began to sob.

"Save your strength," Nathaniel said again.

Behind them, the mounted men were laughing. "There ain't a good-lookin' female in the lot."

Nathaniel moved close to Hannah. "Keep your hair and face hidden. Your hood's slipping."

Hannah tried. Hard to keep things together with Adah in her arms. Finally she hoisted the child higher and hid her face in the golden hair.

The afternoon shadows lengthened. They passed cabins on the ridge to their left. One of them had three sides and no roof, and smoke rose from it. She thought of the cabin Daniel had built for her and wondered if they'd passed it unknowing. Her arms began to ache.

"Do you feel like walking, honey?"

"No." The child tightened her grip around Hannah's neck.

"All right."

Once Diana broke from the group and got down on her hands and knees. She vomited into the grass. Lem went and stood over her.

"Keep moving!" a voice cried.

Suddenly one of the horsemen let loose a string of profanity; a bee had stung him. Hannah heard words she never even knew existed. She marveled that he could hold forth so long without repeating himself.

"Man," Rusty said with a whistle. "He goes on better than old Grandpa Ordwell. I thought nobody could out-swear him."

"Be quiet," Nathaniel said. "You want to encourage him?"

"It's longer'n some prayers I've sat through."

They heard noises ahead, shouts and what sounded like rifle shots. They climbed up over a little hill. It sloped down to a valley with a stand of spindly trees. In the distance, Hannah saw a line of people stretching away to the north, men, women and children in little groups. Some had packs on their backs, some carried bundles and boxes. One man carried a barrel, and another had a feather bed in a wagon. There was a sound of weeping, children crying, voices murmuring. As they drew closer, she could pick out individual voices.

"I'm hungry, Ma. I'm hungry now."

"Sorry, dear—keep walking. There's nothing to eat right now."

"There's been nothing to eat all day!"

"I want my kitty. Can we go back and get her, please?"

All up and down the line, men on horseback were cracking whips, brandishing rifles. They harassed anyone who tried to stop.

Hannah and the others walked without speaking. Nathaniel kept turning to look at her; he seemed to be making an effort to keep pace with her. She tried to slow down, to make it easier for him. They fell into line and became part of the exodus of exhausted, confused people, the string of refugees stretching away to the north. Tiredness became a state of being; aching muscles were all she knew, and yet by some miracle she kept walking, carrying Adah while Rusty carried Jacob and Nathaniel carried pale, limp Pandora.

Once he spoke to Pandora. "It's a rough ride, I know. If you put your arms around my neck, 'twill be easier."

She opened her mouth, and a moan came from her. Nathaniel and Hannah looked at each other.

"I figure the river's not far now." The whipping had reopened the old scar by the side of his mouth—it bled as he spoke. Hannah wished she could wash it clean for him.

When they reached the river, the line of people disintegrated into groups milling around, mothers calling for children, individuals seeking family members.

"Have you seen our Uncle Ephraim?"

"Zeke! Zeke, where are you?"

People were massed on both sides of the river. The regular ferry and two rowboats were ferrying people across. Hannah scanned the crowd till her eyes ached, but no one looked familiar.

"I think we need to cross," Nathaniel said. "But waiting gives us a chance to rest."

He went to a spot under a cottonwood tree and put Pandora gently on the ground. Timothy and Aletha helped their mother to a resting position beside her. Diana and Lem collapsed on the grass close by.

"Here's your mamma, now." Hannah set Adah next to her mother. Diana, too weak to speak, smiled her thanks. Rusty handed Jacob to Lem.

"He's sleeping now."

"It's better so." Lem cradled the boy close to him. Adah put her head in her father's lap.

Nathaniel straightened up. "I'm going to get some water, and see if I can learn what's happening. You stay here—I'll be right back."

Hannah watched him move through the crowd. Then she followed him. She caught up with him when he stopped to talk with a middle-aged man by the water's edge.

"I don't know," the man was saying. He rubbed his grizzled chin. "There's rumors of battles all over the place. I hear they even took some of our leaders and threw 'em in jail. From what I hear, we had no choice but to give up our arms. Then they started burning everything they could find."

Nathaniel turned and looked at Hannah. He was breathing fast, as if standing were an effort. "I looked for you to stay with the others."

"They're all resting."

The older man spoke again. "I hear whole bunches of folks wandered on the prairie for days with nowhere to go. No food or shelter."

Nathaniel's mouth hardened into a grim line. His wound was still oozing. The other man shook his head and moved away.

"Wait, Nathaniel." Hannah reached down, lifted the end of her skirt and tore off a piece of petticoat. He looked at her with a puzzled, wondering expression. She knelt to moisten the material in the water.

"Sit on that stump for a moment."

He did, his arms folded in front of him.

"No—not like that. You have to take off your shirt."

He started to unbutton his shirt. She reached in with the dexterity of a mother and washed the dirt and caked blood from his face. To her surprise, he didn't protest.

"I s'pose it has to be done."

She had to peel the shirt from his back. He made no sound, but she sensed it was like the whipping all over again. She felt a pang in her chest as she saw the raw wounds. She rinsed the cloth and dabbed it at his shoulder.

"Don't be gentle," he said. "I figure the best thing is to pour whiskey over it. But I don't reckon on finding any here."

She grew braver and began to wash his back as thoroughly as she could. "How can we possibly find Daniel in this—this confusion?"

"I wouldn't—ouch—look to meet up with him in the next twenty minutes. But if he's here, we'll find him."

"How?"

"I reckon we all have to cross the river. I'll start making inquiries—might take a few days. Don't you worry."

"I sure didn't plan on this happening."

Nathaniel put his hand to his mouth where the whip had cut him. "I don't think any of us did. There must be law and order somewhere that will put things right."

She looked up from her ablutions. Ten feet from her, Rusty and Aletha stood watching. Aletha had a strained, pinched expression.

Rusty moved toward them. "Pandora's bad. Someone saw her—a leader or somebody. Said we should get her across as soon as possible."

"They have us ready to cross on the next boat." Aletha avoided Hannah's eyes.

Twilight descended before they reached the other side of the Missouri. Someone gave Nathaniel a sheet of oilcloth and some dried pieces of cornbread. He portioned out the cornbread so that everyone had some, except for Pandora who refused to eat.

He spread the oilcloth and fashioned a lean-to between the cottonwoods. "It's lookin' to rain." They laid Pandora on a bed of leaves and moss, and prepared for the night.

15

Rusty Manning liked to study people, observing them when they least suspected it. He'd known, long before she told him, about Hannah's attachment to Brother Perry. He'd overheard Aunt Elizabeth telling his father about burning Perry's first letters.

Hannah was the one he loved best in all the world, now that their mother had died. He'd been eager to accompany her to the promised land and see her united with Dan Perry. But he hadn't figured on Nathaniel Givens.

He was well aware of Nat's fierce devotion. Hard to mistake it. He'd never met Perry—he knew only what Hannah had told him. But he grew more convinced by the day—no one would make her a better husband than Nathaniel.

How could he persuade Hannah to forget about Perry and accept Nathaniel? Rusty pondered it that night, huddled at one end of the lean-to while the rain beat down. Outside, he could see tents among the cottonwoods, and people gathered around campfires.

Under the oilcloth canopy, Pandora lay moaning, covered by her husband's thin jacket. The other women took turns sponging her face. They knelt on the bit of carpeting Nathaniel had found for a floor. At last Hannah turned, the light from the nearest fire flickering over her features.

"Nathaniel—go ask, and see if you can find a midwife."

Nathaniel went out without a word. Rusty could see him tramping from tent to tent, bareheaded in the rain. Finally he returned with a tiny, wizened woman who knelt by Pandora's side and probed her with long, claw-like fingers.

Nathaniel advised the rest of them to get some sleep, as the children and old Mother Beckett were doing. Diana leaned against Lem, and Hannah finally lay down beside Rusty. Nathaniel stretched out on the other side of her and covered all three of them with his greatcoat. Timothy and the midwife sat up with Pandora.

Rusty fell into a light sleep, lulled by the incessant patter of the rain. By morning the rain had stopped.

Everyone left the lean-to except Pandora, the midwife, and the rest of Pandora's family. Nathaniel begged some bacon and cornbread, which he brought back to the little group. He found dried apples and raisins in his knapsack.

"I was hopin' I had some left."

Nathaniel's attitude could not be called cheery. It was more of a good-natured briskness, as if they must do what they could in spite of everything. "Come on." He nudged Rusty on the shoulder. "They're building cabins out of cottonwoods. We're going to help."

"Aren't you sore?" Rusty asked.

"I reckon. But I'm doing a lot better than Pandora is, and so are you. Let's build them a shelter."

Nathaniel had another gift. He could talk easily with people he'd never met before, and the strangers opened up to him as if they'd known him for years. Rusty looked at the tents lining the shore like a camp meeting and listened to the men talk.

"I reckon there must've been fifty of them—maybe more. By the time they got through with them cabins, there weren't nothin' left. No crops, not even fruit trees."

"There's more people comin' over than you can shake a stick at. They want us all on this side of the river."

"You seen Parley Pratt? He managed to get his horses across."

"Some of 'em have wagons. Not much good for keepin' the rain out."

"Dan Perry? Yeah—he got beat up pretty bad when they wrecked the printing office. I ain't seen him, but I seed his folks last night. They're here somewhere. All the Colesville people had to leave."

Just before noon, Lem came to tell them that Pandora's child had been born dead.

"Like as not, it came too soon, and she had no strength. That's what the midwife said. Yesterday just about did her in."

Nathaniel nodded. Lem said, "They're hopin' for some sort of coffin."

Nathaniel said, "I may not be able to do much, but I'll try. Rusty, you stay here and work."

Rusty finished what he was doing, then walked back to the lean-to in time for the burial service.

Nathaniel had fashioned a box out of boards from an abandoned wagon. Pandora was too ill to attend. A few others—the midwife and some strangers—joined the group that walked out on the prairie. The women clung together and wept as Nathanicl and Lem lowered the coffin into the shallow grave.

A breeze ruffled the tips of the long grass. From the river drifted shouts and the neighing of horses, sounds made sweet by the distance. Nathaniel said a brief prayer, and they sang a hymn which Rusty didn't know, something about weeping in the valley of death and roving alone in the wilderness.

Through half-closed eyes he watched his sister as she stood beside Aletha. Hannah's beauty shone around her like sunlight. At that moment, Aletha too looked beautiful, her features no longer pinched and strained.

They turned for the walk back to the river. Nathaniel put his hand on Timothy's shoulder. Whatever he whispered made the bereaved father walk with surer steps. Then Nathaniel dropped back and touched Hannah on the arm, as if escorting her. Rusty saw Aletha's face twist into a look of pure hatred. Her moment of beauty fled like a leaf in the autumn wind.

In a flash he understood. Strange not to pick it up before. Usually, when he discerned anything of this type, he felt great sadness for the victim of the impossible situation, in this case Aletha. But since it concerned his sister, he could no longer see things clearly.

A sudden fear for Hannah sprang up in his mind, a nameless anxiety. He walked close behind them, determined not to let her out of his sight.

****

Dan hunkers shivering in the woods, his back up against a tree. Near him, Pinky hovers, silent, the end of her halter trailing on the ground. He can't make out her shape in the dark, but he can feel the warmth from her body.

From his guess, the raiders struck some two hours after midnight. The first firebrand must have flown through the window into the main room of the cabin. He remembers waking to the room ablaze, his mother screaming his name, both parents rushing through the sparks to the front door.

He relives it in his mind—managing to grab his overalls and boots. Hurrying out the back door. His injured knee twinging as he tries to run. Flames shooting out of the roof. Watching, horrified, as pieces of roof crash into the place where he stood just seconds before. What to do? Nothing anyone can do. At least his parents are safe; he saw them escape.

Little tufts of grass burn all around him. Beyond the stable, the haystack flares up. He sees shadowy shapes of men on horseback, torches in their hands. Their yells echo between the buildings, a cacophony of cries and yelps. If the demons in hell could all give voice at once, he doubts they could sound worse.

He tries to pray, but words do not come. He's always been good in extreme emergencies. And God knows, this is one. He creeps to the side of the stable. Keeping in the shadows, he puts his overalls on over his nightshirt and crams his feet into the boots. A horse neighs in terror.

He has to work fast, before the stable burns too. He rushes inside, grabs the mare's halter and leads her out of her stall. He lifts the bridle from its peg on the wall. If he can, he'll get the saddle later.

He leads Pinky away from the buildings. All around them, cabins blaze. Distant fires glow on the horizon. The air reeks with the smell of smoke and burning leather. Pinky rears up, snorting.

"Quiet!"

Climbing on her back. Cantering over the back hills, toward the woods, away from the road. Dismounting, feeling his way into the shelter of trees. Waiting. Dan watches the burning. He wonders which way his parents have fled.

The yelling grows fainter. The raiders ride off into the night. After a while his heart stops racing; he tries to rest. His knee aches—he straightens it out in the leaves. The mare shifts her weight, and he feels her warm breath on his cheek.

When it is light enough to see, he leads the mare out of the woods. The smell of ashes and smoke hangs in the air. The cabin lies in ruins, blackened, smoldering. Nothing remains of the haystack. To his surprise, most of the stable is still standing. He feeds the mare some oats, then puts the remainder in a burlap sack.

"At least you'll eat."

He saddles and bridles her. What else to take? He moves a board to get at the well. He finds a canteen and fills it.

Silence lies everywhere. He doesn't want to make any noise, fearful of what it might attract. He can see nothing alive—pigs, chickens, geese have all disappeared.

He mounts and rides past the cabin he built for Hannah. A smoking ruin. He looks at it, and a sob comes from deep in his chest. His eyes flood with moisture. He brushes the sleeve of his nightshirt across his face.

They head north along the road. He doesn't feel safe on the road, but he doesn't want to miss his parents either. Maybe the raiders have quit for awhile. He passes two burned cabins, the first completely destroyed. A family with six children lived there yesterday—where are they now?

A lone pig trots out and looks at him. He dismounts and tries to catch the animal—he can carry it in his arms. But the pig refuses to be caught. Dan mounts again and clicks to the horse.

He thinks he hears distant shots, the sounds of a battle. He didn't think to search for a weapon. He feels sleepy, disoriented, too dazed for any fight. But a terrible, righteous anger is building inside him. How dare they do this to his people, his family? How dare they destroy the things he has so carefully built? The cabin for Hannah, even the crops—he trembles with rage.

The sound of horses? A cry for help? He urges the mare over the next hill. Off to the left, he sees four men standing near a tree, two others on horseback.

Then he gasps. A seventh person, a young black man, is tied to the tree. His hands are bound with ropes, and another man is beating him with a stick. The stick makes a cracking sound as it descends. The bound man cries out.

Without thinking, Dan gallops toward them. They look up. The beaten man glances around in wonder.

"What's he done?" Dan asks.

The man wielding the stick has a familiar look—narrow eyes close together, with an impression of emptiness. Dan recognizes the lean-faced man who had beaten him last July.

"So, we meet again, do we?" the man says. "It's our slave-loving friend."

"Why are you beating him?"

"It's none of your business," another man says.

"He stole a chicken!" yells a man on horseback.

Dan says, "Maybe he was hungry. Don't you feed him?"

The lean-faced man spits, then raises the stick. "He needs to be taught obedience."

"Well, you won't do it in my presence," Dan says. "Turn him loose."

The lean-faced man looks puzzled, then grins. "I'll be dad-blamed. Here's a blasted Mormonite trying to tell us what to do."

Dan rides up to the slave. He grasps the knife he carries on his saddle and reaches down to cut the rope. He leans over too far—he feels himself slipping from the saddle. The severed rope dangles from the slave's wrists.

"Nab him!" the lean-faced man says.

To Dan's surprise, the slave lunges out and grips his arm. The knife falls to the ground.

Before Dan can get to his feet, the others surround him. The two riders dismount, and one of them grabs Pinky's bridle.

"I'll take the horse away."

"No," Dan says.

"Why not?" the lean-faced man says. "You won't be needin' it."

"But—I was on my way out of the county. Tryin' to find my folks."

The lean-faced man spits again. "You're on your way out, all right. Looks to me like you wanted a little trouble before you left."

"Aw, let 'em go with the others, Will. Give 'em his horse. It's worth it to git rid of 'em."

The lean-faced man looks at Dan, and his brow wrinkles as he chews. "Let's have us some fun first."

He raises the stick and hits Dan just above the left ear. Dan hears something crack in his skull.

As he slumps down, he has a sensation of people rushing at him, kicking him. Blows rain on his head, his side, his arms. Dust chokes his nostrils. He begins to feel detached, no longer a part of things, even though he knows he is still being beaten. As if his mind has gone somewhere else. When he opens his eyes, objects seem to come close and then recede into a great distance.

His mouth moves. "Hannah."

"Let him be, Will. He's saying something."

"Aw, shut up, Jude. What are you, some blasted Mormon-lover?"

"Will's right. Make it too friendly for 'em, they'll stay."

Time loses its meaning. He cannot tell when the beating stops, or when the men ride away. The one thing he puzzles over is why the black man beats him too. Things keep coming close and going away again, like slow waves. Once he thinks Benjamin is bending over him.

"Brother Ben. I ain't seen you since—since the troubles began." His voice sounds strange, like mumbling.

"Don't talk. As the Lord lives, I'll not leave you."

"Tell Hannah—"

He cannot raise his head. Something has gone terribly wrong. He tries to tell Benjamin, but the words stick in his throat. The wave of closeness comes again, so that Benjamin's face seems to fill his world. Then the distancing part begins. He closes his eyes and gives a deep, shuddering sigh.

****

Toward evening, tiny cabins stood among the tents in the cottonwood bottom. More people joined the ones on the northern shore. Some had supplies—food, grain, blankets. Most had nothing.

Because of Pandora's weakened condition, Nathaniel was able to move his little group into one of the first cabins. The midwife promised to bring soup for Pandora and her mother-in-law. Nathaniel went foraging for more solid food.

He found a man from Clay County with a wagon-load of food for the refugees. He managed to get two loaves of bread and some apples.

"I sure do thank you."

The driver shook his head; he rubbed his hand over his gray-stubbled chin. "A terrible shame, what they're doin'. I never did hold much with Jackson County folks. Bunch of low-down scoundrels—worse than varmints. I hear they're drivin' Mormons outa Van Buren and Lafayette Counties too—won't let 'em stay there."

"I'm sorry to hear that," Nathaniel said.

"'T'ain't right. Tell you what. Meet me here tomorrow morning, and I'll have another load for you. You can help me distribute it."

Nathaniel nodded his thanks.

"Why, land's sakes—we'd be pleased to have folks like you in Clay County. Any of you want to settle here, that's fine by me."

Nathaniel took the food back to the group, ensconced now in the tiny cabin. Here they could keep dry and warm, with more space than the lean-to.

"Come on, Rusty. There's cabins to finish up."

But Rusty sat hunched in the corner, close to Hannah. "I'm feeling poorly this evening. Got a misery in my shoulder."

You need a misery in the seat of the pants, Nathaniel thought as he stamped out. He worked until it was too dark to see what he was doing. Then he went in search of Dan's family.

"Way down at the end," someone told him.

"Don't count on finding 'em too soon. Lyman Wight's been looking for his wife and children for a week now."

After three hours he found the elder Perrys—a stooped man with thick gray eyebrows, and a plump, short woman. Could these be the parents of tall, broad-shouldered Dan? A closer look confirmed it. Their faces had the same gentle, open quality that Nathaniel remembered. The father spoke first.

"We've not seen him—we've been waiting. They chased us out of our cabin, set it on fire. Dan went to the barn to get his horse—he set a store by that mare."

His mother wiped her eyes. "The thing is, he couldn't travel very fast without the mare. He'd have to stop and rest. He hasn't been able to walk any distance since he was beaten."

Nathaniel nodded. "Most likely he'll come in tomorrow or the next day. When he does, tell him his intended is waiting for him."

His mother smiled for the first time. "Hannah's here? My, he'll be glad to hear that."

"I reckon so. She's with a little group at the other end."

Nathaniel trudged back along the shore. Best not to tell Hannah before he knew Dan was safe. She'd only worry. Within sight of the cabin, he fell in step with another man. "You heard any news?"

"There's a bunch of folks gathered over by the Blue River," the stranger said. "Most of 'em are tryin' to get over here."

"I never looked to see such trouble."

"I hear one of the women was raped by a whole mob of 'em. Sent her right out of her head. All she does is tremble and cry."

Nathaniel felt like weeping himself. Suddenly Hannah appeared at his side.

"What're you doing out so late?" he asked.

"I went for some water. What's that about some woman being

attacked?"

"Never you mind." Nathaniel took her arm and led her away from the stranger.

"Are you thinking to shield me, Nathaniel?"

"I do what I think best."

She turned. "Then, promise—if you hear anything about Daniel, no matter what it is—promise you'll tell me right away."

"Of course." They approached the cabin. Suddenly Aletha's voice drifted to them.

"If you ask me, she and Nathaniel have been carryin' on this whole time. Even though she's supposed to have someone waitin' for her."

Diana's voice broke in. "She's right pretty—men are bound to look at her. That doesn't mean anything."

"You can take up for her if you want. But I've watched the two of them."

Hannah glanced at Nathaniel, her lip trembling. He lifted the carpeting which he'd nailed up for a door. Then he pushed past her into the room. There was just enough light to see Aletha's face. She started like a frightened deer, her eyes wide.

His voice shook with anger. "I thought the enemy was on the other side of the river. My mistake. Now I find him right here, in this very cabin."

Aletha's hands fluttered to her throat. "I—I only meant—"

"I heard what you meant. And none of it's true. Have I given you any cause to think such a thing?"

"Well, that is—no."

"So you thought you'd just be malicious. Now, listen to me—all of you."

"Nathaniel—" Diana began.

"I don't have to tell you, these are dreadful times. Terrible things are happening to us—all of us. Don't you see? We have to be kind to each other, treat each other decent. Otherwise we'll lose everything. We won't have any strength or hope left."

Hannah entered with Rusty close behind her. Diana said, "The children are sleeping."

Nathaniel spoke in a lower tone. "I've done, now. Just remember what I've said."

They found places on the dirt floor and prepared for the night. Nathaniel directed Rusty to lie down between himself and Hannah, then spread his greatcoat over all three of them. He felt restless, confused, depressed—what would they do the next day, and the next? Had God forgotten about them? His musings grew jumbled—he drifted into sleep.

He woke to the sound of voices outside. "Look! Look there!"

Someone had opened the entrance flap. He felt a nudge, heard Hannah's voice.

"Nathaniel, wake up! Come outside! You'll never believe it!"

He got to his feet in the darkness and stumbled outside. Rusty, Lem and Diana were standing together in a little clearing.

"What—" Nathaniel began.

"Up!" Hannah said. "Look at the sky."

A trail of light caught his eye, then another and another. The sky blazed with meteors, bright streaks shooting in every direction. One left a long train of light which lingered for seconds, a brilliant arc among the stars. Others flashed around it; then he saw another train of light.

All up and down the river bank, people crept out of their shelters and huddled in groups, looking up, exclaiming.

"Look at that one!"

"Hallelujah!"

"Lord be praised! It's the end of the world!"

Diana said, "Let's get the children. I want them to see this, and remember."

She and Lem hurried back to the cabin. Hannah took a step closer to Nathaniel and touched him on the arm. He didn't move away. Her voice trembled, ecstatic. "Did you ever see such a thing?"

"A marvelous sight." He felt a rush of wonder and awe, one of those moments when people reach out for the nearest human contact. His arm stole around her shoulders; they stood together and watched the sky.

"There's one for you!" Rusty said. Lem and Diana reappeared, each holding a child.

"Shooting stars, honey," Diana said to Adah. The child rubbed her eyes.

"I'll be—it looks like hundreds of 'em," Lem said. "Beats any fireworks I ever seen."

Rusty said, "You can see 'em reflected in the water."

Timothy stood outside the cabin with the slight figure of Pandora in his arms. His mother exclaimed, “Glory be! The Lord is coming!”

Shouts of “Hosanna!” echoed up and down the river’s edge.

Hannah said, “Do you suppose it does mean something? Some sign from God?”

“I reckon it’s just a natural happening,” Nathaniel replied. “Like an eclipse, or a sunset.”

“I think it’s a sign that our troubles won’t last—that God is still with us.”

He said, “I’m sure you’re right—such misfortunes can’t last forever.”

Someone coughed behind him. He became aware of Aletha’s eyes on him. Conscious of his arm around Hannah, he started to move away. Then he stopped. So little time remained—he might have to relinquish her to Perry as early as tomorrow. His days of sorrow and loneliness would begin in earnest. Ignore Aletha—did it matter what she thought? He tightened his arm about Hannah. On the other side of her, Rusty was holding her hand.

“Look at that one!” Nathaniel gestured with his free hand at the trees across the river.

“I reckon that might’ve landed somewheres,” Rusty said. “Seemed so close-like.”

“There ain’t as many now,” someone said behind them. “I figure it’s almost over.”

They watched in silence. After a moment Rusty spoke again. “It’s gittin’ bright just above the horizon, there to the east.”

Nathaniel glanced at the rest of the camp. People were still standing, watching, their eyes wide. Timothy and Pandora sat together on a log; he held her in his arms as they looked up.

The children began to whimper. Diana and Lem carried them back to the cabin. Aletha shook her head and followed her mother back inside.

Nathaniel, Hannah and Rusty stayed in the clearing and watched the last of the meteors.

16

After a few hours sleep, Nathaniel stumbled out of the cabin with Rusty at his heels. They hurried to meet the farmer with the wagon-load of food.

"Right decent of him," Rusty said. They walked in the ruts of the road. On either side, the long grass glistened with dew. "Makes you think there's still some good folks left in the world."

"It's true, and don't you forget it." Nathaniel felt sleepy. The impending loss of Hannah lay like a black shadow at the edge of the woods. With every step it seemed to come closer. As a consequence, everything Rusty did annoyed him.

"This is where he said to meet him." Nathaniel glanced down the road, then leaned back against a tree and shoved his hands in his pockets. Rusty sat down on the grass before Nathaniel could stop him.

"Be careful, lad—it's still wet. Now, look at you—you're soaked. You might as well go set in the river."

Rusty glanced down and shrugged. "I'll dry right soon in the sun."

Nathaniel sighed and looked at the road. A horse neighed. The wagon appeared from behind a clump of cottonwoods. The driver pulled up in front of them.

Nathaniel straightened up. "This here's my friend Rusty." They climbed in the wagon.

"My name's Snyder," the farmer said. "I live about two mile west of the landing. My neighbor, just north of me—he took in a whole family, a woman and some little children—one of them right poorly. He said he'd keep 'em for the winter."

"That's very good of him," Nathaniel said. "I reckon he'll be blessed for his charity."

"That's what I figure," Snyder said. "Do you know any folks like that, sort of sick-like, who'd come home with me?"

Nathaniel told him about Pandora and her family, and how she'd delivered a still-born child just the day before. The farmer frowned, his lips pursed together.

"'T'ain't right she should be in a place like this, with winter comin' on. Once we unload the food, let's see if she and her kin won't come with me."

"I'm sure they'd be beholden," Nathaniel said. It meant getting rid of Aletha. For the first time that morning, he smiled.

As they worked distributing food, he saw other wagons, people bringing supplies from neighboring farms.

"There's old Asher Eberhardt," Snyder said. "Derned if he didn't take in a family last week. He liked 'em so well, he's ready to become a Mormon too. Don't that beat all?"

Later, after the Beckett clan had been loaded in the wagon, Nathaniel and Rusty walked beside them on the way out of camp.

"Sure you don't want to join us?" Snyder asked.

"Yes," Aletha said. "Come with us."

Nathaniel looked straight ahead. "I thank you. But we're needed here, for the moment."

Snyder said, "What do you figure on doing?"

Nathaniel squinted into the sun. "Well, I didn't aim to settle in Missouri. I live in Kirtland, and I expect I'll head east as soon as my obligations here are done."

They said good-bye and wished each other good luck. Nathaniel and Rusty stood watching as the wagon creaked its way westward. They turned back to the camp.

Rusty threw him a sideways glance. "Nathaniel, I'd be pleased if you'd let me travel back with you."

"What—to Kirtland?"

"You see, the way I figure—once Hannah gets settled, I'd just be in the way. One more mouth to feed. It's not like we planned."

"I don't reckon anyone planned it this way."

"It's in my mind to go back and help my father with the spring planting, since I missed the harvest and all. Say good-bye to Hannah and leave."

Speaking of it made it come close. Nathaniel blinked a few times before he answered. "Suit yourself."

"I know you're in a huff about something—I'm not sure what I did."

"You didn't do anything. Be all right in a while."

A group of men stood talking near the first cabin. Nathaniel nudged Rusty. "Maybe there's news."

They moved closer. Words drifted to them.

"Derned if he didn't scoop out the grave with his bare hands. Buried 'em right there, under a tree."

"But the strange thing is, the horse wouldn't leave. Can you beat that? Stayed right there, all that afternoon. Benjamin had to cover its eyes to lead it away."

"What happened?" Nathaniel asked.

An old man spoke. "This young feller on t'other side of the river—he didn't get away in time."

"Or he stopped—no one's quite sure," someone else said. "Benjamin says his head got staved in by a gun barrel."

"Who?" Nathaniel asked.

"Like as not, he was ambushed. They was waitin' for him."

Nathaniel felt the perspiration breaking out on his forehead. "Do they know who it was?"

"Well, who else? A bunch of low-down pukes."

"No. Who was it got killed?"

Someone said, "That young feller—you get his name?"

"Why, it was Dan—young Dan from up by the Blue River."

The words stuck in Nathaniel's throat. "Dan Perry?"

"Was it Perry? Seems to me he said something else."

"If it was Perry, he was a spunky young feller. Big, too. It'd take half an army to do what they did."

Nathaniel said, “I have to be sure.”

The old man spoke again. “You better go talk to Brother Benjamin. He’s just down by the water—real tall feller, black hair. He’ll tell you.”

Nathaniel turned to face Rusty. Rusty looked shaken, his face pale. For once Nathaniel didn’t have to explain what they were going to do. He nodded, and Rusty followed him down to the river front.

Brother Benjamin confirmed their fears. “I just been to see his parents—gave them the horse. They said something about a woman name of Hannah—said she should be told.”

Nathaniel said, “I’d appreciate it very much if you could come with us. This here’s her brother, and I’m a friend.”

He felt dizzy, unsteady on his feet, as if he'd had too much applejack. As he led the way up to the cluster of cabins, he had the sensation of being half-awake, in some dream-like state. Once he glanced back to make sure that Benjamin, with his dreadful news, was really there. Benjamin followed close at his heels, keeping pace with Rusty, both of them grim-faced.

Nathaniel shook his head. How could he prepare her? How would she react? Cry out, maybe, or faint. Maybe he could help her more if he stayed in the background. She appeared in the doorway, wiping her hands on her skirt. His heart gave a lurch. Adah stood beside her, a bit of bread in her hand.

Hannah frowned as she caught sight of them, a shadow crossing her face. Rusty pushed past Nathaniel and took her hand.

“Bad news, Hannah. Adah, go in to your mother.”

The girl obeyed. Hannah looked at Rusty, then at Nathaniel and Benjamin. She drew a deep breath. “No.”

Nathaniel tried to speak, but something caught in his throat. Rusty said, “This is Brother Benjamin—he was with Daniel.”

Hannah gave Benjamin a long look. “He's dead.”

“That's right, ma’am.” Benjamin shifted from one foot to the other. “I’m awful sorry to bring the news. He ran into a bunch of ’em, and—well, I'm not sure just what happened. But they didn't let him git away.”

Nathaniel gave an intake of breath, like a hoarse cough. She didn't look at him as she spoke. “It’s what I figured. I had a strange dream, just the other night—him all in white, and wandering somewhere. I didn't understand it then, but I do now.”

“I’m powerful sorry," Benjamin said.

Nathaniel marveled at her presence of mind as she stood blinking in the road. “His mother and father, now—do they know?”

“I've been to see them—they was the first I told.”

“I’d like to go to them,” she said.

“I'd be pleased to take you over there,” Benjamin said. “We’ll all go.”

Nathaniel still found it hard to speak. He walked beside Hannah as they followed the curve of the river to the other end of the encampment. Somewhere children were playing a game, laughing, running among the trees. Their shrieks mingled with the voices of the adults.

“Lazarus! You come in here this minute.”

The rest of the afternoon passed like a waking dream. Through his daze, Nathaniel remembered Hannah greeting Daniel's parents. She embraced them both, and introduced Rusty, who embraced them as well.

"I think you know Brother Benjamin," she said.

"I do indeed," Brother Perry said. "He's more than welcome. And Nathaniel, again."

Hannah's eyes flew open in momentary surprise. Nathaniel tried to act as if nothing out of the ordinary had been said, but inwardly he felt sick. Should he have told her about his visit to Dan's parents? At the time he'd thought it best not to mention it.

Again Benjamin told them what he knew. In the presence of the older Perrys, Hannah seemed subdued, her voice low.

"It seems like we should have a prayer. Nathaniel, would you?"

He gathered them in a little circle and offered the first prayer, finding his voice at last. He prayed for God's spirit to surround them and sustain them in their time of grief and trouble. Then Benjamin and Brother Perry, both elders, added their prayers. Rusty and the two women listened in silence.

Toward the end of the afternoon, Sister Perry said, "Why, you be just as lovely as Dan said. He vowed he'd never seen such glorious hair. What will you do, my dear? Comin' all that way, just to have this happen."

Nathaniel leaned forward—he cared more about her answer than he wanted to let on. Hannah said, "I don't rightly know. It seems like I can't think just yet."

Dan's mother dabbed at her eyes. "We'd be pleased if you'd abide with us—you and Rusty. We're thinking of goin' north into Clay County, maybe stayin' up there a spell."

"I thank you kindly," Hannah said. "Let me study on it."

They said tearful good-byes and made their way back among the river. Benjamin stayed behind with the senior Perrys. Hannah clung to Rusty's arm, and Nathaniel walked on the other side of her.

"It seems to me," Rusty said. "They've lost everything. We'd just be extra folks for them to take care of."

"I was minded of the same thing," Hannah said.

Nathaniel spoke slowly. "It might be best if you traveled on back to Kirtland with me."

She turned to look at him, her eyes wide. Her face was pale; she had a sick, stricken expression. He went on. "It's an interesting place, Kirtland. There's lots of meetings and such-like, and the House of the Lord being built—"

Suddenly she crumpled to the ground. Rusty grabbed her hand, but it slipped through his grasp. Nathaniel bent over her and gathered her up in his arms. She felt limp; her arms dangled down, swinging. Her head fell on his shoulder as he carried her up the embankment.

"You'd think she'd give us some warning," Rusty said.

"We should've known. Look what she's been through." He carried her into the cabin. "Quick! Some water!"

Diana took the water pitcher and hurried out. Nathaniel nudged the greatcoat with his foot. "Spread that out, Rusty."

He lowered her gently onto the coat. When Diana appeared with the water, he took a cloth and sponged Hannah's face. In an undertone, Rusty told Diana what had happened.

"Best to let her rest," Diana said. "If you wake her, she'll just be grieved."

Nathaniel sat by her the rest of the day and into the night. He took no food, even when the others pressed him. He did not permit himself to lie down, but sat with his back against the logs, his head bent.

Once Adah cried out in the night, but Hannah didn't stir. Nathaniel drifted in and out of sleep, alert for any sound from her. But all he could hear were the shallow breaths of the others, and Rusty's gentle snores. Toward morning his head drooped; he slumped sideways against the logs and slept.

****

"He won't leave her. He went outside once, but derned if he didn't come right back. Don't seem like he had time to eat anything."

"Well, he's gone now. God knows for how long. Seems like he needs help as much as her."

She lay half-asleep as the words drifted to her. She recognized Lem's low, rumbling bass, then Diana's breathless contralto. She wondered who 'he' was. Rusty, most likely. And where was Nathaniel? Never around when you needed anyone.

In seconds the past day's events hit her with final clarity. No longer betrothed, she was alone, one of a group of outcasts, while Daniel lay in an unmarked grave on the other side of the river. She felt she should weep, but she seemed to be in a place beyond grief. She reminded herself that all had suffered, all had lost. She thought of Pandora and her child born dead, of the woman who'd been raped until she'd lost her mind. She thought how Nathaniel had tried to conceal it from her, and how his own face bore an expression of hurt and disappointment that seemed symbolic of all their troubles. She took deep breaths, and it seemed that her personal sorrow took on a universal aspect, as if she grieved with the entire community.

"She's awake," Diana said. "Poor dear. Here's some water—you'd best drink something. Nathaniel's gone to find us breakfast."

Diana sat by her while she drank. Adah crawled around to her other side and snuggled against her. As she lay with the two of them close to her, she felt a strange peace, like the calm in the center of a storm.

"It's been a long spell since I saw Daniel," she said. "It's not like I was married to him."

Diana smoothed the hair back from Hannah's forehead. "It's a hard thing anyway. You go ahead and grieve."

Weak sunlight filtered through chinks in the logs. The shelter, put up in such haste, would not do for very long. They had to find something else before winter set in. She spoke of it to Diana, and Lem appeared out of the shadows. He knelt beside his wife and scratched at his chin.

"I been talkin' with some of the men. They think the best thing is to head north, find some place to stay for the winter. Then maybe—come spring—we can go back across the river."

"Not if they figure on killing us," Hannah said.

"Like as not, they'll be through hating us by then."

Light filled the cabin as the entrance flap lifted. Nathaniel and Rusty filed noiselessly into the room. Nathaniel handed his knapsack to Rusty, who bent to open it.

"What you got?" Lem asked. "More bread and cheese?"

Nathaniel didn't answer. He was gazing at Hannah, his eyes solemn. She tried to smile, to reassure him that she would not need special care because of her loss. He shook his head; he looked as if he'd missed a night's sleep.

"Well, praise the Lord," Diana said. "Let's eat."

They clustered around Hannah and offered her bits of the coarse bread.

"There's butter this time," Rusty said. "And a small jar of peach sauce."

Hannah tried to eat a few morsels to please them, but she had no desire for food. Her whole body felt numb, as if she were in some strange dream. She sipped water from Nathaniel's canteen. His eyes never left her face.

She handed the canteen back to him and leaned up against the logs. Nathaniel opened his mouth to speak, but Diana broke in.

"She needs to rest now. Everyone out. Lem, take Jacob down to see the water. I promised him."

"Boats," the boy said. Nathaniel and Rusty glanced at each other and followed Lem and Jacob.

Hannah lay silent, her head against the logs. She heard the shouts of children outside, the soft sounds Diana made as she straightened up the cabin. They had two tattered blankets now, and an old earthenware pitcher for water. When the children returned, Hannah made an effort to talk with them in her usual way. Slowly the feeling of peace and solace came back to her.

Over the next few days, Nathaniel made several attempts to see her alone, but Diana and the children hovered close to her. She felt little inclination to wander outside; the sunlight seemed to stab at her eyes and make them ache. Once she lifted the flap and saw Rusty and Nathaniel standing together. She heard Rusty say, "Hang it all, man. Just ask her."

She sighed as she leaned back against the logs. So much to deal with. She tried to look at things clearly, but the strange numbness kept getting in the way, like fog during a river crossing. On the fourth day, Nathaniel came in with some exciting news. The farmer Snyder had a brother up near Richmond, and he'd offered to take in a family for the winter.

"I told him you'd be willing," Nathaniel told Diana. "He's coming with a rig tomorrow afternoon."

Diana hurried out to find her husband and children. Hannah found herself alone with Nathaniel. Was she prepared? She thought of feigning sleep, but the intensity of his gaze made her abandon the idea. She spoke first.

"That's wonderful news. I knew we couldn't stay here much longer."

He knelt beside her and gave a little cough. "That's right—we have to move on. Hannah, I—that is, it's been in my mind to speak to you. You know—well, that I care for you. That is, I think you know—"

Beads of perspiration stood on his forehead, though the day was not warm. She wondered if she should make it easy for him.

"Nathaniel, are you asking me to marry you?"

He swallowed. "I'd be very pleased if you'd have me. And—and I know it's sudden-like, so soon after—but these be strange times. There've been babies born, all sort of goings-on in this camp. A marriage would not be unusual."

She looked straight ahead. "I'm sure you'd be a good husband. You've been a most valuable friend."

"I'd take care of you. No one could love you more. Oh, Hannah, I—" He broke off, and his eyes glistened. He wiped at them with his jacket sleeve.

She waited before she spoke. Best to hurry; the others would be coming in. "Nathaniel, I don't really know what's best to do. But I think it's a mistake if I marry you. I'd still be loving Daniel."

"That's no matter. I'd be content. We can even live as—as brother and sister, if it would please you."

She laughed then. "Oh, Brother Nat! Now, why would we do that? I already have a brother."

He reacted as if he'd been struck. "I only meant..." He trailed off, one corner of his mouth working strangely.

How to make things right? She tried again. "Nathaniel, I truly appreciate all you've done for Rusty and me. But I just can't be your wife. It's not fair to you. I—I need time to recover."

"When we get back to Kirtland, you might feel—"

"I'm not going back."

Surprise and shock spread over his face. "But—that is, I figured—"

"I've been studying some. And I think my place is with Diana."

"But—"

"You know her time's almost here. She needs me to take care of the children, and help when the baby comes. Lem's not much use that way. And I think if I do this, my own strength will come back."

He sighed. "I feel responsible for you, is all."

"Well, don't. I'm responsible for myself. I believe this is what I'm called to do right now."

He looked down, his lips pressed together. He fidgeted with the middle button on his jacket. She spoke in a gentle murmur. "Do you understand, Nathaniel?"

He raised his eyes to meet hers. He looked close to tears. "I reckon."

"I know Rusty wants to go back east. Watch over him, will you? Pretend he's me."

He didn't smile. "I could never do that, Hannah. But I'll see that he gets to Kirtland."

She took his hand then. "Write to me when you get there. Let me know he's safe."

He glanced down at their hands, then hurriedly pulled his away. He made a little noise in his throat. "I will."

"Thank you." She leaned back against the logs and closed her eyes. She heard him draw a deep breath and stand up. She opened one eye as he turned to leave. His very posture seemed to carry the weight of despair and bewilderment.

She sighed. She'd never asked him to love her. She thought the matter was settled, but then Rusty caught up with her as she walked in the early evening.

"Hannah, he's a good man. And he dotes on you. You're breaking his heart."

Hannah whirled to look at him. He went on, oblivious of her anger. "It's a big mistake, to refuse him. He'd take care of both of us. We've got nothing—just the clothes on our backs. And he's better than a gold mine—you've seen how resourceful he is."

She tried to choose her words with care. "Don't my feelings count for anything? You speak of broken hearts. Isn't mine broken enough for you?"

"Well, that is—"

"If he put you up to this, he's barking up the wrong tree. How can I marry anyone? When I close my eyes, all I see is Daniel. It's that simple."

Rusty said, "He didn't ask me to speak for him. I just saw the way things were, and—"

"I told him I'd always be his friend. He has to be content with that."

"He will be. I reckon he'll fret for a while."

"He'll be over it before you're out of Missouri. Trust me, Rusty. And trust God."

They stood together looking out over the water. Little waves came rippling into shore. Rusty pulled his jacket around him. "Storm's coming. Feel the bite in the wind?"

"You're starting back tomorrow?" she asked.

"As soon as Mr. Snyder comes to fetch you. I reckon we'll ride with you far as Richmond, if there's room."

"That makes sense. We better get some rest now."

He put his arm about her shoulders as they walked back to the cabin.

17

Rusty thought Nathaniel would break down for sure when they said good-bye to Hannah. She took Nathaniel's hand in her gracious, gentle way and thanked him for bringing them across. He looked embarrassed and mumbled something about sending for him if she ever needed anything.

"I will." She turned to Rusty, and they held each other in a long embrace. When he finally released her, both were in tears. Nathaniel stood by, his head bent, his eyes glittering.

"Mind Nathaniel, now," she said with a little smile. "Stay out of trouble."

Nathaniel nodded to Rusty and the two of them started their trek eastward. Nathaniel looked back at least four times, but Rusty kept his eyes straight ahead. "The missionaries leave their families all the time, so I reckon it can't be that difficult."

Nathaniel said nothing, his lips pressed together. They fell into a brisk, rhythmic walk, keeping to the trails between settlements, following the river east. At first Rusty feared that his friend would mope after Hannah all the way across four states. But Nathaniel did his grieving in secret. They took turns carrying the knapsack. It bulged with provisions from the Snyder brother in Richmond, a farmer they all called 'Rube.'

The first night they camped in an abandoned shed. Nathaniel squinted at the sky. "Storm before morning."

They ate bread and bacon from the knapsack. "I hope you're set for walking," Nathaniel said. "There's no money for any stage."

To Rusty's chagrin, he was the one who broke down. He kept thinking of Hannah and how they'd never been apart before. In the dark, he thought Nathaniel would have no inkling of his weakness; he let the tears run down his cheeks.

Then Nathaniel spoke. "Here, lad."

Rusty felt a rumpled handkerchief being pressed into his hand. Embarrassed, he dabbed at his face.

There was a pause before Nathaniel spoke again. "You'll see her before too long, I reckon. She's kin."

Rusty sniffed. "Maybe you will, too."

"That may be." The rain began drumming on the roof. "But look at it this way. She and the others—they're safe and well-sheltered. They won't be cold any more."

"That's good to know, after they gave away those pitiful blankets."

"They did right. Why, come to think of it, they're warmer than we are. They have a nice fire, and real beds warmed by a warming pan."

"And bread set by the fire so the end is all toasted. All the comforts of civilization."

"That's the way to look at it. Just put her in God's hands—that's all we can do."

They walked through rain and sleet, and spent the nights wherever they could. If they happened upon a cabin or farmhouse at evening, the owners took them in. They spent one night huddled in the side of a haystack after walking long past sunset.

"Too late to ask for proper shelter," Nathaniel said.

Before they slept, they sat and looked up at the sky. Nathaniel pointed out the constellations and the brightest stars.

"See? There's Betelgeuse."

"Beetle what?" Rusty felt ashamed—his knowledge of astronomy ended with the Big Dipper and Orion. "How'd you learn all those names?"

"When I was with the Shakers, I read everything I could find."

Nathaniel told him stories of the Shakers, and early childhood in a cabin in southern Ohio.

"It was wilderness then. No trails, no other cabins—just us and the wild creatures."

The first night in Indiana, their host made them preach for their supper.

"Mormons, are ye? Let's hear some of that angel message. We'll see if you do as well as the last fellers that came through here."

Rusty looked at Nathaniel in consternation. He knew Nathaniel held the office of deacon, and was not a missionary elder. But

Nathaniel stood and gave them an earnest sermon about the finding of the golden plates and the message of the Book of Mormon.

Rusty listened, spell-bound. This man could add preaching to his other gifts. When Nathaniel finished, their host nodded. "That was right tolerable."

As they ate, the farmer said, "There's word of fierce trouble out to the west. Fighting. A Mormon army rising up against the other settlers."

"No, sir. It's the other way around," Nathaniel said.

"Is that a fact? I guess it depends on who's telling it."

The farmer chewed his hard cornbread as Nathaniel told what he knew. "It's true we don't know everything that happened—just what we experienced."

"So the Mormons was all run off their land?"

"I think we can say that." Nathaniel took a drink of cider.

"Rough country out there. I'd sooner tackle wildcats than a bunch of Missouri pukes."

They chewed in silence. The farmer wiped his mouth on his sleeve. "Tell you what. You look like good, strong fellers. I've had a powerful rheumatiz in my back for nigh on to two months now. I got me a bit of coinage—been savin' it. If you finish fillin' up my wood pile, I'll give ye enough to get back to Ohio."

Nathaniel and Rusty worked felling and splitting logs for the rest of the week. They continued their journey. Rusty said, "If we're lucky, I'll be in Pennsylvania come Christmas."

"You might be a bit late."

"Blame it," Rusty said. "If only she'd come back with us."

Nathaniel's dark eyebrows drew together. "She made up her own mind. And maybe it's for the best. As long as she stays with Diana and the children, she'll be safe enough."

"Like as not, that baby's been born already."

"I reckon."

They had an argument about the money. Rusty wanted to get on a stagecoach right away. "My feet are like to drop off. We got enough to get us most of the way to Kirtland."

"Not if you want to reach Allegheny County in good time."

Rusty looked at Nathaniel, puzzled. "What d'you mean?"

"I mean, you can't go to Kirtland—it's too far north. Best to catch the stage at Dayton, or maybe Springfield. If we don't spend all the money now, there'll be enough to get you right across to where you want to be."

Rusty strained to imagine a map in his mind, then nodded. He paused before he spoke. "But what will you do?"

"Don't worry about me. I can take care of myself."

As they neared their destination, the weather worsened. The wind had an edge to it that made them shiver. Rusty felt ill-prepared for winter. Nathaniel found a burlap sack and fashioned a coarse shirt for him. An old piece of blanket, tied in front, formed a make-shift cloak. They took turns wearing it and the one greatcoat. On some days they hitched rides with local farmers.

They spent the last night in a farmhouse on the outskirts of Dayton. As they prepared to share the spare bed in the loft, Rusty said, "I was just minded of Hannah and me—how we came out here talkin' about the promised land, and a place where we'd all be safe."

Nathaniel looked at him, as if waiting. Rusty said, "Do you figure they got it wrong, and Zion was supposed to be in another place?"

Nathaniel paused a long time, and Rusty began to think he hadn't heard the question. Then Nathaniel sighed. "Something went very wrong, but it's not the location. Maybe it's us—we aren't ready to live there yet."

"But then, why—"

"And maybe Zion is more than just a location, a physical area with boundaries. I don't rightly know. I'm not sure it's supposed to be free of all dangers—no place is."

Rusty crawled into bed and lay looking up at the rafters.

"Move over." Nathaniel blew out the candle. "Maybe Zion is something more than we ever thought or dreamed. But don't be giving up just yet. I expect we'll get back in there. I reckon those high-priced lawyers will know what to do."

In the early morning they walked to the stage stop. "You stay here." Nathaniel went inside to see about the fare. He appeared carrying a mug of warm cider and something wrapped in white cloth. "Your stage is due, about ten minutes. Here." He offered the mug to Rusty.

Rusty took a swallow of it and felt as if his throat were on fire. He choked, and tears came to his eyes. "That warms you clean through."

Nathaniel took the mug and put it to his own lips. A startled look spread over his face. "That's practically applejack! No more for you."

"What—you're gonna drink it all?"

Nathaniel wiped the back of his hand over his mouth. "It wouldn't do for Hannah to think I got you drunk on our last day."

"I won't tell her."

The stage rushed in with a rumble of wheels and the neighing of horses. Drops of mud splattered everywhere. The lead horse, a magnificent black animal, pawed at the ground.

"Here, Rusty. Up you go." Nathaniel handed him the bundle of cloth.

"What—"

"It's some food for the journey. Godspeed, son. Get in, now, and find a place."

Events seemed to be speeding by him. Rusty blinked. When he looked again, Nathaniel had gone; he'd taken the mug of cider back inside the building.

As the coach started to move, he remembered that he hadn't even thanked his friend for all his trouble. He looked at the bundle, opening it at the side. Warm biscuits and a bit of cheese. He reached for a biscuit and felt something else—a knotted handkerchief. The same handkerchief Nathaniel had handed him that night in the abandoned shed.

He unknotted it. There, spread out in his lap, were the rest of the coins the farmer had given them. He covered them in haste, but in one glance he knew that Nathaniel had taken nothing for himself.

He knotted up the handkerchief and put it back with the biscuits. His eyes burning, he looked out the window. He tried not to think when he would ever see his friend again.

****

Dizzy..feeling faint. A slowness in his arms and legs. The snow, maybe. Falling since first light, great white flakes out of a leaden sky...drifting, growing deeper by the hour. Wet, heavy snow, reaching well above his ankles. Feet numb with cold. Fighting to keep going.

Wind driving against him in the open spaces, whipping his back with blasts as fierce as the Missouri man's whip. His coat flapping wildly. Spent, exhausted, since he put Rusty on the stagecoach. Weakness growing, a cough wracking his whole body.

What to do? Somewhere ahead of him lies Kirtland—he tries to estimate how far. If this next settlement is Mansfield, he is about eighty miles to the southwest.

Staggering now, making his way toward a cluster of log buildings. One, larger than the rest—some sort of general store or gathering place. All his strength—pushing open the heavy door, stepping inside.

A short, stocky man leans against the counter. "Hello, there, stranger. Welcome. It's not fit for man nor beast out there."

"And it's gonna get worse," another man says. "One of them all-fired white-out blizzards, I reckon."

Nathaniel speaks with an effort. "I don't want to trouble you none. But I been travelin' a long time, and I'm feelin' plumb tuckered out. I figure I need a few day's rest."

"Well, you can't go on in this weather; I'll say that much."

Nathaniel continues. "Do you—do you maybe know of any Mormon families in town?"

The proprietor wrinkles his brow. "Seems like there was some, but I don't rightly remember—"

"There's Quakers living down by the bridge there," the second man says. "Old Man Simms. He'll put you up—he's partial to strangers. And if it's Mormons you want, he's like to know some."

They give him directions and he sets out again. When he finally finds the Simms' house, he can no longer feel any sensation in his hands and feet. His face stings from the wind. The residents, an elderly couple, welcome him. After one look, the householder insists that he stay with them and not seek any further for shelter. They feed him hot broth and give him a bed in a tiny room close to the hearth.

"Warmest place in the house," Simms says.

"I sure do thank you."

Those are the last words Nathaniel is able to speak. He sinks into a deep sleep. Every once in a while, a spasm of coughing shakes him. He seems to hear the sound from a great distance, as if someone else is doing it. He lies, as if paralyzed, in too much of a stupor to move. Burning, drenched in perspiration, he falls back into sleep again.

He forgets about time, even forgets about his uncompleted journey. He does not know how long he lies there; he has a dim realization that he is ill, with a terrible weakness in all his limbs. Like the storm outside, images whirl in his brain, scenes of Missouri, walking, tramping through endless wilderness. In his dreams, Rusty walks beside him, and Hannah, always Hannah—he hears her laughter, feels her hands on his forehead.

He opened his eyes to find the Quaker lady bending over him, her hand on his brow.

"Thee is awake." She had tiny wrinkles all around her mouth and eyes.

"How long have I been like this?"

"Thee had a powerful sickness. Thee must have been exhausted."

"I've come from a terrible time in Missouri. My people were driven from their homes."

"Hush, now, and don't talk so. Dreams have troubled thee. The fever's broken, but thee must rest."

He learned later that he'd been ill for the better part of three weeks. Christmas and New Year's Day had passed without his knowing. In the next few weeks, he had a slow return to health. He tried to do as many chores for his hosts as he could, to repay what they'd done for him.

"Thee mustn't tire thyself out," the old man said. "Thee needs strength to get home."

A neighbor, taking a wagon-load of goods to Wooster, offered Nathaniel a ride. He accepted, and spent the last evening telling the Quaker couple about his religion. As eloquent as he was, his missionary efforts fell on deaf ears. The old man spoke for both of them.

"We don't hold much with ordained clergy. What thee calls 'priesthood' sounds more like the same old priestcraft. And angels and such-like—I'd have to see one before I believed."

In the morning, Nathaniel thanked them again and climbed into the wagon. On the outskirts of Wooster, he caught another ride.

On the day he planned to walk into Kirtland, he stopped to barter for some food. A small mirror hung just behind the counter, and he glanced at it. A stranger's face looked back at him. The scar was still there, white against his lip, and the shaggy black hair. But the face itself appeared altered—thin and drawn, with hollow places under the eyes. 'Peaked,' as the back country folks would say. His whole frame—at least the top half—looked emaciated, even frail. It hit him with a sinking feeling—the person he had been was no longer in the world. Hannah wouldn't know him now.

He made his way to his favorite watering place, thinking to get the news before he walked out to Crawford's. As he entered the public house, he wondered if people would even recognize him. "I'll be dad-blamed if it ain't old Nat! Where you been?"

"You look like death warmed over. Been tangling with bears, or what?"

"Boys," Nathaniel said to the three that were there. "I've been to Missouri and back."

"No foolin'?"

"Don't look like it did much for you."

Nathaniel said, "Now, Brother O'Neill—how about some of that cider on credit? I have a powerful thirst. There's big trouble out there. Most everybody's left Jackson County."

"We know." Brother O'Neill reached for a mug. His round, ruddy face shone from the heat of the fire. "They sent two men out there—

David Patten and William Pratt—with a bunch of clothing and provisions. Let's see—when did they leave?"

Brother Henley, the second man, spoke in a rough, gravelly voice. "I reckon it were around mid-December."

Nathaniel said, "With the storms and all, it'll be March before they get there. That's no help at all."

"Better'n nothin'," the third man remarked. He had a long nose, and a thin, wide mouth. The only thing Nathaniel remembered about him was his name—Zedekiah.

"But they need more than that, and soon," Nathaniel said. "What does Brother Joseph say?"

O'Neill set the mug of cider before him. "As a matter of fact, the prophet told somebody he warn't sure about what had happened. So he didn't think he should advise them what to do next—not without knowing more details, like."

Nathaniel cupped his hands around the cider mug. "So no one knows what really happened?"

"Well, you wuz there," Henley said. "Can you figure it out?"

"Not for certain. But they're in a terrible plight—most of them have lost everything."

O'Neill nodded. "I reckon we didn't know things was that bad. Seems like there's enough goings-on around here to keep folks occupied."

"Like what?" Nathaniel sipped the cider.

Zedekiah said, "Ain't no one told you about the House of the Lord?"

Nathaniel put the mug down. "What about it? This the first I been in town."

O'Neill leaned on one elbow and scratched behind his ear. "Well, you knew some folks weren't too happy about the whole idea. They ridiculed it from the beginning. There was attacks on the work site way back last year. But on January seventh—"

"It were the eighth," Henley said. "I remember like it was yesterday."

"Well, you tell it, then."

Henley said, "About one o'clock in the morning, it happened. A tremendous noise, like all hell breaking loose. Derned if that mob didn't fire off thirteen rounds of cannon."

"Where?" Nathaniel felt a tightening in his stomach.

"They wuz on the hill—about half a mile northwest of town."

Nathaniel said, "Did they hit the building?"

Henley laughed. "I don't think they could hit the side of a barn. But it sure stirred folks up."

"It were a warning—don't you see?" Zedekiah said.

"So now the men are keeping a close watch on the site at night. A lot of 'em are sleepin' in their clothes, with their firelocks close by."

The news, coming so soon after his experiences in Missouri, flooded him with misgiving. "Do we have to give this up, too?"

"What do you mean?" Henley said. "No one's givin' up anything. Everybody's fightin' mad. People are fixing to work on that building who swore they wouldn't lift a finger. Even the women—they're all knittin', spinnin' wool and sellin' it, making drapery and carpets for the building. And clothes for the workmen."

O'Neill smiled. "You'll get yourself a new suit, Nat. Looks like you could use it."

"That house is goin' up," Zedekiah said. "Ain't nothing gonna stop it now."

O'Neill said, "Another thing—they finally got the press set up. 'The Morning and the Evening Star.' Dedicated it December 18."

Henley said, "You got it wrong again, Pat."

"Whaddiyuh mean? It was so the eighteenth."

"It's 'The Evening and the Morning Star.' You said the other way around."

"Huh!" O'Neill said. "Seems like it orter be Morning and Evening. I mean, morning comes first, then evening."

"Depends on when you get up," Henley said.

O'Neill said, "Leastways, I got the dedication right. The same day they set apart Joseph Smith, Sr. as the Patriarch of the church."

"Now, what in tarnation is a Patriarch?" Henley asked.

O'Neill blinked. "Well, I expect he sets around looking solemn, and prays for folks if they want it. Or even if they don't want it."

Nathaniel paused with the cider mug halfway to his mouth. "Like the name says, he's a father to his people. A spiritual adviser. And Lord knows, most of us need one."

O'Neill smiled. "We've missed you, Brother Nat. Someone to set us straight about things."

Nathaniel drank, then set the mug down. "So what else has been happening?"

O'Neill wiped his hands on a white cloth which he kept behind the counter. "Let's see—the prophet and Sidney Rigdon went up into Canada and baptized a whole bunch of people. And there's someone named Doctor Hurlbut—he warn't a real doctor, but his mother wanted him to be. So that's what she named him. He's been stirrin' up folks, spreading lies about the Saints."

Zedekiah snorted. "And you know why? The leaders cut him off for immoral conduct!"

O'Neill said, "Speakin' of trouble, you been out to Crawford's yet?"

Nathaniel threw him a quick look. "I'm just going over there now. Why?"

O'Neill pursed his lips as if he were about to whistle. "Well, there's nothing big. Leastways, not right off. Things is just different."

Nathaniel tried to conceal his impatience. "Nothing's happened to Brother Owen, I hope?"

"Oh, no. It's like—well, he's gone and got hisself married, is all."

"Married!"

"Well, yes. It do happen. He figured he'd been a widower long enough."

"So who'd he marry?" He felt dazed, unprepared for this development. Did he still have a place to live?

Henley said, "Name's Polly. Sister Polly Brackett, she was. She be younger'n him, sort of pretty, if you don't look at her teeth."

"She's plump," Zedekiah said. "Well-fed, you might say."

"The thing is," O'Neill said. "She thinks she knows everything about farmin'. And she's kinda critical about how he does things. The looks of the place, and how it could be fancier-like."

Nathaniel spread his hands, a little puzzled gesture. "But it was in fine shape when I left—everything in good repair."

Henley smiled. "That's your way of thinkin'."

Nathaniel rubbed his hand across his mouth. "But what does she—"

"Tell about the dog," Henley said.

O'Neill leaned over the counter. "She has this feisty little dog—brought it with her. First thing it does is bite Crawford in the seat of the pants. He was ready to kick it to Kingdom Come. They had quite a row."

"And the young fellers," Henley said.

"Oh, them two. Well, we better back up a bit. See, there wuz these two new fellers—"

"They showed up here around the middle of December,"

Henley said. "A funny little French feller—not very old, and a young man of color. A freed slave. They was friends, new converts. Well, Crawford took 'em in and put 'em to work on his place. Gabe—that's the Frenchy—he did most of the work on account of the freed man had a bad arm. Broke or something."

"He's gettin' some better," O'Neill said. "Totin' wood, the last I seen of him."

Henley went on. "Well, now the new missus is after Crawford to get rid of them two, and bring her own relatives in to work the farm. And Brother Owen, he don't want to let 'em go. He's taken a liking to both of them, 'specially since they're newly baptized and all."

Nathaniel nodded. "That doesn't surprise me none."

Henley said, "He's afeard, if they work on another place, they won't be treated right. Gabe's real young, like I said, and Eb's got that injured arm. Crawford wants the arm to heal up good before they go off somewhere's else."

O'Neill said, "I hear tell they aim to open up a blacksmith shop some day. Savin' up money."

Nathaniel said, "That'll take some doing."

"So the Crawfords is going 'round over these two young'uns. And with that dog bitin' everyone it sees, I reckon you're in for a lively time."

Nathaniel stood up and fastened his coat. "It sounds like I better head on out there—see if I still have a bed to sleep in. Thanks for the cider. I'll be in with the money as soon as I get my hands on some."

O'Neill smiled. "Forget it, Nat. It's on us this time."

"Watch out for Sister Polly, now," Henley said.

The room rang with the sound of their laughter. Nathaniel opened the door and stepped out into the cold.

18

Nathaniel tramped toward the farmhouse in the early dusk. New snow was falling. He went around to the back door and knocked.

A flurry of barks sounded from inside. Curious to see the dog. The lady, too. He hoped Brother Owen was close by. The door opened.

A stout woman stood looking at him with little, close-set eyes. Henley was right—she had a pleasing plumpness, even though she didn't smile.

"We've no room for strangers here."

"I'm no stranger," Nathaniel replied. "I'm Brother Nat Givens. I be workin' for Brother Crawford for nigh onto two years now."

She swallowed and looked less certain. He said, "I've been away for a while. Is your husband at home?"

She sighed and opened the door wider. "You might as well come in."

He entered the cooking area of the keeping room. "You've been baking. I declare, I haven't smelled bread that good since my Shaker days."

Sister Polly wiped her hands on her apron. "And don't think you're gonna get any, either. There's just enough for us and the boys."

He tried to maintain his composure, but he hadn't eaten since early morning. "I reckon the smell of it will have to do."

She moved toward the front of the house. "Owen!"

A small black-and-white dog scrambled out from under the table. Nathaniel stood his ground as the dog advanced. She—for he saw it was female—sniffed the edges of his boots. He reached his hand down for her to smell. The dog sniffed the ends of his fingers, then gave a twitch of her tail. She retreated under the table as Crawford hurried in.

"Nat! I'll be hornswoggled! I didn't look to see you before planting time!" Crawford appeared hearty enough, but there was a strange, perplexed look about his eyes, like a shadow.

Nathaniel shook his hand. "Congratulations, brother—I see you've found yourself a wife. And my congratulations to you too, ma'am." He nodded to Sister Polly, who had followed Crawford in.

"Oh, yes!" Crawford stopped to introduce her.

She cut him off with a sour expression. "We've met."

Crawford turned back to Nathaniel. "But ye look much altered, my friend. You be thin as a rail."

"I took sick on the way back from Missouri." Nathaniel felt he would faint if he didn't get something to eat soon. "A right powerful misery."

"Well, here," Crawford said. "Let's cut you some of this bread."

Polly tightened her lips in a straight line as Crawford cut the loaf. He put the crusty heel on a plate and slathered butter on it. "Come sit down. Let's have some of that fresh milk, Poll. And you might as well call the boys—we'll feed 'em now and get it over with."

Nathaniel and Crawford sat down at the kitchen table. Nathaniel looked at the butter melting on the new-baked bread. "God bless you, Brother Crawford."

By the time Polly returned, Nathaniel was on his second slice. She began putting plates on the table with a clatter and getting things from the pantry—milk, cold ham and cheese, applesauce. Nathaniel felt the dog sniffing at his ankles.

Crawford was talking about the House of the Lord and how things were progressing. "When the winter's over, they'll start up again. It looks like they'll be getting to the interior finishing work before long. And the rest of the masonry work."

Nathaniel spoke with his mouth full of bread. "I reckon I've come back in good time."

He glanced up as the two newcomers entered the room. They looked just as he'd expected—the first one short, dark-haired, not much older than Rusty, the second man tall, muscular except for the emaciated right arm. He couldn't explain why, but he took a liking to the pair right away. Crawford gave brief introductions.

"So you're Gabriel." Nathaniel gestured with his dinner knife. "And you must be Eb."

Gabriel gave a shy smile and sat down. But Eb shot him a

suspicious look. Slow to trust people, Nathaniel thought. Afraid of strangers, like the little dog.

As they ate, he told them about Missouri and the journey. He omitted the most significant aspect—his feelings for Hannah and how they were becoming stronger instead of diminishing. Polly sat with her same tight-lipped, annoyed expression. Eb still looked suspicious. Gabriel began to speak.

"That puts me in mind of our own journey—from Gallipolis, way to the south. For Eb, it was even longer."

He told about discovering the Book of Mormon, and how reading it had persuaded him to abandon his ancestral faith and seek a new one. He told about finding Eb on the river bank, and how they'd made their way north, from one safe house to the next. As he spoke, he gave quick, little gestures with his hands. Nathaniel remembered seeing Hannah do the same thing. He watched, fascinated, as the image of his beloved came close in his mind.

Eb sat looking embarrassed, as if he were unused to sharing the story with a stranger. Owen Crawford had his usual kind, paternal expression. Sister Polly stifled a yawn; she looked irritated, a bit bored by the tale which Nathaniel had found brave and moving. What did interest her? The dog, maybe.

"That's a right pretty little dog."

"She's valuable, she is. She catches rats. When she has pups, I aim to sell 'em for two dollars apiece."

"I don't know who's gonna pay that much for a dog," Crawford said.

"Well, now," Nathaniel said. "A purebred rat catcher."

Gabriel and Eb began to laugh. Polly reddened and looked down. Crawford said, "Trust old Nat to put things in their proper place."

Polly raised her head and glared at her husband. "How long's he staying?"

The others stopped laughing. Nathaniel drew in his breath. Crawford looked at her. "Well, he's been biding with me since he left the Shakers. I reckon he can stay a little longer."

"He'll have to bunk with them, then."

Crawford gave him an apologetic look. "I put these two in your room—I didn't know when you might be comin' back."

Nathaniel managed to smile. "That's fine. I been in close company so long, I'm not used to anything else."

Polly went on. "And I hope they all realize it's only temporary."

Crawford looked embarrassed. "We can talk about it later." He shuffled his feet. "Now, I—"

The dog gave a high-pitched yelp and shot out from under the table. Forks and spoons went flying. "Tarnation!" Crawford shouted. "I forgot she was under there!"

Polly jumped up. "You did that on purpose! Yes, you did!"

Eb and Gabriel stood up in a hurry. The dog cowered by the hearth, whimpering. Polly said, "Him and his big feet! I never saw such a one for putting them anywhere."

"He didn't do it deliberately," Nathaniel said. "I know he wouldn't." He clicked to the dog and held out his hand.

Polly shook her head. "She won't pay you no mind. She'll only come to me, and I have to wait till she calms down."

By the time she had finished speaking, the dog was at Nathaniel's feet. He went down on one knee to stroke her head. "We're sorry—it's all right."

"He has a way with creatures," Crawford said to Polly. She sighed and made a funny rolling motion with her eyes.

Nathaniel and the other two retired to the small spare room.

Eb said, "Since he got married, it seems like they go to bed with the chickens."

Nathaniel smiled. "Maybe if I was married, I would, too." He put the single candle on top of a small chest of drawers. The one large bed took up most of the room.

"I reckon that'll hold all three of us," he said.

Gabriel nodded. "It's bigger than most beds."

Nathaniel removed his shirt, now threadbare. "I've slept in a lot worse places. The backs of wagons, haystacks and such." He needed new clothes, but there were no Shaker sisters to sew them for him. He would have to make his own. He'd left his old nightshirt in the bottom drawer. With luck, it was still there—Crawford wouldn't have touched it.

He bent over to open the drawer. Behind him, Eb gave a gasp.

"What?" Nathaniel asked. When he straightened up, both Eb and Gabriel were staring at him.

"Your back," Eb said. "It's worse than mine."

"Back?" Nathaniel put his hand to his shoulder and craned to look.

“I’d say you took quite a beating,” Gabriel said in an awed voice.

“I was hopin’ it was all healed by this time.”

“How’d you come by those?” Eb sounded angry. “You was never a slave.”

“No, it was—I didn’t say it before, but—that is, when I first set foot in Jackson County, they tied me to a wagon. See, they were chasin’ all our people out, and they figured...” His voice trailed off, and he shrugged. “It was just their welcoming committee.”

“Because you was a member of the church,” Eb said.

“Well, I reckon.” Nathaniel felt embarrassed; he reached for his nightshirt.

Eb spoke again. “You an all-fired hero. A—what do you call them? A martyr.” His eyes shone, all signs of suspicion gone.

“Oh, no.” Nathaniel pulled his nightshirt over his head. “I was just—in the wrong place at the wrong time.”

Gabriel was smiling. “If you say so. They’re healing up just fine, by the way.”

The candle out, they settled themselves side by side in the bed. Something bumped against the door. It opened, and they heard the sound of claws clicking on the floor boards.

“The dog,” Nathaniel said. “What’s her name?”

“Derned if I know,” Eb said.

Gabriel yawned. “I think it’s Nell, but I can’t be sure. Mainly they just yell at her.”

“Well, come on, Nell.” Nathaniel patted the bed. The dog jumped up and lay across their feet, her head resting on Nathaniel’s ankle.

“Leastways she’ll keep us warm,” he said.

“She better not bite me,” Eb said. “I’ll wake the dead.”

“She’s not biting anybody. She might, though, if you put her off the bed.”

Through the open door, the firelight flickered on the walls. After a moment, Gabriel said, “I don’t think we can stay here much longer.”

“I know,” Nathaniel said. “I reckon Brother Owen will let us be till spring. Then I know some folks in town—one brother has an old house on his property. Like as not, he’d let us move in if we fixed it up for him—did some extra work and such.”

“Our own place,” Gabriel said. “How about that, Eb?”

Nathaniel said, “I’ll see if I can find us some small jobs in town. We’ll save all the money we can. And when they start up work on the Lord’s House, we’ll be able to give them our one in seven.”

“Our what?”

He explained. “For every seven days, you put in a day’s work on the building. You help with whatever they’re doing—hauling, quarrying. When they start on the interior, I’ll be working there most of the time.”

19

"So, Brother Parley—how did they decide about Zion's Camp?"

"Well, it was obvious that something needed to be done. Now, that winter of '34, we held a general conference at my house. The group decided that two of us should go to Ohio, to seek help and advice from President Smith and the church there. They asked for volunteers. Finally Lyman Wight and I offered our services.

"Now, I want you to know we had nothing—no clothing, horses, or money for the journey. It seemed impossible, but all those things fell into place. We rode hundreds of miles through a wilderness country. We traveled every day, in all kinds of weather, and arrived in Kirtland in February."

"I reckon they were glad to see you."

"I want to tell you! When we told them about the persecution, they grieved as if they themselves had gone through it."

"So then you organized Zion's Camp?"

"Wait a minute—I'm coming to that. First the President inquired of the Lord, and received, among other things, assurance that we would possess that land. Then we were told to gather a group of men, preferably five hundred, but not less than one hundred—"

"Five hundred! You sure didn't get that many."

"No—I don't think it was much more than a hundred and twenty. I visited churches in the eastern cities, to persuade people to be part of it. I traveled with Joseph Smith, and Lyman Wight went with Sidney Rigdon. There were others of us, trying to find enough men to fulfill the commandment."

"And you did, it seems."

"Just barely. I have to tell you, I was mainly involved in the recruiting end of things. I didn't spend much time with the camp at first. I would visit the churches along the route, preach and plead with them, and return to the camp with additional men, arms, supplies, sometimes even money."

"But you didn't get enough. If you'd had five hundred, or even four hundred, you coulda made hash out of those outlaws."

"Now, wait, son. It wasn't our intention to 'make hash' out of anyone. That's what folks keep forgetting. We were supposed to be carrying supplies to the Missouri saints, and to reinforce and strengthen them. We hoped to influence the governor to call out additional troops, and then, with a sufficient number of men, we'd be able to help the people reclaim their land."

"So you didn't plan on killing anyone?"

"Certainly not. Not if we didn't have to."

"Oh." The young man looked disappointed. Pratt ignored him and went on. "Now there were two groups of marchers, to begin with. See, Hyrum Smith and Lyman Wight went up to the northwest looking for recruits, by way of Michigan and northern Illinois. They had a wagon for hauling supplies, and orders to go on to Missouri and meet up with the men from Kirtland around the first of June."

"But that wasn't the main party."

"I'm comin' to it. The main group left New Portage the second week in May. But it took some doing to assemble all the marchers and get supplies and money together. Why, it was mid-April before Brother Joseph knew he had enough men and resources for such an expedition. Then he decided to go ahead, and lead the march himself.

"Now, soon as they started, late-comers hurried in from all directions. A bunch of brethren from the eastern states joined us at Richfield, some with wagons and supplies, some with cash. Most of them had very little at all, and as for weapons, it was laughable. Some had rusty swords, others had hunting knives. I swear, one had a musket that hadn't seen action since the Revolution. I remember the rejoicing when that group of eastern Saints came in. And eight German brethren, all from Stark County."

"Did you get any more?"

"I hope to tell you! Recruits joined us all along the way. We even had families following us with the idea of going up to Zion and settling, once things had quieted down. Yes, sir. When you look back on it, that camp was really something."

****

The morning routine. It reminded Nathaniel of the Shakers, except that it seemed less rigid. They woke at sunrise to the sound of the trumpet, in this case a battered French horn. The company commanders roused their squads, and the camp began to stir. After prayer, in which everyone knelt to ask the Lord's protection for that day, the men washed in the nearby stream and began their assigned duties—cooking, gathering wood, fetching water, and taking care of the tents, horses and wagons.

Nathaniel's company consisted of six, less than the usual ten or twelve. He and Gabriel had charge of cooking for the company. When Gabriel wasn't busy with food preparation, he helped Eb gather firewood. The three others took care of the tent and carried water. Since they had no horses or wagons to look after, they escaped that particular detail. They had only to see that their tent and personal belongings were properly stowed in the designated wagon before breakfast.

Lucky this morning—biscuits and bacon. Nathaniel mixed up the dough and shaped biscuits as Gabriel started the fire. Nathaniel cut strips of bacon and laid them in a three-legged skillet which his mother had always called a 'spider.' Gabriel bent over the pile of twigs and fanned the flame, muttering something in French. Trouble with the wind. Nathaniel moved over and stood between the fire and the wind.

As he waited, he glanced at the surrounding woods, the dark figures darting among the trees as they hurried to complete their duties.

"Chilly this morning." He got down on one knee and set the spider over the fire. He put the biscuits to bake in a covered pan. As he cut more bacon, Gabriel laid wood on the fire.

"You'd think I could get it going quicker than that, being raised in a blacksmith shop."

Nathaniel didn't answer. Thinking again—in two minds about Zion's Camp.

As a Shaker, he'd learned a strict pacifism. To take human life under any circumstances was unthinkable. In the collected revelations which would have been published last summer in Independence, the taking of life was forbidden.

Yet here they were, marching as a body to reclaim their lost land. Outwardly a mission of peace, an act of encouragement and support for the refugees. The wagons had supplies, to be sure. Old blankets, coats that had outworn their usefulness. But Nathaniel thought of the weapons—each man armed, from firelocks and horse pistols down to his own butcher knife. A shudder ran through him as he turned the bacon.

He could not take life. He would die first. In spite of his beating, and Hannah losing not only her intended, but the land she would have lived on in Missouri—he had no desire to fight.

Gabriel felt differently, he knew. They'd talked about it. "I can't abide slave-holders. I could kill the whole lot of 'em, and they'd deserve it." And Eb had agreed.

Nathaniel felt even more uneasy since he was the one who'd

encouraged Gabriel and Eb to join the expedition. They'd just completed their move to a small structure near the House of the Lord, part of a group of out-buildings on one of the farms. The Crawfords had given him the dog Nell as a farewell present, since all she did was to wait for Nathaniel and follow him. He'd never known such devotion from an animal; it embarrassed and humbled him at the same time. The Crawfords had agreed to keep her till his return—maybe she wouldn't even recognize him by that time.

Why had he volunteered? A good question. Aside from the fact that he loved the prophet and trusted his leadership, he ached to see Hannah again. This expedition should bring him well into Hannah territory—Clay County, where most of the outcasts had gathered.

He hadn't thought of what he would say when he found her. Enough just to behold her face. Pain and anguish it would bring him, to be sure. But he was used to concealing such things. Seeing her would be like completing a circle, or a convoluted journey.

The others gathered around the fire. They rubbed their hands together and held them close to the flames. He opened the biscuit pan, catching the handle with the tip of his knife. The men helped themselves to biscuits and bacon. Eb scooped up some of the grease to smear on his biscuits, and the others did the same. They drank water out of a dented tin cup and passed it around.

They talked, but Nathaniel didn't listen. He was thinking how he'd written to Hannah after his return from Missouri—a brief note, telling her how he'd put Rusty on the stage to Pittsburgh. He'd apologized for not writing sooner, and explained how he'd become ill before he reached Kirtland.

To his surprise, he'd received a reply. It arrived just as they were moving their belongings into the new house. Gabriel had brought it to him. "Something from the post office."

He'd memorized it: *Dear Brother Nat,*

It was so good to get your message. I have received a letter from Rusty. He arrived home in time for Christmas. They had a pleasant holiday because my Aunt Elizabeth, who is opposed to any idea of 'Mormonism,' has gone off on another lecture tour. They are hoping she will settle closer to New York City, as her editors have advised.

I hope you have recovered from your illness. Everyone here is as well as can be expected, but doing without many things that would make life easier. We had quite a scare with little Jacob. He fell ill after the first of the year, but is in good health now. Diana's new baby boy is very strong and healthy, with a good pair of lungs. They have named him Joseph.

Lem wants us all to move up north of Richmond. He feels we have been beholden to the Snyders long enough. I wish you good luck and good health as you help build the House of the Lord. I remain always your friend,

Hannah Manning

A hand on his shoulder. He turned. Gabriel stood watching him with an expression of concern.

"You aren't eating. What's wrong?"

"Oh—nothing. I was just—well—"

"I saved some bacon for you. And you'd better enjoy the biscuits, 'cause there'll only be corn dodger and johnny cake soon. That's the word from the other companies."

"Oh." Nathaniel sat on a log to eat. Gabriel began pouring water on the fire. Nathaniel watched him. Despite his impulsive nature, the young man seemed to have intuition, and a keen sense of what needed to be done. Not like Rusty. Nathaniel felt the familiar ache in his chest. Missing Rusty, not to mention his sister. A little more time with Rusty, and he could've taught the boy how to get along in the world. Things Gabe already knew.

"Coffee, anyone?" A cook from another company held up a pot. Eb and two others hurried over to get some. Gabriel gathered up the cooking pots and went down to wash them in the stream.

Nathaniel tramped to the water's edge to wash his own plate and utensils. Then he stowed them with the other gear in the wagon. The men waited. Some wrote letters home; others wrote entries in their journals.

"All right, boys!" a voice called. "We're moving out!"

A horse neighed. Wagon wheels creaked. Nathaniel straightened up and fell into step beside Gabriel. Eb followed close behind with the three others. They walked behind the wagon containing their gear; it moved into place with the other wagons. Soon they were all moving, some mounted, most on foot. They walked first as a tight cluster, then some lagged behind, stringing out in a long line through the trees and out across the prairie.

They followed the usual procedure of breaking up and going through the settlements in small groups, like other migrants heading west. In the open spaces they kept closer together. Some of the mounted men rode up and down the line of march to see that everything was as it should be.

Just outside town, a road led in from the east. Nathaniel could see a small, weathered wagon, hardly more than a cart, behind two bay horses. In the wagon sat a middle-aged man, solidly built, with thick gray hair and wide-apart eyes. A younger man stood by the horses as they waited for the procession to pass. Something about the youngster made Nathaniel pause. Suddenly his heart lurched in his chest.

"I'll be back." He left the march, not daring to believe it. He hurried, tripped over a root, regained his footing. "Rusty?"

"Dad-blame it, if it isn't Nat!" Rusty grasped him by the shoulders, and Nathaniel saw that the boy had grown by at least four inches.

"I'd know that hair color anywheres."

"Papa," Rusty said. "This's my friend, the one that took us to Missouri. Brother Nat."

The man was standing up in the wagon. He had a squarish shape to his face, a broad nose and dark, arched eyebrows. "This Zion's Camp?"

"You better believe it. You come to join us?"

"'Course we're joining. Been lookin' for 'em for two days." Rusty's father leaned over to shake Nathaniel's hand. "Calvin Manning here. I'd hoped to meet you and thank you for all you've done."

Nathaniel still couldn't believe it. Rusty shook his head and laughed again. “You’ll never guess all that’s happened. Do we just follow along here?”

“We’ll get you a place.” Nathaniel held up his hand at the next wagon, then pulled the Manning team and wagon into a position just ahead of it. “Like it or not, you’re now part of us.”

Rusty nodded, then frowned. “You look plain tuckered, Nat. Thin as a rail. Get into the wagon. You can rest while we tell you how we come to be here.”

Nathaniel climbed up beside Calvin. “I want you in my company. We’re only six, so we’re short some.”

“You the leader?” Rusty asked.

“The captain—yes. The others voted.”

“They could do worse.” Rusty walked beside the wagon, and together he and his father related their story.

Calvin began. “It was the Ordwells, started it. All the talk of going up to Zion. Then it was Zion’s Camp—going to help the ones who’d lost their lands. Maybe get them back. Then the missionaries—the two Orsons.”

“Pratt and Hyde?” Nathaniel asked.

“The same. They pleaded up and down—I never did hear such preachin’. I reckon they could even persuade the dead.”

Rusty nudged Nathaniel. “He was baptized the Sunday before we left. But it took some doing.”

Calvin said, “We better backtrack some, to when Russell came home. We did the planting and the necessary chores. My sister Elizabeth had gone off somewhere—one of her holy crusades—and it gave us a chance to think some. Why keep our farm and livestock when maybe we could be helping Hannah and her friends out west?"

Rusty said, "That letter came just the right time."

"From Hannah?" Nathaniel asked.

"No. Aunt Elizabeth, telling us she wouldn't be coming back. We shipped all her things to New York. We did it in a hurry, so she couldn't change her mind."

Calvin ran a hand through his hair. "Then we heard about the Jackson County people, and how wide-spread those troubles were. I tell you, those preachers made it seem as if you was right there. And of course, Russell was in the thick of it. You too, I understand."

Nathaniel nodded and looked straight ahead. He longed to ask about Hannah, but decided to wait till they finished. Calvin shifted the reins to his left hand.

"Well, it didn't take long for us to sell the farm and all the stock. Kept some of Hannah's things—they're packed in the wagon. Got a good price for the farm. Gave most of it to the missionaries to help with the camp. Kept some—kept our matching team and the wagon."

"And here we are," Rusty said. "Ready for whatever happens next."

"That was right generous of you," Nathaniel said. "Giving the proceeds to the redemption of Zion."

"I wasn't even thinkin' of that," Calvin said. "It was mainly for Hannah—my wayward child."

Nathaniel smiled. "Not so wayward. You'll be blessed, nonetheless." Before Calvin could speak again, he said, "You heard from her?"

"Lord, yes. She's written at least three times."

Nathaniel said, "She mention going further north?"

"No. She—let's see, what was in the last letter?"

Rusty said, "Rube Snyder and his family are treating her real nice. I figured they would. But she doesn't know a thing about Papa joining the church, and us selling our property. And she doesn't know about us joining Zion's Camp. We'll just go out and surprise her."

"Oh, she'll be surprised, all right," Nathaniel said.

Calvin gave a little cough. "Well, we figured she'd worry some if she knew. And she's had enough to burden her, with her young man dyin' and all."

"Yes—I've feared for her," Nathaniel said.

"Oh, she's strong—you can bet on that. And stubborn. If she ever does marry, she'll have some young feller jumpin' through hoops."

"Oh, now, Papa," Rusty said.

Calvin clicked to the horses. "But we didn't want her to grieve on account of us."

"Yes—that's best," Nathaniel said. "Wait and see how things work out."

20

Whatever Rusty expected, Zion's Camp wasn't it. Even though he'd been in Missouri and knew what lay ahead, he'd hoped the expedition itself would be more light-hearted, less disciplined. In a word, more fun. But whenever he tried to liven things up, he got a reprimand from his captain.

Nathaniel seemed changed—leaner, older, more serious. Too much authority, Rusty thought. At the same time he sensed something else—a strange, brooding sorrow.

"I hear he took powerful sick, comin' home from Missouri," Gabriel said as they washed the cooking pots from the evening meal. "He's put on a few pounds since I first met him."

"He seems so somber-like," Rusty said.

"That beating sure didn't help him none. But I figure it's some woman he's pining after, out there in Missouri."

Rusty looked at him. "After all this time? You can't be serious."

"All I know is, she sent him a letter. After that, he started acting all moody—like his mind was someplace else. Eb thinks he's lovesick for sure."

Rusty blinked and shook his head. "For Hannah?"

"H. Manning—that was the name on the outside of the letter."

"That would be my sister."

Gabriel raised his eyebrows. "*Eh bien.* Is she pretty?"

"Folks say she's real good-looking. But she's more than that—I can't describe her."

"She must be something, to keep him stirred up like that."

Rusty looked at the shadows in the water. "She'd be grieved for certain if she thought he was taking on so."

They made room for Rusty and his father in the tent. The first night, Rusty lay awake and listened to the night noises. Close at hand he heard crickets and locusts. A chorus of frogs echoed from the creek's edge. Rusty thought about getting Hannah and Nathaniel back together. She might look at him in a kinder light if she knew he still cared for her. He sighed and turned over.

An ear-splitting shriek rent the air.

"Now what in tarnation was that?"

"Somebody step on a rattlesnake?"

Above the murmur, Nathaniel called out. "Land's sakes! Ain't you folks ever heard an owl before?"

"Owl?"

"That was an owl?"

"Little ol' screech owl. Go back to sleep."

Rusty began to laugh, a suppressed series of snorts. He heard

Gabriel laughing too. Eb said, "If that don't beat all."

Then Nathaniel got to his feet and stood over them. Rusty stopped laughing. Nathaniel spoke after a moment.

"What do you aim to do? Tell our enemies right where to find us?"

Rusty didn't reply. Nathaniel waited, then sighed and lay down. Enemies? Rusty stared up into the dim light, wondering.

Did fear stalk the camp? Was that why they split up into small groups to go through the towns? It explained the weapons. Joseph himself had a rifle, a four-foot sword borrowed from Wilford Woodruff, and a brace of pistols which someone said had been purchased on credit. In days that followed, Rusty observed how any stranger approaching the camp drew suspicious looks from the marchers.

"Might easily be a spy," Nathaniel said.

They began referring to Joseph as 'Squire Cook' in an effort to protect his identity. As they crossed over into Indiana, they posted sentinels nightly to guard against spies. Rusty tried to joke about it.

"I reckon that big dog is a spy. And the lead horse on that wagon."

"I'd be careful if I was you," his father said. "Don't call up more trouble than we've got."

Rusty tried to shake the feeling that he had two leaders—his father and Nathaniel. Best to co-operate. He stopped joking, and made an effort to win Nathaniel's approval. But Nathaniel kept catching him in acts of carelessness—dropping cooking utensils, or spilling the water they'd just hauled from the stream. Once, he and Eb ran into each other and scattered firewood, as Eb said, "from here to breakfast."

Nathaniel sighed. "All right, Rusty. You go see to the horses—I reckon you'll be more use there."

Rusty hurried to help his father with the horses and wagon. He hated being exiled from the kitchen area—it meant he didn't have first chance at the food. And Nathaniel no longer trusted him to do anything right.

True—Nathaniel tried to take care of them. Rusty remembered the fording of the Miami River, and how he'd stood on shore watching the baggage wagons splash into the water. The air echoed with the sound of horses neighing and men shouting. His father and Eb started their own team across.

"Hurry up, Rusty!"

Rusty looked at the water as it swirled around the wagon wheels. If he stepped into a hole, he wouldn't be able to swim. Some of the men were carrying others across on their backs. Rusty had just decided to strike out on his own when Nathaniel's hand gripped his shoulder.

"Come on, lad. Climb up on this rock, and I'll get you across."

Nathaniel carried Rusty across. Then he went back again for Gabriel.

That same day, Rusty managed to be first in line for some milk given them by the local people.

"Be careful," one of the men said. "There's like to be sickness in that milk."

"How do you know?" someone else said. "God tell yer?"

"The cows is all sick, and there's people afraid to drink it."

Toward evening, Eb stood up from his meal. "A misery in my innards." He hurried into the bushes.

Rusty began to feel uneasy. He'd had more milk than anyone. He noticed men in other companies looking pale and ill, some heading into the woods. Two of the captains came over and spoke to Nathaniel in a low voice. Nathaniel nodded and set his bowl of cold stew and cornbread on a stump.

"You boys see to the kitchen. And take care of Eb." He turned and followed the other leaders toward the center of the encampment.

"What's that all about?" Rusty said.

Gabe shrugged. "Hanged if I know. Doesn't look like anyone's hungry—that's not a good sign."

By the time Nathaniel returned, they had the cooking utensils cleaned and the fire laid for the morning. Eb sat with his back against a tree, his legs stretched out in front of him. Gabe sat cross-legged beside him, and the rest made a little semi-circle around the fire pit.

Nathaniel's eyes scanned the circle. "Everyone here? Good. How you makin' it, Eb?"

"I'm fine now. Long as I don't eat."

Nathaniel propped one foot on a log and leaned his elbows on his knee. "A bunch of us went over to consult with Brother Joseph about this 'milk sickness' story. Seems like some folks figured our enemies had maybe poisoned the milk and gave it to us. Well, the prophet studied it some. Here's what he said—we shouldn't fear. If we follow his counsel and use all we can get from friend or enemy, it will do us good and no one will be sick as a consequence of it."

Some of the men mumbled among themselves. Finally Rusty's father spoke. "Well, I'm willing to believe it. After all, what can we do? We have to depend on the local people for most of our food."

Eb said, "I feel some better now. I reckon I could try eating."

"Best you wait till morning," Gabe told him. "Just have some water for now."

On Monday, May 19, they marched for Indianapolis. Another rumor reached their ears. The Indiana governor planned to stop them at the capital city, acting in his official capacity to turn back any belligerent force which had no government sanction.

"They say he can keep us from goin' anywhere," Eb said. "This a neutral state, and he don't want no armies passin' through."

Rusty felt a shiver of fear. "What do we do?"

"Jest keep marchin'. Or git in the wagon if you want."

Climbing into the wagon meant taking orders from his father. He'd had enough of that yesterday. Since it was Sunday, they hadn't done any traveling. They'd had communion together in the morning, and spent the rest of the day baking bread, mending clothes, catching up on what needed to be done. Some had gone hunting and fishing, without much success.

He'd planned on a snooze in the wagon, but his father and captain had other ideas. They had him cleaning and greasing wagon wheels, unpacking and scrubbing the interior.

"I was hopin' for a nap," he said at last. "It's supposed to be a day of rest."

"I'm glad you're not a lazy person, Rusty," Nathaniel told him. "That would really grieve me."

When they'd finished working him, it was time for the firewood and cooking pots.

At the next stop, Nathaniel gathered his company together.

"I don't know just what you've heard. But Brother Joseph has prophesied that we'll march through the city without the people knowing it."

The journey resumed. "That'll be some trick," Rusty said to Gabriel. "Maybe we'll all be invisible."

At the final stop outside the city, orders came. "We're to get into the wagons," Nathaniel said. "As many of us that can. The rest will walk in scattered groups, and take different routes through."

Rusty rode up in front with his father. Behind them, under the burlap and bedrolls, crouched Gabriel, Eb, and three others. Nathaniel walked beside the horses.

"Wait," he said. "We want lots of distance between these wagons."

From his wagon seat, Rusty could see townspeople in little clusters by the road's edge. To his mind, they looked even more fearful than the marchers. At first he thought it was his own apprehension, reflected in what he was seeing. Then Nathaniel spoke in a low voice.

"I swan, they look like they're seeing ghosts. That one on the end—he's pale as a sheet."

Rusty heard a low murmur of voices, then a silence, broken by the clomping of the horses' hooves. The stillness seemed to follow them as they passed through.

Once out of the city, Rusty let out his breath in an audible sigh. He and his father exchanged glances. Calvin's lips formed a smile, and Rusty saw a dampness under his eyes. Nathaniel looked stern, as if this were not the time to show one's feelings. They stopped in a stretch of woods, and the others crawled out of the wagon.

After that, Rusty heard very little criticism of their prophet and leader.

Even with the guards posted around the camp at night, fear prevailed. An edict from the camp headquarters prohibited any fraternizing with strangers. At one point, Joseph declared that the angels of God were with the camp, for he had seen them. If this was an attempt to allay their fears, it didn't work. To their minds, spies lurked behind every bush, strangers waiting to report their every move to the Missourians. Reports reached them of spies boasting in the towns about "fooling the Mormons," and preparing to return to Missouri to organize an army of resistance.

May 25. The full moon shone through the trees, casting spots of light on the forest floor. The sentries thought they saw the fires of an enemy close to the encampment. Alarm guns roared, three in quick succession.

"That's it!" Nathaniel shouted. "Up, all of you!"

The men fumbled around for their clothes, shoes and weapons.

"Where's my hat?" Gabriel asked. "Eb, you got it!"

"Well, you're wearing my coat!"

By the time the others were up and in formation, Rusty was still hunting for his clothes. He had not even finished dressing before word came that the danger had been imaginary, in the minds of the guards. He was not the only one caught unprepared.

"Like the ten virgins," someone remarked. "Nothing in readiness."

How could they face an enemy with such a lack of discipline?

The camp leaders decided to begin a training program which would help prepare them in the face of an attack. After crossing the Kaskaskia River, they divided into three units for the preparation and staging of a mock battle. Nathaniel's company marched with the first two divisions into the woods.

At the signal, they attacked the remaining division from different directions. They proved so enthusiastic that one man was injured.

"Captain Heber Kimball," someone said. "He grasped Captain Zabriskie's sword, to take it from him. Derned if he didn't have the skin cut from the palm of his hand."

This incident prompted Brother Joseph to caution them. "Control your spirits under all circumstances so as never to injure each other."

"Well, we know now they can fight," Rusty's father remarked.

"That's true," Nathaniel replied. "Even Joseph said so. Did you hear? He said many of the captains showed more tact and acquaintance with military matters than he'd expected."

"I'm not sure he expected too much."

Tired as they were, they seemed to move with new confidence

after the exercise. On Sunday, June 1, they prepared for a preaching service just outside Jacksonville. Since the local people seemed friendly, the men of the camp invited them to the service. As a result, two hundred curious people came out to hear them.

Not wanting to reveal themselves as Mormons, the leading men of the camp assumed different religious identities. Each man gave a talk typical of the denomination he had chosen to portray. Joseph Smith spoke as 'Squire Cook' and presented himself as a liberal free-thinker. He spoke for about an hour, followed by John Carter, a former Baptist, who discoursed on Baptist beliefs that agreed with the Restoration.

The word spread among the local inhabitants. That afternoon a large crowd gathered to hear the rest of the preaching. Joseph Young, Orson Hyde, Orson Pratt and others held forth on various portions of the gospel, each from a different religious point of view. The crowd listened, fascinated.

"I reckon they had fun doing that," Gabriel said afterward as they sat around the wagon.

Eb leaned back against the wagon wheel. "And no one let on who we really were."

"Like as not, some of them knew," Gabe said. "Don't you reckon they figured it out?"

"I suppose so." Rusty, seated on a stump, glanced up as a shadow fell over them. Nathaniel stood looking down at them. He didn't smile.

"Something wrong, Captain?" Gabriel asked.

"It's time to eat, and the fire's not even laid."

"We'll see to it," Gabriel said. Nathaniel turned and strode around the back of the tent. They watched as he walked toward the place where the horses were tethered.

"What's up with him?" Rusty asked.

"The usual. Takes his job too seriously," Gabe said.

Eb stretched his legs out in front of him. "You figure that's all?"

Gabe said, "No. I reckon he's thinkin' he might actually have to fight the Missourians. And he doesn't want to do it."

"I'm not too keen on it myself," Rusty said.

Eb grunted. "I've seen enough bad things in my life. I don't need no more."

Gabriel gestured. "Nathaniel not only doesn't want to fight, he doesn't want us doing it either. He told me himself."

"That's like him," Rusty said. "Takin' responsibility for everybody."

Gabriel shook his head. "No—it's just us. We're like his family."

Rusty shuffled his feet in the pine needles. "Well, I wish we didn't have to."

"Maybe we won't," Gabe said. "What does your father think?"

"He'll go along with whatever the leaders say. But he'd just as soon not kill anyone."

Gabe gave a little laugh. "Some military force we are."

Rusty said, "Listen—I have an idea."

Before he could explain it to them, Nathaniel appeared from around the side of the tent. This time he looked angry; the veins stood out in his temples. “Why isn’t this fire going? Why are you still sitting here?”

They jumped up and began gathering the firewood. Nathaniel looked at them and shook his head. He went to get the cooking utensils out of the wagon.

“Seems all I can see is fear,” Rusty remarked as they built the fire.

“Oh, no,” Gabe said. “There’s other things. Like the snakes. Remember?”

“What snakes?”

“Brother Brigham found this ol’ rattlesnake while he was marching. Instead of killing it, he made one of his men carry it off. He said to tell it not to come back again, and to say to its neighbors not to come into our camp tonight or someone might kill them.”

Rusty blinked and wondered why Gabe would remember such a thing. Gabe went on.

“Then ol’ Brother Parsons, he woke up from a nap and found a snake in the bedroll with him. Some wanted to kill it, but the brother said that they’d just shared in a good rest together. They let the snake go away unharmed.”

Rusty looked at him, puzzled. “What of it?”

“Don’t you see? It explains a lot of things. We’re seeing God in nature. If he’s everywhere, he’s in the snake too. And the deer. Do you wonder why we don’t hunt very often?”

“We don’t want to get the local folks excited.”

“No. It’s more than that. It’s—well—like a kind of connection with all created things. And what we’ve been talking about. No one wants to take life. It's—"

"That fire ready yet?" Nathaniel demanded.

As they neared the Mississippi, they heard rumors of four hundred of the enemy positioned on the other side of the river.

"Just layin' for us," Eb said. "Waitin' to tear us apart."

Rusty's father reined in his team. "Luke Johnson says they aim to pick us off as we cross."

"Why worry about them?" Gabriel said. "We got folks taking shots at us most every night."

It was true; they'd even redoubled the guard. At one stop, the camp members heard guns firing in all directions throughout the night. Weary from traveling and lack of sleep, they grew edgy with the repeated threats. Tempers flared. New quarrels broke out among them. Even Nathaniel spoke only to reprimand and bark orders.

They had an added worry. Brother Joseph had stated in the name of the Lord that if they didn't stop murmuring and finding fault, a severe scourge would come upon the camp, and the men would suffer chastisement for their wickedness and lack of humility. He advised them to repent and engage in prayer. Now, if any accident or unfortunate event happened, they attributed it to God's wrath.

"I fell in that last creek, tryin' to git me some water," Eb said.

Gabriel gave a short laugh. "I reckon you haven't been humble enough."

When they reached the Mississippi, all levity ceased. On the afternoon of June 4, they began the crossing in a single ferryboat. No sign of any enemy. By evening, they had only managed to get half of the baggage wagons and men across.

"I figure that's a mile and a half of water," Gabriel said.

Nathaniel and his company camped with the first group on the Missouri side, while the rest remained on the Illinois shore. Once across, the men rested and waited for the others. Some went hunting or fishing, others wrote to their families whom they hadn't seen for a month.

Nathaniel's company relaxed around the fire that night. Nathaniel joined them, for some reason acting more affable than he had in weeks. Eb leaned up against the wagon wheel. "I reckon those four hundred men was waitin' further down the river."

Nathaniel smiled. "Maybe they weren't waiting at all." Then he looked serious. "Tell me, Calvin—what do you aim to do when all this is over?"

Calvin's brow furrowed. "Over?"

"When they settle the land issue and disband the camp. We don't have much further to go, you know."

"Well—if there's any fightin'—"

"There may not be. That's just a feeling I have."

Rusty said, "I sure hope you're right."

"We ain't fighters; that's certain," Eb said.

Rusty's father rubbed the side of his nose. "Well, I don't see myself as much of a pioneer either. Rusty and I—we'll most likely go settle somewhere near Kirtland. He says it's good country. We'll look for a bit of land to farm."

"In that case, I have a place for you," Nathaniel said. "You can stay with me and the boys as long as you want. It's a snug little house—you can have the whole upstairs."

"That's right decent of you," Rusty's father said. "It'll take care of us for a while—till we decide what's best to do."

"I'm pleased to offer it," Nathaniel said. Gabe and Eb glanced at each other as if they shared some private joke. Rusty wondered what it meant. Then his father sighed and spoke again.

"'Course, more than anything else, I long to see my daughter. I was thinkin' it'd be at the end of this journey, when we get near Richmond. That's where she was when we last heard."

Nathaniel nodded. "I know. But it's powerful risky, leaving the main group. If they catch you off alone, you haven't got a chance."

Again Gabe and Eb looked at each other, Gabe with his eyebrows raised. Rusty tried to ignore them, but he felt uneasy.

"All I want is to see Hannah again," he said. "She's right special, for a sister. I don't reckon I can explain. But I miss her more than I can say."

His father reached over and patted his shoulder. Nathaniel sniffed as if he had a cold. Gabe spoke, his voice gentle.

"I reckon I know how you feel. I have a sister too—'course I have three sisters. But there's one that's close to me—she's special. Sometimes it was like we were one person, the way we thought and spoke. I don't expect I'll ever see her again."

"You can't tell," Nathaniel said. "Stranger things have happened."

The rest spoke in turn of the ones they wanted to see again, and the things they hoped to do. Rusty knew they were all thinking of what might lie ahead. Gabe mentioned his desire to be a healer, and his idea of opening a blacksmith shop. Eb spoke of his wife, his Jess.

"I expect she looks up at the stars and wonders where I am—if I ever got north to safety. I hope something whispers that I did."

Finally everyone had spoken except Nathaniel. Instead of saying what he wanted, he led them in prayer for each of their plans, and for their loved ones. When he mentioned the name of Hannah, his voice broke. He recovered, and encouraged each one to pray in turn. Rusty, leaning close to his father, felt peace settling around them with the darkness.

The next morning Rusty helped Gabe build the fire.

"Why did you and Eb think it was such a joke when Nathaniel offered us a place to stay?"

Gabe looked around before he answered. Nathaniel had gone over to get something from the wagon.

"It's not a joke, and you'll be more than welcome. But, the thing is—he thinks so much of your sister that he'll do anything if he figures there's a chance of pleasing her. And giving you a place—well, that's sure to win her approval. Eb and I had to smile. Ol' Nat's really trying."

"So that—so that's why—"

"*Tiens.* Here he comes." Gabe bent to light the kindling.

After breakfast, Rusty and Gabe washed up the dishes in the river. They stayed at the water's edge to watch the crossing.

"I reckon they'll be most of the day gettin' those wagons across," Gabe said. They sat on a log jutting out from the bank and dangled their feet in the water. Sounds drifted from across the water, shouts, horses neighing. The wind sent tiny ripples into shore, and Rusty told Gabriel his plan.

"I'd like to leave the camp for a few days when we get closer to Richmond. I'm going to see my sister even if I die in the attempt."

Gabe looked at him. "You're really set on it?"

"I reckon so."

"Nat said it was dangerous."

Rusty looked straight ahead at the far shore. "He's most likely right. But I'll take my chances."

"What about your father? He know what you aim to do?"

"He'd never leave the camp without permission. And he'd fret if he knew. Like Nathaniel, he'd forbid it."

Gabe waited, then shrugged. "Well, from what I see, folks come and go all the time. I heard one fellow say he was disillusioned with the whole idea, and he'd been away from his family long enough. I don't reckon he's still here. And there's scouts goin' out, others comin' in. Men are still joining the march."

Rusty looked at Gabe. "What are you telling me?"

A little breeze ruffled the hair on Gabe's forehead. "If you want to leave, just do it. But be careful."

"I was hopin' you and Eb might come along. You'd like Hannah; I know it. She'd even speak French with you."

Gabriel nodded. "I'll go with you, if you like. But we can't take Eb. Don't forget—Missouri's a slave state. If they caught us, you and I—we'd probably be all right. But for him, it'd be terrible."

“They’d kill him?”

“No. He’s valuable. They’d most likely beat him and then sell him. We can’t take that chance.”

Rusty nodded. “Just us, then. You afraid?”

“No. There’s no need to be. I’ve led whole bunches of folks to safe houses, even while men were looking for them. I can slip through the woods good as an Indian. I’ll teach you how.”

They watched as the ferry came to shore. Gabe spoke out of the side of his mouth. “You know where in Richmond?”

“Home of Rube Snyder. When we reach town, I can take us right there.”

“Well and good. We’ll stick with the march as long as we can—maybe another two hundred miles. Then we’ll sneak away.”

“I wish we could tell somebody,” Rusty said. “Nat, he’ll worry. And my father.”

Gabe frowned. “I wouldn’t. If Eb knew, he’d want to go with us. Thinks he’d be protecting me. We’ll be back before they even know it.”

Nathaniel’s voice spoke behind them. “Just sitting here? Why aren’t you over there helping?”

Gabe started as if a rifle shot had gone off in his ear.

“I—I don’t know, sir. I reckon they’re doing fine without us.”

“We were finishing up the dishes,” Rusty said.

“Takes you long enough.” Nathaniel turned and tramped toward the ferry.

Late in the afternoon, others lined the shore to see the final ferry load come in. The last company, under the leadership of Sylvester Smith—no relation to the prophet—stepped off the ferry. The men formed a single column.

"Listen." Gabe held up his hand. "Hear it?"

The strains of a fife drifted to them. Rusty parted the branches for a better view.

Levi Hancock marched out in front of the company, blowing a fife he'd managed to carve while he waited to cross. The rest high-stepped behind him as they made their way into camp. Applause and cheers resounded from the on-lookers.

Suddenly a ferocious barking broke out.

"Oh, no," Rusty said. "The dog."

They'd forgotten about the bulldog, a gift presented to Joseph Smith for his protection at the beginning of the journey. Unnerved by the fife and the cheers, the dog raced into the group. The column scattered and ran in all different directions. The dog chased them, barking. The cheering changed to shouts and yells.

"That dog is not a music-lover," Gabriel commented.

The shouting grew louder. Two men were hurling insults at each other.

"What're they saying?" Rusty asked.

"I don't know." Nathaniel backed away from the waterfront. "One of them sounds like Brother Joseph."

"It's him and Sylvester," Eb said.

Rusty stood up and waded ashore. Gabe stepped up on the log and made his way to the bank. They hurried toward the spot where the column had come to such an abrupt dispersion. They could hear Sylvester yelling something about poor administration, and how the leaders had stirred up intrigue that would make the camp fail.

"And that blasted dog is a menace! I'd kill it in a minute if it comes after me!"

Then Joseph was shouting back, something about anyone harming the dog would have to deal with him.

After a few more exchanges, Nathaniel yelled, "It's time to eat!"

A chorus of cheers greeted him. "Amen!" someone said. Men stepped up and separated the two Smiths.

"Things is really gettin' bad," someone else remarked, "if a dern fool dog can set 'em off like that."

Nathaniel gathered his company and made them begin their evening chores. "Let's get this fire lit." If they talked among themselves, he cast stern looks in their direction.

"Easy to see which side he's on," Gabe said.

"The worst thing about a public quarrel like this," Rusty's father said. "It erodes confidence in the leadership."

The next morning, the fight resumed. Sylvester declared again that if the dog bit him, he'd kill him.

"If you kill that dog, I'll whip you!" Joseph shouted.

More heated words flew between them. Finally each one stormed off to opposite ends of the camp. Nathaniel sighed, shaking his head as he stowed the gear in the wagon. Rusty went to stand beside him.

"I reckon we're all human," Rusty said. "Even prophets."

Nathaniel looked up and met Rusty's gaze. "If someone

threatened to kill my dog, I'd be madder'n a drenched cat."

"Well, Sylvester only said it because he thought he was being humiliated in front of his men."

Nathaniel gave him a fierce look. Rusty figured it was a good time to keep silent.

"I'm ready to head out now," he said to Gabriel.

"Don't be foolish. It's not time. And don't mention it again. You'll get people more suspicious than they are."

A few days later they joined the second portion of the camp, led by Hyrum Smith and Lyman Wight, at the rendezvous point on the Salt River. They spent five days getting ready for the final leg of the march. The leaders reorganized the camp so that each captain had exactly ten men under him. Clothes, weapons and gear were put in order for the last time. They even held a military exercise, a sham battle in which swords were broken but nobody was hurt.

As they started across Missouri to the sound of Levi Hancock's fife, they marched under a flag also fashioned by him. It had an elegantly decorated staff and a square piece of white cloth with an eagle painted on it, and the words 'PEACE' painted in large letters. Hyrum Smith, the official standard-bearer, began delegating the duty as a reward to others who had performed well on the march. Once Eb had the honor of bearing the standard, which delighted his whole company.

"There was folks by the wayside," he said. "They seen the banner and said to each other, 'Peace.' Then they walked off."

They learned that their prophet had sent two of their most trusted leaders, Orson Hyde and Parley Pratt, to meet with Governor Dunklin in Jefferson City.

21

Governor Daniel Dunklin, forty-four years old, stood up from his desk and sighed deeply. He strode to the window and looked out at the street below. Nothing out of the ordinary—the usual line of horses tied up outside the public house. As he moved, he caught his reflection in the corner of the glass—a strong, resolute face, deeply lined.

Sleepless nights. Anxious days. Everywhere he turned, the question confronted him. *What to do about the Mormons?*

On his desk, piled high with reports and copies of letters, lay the newspaper clippings. An armed force, estimated to be at least five hundred men, was even now on Missouri soil.

Where did they get the idea that sending a body of armed men would help their cause? Somehow, some lesser official had led them to believe that once they arrived, a state militia would relocate them on their lands. He himself had never promised such a thing. And once he found that official, the man would wish he'd kept his mouth shut.

He'd already made the mistake of admitting that the Mormons had been wrongfully and illegally treated. He'd even written that they 'deserved to be put in possession of their homes, from which they had been expelled.' Was it his fault that the ones driving them out were among his staunchest supporters?

He sighed again and moved away from the window. Up to this point he'd managed to side-step cleverly. When the Mormons first petitioned him to help regain their rights, he'd replied in a non-committal way. He'd advised them to obtain satisfaction through the courts, and if that proved futile, he would then enforce the execution of the laws. He knew that this course would involve a lengthy process before he had to do anything. At least he'd bought himself some time.

Now the period of indecision, in which he had neither angered his supporters nor aided the refugees, had come to an abrupt end. From what he understood, deputies from the Mormon camp were en route to Jefferson City, to see him and demand action. He looked down at the mounds of papers, wishing he didn't have to deal with any more of the fanatics. What, indeed, could he tell them?

He'd considered other actions. If they could be persuaded to sell their lands in Jackson County and settle somewhere else, a compromise might be possible. If they refused, and the gentile population would not rescind their illegal resolves, there was not a lot he could do. He didn't want to authorize military force, or involve the state more than necessary.

"What is my duty?" It became fuzzier and less distinct by the day. Any action he took would have disastrous consequences, for him if for no one else.

When the two Mormons arrived, he didn't feel ready to meet them. He tried to assume a benevolent, helpful expression as they entered the room.

"Good afternoon, gentlemen. You must have had a long ride." *Get them talking. See if they're capable of listening to reason.*

"All the way from Ohio." *The taller one shuffling his feet, speaking with a backwoods twang.* No genius here.

The second stepping forward. Short in stature, broad-shouldered. Direct eyes blazing out of a shrewd, intelligent face. In addition, dapper in appearance, good clothes, suit of black broadcloth. How much did this one understand? *Suddenly on guard, sensing trouble.*

"Indeed, we've come quite a distance. I'm Parley Pratt, and my companion is Orson Hyde." Pratt reached out a firm hand. *Stall for time. Accept the handshake slowly.*

"Yes, gentlemen. I'm sure you're right thirsty. Let me offer you some brandy."

Pratt spoke again. "No, thank you. River water's good enough for us."

"Oh." *Remembering then—Mormons not drinking spirits.*

"We'll get right to the point, if you don't mind, sir," Pratt said. "We're ready to make the final arrangements for the reclaiming of our property in Jackson County. You know the whole story of events, I'm quite sure. If you'll inform us where our men can rendezvous with your troops, then we'll be ready to go in and resettle the area."

"Uh—wait a minute." *Feeling rushed, nervous as he tried to explain.* "You apparently feel that a state force should help you. But I—I never promised any such thing. It would—it would be folly to attempt it."

A look between Pratt and Hyde. Pratt stepping closer, his eyes narrowing. "Sir, we have every hope that you will arrange for troops to assist us. In fact, our leader, Joseph Smith, expects your full co-operation. We assumed the matter was settled. Our cause is just; you have declared it yourself."

Giving a little cough. "Mr. Pratt, believe me—I do sympathize with you."

"And it seems only right, in addition, that you should take some steps to punish our persecutors."

"We submit this as a personal request," Hyde said. "Our people have suffered beyond belief. And, sir—I would say that they've waited long enough."

Clearing his throat, shuffling papers on his desk. Not wanting to meet their eyes. "Gentlemen, I fear I have only one recourse. And that is, to refer you to the courts of the respective counties in which your aggrievances originated."

Hyde frowning, gesturing. Willing to argue. "But, sir—"

"Now, I have no doubt but these courts—which have, I may add, full jurisdiction—will do you ample justice in your case."

Hyde swallowing, as if searching for words. "Sir, surely you are aware that everyone—magistrates, constables, judges, sheriffs—were all engaged in that mob. Sworn to destroy us."

Looking up, managing to meet his eyes. "I'm sure you're

exaggerating, my good man. Now, considering the facts..." *Intoning, assuming a calming, pontifical air.* One of his gifts—rambling on as long as necessary, and never running out of polysyllable words. Parley Pratt listening, his arms folded, his head on one side.

Dunklin began to outline the idea of selling their Jackson County lands and moving somewhere else. *Pratt looking at Hyde in disbelief. Straightening up suddenly, spreading his hands as if he were delivering a sermon.*

"Sell our lands? What are you suggesting? That we hold terms with these—these land pirates and murderers? I'll say right now—if we can't be permitted to live on the land which we purchased of the United States, and be protected in our persons and rights, then it will at least make a good burying ground!"

Eloquent fellow. He can't possibly be serious. "That would be even greater folly. Do you want to involve the whole countryside in war?"

"We can't retreat now. By God, we'll hold on to our lands in the county of Jackson, if for no other purpose but this—a place to lay our bones!"

Really means it. How to divert him? "I'm sorry, gentlemen. I do acknowledge the justice of your demand."

"So you will furnish us the necessary troops?" Hyde asked.

"Frankly, I dare not attempt the execution of the laws in that respect. Feelings are running too high. We'll have nothing but civil war and bloodshed."

Hyde and Pratt glancing at each other. Anger taking the place of shock. Struggling to accept it. As he watched Pratt suck in his upper lip, the governor felt the stirrings of regret that he couldn't help them. *Don't be foolish. Political suicide.* Hyde shrugged. "It seems that we're compelled to return with the same knowledge we had before. God is with us, and everybody else against us."

Shrugging himself. Uncomfortable, wishing the interview were over. "I hope you realize my position."

Pratt fixing him with a final look. "We realize more than you think." *Looking at Hyde.* "Well, then—good afternoon, sir. I hope you don't regret this as much as we do."

"Good day, gentlemen."

Departing. Footsteps receding down the hallway. They'd left the door ajar. The governor waited, then left his desk and walked across the room to close it. As he grasped the door knob, he heard their voices from the end of the hall.

First, Hyde: "I didn't know the governor had so little power."

Then Parley Pratt spoke. "The poor coward! He ought, in duty, to resign. He owes this, morally at least, in justice to his oath of office."

Coward. The word struck him like a knife wound. He felt strength and resolve ebb out of him. Pratt, an ignorant minister of a deluded, hated sect—how was it possible that he knew? As if he could read a man's very soul.

He leaned against the door, breathing hard. The speech could not have had greater impact if it had come from God himself. *Strange.* He knew he'd prevailed, but for a moment he felt as if he'd lost everything.

****

No time to lose! Nathaniel hoisted his bedroll over his shoulder and tossed it in the wagon. Roused at daybreak, they'd been ordered to resume their march with all possible speed. No prayers or breakfast that morning.

Eb sat up in the wagon and stowed the items that were handed to him. He wore the dazed, hurt expression he'd had for two days. Nathaniel shook his head. Best to appear stern. The only way to conceal his own grief and anxiety.

Rusty and Gabriel had left the camp. They'd managed to sneak off sometime on the seventeenth. There'd been a heated discussion over where to make camp. He remembered how the marchers had followed the north bank of the Wakenda River that day. William Smith had killed a large deer, which made nourishing soup for everyone. Then, when it was time to camp for the night, Joseph thought it best to go out on the open prairie where their enemies could not surprise them. Lyman Wight and Sylvester Smith wanted to stay in the timber, near firewood and good water.

Lyman, Sylvester and about twenty others camped in the woods. Joseph took the rest out on the prairie. When Rusty and Gabriel couldn't be found, Nathaniel assumed they were with the smaller group.

The next morning, both Sylvester and Lyman received a severe reprimand from the prophet. Nathaniel agreed; the camp could only have one commander, and anything else amounted to insubordination.

As he looked at the ones who'd spent the night in the timber, his heart sank. Next to him, Eb gave a little gasp.

"They've gone!"

Nathaniel tried to act calm. "I reckon I know where. Off to Richmond—they'll come back."

"Hannah." Eb smacked his hand against his forehead. "Of course."

"And if they don't do it soon, I know where to go looking."

"But they be in danger! They's enemies all around us."

"Gabriel's clever," Nathaniel said. "He'll get through."

"With Rusty? He's clumsier than a hog on ice."

"They'll be fine." Nathaniel tried to speak with finality. He had to cover the same ground with Calvin. Rusty's father rolled his eyes.

"They'll get caught for sure! That boy's about as quiet as a cat in mating season!"

Nathaniel sighed. Bad enough that they were advancing across Missouri without the expected help from the governor. When the messengers reported that he'd refused to send state troops, the leaders had met for two hours while the camp waited. Finally the word came. They were to continue "armed and equipped to Jackson County."

As much as he loved his prophet, Nathaniel had felt his confidence wavering. An armed confrontation most certainly lay ahead. And his two young charges were off where he could no longer protect them.

"Hurry up! Move 'em out!"

Calvin sat holding the reins, swaying a little. He looked pale and tired. No sleep for him either. Nathaniel climbed up beside him and took the reins. Calvin surrendered them without a word.

They passed quickly through Richmond before most of the people were awake. A slave woman called to Luke Johnson, and he went over to talk to her.

Nathaniel heard later that she'd warned them of a group of men calculating to kill them as they passed through.

"That's nothing new," someone said. "They've been sayin' that right along."

They halted for breakfast some eight miles west of the city. A farmer furnished them with milk to wash down their bacon and corn dodgers. He warned them of trouble. "It's a derned shame that every man can't enjoy his religion and everything else without being molested."

"At least we have us some friends," Eb remarked.

They camped ten miles from Liberty, fifty feet above the flood plain between two rivers.

"There's the Little Fishing River we just crossed, and the Big Fishing River a half mile yonder," Calvin said. "That's what I heard, anyway."

Eb snorted. "Some river. The water didn't even come over my boots."

As they set up their tents, Saints began pouring into camp from the surrounding area, people prepared to march in and reclaim their land. Strangers came in too, with offers of help and supplies.

"I hope the boys know where to find us," Eb said.

"By this time, all Missouri knows where we are," Nathaniel replied.

"I wish they'd taken me with them."

"I reckon they had good reason to leave you behind."

With all the Saints and friends gathering in, Nathaniel sensed a new spirit of optimism, of euphoria. People spoke of a victory march. He left his company and moved among the groups of newcomers. He searched for familiar faces, for Rusty or Gabriel, or possibly Hannah. A slim hope. Most likely Lem would not bring the women and young children on such a venture.

He found someone from Richmond, an older man with clothes shabbier than his own. The man chewed on a piece of prairie grass.

"You can't imagine what folks is goin' through. Not enough food to go around. Everything you care to name's in short supply. Families living in tents, abandoned sheds. Crowded into tiny little cabins you wouldn't keep a dog in. They can hardly wait to git back across that river." He spat.

Did he know the Wheeler family? Lem and Diana, a young couple with three children?

"Livin' with Rube Snyder, you say? I reckon I do. And that pretty little gal—Hannah. They say Rube's just plumb crazy for her."

Nathaniel felt as if a boulder had been dropped on his stomach. "I thought he had a wife."

"She died in early spring."

"And—and so now he's after Hannah?"

"Well, you know how folks talk. From what I heard, she's not much interested, and him so rich and all. 'Course if she gets hungry enough, she may change her mind."

Before Nathaniel could digest this bit of news, he heard hoof beats. A horse whinnied. He looked up. Five men rode into camp. He knew from their angry looks that these were not Saints or friendly Gentiles. They reined in their horses as Joseph and Hyrum walked toward them. Everyone fell silent.

The first rider, a heavy-set man, looked around at the crowd. He prefaced his message with a string of profanity.

"You fellers is gonna see hell before morning, derned if you ain't. You ring-tail roarers are gonna get the fight you came fer."

Another said, "I reckon you'd like to know what we got. There's sixty men from Ray County, forty from Lafayette and seventy from Clay, ready to kick your sorry hides to Kingdom Come!"

"And don't forget the two hundred comin' over from Jackson," the first one said. "There won't be a blasted one of you left by morning." He let forth another string of oaths.

As they left, someone said, "That's pretty fair cussing, you got to admit."

Other voices began to murmur. "I reckon they mean to send us to the next world before sun-up."

"We're outnumbered, that's certain."

Joseph held up his hand and spoke to those around him. Nathaniel couldn't catch the words, but the voice sounded calm and reassuring. They should be used to threats by now. He turned to go back to his company.

He saw it then—a dark cloud rising in the west, its top just above the level of the trees. The last light glinted on the edges of it. The sight gave him a strange, shivery feeling. He walked toward the tent, glancing over his shoulder at the cloud. His anxiety deepened; he tried not to think of the boys somewhere out there where the enemy forces were massing. If they attempted to sneak back into camp, they'd be stopped by the guard. Maybe shot by their own brethren.

Sick at heart, unsettled even more by the news about Hannah, he prepared for the darkness. Another night without sleep, and he'd be no use at all. As he closed his eyes, he heard the first drops of rain on the tent.

He woke to the sound of the wind rising. A horse whinnied close at hand. He pushed himself to a sitting position and felt his hand sinking into dampness. "We're in mud!"

Lightning flickered. It revealed both Eb and Calvin sitting up, the others stirring. The front edge of the tent began to flap. Thunder crashed overhead.

"I reckon we're in for it now," someone said.

"We'd better secure that flap," Nathaniel said. Before they could move, the heavens let loose. The rain hit them in torrents, like buckets of water being thrown at the tent. Nathaniel heard it splattering on the ground outside. The next flash of lightning showed the canvas drooping under the onslaught. The earth shook with the thunder crash.

"That be some storm," one of them said.

"All right, men," Nathaniel said. "We're gonna be mighty wet if we don't do something. I'm gonna go out and dig a ditch around the tent. Eb, you get that flap tied down."

Water sloshed into the tent as Eb got to his feet. "I think we're gonna get wet anyway."

The deluge continued. Nathaniel felt it pelting his back as he tried to ditch the tent. The repeated lightning flashes made one continuous flickering. He could see little streamlets running every which way on the ground. He attempted to divert some of the water from the top of the tent.

"You could float a boat in here!" Calvin yelled.

Then the wind hit. The sides of the tent began to flap like a sail. Nathaniel threw down the shovel and grabbed at the canvas. "Come help me hold it!"

He heard them scrambling around inside. The tent started to lift. He sensed someone moving at his side, felt another pair of hands gripping the tent. A tremendous lightning flash lit up the sky. A tree come crashing down. Then he blinked, too astonished to speak.

Gabriel stood beside him. "We better take her down before the wind does."

The next flash revealed Rusty hauling at tent ropes on the other side. Both of them looked like they'd been in the river. But they were safe; relief flooded his mind. He felt the rain pouring from his hat down over his face, down the back of his neck. "How'd you find the camp?"

"No trick to it," Gabriel said. "The hard part was gettin' across the river."

Eb had just emerged from the tent. "That little creek? What are you saying?"

"Creek, my hind leg! You oughta see it now."

By this time everyone had crawled out of the tent. They fought to take it down. Finally the wind collapsed it for them. In the flashes of light, Nathaniel saw men in the other companies struggling with their tents and bedding. One of the captains tramped over and said something to Calvin. Calvin nodded and hurried toward Nathaniel.

"What?" Nathaniel asked.

"He said we're to leave everything—no sense in getting any wetter. They're all heading for this church they seen a little ways up."

Nathaniel remembered the church—no one had paid it much attention except to remark on it.

"Funny old building—out here all alone."

They trudged through the mud toward the church. Rusty was one of the first ones there; Nathaniel hadn't known he could move so fast. To their relief, they found the door open. They hurried in, dripping, looking at each other as the lightning flashed.

"It's a Baptist meeting house," someone said. "And it's big. Room enough for all of us."

Men stretched out on the benches while the water dripped from their clothes. Hyrum Smith laid his hand on Nathaniel's shoulder. "Your company all accounted for?"

It was; he'd stood just inside the door to make sure they'd all come in. Joseph entered the building. He shook the rain from his hat and clothes.

"Boys, there's some meaning to this. God is in the storm."

Outside, the rain descended with increased fury. They could hear it drumming on the roof. Inside there was silence; the men sat contemplating the words they had just heard. Nathaniel went to find a place near Eb and the others. Someone began singing a hymn. Someone else joined in, and another, until they were all singing, full-voiced, praises to God.

Nathaniel couldn't remember how long they sang, or even which hymns; he only knew that they were safe, out of the rain, and if any enemies got through now, they'd have to be part amphibian. He believed for the rest of his life that not only were their foes deterred by the storm, but the Saints themselves were kept from the shedding of blood.

The storm lasted until dawn. The sun rose on a scene of devastation. Nathaniel walked around the camp looking at the tents blown down, the twigs and branches littering the ground. No dry wood for cooking. All their bedding and supplies soaked.

Reports of the destruction began to come in. Lyman Wight said that he'd found hailstones the size of rifle balls and turkey's eggs, just three miles from the encampment. Charles Rich said the hailstones had actually split large planks. The hail had cut down corn and vegetable crops, and even cut limbs from trees. In addition, the wind had twisted trees into strange shapes, 'withes,' as Joseph said.

The men talked among themselves. Each one had a story of how he'd survived the deluge.

"I was doin' fine till I tripped. It was like falling in the well."

"That river's riz thirty to forty feet."

"It's the worst storm I've ever seen."

Nathaniel began setting up the tent to give it a chance to dry. Out of the corner of his eye, he saw Eb and the two boys walking toward him. They deserved a reprimand. He debated what to say to them.

Rusty gave him a smile. "Mornin', Nathaniel."

Nathaniel didn't meet his eyes. "We've got work to do."

"Don't you want to know what happened to us?" Gabriel asked.

Nathaniel stopped and looked at him. "All I know is, you left without any warning. Not telling anybody."

"We were in Richmond before sundown," Rusty said.

"I don't want to hear it," Nathaniel said. "You were wrong to go off, and you know it. I don't care what you did."

In the silence, Rusty and Gabriel looked at each other, Gabriel with his eyebrows raised. Gabriel shrugged, and a little smile played at the corners of his mouth. "In that case, we won't tell you how we tried to find Hannah and couldn't."

"She wasn't at Rube Snyder's," Rusty said. "They'd moved on north—Rube told us where."

"But he doesn't want to hear that," Gabriel said.

Nathaniel paused, looking at them. "Well—did you find her?"

"Yes—it was about dark when we reached the cabin," Rusty said. "She was mighty glad to see us. She said—oh, you don't want to know that."

Nathaniel resisted the impulse to shake him. "Hang it, man—what did she say?"

Gabe spoke quickly. "She's well and all. She wanted to know about the camp, and how her father was. We talked about what happened over in Liberty. They arranged a meeting between the Saints and Gentiles about the land. About a thousand men tried to swarm into that courthouse."

"And what happened?" Nathaniel asked.

Rusty said, "Nothing much. Lem said the biggest excitement was when this fight started outside the building. Someone yelled, 'A man's been stabbed!' Everybody ran out of the courthouse to see. Lem said the crowd was all hoping some Mormon had got killed, but it was only one Missourian dirking another."

"That broke up the meeting," Gabriel said. "The Jackson County boys were all hot to get back across the river. There was a race to get to the ferry boat. And I guess you heard about the last boat sinking with most of the committee members on her. It's reported that about five of them drowned. And now they're saying we sabotaged the boat."

"That's not possible." Rusty scraped the mud from his boot with a stick. "Leastways that's what Lem said. None of our people would do such a thing."

"I don't see how they could," Gabriel said. "That boat went back and forth all evening without anything happening."

Calvin walked up and stood beside them, a piece of paper in his hands. With a pang Nathaniel recognized Hannah's handwriting.

"Did you give him his letter?" Calvin asked.

"Letter?" Nathaniel asked quickly.

"He didn't appear to be much interested," Rusty said.

"Nonsense. Give it to him."

Rusty looked in his pockets. "Do you have it?" he asked Gabriel.

"I thought you did. Unless you put it with the biscuits."

Nathaniel gave a sigh. "What biscuits?"

Rusty reached inside his shirt. "Hannah gave us some fresh biscuits and bacon. There was twelve biscuits—one for all the company, and extras."

"And where are they?"

Gabriel said, "Rusty ate three of them—his own and the two extras."

"They were good," Rusty said.

"Then—just before we reached the river, a bunch of fellows grabbed us. They wanted to know what our religion was, but we acted as dumb as we could."

"That couldn't have been too hard," Nathaniel said.

"Don't be mad," Rusty said. "They got the food, but it would have got soaked anyway. And here's your letter, safe and sound."

He produced it with a flourish. Nathaniel took it without a word. He left them to finish putting up the tent and moved off under a tree. On the folded part she'd written, 'Captain Nat.'

"A lot of thanks we get," Rusty said.

He walked a few yards further into the woods and leaned against an oak to read it.

Dear Brother Nathaniel,

Russell tells me that you are still taking care of my family, in the capacity of leader as well as friend. For this, I thank you.

I am so glad to know that my father has united with the church and the cause of reclaiming the confiscated lands. I have written a separate letter to him. I pray that there will be no bloodshed, and that you will all be kept safe.

I have only a few moments to write these words. We are living in a tiny cabin, the six of us, having left the Snyder farmhouse just before spring planting. I sleep in a loft with the two older children. Russell will tell you more. We are all well for the moment.

That you will be sustained in all you do, is my hope and prayer.

Always your friend,

Hannah

He couldn't believe she'd sent him such a letter. Concern, thanks, friendship—all there on the single page. He was reading it for the third time when he heard his name called.

"Nat! Brother Nat!"

He looked up. Lyman Wight stood in a clump of ferns. "We've been ordered to discharge the firearms and reload. See how many are still in working order."

Nathaniel nodded and stowed the letter in his shirt, next to his chest. He rounded up his men and had them check each firearm. To their surprise, all of the weapons fired except one.

"That's surprising," Calvin said. "You'd think nothing would work after that drenching."

Men in other companies had similar reports; roughly two thirds of the weapons had discharged. It appeared that little damage had occurred to either men or equipment.

They packed up and prepared to march. They'd originally intended to head for Liberty, but the flooded river prevented it. The boats had all sunk or drifted away, so ferrying across was out of the question. They went north, toward the headwaters of the river.

"I reckon they aim to go around and then head south," Rusty said from the back of the wagon.

"It's not like we have a choice," Nathaniel replied as he walked beside the wagon. He reached inside his shirt and felt his fingers brush against the letter. "Every other way's flooded."

Calvin sighed from the wagon seat. "I'd sure like to visit Hannah the way the boys did."

"I'd like that too." Nathaniel saw Gabriel and Eb exchange amused glances. He tried to ignore them. "Tell you what. I figure there's not much more to do—distribute the food and settle the land issue. After that, we'll go see her."

"She'll like that," Rusty said. "She'll be right surprised. In fact, it's a good time for you to do it, Nat."

Gabriel flashed Rusty a warning look. Nathaniel frowned, puzzled. "What do you mean?"

Rusty said, "Well, when she asked how you were, he said—"

"I didn't say it!" Gabriel gestured, his long fingers shaping the air. "*You* did."

"I did not. You mentioned it first."

"What did you say?" Nathaniel tried to sound patient.

"He said you were pining after her."

Gabriel started to stand up in the wagon. "*He* was the one who brought it up."

Nathaniel couldn't believe it. "Hang it all! Why'd you go and tell her something like that for?"

Gabriel sat back down again. "Isn't it true?"

"If it is, she doesn't have to know it."

"That's where you're wrong," Rusty said. "We had good reasons for sayin' it. For one thing—after that, she went and wrote you that note. If we'd kept still, it's a right smart chance she wouldn't a sent it."

Nathaniel sighed and shook his head. "Well, I suppose it's done now."

"It'll be all right," Rusty said. "Trust us."

Gabe gave a little laugh. "I hope she'll make more biscuits when we get there. I only got to smell the last lot."

They made camp in a field near the home of Brother John Cooper. The leaders ordered guards posted in case of another attack. Scouts came in with more news of the storm, and how it had affected their enemies.

"I hear tell that most of those fellers got so wet they could hardly carry out a retreat."

"I reckon they were pretty glad to get themselves back to Jackson County."

From the reports, hail struck with such force that it tore holes in their hats, and even broke the stocks off their guns. One man was reported killed by lightning, and another lost a hand while trying to control a horse terrified by the hail.

"What hail?" someone asked.

"We sure didn't see any."

The next day, visitors rode into camp. Some of the principal citizens of Clay County came to learn the intentions of Zion's Camp. A contingent from Richmond, Colonel John Sconce and two other men, arrived the same day. Assured that the mission of the camp was peaceful, the visitors rode away. The latter group even pledged their support to help pacify the local population.

After a short preaching service the next day, the sheriff of Clay County, Cornelius Gillium, addressed the entire camp. He urged them to pursue a moderate course of action, for their own safety. The event the men remembered most was a revelation dictated by Joseph later in the day, in which they were instructed to 'wait for a season' in regard to the redemption of Zion, and prepare themselves. They were to expect a 'great endowment and blessing'—an outpouring of the Holy Spirit—and they were to 'sue for peace.'

"I like that part," Nathaniel said later as they gathered around the fire. "We're to 'make proposals for peace unto those who have smitten' us."

"I don't know," Rusty said. "I was about ready to smite them back."

"You don't know what you're saying," Calvin said. "We wouldn't have a chance in Hades against some of these fellers I've seen."

Rusty ran his hand through his hair. "It's just that when—when I saw the conditions they were living in—Hannah and that whole family in a place hardly bigger than the tent—"

"*Tiens*, so *now* you're ready to fight?" Gabriel sounded amused. "As if facing murderers and slave-holders wasn't enough for you."

"Well—"

"That's enough," Nathaniel said. "We're to seek peace, and that's that. No more talk of revenge or war."

Eb stood up and leaned his hand against the wagon. "I don't know about you. But since I ate that stew, I be feelin' faint and sick-like."

One of the others, an older man named Elijah, spoke up. "There's men feelin' poorly in at least three other companies. I heard when I came back from the horses."

"Like as not, we could all do with a few days rest," Nathaniel said.

"I reckon you're right." Gabriel got to his feet and followed Eb toward the tent. The rest clustered closer around the fire. They watched in silence as the circle of light flickered and grew feeble. At last it gave way to the darkness.

22

"Brother Parley, what are you telling me? While you were negotiating about the Jackson County lands, you had to deal with cholera too?"

"Well, yes. Cholera struck that camp around the twenty-second of June—Sunday evening, as I recall. That was the same day Brother Joseph gave Sheriff Gillium a set of proposals to take back to Liberty."

"What proposals?"

"Oh, they were widely published. Let's see—he recommended that twelve men be appointed, six from each side, to assess the value of the non-Mormon possessions in Jackson County, or those of anyone not willing to live among the Saints. The church would then buy this property, the full amount to be paid within the year. An assessment of damages would be subtracted from the sale price. Again, he emphasized that we wished to live in peace, and were willing to live alongside the Missourians, if they would permit it."

"And what happened?"

"The Jackson County committee refused to consider it. They still believed that we intended to reoccupy those lands by force. The Clay County elders had just turned down the committee's offer to buy the Mormon-owned lands. So you see, things had reached an impasse."

"And then the cholera hit."

"Now, I left the camp at Fishing River and went back to my family in Clay County. So I missed the worst part of it. But those who lived through it told me what happened. Come Monday, they had to deal with the sickness in earnest. That was the day they started to march toward Liberty. Five miles north of town, they were met by our lawyers, Doniphan and Atchison. The lawyers advised them not to go into town because of the outraged feelings of the people."

"So what did they do?"

"As I recall, they turned left to Sidney Gilbert's homestead, near Rush Creek. The cholera was raging by that time—even Brother Gilbert came down with it. The expedition made camp on the bank of Rush Creek, in Brother Burgharts' field. That's where they carried out the distribution of food and supplies to the impoverished Saints—the last thing they had to do."

"How did they travel with so many sick?"

"Well, they tried to keep them isolated. Eventually they broke up into small groups, so the disease wouldn't spread. One of the people in the settlement had a spare room, and they put the sick in there. The healthy ones stayed up nights trying to help them. Nothing seemed to help, not even the laying on of hands and prayers over the sick. About the middle of that week, men began dying of it."

"There wasn't anything they could do?"

"Didn't seem like it. They rolled the dead in blankets, carried them about half a mile on a horse-sled. Buried them on the bank of a stream that fed into Rush Creek. They dug the graves in darkness, except for a torch light. They tried to keep the epidemic a secret as long as possible, hoping to delay any panic among the settlers. I heard that each group held prayer services afterward. Brother Kimball, he said the scenes of grief were truly beyond expression. All he wanted to do was live to see his family again. You can bet everyone else felt the same way. But even at these services, men were being struck down."

"How many took sick?"

"Oh, lord—dozens. Over sixty, I'm sure. Not everyone died. All told, they lost twelve men and one of the women. Two Clay County Saints died—one of them Brother Gilbert. What's the matter?"

"It seems so senseless, like. To travel a thousand miles and meet their deaths that way."

"Son, I can't answer that. I reckon only God knows the reason. Cholera was everywhere, all through that area. Joseph did warn of a scourge that he couldn't prevent. But one thing it did—it united that group into a solid unit. They felt bound to each other with ties of brotherhood so strong that nothing could break them."

"So, that was the end of Zion's Camp?"

"Just about. The various companies had to find their own food and care for their sick. They officially disbanded the camp on June 30."

"And what did they do?"

"Some of them, like me, stayed in Clay County. The rest started back east in little groups. Everybody knew about the cholera epidemic by that time, and the Missourians avoided anyone they suspected of being a Mormon. No danger of attack on the way home."

"So that was the end of it? They went out there armed to the teeth, didn't even fight, and returned home?"

"Well, son—I reckon there was more to it than that. I don't think God ever intended us to fight—at least, not then. One more thing—we were told that in order to live in the promised land, we'd have to prepare ourselves spiritually. On July third, thirty-five men met in Liberty to organize a group designed to help with the preparation—the High Council of Zion."

"Another high council? It sounds like all they needed."

"Yes—there was one already functioning in Kirtland."

"What did all this have to do with Zion's Camp? I mean—"

"Now, hold on a minute. One of the first things they did was draft an appeal stating that the purpose of Zion's Camp in coming to Missouri was strictly peaceful—they'd been falsely accused of trying to incite civil conflict. Emphasizing again, you see, the desire for peace."

"I still think they should've fought. I bet those camp members didn't wait around in Clay County while this council tossed words around."

"Some did. As I said, some had already left."

"I reckon they couldn't get out of there fast enough."

"I'm sure they were anxious to start home. Don't go thinking they had an easy time of it. From what I hear, they didn't. Some walked, some rode in wagons—"

"You just said they didn't have to fight anyone."

"True. But none of them had much money, and few strangers wanted to help them because of fear of the cholera. What with some still sick, the heat, the dust and the rough roads, it sure wasn't any Fourth of July picnic."

****

Wheels creaking, the wagon shifting from side to side. Horses' hooves on gravel. Pain and weakness washing over him like a wave. If the jouncing would stop.

Gabriel groaned and put his hand on the side of the wagon. Splintery boards cold under his fingers. Opening his eyes. Blue sky overhead, pine branches waving. Eb's face filling his field of vision.

"How you makin' it, Gabriel?"

Not answering. What to say? Breathing fast, clutching at the wagon boards. Aware of Calvin on the front seat, Nathaniel and Rusty walking beside the wagon. He tried to summon his rational mind, tried to comprehend what had happened.

That he should get sick. He, the care-giver. The expert, the healer, who had nursed the rest of them. Unbelievable. Like lightning, it had struck.

Remembering. First Rusty down with the disease. Then Eb, then Calvin. Then two others in the company. He'd sat up with each one, giving water, holding the cup to lips parched with fever, sponging skin dry to the touch.

Rusty and Eb recovered after a few days. Calvin took longer. Worried about Calvin...older, not as strong. He and Nathaniel took turns sitting with Calvin. Hannah's father...mustn't die. Remembering...Calvin at his worst, Gabriel whispering through the night. "Hannah wants to see you again. Must get well so you can go to her."

Toward early morning he was murmuring it in French. Calvin lay quiet, in a stupor, the cramps lessened. Nat stayed with him while Gabriel tended the others.

At the end of the week, Nat said in passing, "I don't see how we can visit Hannah now. I reckon I'd rather die than see her down with this."

"They might all recover in good time," Gabriel replied. "Eb and Rusty are coming along—a bit shaky on their feet. Calvin needs a good deal of rest."

Gabriel suggested that the captain get some rest too. Nat appeared not to hear. Gabriel expected Nat to come down with the disease, but he remained healthy. By the time Zion's Camp disbanded, the ones in their immediate group had recovered. Then, on the way to Richmond, they stopped for the noonday meal. Gabriel walked down toward the little stream. As he stepped into the woods, the cramping seized him. He fell in the road. He remembered Eb crashing through the underbrush to reach him. After that, everything seemed to blur together.

Trying to give instructions. Too ill to know if they were carried out. "Whiskey. Whiskey and flour. Make a mixture, feed it to me. Water. Here, on my head."

Once he woke in a horse-stall with Eb bending over him. He felt bits of straw prickling the back of his neck. "Where—"

"Hush. You in a barn. A brother let us bide here while the others went to find Hannah. We're to stay put till they get back."

"I reckon I'm not going anywhere."

But they had not seen Hannah. Through waves of sickness, he heard what had happened. Voices echoed in his mind. First, Rusty, explaining to Eb: "That cabin was deserted. No sign of anyone."

"I reckon they'd been gone about three days," Calvin said.

Nathaniel sounded matter-of-fact. "The nearest neighbor said Lem was so scared he could hardly see straight. He didn't want any part of a Mormon war. So he borrowed a horse from Rube Snyder, a wagon from somewhere else, and took the whole family up north of Clay County."

"And Hannah—" Calvin's voice broke.

"Hannah went with them," Nat said. "And if Lem's that scared, you can bet she's not in any danger."

Gabriel sighed and turned to face the side of the stall. If he hadn't fallen ill when he did, maybe they would've found her.

Eb put an arm around his shoulders. "Come on. Let's get you back in the wagon."

Gabriel liked to think how he'd tended five men through the outbreak, and not one had died. But as night descended, he began to worry. The sixth man, the self-styled physician himself, hovered near death. He sensed strength ebbing from him, his will to live slipping away. Like a swimmer battling waves too strong for him, he felt his body succumbing, going under. The men were right; he'd heard them describe the disease as a malevolent spirit, a living entity which struck indiscriminately and without warning. Fighting it was like dealing with a malignant force.

Flinging off his blankets. "Eb! Nathaniel!"

They bent over him. "Water!" he gasped. "More water!"

He heard Eb dipping the cup into the pail. Then he felt Eb's arm under his shoulders. Eb lifted him to a sitting position. He drank.

"No matter what I do or say, keep giving me water."

Eb dipped into the pail again. Gabriel struggled to tell them the last thing.

"Nat—listen. If—if I don't live, do this for me. Write—"

"You'll live," Eb said. "If you die, I'll never forgive you."

"Listen, Nat. I have a sister, in Gallipolis. Name's Marie-Françoise. Write, tell her what happened. Tell her I—"

"You're not gonna die." Eb's voice sounded fierce. "Don't even speak of it."

"Wait," Nat said. "Marie-Françoise—"

"Get Rusty to spell it for you. Last name's same as mine. Tell her I—I thought of her every day. I died thinking of her."

"If you say 'die' one more time, I'm gonna wallop you," Eb said.

Nathaniel said something to him in a low voice. In a few seconds Gabriel heard them all praying for him, first Nat, then Eb. As Rusty began, Gabriel said, "Pray all you want, but keep feeding me water."

After the prayers, he lay silent. This was his battle; he'd brought the others through, but he had to fight the malevolence by himself. He tried to form a prayer in his mind. If he lived, he would be God's person, a special servant. No one would serve with more diligence—he'd work extra hours, whole nights, offering everything he had. They hadn't named him Gabriel for nothing. *Man of God*.

Toward morning he had an overwhelming desire for water. More water than they could possibly give him. He wanted to plunge into that river he'd imagined, sink beneath the waves, if need be. He threw the blankets off and staggered up.

"Where do you think you're going?" Eb asked.

"To the river. The water."

"There ain't no river. Just a piddling little stream."

"Take me to it."

"He's delirious," Rusty said. "Out of his mind."

Then Nathaniel spoke. "Do what he says. Let him sit in the creek if he wants."

With Eb and Rusty on either side of him, Gabriel stumbled to the stream's edge and down into the water. It felt cool around his ankles. He sat down among the rocks and splashed water on his chest, his head.

"It's icy cold," Rusty said.

"Don't come out in it," Gabriel told him. "Leave me be."

After a while Rusty left, and only Eb remained on shore. Gabriel immersed himself in the stream and let the ripples wash over him again and again. The terrible heat left his body, and his mind felt clear for the first time in days. In the faint light of dawn he saw Eb huddled at the water's edge.

"Get to bed, Eb. You want to get sick again?"

"You didn't leave me in the river, and I'll not leave you."

"Don't be ridiculous. Go back to the wagon."

"No. I'm free now, and I do what I please."

For Eb's sake he left the water sooner than he intended. As he climbed on shore, he knew the fever had broken.

"Now I'll live."

Eb stepped to his side and took his arm. "You'd better."

Eb slept beside him in the wagon as they headed east. Gabriel felt exhausted, but his mind remained clear. He listened, on the edge of sleep, as the others talked.

"I wish we knew where she was," Calvin said from the wagon seat. "It's like she's gone off the face of the earth."

"She knows how to reach us," Nat said. "And—depend upon it—she will. I reckon her first letter will get there before we do."

"She can't be lost forever," Rusty said. "I just know she's not."

The waters of sleep swirled around Gabriel's head. When he woke, they were talking about a very different matter.

"We went out there to reclaim those lands," Rusty said. "No other reason. All the arms, the military drills—"

"I have to say you're wrong." Nathaniel spoke with passion. "That mission was peaceful. All our communications spoke peace—the letters and proposals. That revelation. And this—this spirit of war is something you're interjecting—"

"Interjecting, my foot! Nat, you're no longer my captain. I can speak plainly."

"You always could."

"In that case, listen. I talked to enough men to know. They were ready to fight."

"Then they were extremely wrong and wicked," Nathaniel said. "I hate to say it, but maybe that cholera was sent as a warning. Or a punishment."

Gabriel struggled to sit up, then fell back. Stunned by the extent of his weakness. Too tired to even form an opinion, let alone deliver it. He sighed and stretched his legs out. Nathaniel was saying, "If we can't get those lands back without shedding blood, then I reckon we don't deserve them."

"Well," Calvin said. "It seems to me like we're too much involved in secular affairs. That's what all this trouble is about. If we spent more time praying and less time trying to form communities, we'd be better off."

As Gabriel recovered, he learned that provisions remained a constant worry. They pulled up at one farmhouse only to meet the farmer with a shotgun.

"Keep moving. We've got nothing for you. You be Mormons, I know it. And ye've got cholera."

They took to camping just outside town. Nathaniel would leave the wagon and take his bag of tools into the settlement. There he would barter work for food, and return with bacon, eggs, bread, or flour. Sometimes he brought cider or milk. He kept silent about his religion.

"In the public house, they were telling how a fierce Mormon army marched through with four cannon—how many cannon did you see, Rusty?"

"Why—none at all."

"Neither did I. They must've been invisible—cleverly concealed. And how many of us? They said five hundred, all on horseback."

"One hundred and twenty, more likely," Calvin said. "Maybe a few more. Most of 'em walking."

Nat sighed. "I reckon our reputation for militancy far outstrips the truth. Here—have some bacon."

****

A gray day, chilly. The prow of the boat cutting through the smooth water-surface. Bethia clutching the railing, a slim girl of medium height, just past her seventeenth birthday. Watching the ripples break the dark reflection of the hull. A sudden lurch. Leaning against the railing, peering out into the mists.

Fairport Harbor close ahead. The captain's words. She can see no sign of land; fog surrounds them. Wrinkling her nose at the scent of fresh water, the faint, fishy odor mingled with the smell of the boat's engines. Stepping away from the rail. Best go back to her aunt and uncle. Uncle Jake feeling ill ever since they'd left Buffalo.

The fog lifts. The near shore emerging, the great wooden pier running out into the water. The expanse of lake shimmering before her, grayish-white. Sky pearly gray like the underside of a dove's wing. Three gulls soaring overhead. Their strange, wild cries filling her with joy. A greeting. Can they know? After a watery journey, by canal boat and steamer across Lake Erie, she is about to see Kirtland at last.

Thinking back. Incredible. Her aunt and uncle, of the religious persuasion known as 'Seekers,' finally accepting the church she discovered over four years ago. That was when she first saw Joseph Smith—they heard him speak at a meeting in Fayette, New York. She remembers how pleasant and personable he seemed—not like any other minister she's met.

And she's met a great many. In their search for the divinely restored church of Christ, they attended every denomination they could find in that part of western New York. Unlike most Seekers, who refused to have anything to do with established churches and simply awaited the final restoration of the New Testament church, her aunt and uncle actively sought.

She thinks of the countless discussions she's overheard—the things which Seekers hoped for.

"Now, see here, Jake. There has to be a restoration of apostolic authority. Ministers divinely appointed. Nothing else will do."

"I agree, brother. There's no other way. When true authority is restored, we'll have baptism and communion, the way it was done in the New Testament."

"And the literal return of Christ. Now, the reformers and

primitivists all say that the Bible contains the necessary authority for restoring. That is, they believe it's possible for the existing church to change into something new and spirit-filled. But how? By their own efforts?"

"Impossible. The apostasy of that early church was complete—total. Only God can restore what's been lost."

After searching and praying, her aunt and uncle examined at last the new sect calling itself the Church of Christ. In their own community, the town of Palmyra, they found the desire of all Seekers—the news of direct revelation from God. Newly baptized, they sought the company of a larger body of believers. Bethia, whose parents had forbidden her baptism, made up her mind to go with them.

"Go ahead, then, if that's what you want," her father told her. "But don't come back here when you discover your folly."

A hard thing, to leave her family—her parents and brother. But hadn't Sister Emma Smith done the same? Trying not to show any uncertainty, Bethia prepared to travel west. Kirtland, where the law would be given and the Saints blessed with a spiritual endowment.

"Bethia, where've you been? We're ready to get off the boat, and here you are, doing I don't know what." Aunt Sarah stands frowning, thin-lipped. She is stout, of medium height, her round face framed in a cloud of grayish hair.

"I was just watching." Hurrying toward them. "Looking at the shore."

"Wool-gathering, most likely."

Beside her, leaning in the doorway, is Uncle Jake—her father's older brother. White-haired, he has a bushy, white mustache to match. He looks pale, not his usual, energetic self.

"You're going to have to help with the trunk," Sarah says. "Jake can't manage it right now."

Together the women carry the trunk down the gangplank, each gripping a leather handle. Bethia wants to stop, intrigued by the sights and sounds of the port, but she has to keep carrying the trunk. A striped tabby cat crouches beside a pier piling. She aches to pet it, wonders if it has a home.

"Watch where you're going. Here. Set it down."

No carriages or wagons to be found. Sarah leaves Jake and Bethia with the trunk and goes to consult the man selling tickets. Jake looks frail and tired. Bethia tries to remember—ten years older than her father. Almost fifty. He seems to read her mind.

"Not as young as I used to be."

"Are you going to be all right?"

"Well, my dear—I certainly hope so. The worst part of the journey's over. I don't know why I feel so weak-like."

Sarah returns with the news. "The man said most folks just walk to Kirtland. It's twelve miles."

Jake's mustache quivers. "That's not far."

"Do you want to rest a while first?"

"No. Sooner we start, the sooner we'll get there."

"He said we could leave the trunk inside and fetch it later."

They begin to walk along the pier toward the town. Their steps make a hollow clunking on the boards. As Bethia looks up, she sees the gulls flying over—two this time, dipping and soaring. Joy is gone; she feels a vague emptiness. They find the road to Kirtland. Eight other people walk with them on the journey. There is a family with young boys, a single woman, another one carrying a baby in her arms.

After a few miles, Jake lags behind. His face is deathly pale. "Go on. I'll rest a bit."

Sarah sighs. "What are you thinking? We won't leave you. We've come this far."

"Maybe you could go there, and—and hire someone to come fetch me."

A horse neighing, hooves clopping on the dirt road. The wagon comes up beside them.

Jake speaks with an effort. "Good morning, sir."

"Mornin'." The driver is heavy-set, burly about the shoulders. His long hair falls down over his collar.

"Could I hire you to take us into Kirtland?" Jake asks. "I'm feelin' poorly, and it's a bit of a walk. But I'll pay you well."

"You be Mormons, ain't ye?"

"That's right. If we could have your help, we'd be most obliged. And, like I said—"

"I ain't givin' rides to no Mormons."

Bethia looks at him, incredulous. "Please, sir."

"Go on with ye. I'll not do it, even for a pretty girl. You kin walk, and see how you like it."

They stand still as he drives away. Bethia watches as he passes the rest of the group. The walkers move to the side of the road. His whip flicks over the horse's back; he doesn't look at them.

"Well, now," Sarah says. "I reckon someone else'll feel more hospitable."

Jake shakes his head. "I don't understand. We have plenty of money. We could've paid—" Suddenly he clutches his chest, sinks to the ground.

"Uncle Jake!" Bethia kneels in the mud, heedless of her new traveling dress.

"Get up," Sarah says. "Jake, what's wrong with you? Stop that!"

"Aunt Sarah, don't make him get up. Let him rest. Stay with him. I'll walk into Kirtland, get help."

No choice. Sarah nods, her lips pressed together. Tears course into the wrinkles of her chin.

Bethia hurries, tries to catch up with the other walkers. They are too far ahead. She is breathing fast; she feels a catch in her side. Looking around. Frantic. She can no longer see her aunt and uncle. "Oh!" Beginning to cry, her sobs mingling with her gasps for breath. She's heard of persecution, that certain people hate Mormons, but she doesn't know it is like this. So soon, so sudden. Nothing to prepare her.

Since she is not baptized, she is not really a Mormon. She will tell the next person she meets that she is a Seeker whose uncle needs help. The forest ends; cleared fields stretch on either side. On a little hill just ahead stands a building. A strange-looking farmhouse. As she hurries toward it, she sees that it is a public house, painted green, with a long porch across the front of it.

Running again. Side aching. She stumbles up the two wooden steps and stands panting. Feeling faint. She puts out her hand and clutches the beam supporting the porch roof.

A voice speaks behind her. "I wouldn't lean on that too hard. It wants some repair."

Whirling to face the speaker. He walks toward her from the end of the porch, a slender man in his mid-twenties, clad in the shabbiest work clothes she's ever seen. Sawdust lies in all the folds of his smock. The knees of his trousers are worn through, and the cuffs of both pants and sleeves are ragged.

She lifts her eyes to his face. "I—I wasn't."

Despite the patch of dirt on his cheek, he looks good-natured, kind, even concerned. Then she sees the jagged scar on his lip. A result of some barroom brawl, no doubt. Best to get away from him. Most likely too poor to help anyone.

A puzzled look crosses his face. She is suddenly aware of her own appearance—her mud-stained dress, the tear-streaks on her face. Panting like an animal.

He frowns. "Here, now—what's the matter?"

"Nothing. That is—I was just going inside."

"Go ahead, if you want. I think it's empty, except for my assistant. A bit too early for most folks."

"Oh." Before she can stop herself, she is sobbing. She stops for breath. The man is watching her.

"When you get tired of doing that, you can tell me what's wrong.

I might be able to help."

What to do? Turning, wiping her eyes. "Oh, sir, I don't want to trouble you none. We just got here, on our way to Kirtland. My uncle collapsed—he's back there, about a mile. But no one wants to help us because we're—we're Mormons. That is, they're Mormons, and I'm a—I'm—"

"Why didn't you say so right off?" He takes her by the shoulders. "You stay right here. There's no need to cry. I'll get Gabriel and the team—we'll go fetch him."

"Team?" she asks, sniffing.

"Yes. We did some hauling for the Lord's House early this morning. We had all our tools in the wagon, so we just drove it to our job over here."

"You're Mormons!" She is incredulous.

"There's no time to waste. Don't go anywhere." He hurries around the corner of the porch. She hears him calling. "Gabe! Leave everything and get the wagon! Someone's in trouble on the road."

She sighs, still not certain, and crosses the porch. She looks to see that no one is watching. Then she takes the two steps in one bound. She waits in the shadow of the building, feeling the breeze on her face. By the time the wagon rumbles up, she is composed, her tears dry.

"What lovely horses," she says to the one leading them. At first she thinks it is the man who spoke to her on the porch. Her mistake—this one is younger, shorter than the first. As he stops beside her, she sees that his height is the same as hers.

"You like them? They're a good team. This one's Jeb, and that's Jenny."

"They're beautifully matched."

"Like brother and sister." His eyes are dark and intent, his face so pale that she can see the veins beneath the skin of his temples. His hair hangs over his ears like some kind of black mop. His clothes are thread-bare, covered with sawdust like the first man's.

She says, "You must be Gabriel."

Just then he smiles, and an expression of impish delight spreads over his face. In the sunlight he looks charming, as winsome as a prince. "That I am. At your service."

"You're an angel indeed, to help me like this."

He laughs this time, throwing his head back. When his companion joins them, he says, "Nat, you didn't tell me we had a damsel in distress. And such a lovely one."

"Stop rattling on, and get in the wagon. Jump in the back and make a place to lie down—spread out the blanket. And you, miss—up in front with me. What's your name?"

She tells him. Gabriel says, "I reckon her name be as lovely as she is."

"Pay no mind to him." Nat helps her into the front seat and climbs up beside her. "He can't help his behavior—he's only seventeen."

Bethia laughs for the first time that morning. "Why—so am I!"

Nat smiles and brushes his hand against the facial scar. "I reckon I'm outnumbered."

He guides the horses into the road and turns them toward the harbor. She begins to relax; these strangers, though poor, seem to know what to do. Curiosity goads her—how is it that they are driving such a handsome rig, with painted wagon and matched horses?

"Are the horses yours?"

Nat clicks to urge them on. "They belong to a friend—all he has left from the sale of his farm."

"And he lets you use them?"

"Oh, yes. We're boarding them, so to speak. He's working on the House of the Lord today, so he has no need of them." He frowns, squinting in the misty light. "Is that your uncle—just off the road there?"

Anxiety makes her throat tighten. Uncle Jake lies where she left him, not moving. Her aunt is kneeling, mopping at his face with a handkerchief. Nat slows the wagon. Then he jumps down, flings the reins over a branch and ties them. Gabriel leaps out on the other side and rushes to her uncle.

She is left to climb down by herself. Annoyed now. Irritated at the way Nat seems to step back and defer to Gabriel as if the younger man is in charge. What does he know anyway—a seventeen-year-old like herself?

Nat is speaking to her aunt, soft words which Bethia cannot hear. Gabriel kneels on the ground, unloosens Uncle Jake's collar, bends to listen at Jake's chest. After a moment he puts his ear to her uncle's mouth and waits. He straightens up and lifts one of Jake's hands, pressing the wrist with his fingers. Bethia catches her breath; everyone is watching Gabriel. His expression is all bewilderment and sorrow. His dark eyebrows knit together; to her astonishment he makes the sign of the cross. Then he looks at Nat and shakes his head.

"What?" Aunt Sarah gasps.

Nat swallows, then speaks. "My dear sisters—we're so tremendously sorry."

"He's—he's gone?"

"There's nothing we can do," Gabriel says. "It seems to have been—very quick."

Sarah is crying now, and Bethia feels tears streaming down her own face. Nat shakes his head. "I reckon—that is, he's been called home to his Creator. That's the only way to look at it."

Sarah keeps crying. Through her tears Bethia looks at her uncle. A pale echo of what he was, like a reflection in cloudy water. An illusion, a joke. *Death a terrible joke.* Nat moves over by the horses. Gabriel gets to his feet and waits while Sarah wipes her eyes. Finally Nat speaks.

"We'll take him into town—it's not far. And we can deliver you to where you were going. Is someone expecting you?"

Sarah lets out her breath, a long, shuddering sigh. "No."

"No one knew you were coming? No family?"

"No."

The side of Nat's mouth twitches. "Well—what did you figure on doing when you got there?"

"We were just going to go in and find a place to live. Rent something, if we had to. Then look for a house."

"I don't know," Nat says. "Places to live aren't that easy to come by these days. Leastways on such short notice."

"What do you mean? We have plenty of money."

"I wouldn't say that too loud, if I was you. Prices are high enough. It's not money we're troubled about."

She sniffs. "Then what is it?"

"There's just not enough room. You see—with the building going up, the town is gettin' crowded. Folks comin' in from all over."

"Oh." Crying again. "What shall we do?"

Nat's mouth works as he thinks. His brow wrinkles. "I reckon we should go on in and arrange for a burial. Then I figure we can make room for you until you find a place."

Sarah stops crying. "That's right kind of you. We'd be pleased to rent a room from you, till we can think what to do."

The two men carry the body and lay it gently in the wagon. Gabriel covers it with a burlap cloth. Bethia feels shy with Gabriel now—he apparently has some knowledge about medical matters that she didn't suspect. He in turn treats her with quietness and respect, no longer joking. He touches her arm. "Let me help you up."

Nat helps Sarah into the front seat, then sits on the end beside the two women. Gabriel rides in the back of the wagon with Uncle Jake.

Bethia enters Kirtland in a state of shock. Everything coming at her through a haze of grief. Log houses, a general store, a public house. A row of little buildings, then a hill beyond, and the skeleton of the house of worship. Biting her lip. Trying to keep from crying as the wagon stops at last.

23

From the back step, Bethia could see the place where her uncle lay buried. First there was a worn split-rail fence and the shed where they kept the horses and wagon, then other houses and outbuildings. Beyond that, the land rose in a gentle elevation, and on this spot stood the House of the Lord.

"You're looking at the back of the building," Gabriel had told her.

The graveyard lay not far from the construction site, off to the left, and here Jacob Paige rested from his seeking.

"I reckon he'd be right proud to lie in the shadow of the House of the Lord," Aunt Sarah had remarked.

They had accepted Nat's invitation, there being no other choice, and settled in. He had given them his own room, just off the keeping room and to the right of the fireplace. He moved into a storage area on the other side of the hearth. When Calvin suggested that he take the spare room upstairs, he declined.

"We may need that for someone else."

With the money Sarah offered for rent, they bought chickens and enjoyed foods they had not been able to afford before.

"I was gettin' mighty sick of corn dodgers," Eb said.

Sarah urged them to spend her money, to make the house pretty and spruce things up. The younger ones greeted this offer with enthusiasm, but Nathaniel held back.

"Best we take things slowly, and buy just what's needed."

"But we want to be comfortable," Sarah insisted.

Nathaniel made no reply. The others accepted his decision. All except Sarah, who believed in living with more amenities than they had. She began a half-hearted search for another place, but Nathaniel had been right about the scarcity of rooms. Bethia didn't want to move; in spite of their poverty, she found her new companions lively and fascinating.

She'd never lived with so many people under one roof before. First there was energetic, wiry Gabriel, her first real friend in Ohio, who treated her with a mixture of kindness and amusement.

"You've not been baptized? Well, I reckon you came to the right place. If you can wait a while longer, Eb or I can take care of it. We're both called to be priests, but we're not ordained yet."

"Have to chop a hole in the ice, if she waits too long," Eb said.

"Won't I get cold?" she asked.

Rusty said, "For some reason, you don't feel the cold. Leastways, I didn't."

It was like having three brothers—one dark-haired, her own age, one older, patient, good-natured, with black skin and eyes, the third younger, his hair as red as his name, full of adolescent awkwardness. She loved the stories of their separate lives, and how they had come to share living quarters. In their conversations, she picked up things she hadn't known.

"You mean—the persecution goes on all the time?"

Rusty said, "Let me tell you. What happened to you—the fellow with the wagon—that's commonplace."

"Sometimes they won't even grind grain for folks," Eb said. "The miller gets all worked up about Mormons, and how there's too many of us."

"We tried to work in the blacksmith shop, Eb and I," Gabriel said. "They let us go when they learned what our religion was."

And her response: "But that's not fair!"

They laughed, Eb wiping tears from his eyes. "Not a lot of things are."

Gabriel said, "The main trouble is with the Lord's House. There's folks that just don't want it built. Why, there's been shooting, raids on it at night. People stealing things, sabotaging, trying to slow down the work. Ol' Sidney Rigdon, he goes up there nights and cries over the walls, folks say. Weeping and praying that it'll get built."

"Is that so?"

"And you'd be surprised at the fellers that sleep with firearms close by, in case there's another attack on it. Why, ol' Nat, he doesn't have a gun. But he sleeps with a pitchfork beside him—as if that's gonna help."

Rusty laughed. "Can't you see him out there in his nightshirt, hopping around with a pitchfork?"

As she stood on the step, Bethia offered an inward prayer that Sarah would not find another place and they could stay here a while longer. She turned and opened the back door. Selfish of her. She should be praying for the House of the Lord and its speedy completion, not for where she wanted to live.

"Where have you been?" her aunt demanded.

"Feeding the chickens. No eggs this morning."

"Takes you long enough. Set the table—the men will be comin' in to breakfast."

The 'men' included everybody else—the three she considered her brothers, plus Calvin and Nathaniel. Bethia got dishes from the cupboard and set them on the table. Nathaniel—he was an enigma. Not much older than Eb. While the others talked, he had a habit of gazing absently into space, as if absorbed by something else. Yet he acted firm when it came to keeping order in the household. When she had asked, Gabriel told her about Hannah.

"He's worried there's been no word from her. I reckon he's about ready to go looking for her."

When she mentioned it to her aunt, Sarah snorted. "Ridiculous. Wanting someone who's most likely got herself married by this time."

The men trooped in and sat down. Sarah frowned. "Where's Nathaniel?"

"Like as not, he's chopping wood," Rusty said. "He figured we needed some."

"The wood box is full."

"Well—he likes to keep a little ahead."

Sarah brought the large skillet to the table and dished out the food. "Nathaniel's not been himself lately. He hardly touches his food."

Calvin said, "He has his heart set on a young lady in Missouri. As a matter of fact, my daughter. I reckon she's safe enough, but he's beginning to fret."

"'Heart set,' indeed." Sarah set the empty skillet on the sideboard, then took her place at the end, opposite Nathaniel's chair. "It's time someone spoke up, and it might as well be me. Hannah's right pretty, from what I hear."

"Oh, she's good-looking," Gabriel said. "But she's got something more—a certain graciousness."

"Whatever it is," Rusty said, "it makes her seem prettier, somehow."

Bethia thought she heard the back door opening. But no sound of footsteps followed. Sarah shook out her napkin. "And you expect me to believe that someone like her, both beautiful and gracious, is going to look twice at Nathaniel?"

A shadow appeared in the doorway. Sarah went on. "Why, he'd be better off pursuing one of the local women. I reckon he'd be lucky to get anyone, ugly as he is—with that raggedy scar across his mouth."

Bethia spoke with a warning voice. "Auntie—"

Too late. Nathaniel entered the room, his arms full of split logs. The rest sat in stunned silence. Gabriel and Rusty exchanged glances. Nathaniel didn't look at any of them; he piled the logs beside the wood box. Bethia felt a tremendous sorrow for him as he sighed and straightened up. Had he heard everything?

Sarah broke the silence. "Sit down, Nathaniel, and eat."

He turned, his mouth tightening. His voice sounded hurt and subdued, not angry. "I'll eat when I've a mind to."

He tramped off to his place in the storage area. Bethia looked at the three young men. Eb sat, his eyes lowered, his dark brows meeting in a frown. Gabriel sighed and opened his mouth, as if he were about to speak. Rusty shrugged; he began to eat again.

"Well, it's the truth," Sarah said. "And he might as well know it."

Rusty paused between bites. "I reckon Hannah might not mind his scar. She never mentioned it."

"It wouldn't hurt none to apologize to him," Calvin said gently. "We all have to get along."

"Yes, Aunt Sarah," Bethia said. "Tell him you didn't mean to hurt his feelings."

Gabriel wiped his plate with a piece of bread. "I reckon after all he's been through, his feelings will survive. But I wouldn't mention it again."

Bethia knew how difficult such a thing would be. Once Sarah got hold of something, she rarely let it go. They finished the last of their breakfast. Nathaniel's dog Nell padded over and scratched at his door.

"At least his dog loves him," Rusty remarked.

Nathaniel opened the door and strode toward the front of the house. As he passed the table, he looked at the men.

"Come on, boys. It's time to work on the building."

Nathaniel left the house. As the others got up, Bethia felt Nell pawing at her skirt. She reached down and sank her fingers into Nell's soft fur. She wished that Nathaniel's feelings could be soothed as easily as his dog's.

"Will you leave off playing with that animal and help me with the dishes? She belongs outside, anyway." Sarah's lips formed a thin line.

Bethia sighed and rose from the table. Since Sarah was thought to be still mourning, people hastened to avoid upsetting her further. But no one imagined that she, Bethia, might be grieving too.

****

When Hannah reached the outskirts of Bucyrus, well into Ohio, she did the thing she had put off doing. She sat in the smoky public house and wrote a letter to her brother. The pen scratched over the paper; she was aware of the proprietor watching her. She'd had to beg him for paper and the use of pen and ink. She forced herself to concentrate, in spite of the noise and the strange, hazy light. At last she looked at what she had written.

Dear Russell,

This letter will most likely not be a surprise to you, but I think you should prepare Papa for the news. I am on my way to Kirtland!

The way it happened is this; we were very crowded in our new place, and I feared I was becoming a trouble to them. Diana is much stronger and able to look after her children. Also, there are neighbors to help if she gets too tired.

I wanted to get back to Kirtland because of you and Papa. I had thought of asking your help in making the journey. But then I heard of a disaffected family—Brother Aaron Levering, his wife and aunt. They wanted to go back to New York State, having had enough of clashes with the Missourians. I asked if I could travel with them. They agreed, and so here I am.

I hope to be with you before the snows fall. I will be very happy to live in a house again instead of a wagon.

Tell Papa in a gentle way, and help him not to get upset or worried. I am very well, and feel 'strong as a horse,' as they say.

She sucked in her lower lip and added the final words:

That I might see you all again is my earnest hope.

Your sister, Hannah

P. S. My best wishes to Gabriel and the captain.

She looked up. Two others were staring at her, rough-looking men in work clothes. One looked old enough to be her father, but his gaze was not fatherly. She sighed. One reason why she'd put off writing the letter. But it had to be done; she couldn't descend on her family without warning.

Too many men had looked at her with that expression. Almost as if they were hungry or had some internal discomfort. First there was Rube Snyder, then Lem, husband of her friend Diana—one of the main reasons for leaving Missouri. Aaron Levering was beginning to have that look, and now the proprietor, and these two strangers.

In a similar fashion Daniel Perry had looked at her, and Nathaniel—but they were different because they had seemed to see her as a whole person and not just a pretty face. She wondered that she could still look attractive after all she had gone through. But apparently it was enough for the men in the public house.

She longed to get back to Kirtland at last, so she could be with her family. They would protect her; they would value her for who she was. And—she hesitated to contemplate it. If Nathaniel still wanted her, she would not discourage him. By this time he'd probably found someone else. But if he hadn't—

She found herself wondering what to do if he had. She'd had too much disappointment to be devastated by anything more. She would simply go and live somewhere with her father and brother, and keep house for them. The trouble was, she felt ready to settle down and have children of her own. And Nathaniel was the best choice she could think of.

She folded and addressed her letter. Then she took the pen and ink back to the counter. Aware of the eyes upon her, she spoke with dignity. "Will you see that this is posted, please?"

"Of course, ma'am. Is there anything else?"

There wasn't. She walked outside to the wagon, where Aaron Levering waited to help her in.

24

They drove into Kirtland on a gray day, the wind at their backs. She remembered her promise to get there before the snow fell. Not a moment too soon. A flurry of tiny flakes descended as they stopped in front of the public house. She grabbed her few belongings, a leather bag with a strap and a burlap sack. Then she said good-bye to the Leverings and went inside.

"Excuse me," she said to the proprietor. "Could you tell me how I can find Nathaniel Givens' house?"

The man's ruddy face creased in a smile. "Why, Nat's over working on the chapel. Want me to fetch him for you?"

"No—not if he's working. Just tell me where his house is."

"Well, you go up to the crossroads, then turn right up the hill—here. I'll get one of the boys to take you over there. And if you're the one they've been looking for, I expect Nat would like to know. I'll send word to him."

She looked at him, puzzled. "I'm Hannah Manning."

"Land's sakes, miss. I reckon they have the whole town on the lookout for you. Sandy!"

A tall, lanky youth got up from one of the tables. The ruddy-faced man said, "Take this lady up to where Nat Givens and all those fellers are living. You know—just behind the Greene place."

As they trudged up the hill, she could see a large building off to the left, with scaffolding along the walls. The wagon road, deeply rutted, felt hard under her feet. Tired, she tried to remind herself that she'd all but reached her destination—they'd received her letter, knew she was coming. She took deep breaths of the pine air, brushed the snowflakes from her cloak. A few more steps. Not much farther.

"There." The young man pointed to a dark frame house which looked more like a shed than a dwelling.

"Thank you. I wish I had something—here, let me give you this." She searched in her bag for a coin.

"Forget it. Nat's been good to me."

She stepped up on the wooden porch and knocked at the door. Footsteps sounded inside. She wondered who would appear first. Rusty, maybe? Or Gabriel.

The young man had left by the time the door opened. Hannah blinked. In the doorway stood a young woman, sweet-faced, with large brown eyes and dun-colored hair.

"Oh." It took Hannah a few seconds to recover. "I—that is—is this where Nat Givens lives?"

"Yes."

"And—and are you Sister Givens?"

Her lips curved in a smile. "Oh, no. There is no Sister Givens—that is, he's not married, and neither am I."

Hannah tried to conceal her bewilderment. "But—"

The young woman spoke quickly. "I'm Bethia Paige. My aunt and I are boarding here—Brother Givens took us in when my uncle died."

Two unmarried females under Nat's roof! What to say next? "Please—are the Mannings still here? Rusty and his father? I heard—"

"Yes—they all live here."

Hannah considered the size of the place and was about to ask how. "I—I suppose they're out working."

"Nobody's here except me and Gabriel. My aunt's gone to the market—Eb drove her down there."

"Gabe's here? Where?"

"Out in back, working on the shed. Repairing a window."

"Well, I'm Hannah—Rusty's sister. If I could just see Gabriel—"

"Why ever didn't you say so? Come in. They've been expecting you for days!"

In a matter of minutes she was sitting at the kitchen table. She sipped peppermint tea while Gabriel talked and made excited gestures.

"I'll vow, we have the fatted calf all ready—in this case, a chicken. Your father and Rusty are holding up all right. But Nat's getting edgier by the day. Worried that you'd be caught in bad weather."

"I almost was." Hannah set her cup on the table.

"They had this big row about cleaning up the place. Nat made

Rusty do more floor-washing than he would've liked. The thing is, there's not that much difference."

Bethia gave a soft little laugh. "I don't reckon you're supposed to mention that."

Hannah had the distinct impression Gabriel was trying to tell her something else. To prepare her—for what? He'd already said her father and brother were all right.

"Are folks as poor here as they are in Missouri?"

Gabriel shook his head. "We have a place to live, as you see. But provisions are scarce. Everything's going into building the House of the Lord."

"My aunt has a little saved," Bethia said.

"Yes, and they've been after that to help with the construction costs. I reckon it's a bigger project than anyone figured. And there's not that many people to work on it."

"Aunt Sarah's stubborn," Bethia said. "And smart. She's not going to give them everything."

"There's someone else just as stubborn," Gabriel replied. "Your friend Nathaniel."

"Oh." Is this what he was trying to tell her? Some kind of power struggle between Nathaniel and Bethia's aunt?

"Don't look so dismayed," Gabriel said. "Things aren't ideal, but they're not impossible. Nathaniel—he's a good leader. A strong brother in the faith. He'll bring us all through, whether we want it or not."

"Leader?" Hannah asked.

"He's our spiritual head, counselor, advisor—as a matter of fact, he's been called to be an elder. And I reckon he'll be a good one."

Heavy footsteps sounded; the back door banged against the side of the house. A little dog shot out from under the table and ran barking onto the back porch. Rusty tramped into the room, breathing hard, his face red from the cold.

She got to her feet. Behind him stood her father and Nathaniel. She grasped the back of the chair. She felt weak, her heart pounding as she realized that the awaited moment had arrived at last. She sought her father's face; their eyes met, locked.

Rusty hesitated, as if waiting for someone else to move. Then he shrugged and rushed around the table to her, his arms spread wide. They met in front of the hearth and stood wordless, hugging each other. Gabriel moved over beside Bethia, who sat watching. Rusty took Hannah's hand. They hurried to their father, who stood with tears streaming down his face.

By this time she was weeping herself. "Oh, Papa." She flung her arms around him. He held her close, and she smelled again the familiar odors from childhood—leather and horses and damp earth. She detected something else—the scent of fresh-cut lumber. He drew back to look at her.

"My dear child—I never thought to see you again."

"I know, Papa. It's been quite a journey. And I'm sorry for running off, the way I did. But I'm here now."

"You've grown up. I didn't think you'd look so much like your mother."

To her he seemed older, not as robust. Rusty threw his arms around both of them and they stood together in silence. She could hear muffled sobs. Then she realized the onlookers were weeping too; Bethia's face was tear-strained, and Gabriel was wiping his sleeve across his eyes. Just behind her father, Nathaniel stood unmoving, the corners of his mouth twitching. His eyes looked red.

She stepped back, and her father released his hold. "So much to tell you," she murmured.

"There'll be plenty of time." He dabbed at his eyes. Hannah moved over to Nathaniel.

"Brother Nat." As she spoke, she put a hand on his arm. She reached to give him a brief kiss on the cheek, but he turned his head and their lips met. An expression of surprise and wonder rushed over his face; he flushed with embarrassment. She spoke quickly, to cover his agitation. "It's good to see you again."

He nodded and tightened his lips, as if searching for words. She said, "Papa, this is the man who did so much to help us. I doubt we would've made it to Missouri without him."

"I know, child. Rusty told me."

"Why don't we go into the parlor?" Nathaniel said. "Then we can have a good long talk while Gabriel starts dinner."

"I'd be glad to help," she said. "I can make biscuits to go with the chicken."

Gabriel looked hopeful. Rusty said, "No—you're to do no work tonight. Those are orders."

"Whose orders?"

"Never mind." Nathaniel's arm tightened around her shoulders. "Gabe will take care of everything. And Eb will help, once he's home."

"I'd like to meet Eb," she said.

"I reckon you will." Nathaniel led her toward a room at the front of the house.

"My gracious. You do have a parlor." She tried not to sound surprised as she looked at the room with the front window. It had two wooden chairs with armrests, a bookshelf and a settle. A rag rug with faded blue stripes lay on the floor. She thought of Gabe's story about house cleaning. "My, that floor is clean."

Rusty gave her a startled look. Nathaniel said, "See? I told you she'd notice."

Hannah tried not to laugh outright. She sat down on one end of the settle.

"No," Nathaniel said. "You've had enough of sitting on a wagon seat. Take one of the chairs."

Not wanting to argue, she moved to a chair. Her father took the other one. Nathaniel and Rusty sat together on the settle.

"How was your journey, my dear?" her father asked.

"Fine. They let me do most of the cooking, to earn my way. They gave me a sack of flour as a parting gift. They thought they had enough to last them to New York."

"It was comfortable?" her father asked.

"Yes—better than I expected. It got a mite cold this last week. I figured I'd get used to it, but I never did."

"Be you cold now?" Nathaniel asked.

She rubbed her upper arms. "Just a bit. But I reckon I'll be all right.

Nathaniel got up and walked into the keeping room. Rusty said, "Well, you sure do look good. As refreshed as if you'd slept all afternoon."

Nathaniel returned with her cloak. He put it around her shoulders. She met his eyes. "Thank you—you're more than kind." To Rusty she said, "I reckon I'll sleep sound tonight."

As they talked, she learned that Rusty and her father had a large room upstairs. "And there's a little one for you, up next to the chimney. You'll be warm enough."

Curious, she asked about the downstairs sleeping arrangements. As Rusty talked, she tried to keep things straight. Bethia and her aunt in the large bedroom, Gabriel and Eb in a smaller room, Nathaniel and the dog in the storage area. She looked across at him, smiling. "Nat, you haven't left yourself any room at all."

"Don't need much."

Rusty's eyes crinkled at the corners. "'Course if you wanted, we could put Nat in with you."

"Bundling?" She laughed. "Well, if we had to, I'd be willing. I'd sew him into the sack myself." Then she paused. "When you think where Nat and I have been, and the nights we've spent, bundling seems rather silly. We've slept in stage coaches, wagons, a lean-to, a tiny cabin—"

"I was there too," Rusty said. "There was always other folks around."

"I'll say," she replied. "You couldn't even move without stepping on someone."

They laughed briefly. Outside the window, the sky to the west glowed pink and red as the sun illuminated the cloud bank.

"Sarah should be home soon," her father said. "And I reckon I might as well tell you now."

Her throat tightened. "Tell me?"

"Sarah and I—we've been thinking maybe of getting married before too long."

She gasped. "Married!" She glanced at Rusty and Nathaniel, but they didn't appear startled.

"I've been so lonesome-like," her father went on. "And she has, too. It seems to make sense—that we should be together."

Dizzy. Trying to find words. "I—I reckon there's nothing wrong with marriage. It's a good institution."

"It's ordained of God," Nathaniel said.

"Yes—I—I suppose. Well, I've not met her, Papa. But I wish you all the best."

She looked at Rusty and Nathaniel for help. Rusty had an amused, resigned expression. Nathaniel leaned forward, his eyes intent; she sensed concern and sympathy emanating from him. Silly of her, to react in such a way. But the suddenness of it had the force of a physical blow. She brushed a tear from her chin.

Then she felt annoyed—she shouldn't need anyone's concern. After all, it sounded reasonable that her father should remarry. A horse neighed outside. Wagon wheels crunched on the dirt. She heard the front door opening, the dog barking.

"Oh, hush," someone said. Then a short, stout woman appeared at the parlor entrance. The woman undid her bonnet, flung back her cloak. "Why, we have a visitor. It's right cold out there."

By this time the three men were on their feet. Hannah rose from her chair as her father said, "Sarah, come meet my daughter Hannah."

The two women looked at each other. Hannah saw that the other had graying hair and a face full of wrinkles, the mouth set in a prim, determined line. The eyes, gray and close together, seemed to have an expression of permanent disapproval. She wore a dress of blue gingham material, but there was no delineation of a womanly figure beneath the starched lace front.

Hannah blinked, dismayed at the contrast between this woman and her own slim, willowy mother. Then she realized the thought was ungenerous. She smiled and held out her hand. "I'm most pleased to meet you."

The woman ignored her hand. "Well, it's high time you got here. These folks have been on pins and needles for days. Especially one of them."

She paused; Hannah wondered which one she meant. Nathaniel gave a nervous little cough. Sarah spoke again. "Well, don't be all a-standing there. Sit down."

Hannah put her hand to her side and sat down again. Sarah was watching her. "From all they said, I must say I was expecting a great lady. But you—why, you look like the rag-picker's child. No offense, of course."

Startled, Hannah looked down at her clothing. "Oh—these are my traveling clothes. I have one other dress, for meeting. I—I didn't have time to sew much for myself."

"So it would seem. Well, you'll have plenty of time now, because these men-folk go to classes most every evening."

"But not tonight," Nathaniel said.

Hannah no longer knew what to say. She sat silent as Sarah talked about her shopping, and what she had discovered in town. Suddenly Sarah stopped and looked at Hannah.

"What's the matter—the cat got your tongue? Or is your mind so full of Nathaniel that you can no longer speak?"

Hannah felt completely at a loss. "I—I beg your pardon?"

"Everyone knows he's just crazy for you. Look how thin he is—plumb wasting away. And if he's too shy to speak to you, then I reckon I'll do it for him."

Hannah tried to find words, but her mind was in shock. "I reckon no one needs to speak for him." She glanced over at Nathaniel. He sat looking at the floor, his lips pressed together.

Rusty stood up. "It's getting cold in here. Let's move into the next room—it seems like dinner should be ready soon."

Sarah turned and led the way into the keeping room. Rusty and her father followed. Hannah put her hands on the armrests and rose from her chair. Nathaniel leaned to pick up her cloak as it fell.

"Thank you, Nat." She looked up to meet his eyes, then asked in a low tone, "Is that woman really going to marry my father?"

He smiled. “Remember—it’s his choice.”

“But—”

“She’s outspoken. It’s her nature.” He followed her into the next room, where Gabriel and a young black man were putting dishes on the table.

“Oh, you must be Eb,” she exclaimed. “I’ve heard so much about you.”

Eb stopped and smiled. “All good things, I hope?”

“Of course. It’s good to meet you, finally.”

“Well, aren’t we the fine lady?” Sarah remarked. “‘Thank you’ this and ‘good to meet you’ that. We’ll just seat you right here, next to the one who dotes on you so much he can scarcely eat. Then you can work your charms on him.”

Hannah moved toward the chair offered to her, feeling dazed. She looked down at the back of the chair. Her eyes traced the lines of the wood grain as she pondered her next move.

Too long a journey. Running away from her father’s farm, traveling across three states to Missouri, to find her beloved slain, the home she was seeking as insubstantial as a dream. Now returning to her family, hoping for peace at last, order in her father’s house, a place where she would be loved and treasured...

Not to be. Here was this woman, every bit as difficult as Aunt Elizabeth...narrow, superficial...

Aunt Elizabeth—of course! A clue to how she should treat this person who would soon be her father’s wife. One thing was certain—she’d endured too much to take abuse from anybody. Putting aside her initial disappointment, Hannah sighed and raised her eyes.

Nathaniel sat at the head of the table, to her left. Across from her was Gabriel, then Eb and Bethia. Sarah presided at the other end, with their father to her left. Rusty sat between their father and Hannah.

Then she looked at the table. It had candles at each end, with roast chicken, baked potatoes and corn pudding in the center. Bread and applesauce completed the meal. She knew it was prepared in her honor, and she tried to smile.

"Gabriel, you've done yourself proud."

"*Merci, mon amie*. I had help."

Sarah gave a little cough. "Well, let's pray over it so's we can eat it. Calvin, will you?"

After the prayer, they began to pass the dishes around. Hannah said, "This is indeed a feast."

Sarah took a piece of chicken. "Don't you be thinkin' we eat like this all the time."

Hannah said, "Oh, I wasn't. That makes it all the more special."

Sarah eyed her. "Well, pile some of it on Brother Givens' plate. Most likely he'll eat, now that you're here."

A pause followed. As Hannah helped herself to the potatoes, she looked at Nathaniel. "I understand you're to be an elder."

He met her gaze. "It's true. I've accepted the call."

"I hope I'm in good time for the ordination."

He smiled. "I'll see that you're there."

"Good. I wouldn't want to miss it."

She wanted to tell him how glad she was for him, that she looked forward to his ministry. But she held back, not wanting to provoke an adverse comment from Sarah. There was another pause, filled with the clinking of forks and knives. As she feared, Sarah broke the silence.

"If you ask me, he needs a wife more than he needs ordination."

Hannah took a deep breath. "No one's asking you."

Both Gabriel and Eb leaned forward, amused anticipation on their faces. Sarah reddened. "I'm telling you, then."

Hannah said, "How do you know what he needs? In time, I reckon he'll have both."

"Oh, and are you fixin' to fill the position?"

Hannah put down her fork. She tried to speak with dignity. "I reckon that's between him and me. I don't know why you're so interested—it doesn't concern you in the least."

Gabriel made applauding motions from across the table. Rusty gave a little laugh, and their father said, "Don't rile the waters." Was the admonition intended for Rusty or herself? She shrugged and asked Nathaniel to pass the corn pudding.

Sarah's voice cut across the other sounds. "Just what do you mean by that? Of course it concerns me—I've seen him gettin' thinner and paler by the day, just because you were too selfish to write."

What sort of reply did that deserve? She glanced at Nathaniel, who sat looking uncomfortable. Eb said, "I reckon he survived."

"And don't think you fool me, with all your fancy airs. You're leading him on, is what you're doing. Trying to play the fine lady, smiling at him. He'll be thinkin' you're ready to have him, and when he finds out the truth, like as not it'll break his heart."

Hannah felt on the verge of tears. If she had any chance with Nathaniel, it was being spoiled now. What did the woman have in mind? She managed to say, "What—what truth?"

"Why, that you couldn't possibly care for him. Look at him. He knows it—he just won't admit it to himself."

Nathaniel sprang to his feet. "Stop it! That's enough!" He flung his napkin down on the table. His face looked ashen; a red blotch began to spread around his mouth. The scar stood out angrily. "Excuse me."

He turned and strode out to the back porch. The door slammed. Too late, Hannah realized her error. Sarah was one who had to have the last word. A mistake, to stand up to her.

Hannah shot a questioning glance at Gabriel. He shrugged and shook his head. For a split second she debated whether to follow Nathaniel or stay at the meal in her honor. She swallowed and looked at Sarah. "I've never seen him so vexed. Now, why in the world would you say such a thing? He's—he's been so generous and good to us all."

"I reckon he'll come back in," Gabriel said in an undertone. "Soon as he calms down some."

Sarah was saying something else, but Hannah no longer heard the words. If she truly cared for Nathaniel, she would go out to him. She stood up. "I'll be back."

"Take the lantern," Gabriel said. "You don't know that back area like we do."

Hannah draped her cloak around her shoulders. Gabriel came out to the porch and helped her light the lantern. She whispered her thanks and started down the back step.

The door closed behind her. She looked around. A soft twilight lay everywhere; she scarcely needed the lantern. At her feet, the ground sloped down to a split rail fence and a shed off to the left. A dark figure was leaning on the fence near the shed. As she moved closer, she saw that he was looking off into the distance, to a hillside full of houses. Feeble squares of candlelight shone from the windows.

She set the lantern on the ground. She reached the fence, put her hand on the rough rail. "Nathaniel?"

He turned quickly. In the half-light she saw his eyes glittering, his mouth in a firm line. "Nat—I'm so sorry."

He waited before he spoke. "You needn't be. It's not your fault that—that I'm so poor at hiding my feelings."

He looked out at the hillside again. She wondered what to say next. "I—I wasn't going to—that is, I was hoping the subject would come up more natural-like. But since it's been mentioned in such an abrupt—even cruel—way, I—I feel we should talk about it now."

Again he paused. When he spoke, he didn't look at her. "If you wish."

She took a deep breath. "I'm going to ask you a question. I know you'll give me a true answer."

"Go ahead."

"Nat—a year ago, you asked me to marry you—remember?"

"How can I forget?"

So far, so good. She felt courage returning. "Nathaniel, look at me. Are your feelings the same as they were last year?"

He glanced at her, and the corners of his mouth twitched. He looked away again. "No."

Her spirits sank; she'd miscalculated. "Very well, then. I shan't speak of it again." She turned to leave.

He spoke in a low, hesitant voice, as if searching for words. "They're stronger. Not a day's gone by when I haven't thought of you. And I know there's no end to it." His hand left the fence in a little gesture. "I thought in time it would go away—I'd be free. But, seeing you again—being with you—I don't know what I'm going to do. I feel I'm like to die."

She put her hand on his. "Well, we can't have that, can we?"

He was looking at her with a perplexed, hurt expression. She drew in her breath. *He thinks I'm laughing at him. What to do now?*

"Oh, Nat—all the way back, I—well, I was thinkin' of my father and brother, of course, and being reunited with them. But I kept hoping you still cared for me—knowing I'd give you a far different answer than I did before."

She could no longer see his face in the darkness. His voice sounded muffled. "Do you mean that?"

"Of course I do, Nathaniel." He said something else while she was speaking, and she had to ask, "What?"

The words seemed to come with a great effort. "You—you'll marry me, then?"

In the pause, the lights on the hill twinkled like bright jewels. "I will, Brother Givens."

He moved closer to her. She thought he intended to kiss her, but instead he clasped her in his arms and buried his face in her hair. She hugged him back. He stood not moving, still holding her, and after a moment she realized he was weeping. Wondering, she patted his shoulders, smoothed the hair on the back of his neck. When he spoke, his voice had the same muffled quality. "I—I didn't look to be this happy."

"Come to think of it, neither did I."

It was obvious; they couldn't return to the others right away. She began to feel tearful herself. By the time he had recovered, she was wiping her eyes. He kissed her twice on the mouth and once on each eyelid. They held each other and looked out over the hillside.

After a moment he said, "See up there—where the lights end? That's where the Lord's House is. You can't make it out in the dark, but it's there."

"I'll be sure to look tomorrow morning. First thing."

"How soon do you reckon we can be married?"

She put her lips close to his ear. "Since I'm living under your roof, I think it should be as soon as possible."

His arms tightened around her. "You mean—like this week?"

"Why not? Or next, if you like."

"I expect if I ask someone like, say, Brother Sidney Rigdon, he could do it. He marries a lot of folks. Is Saturday all right?"

"That would be fine, Nat. It would give us time to make some plans, maybe improvise a dress. Then I won't look so much like the rag-picker's child."

He gave a short laugh. "Don't pay Sarah no mind. That's what I try to do."

"Nat, that woman's pure poison. I don't know what's come over my father. But I'm going to have trouble getting along with her."

He paused. "I—I see."

"Well, don't you find her comments offensive?"

"Maybe so. But—well, when I first took them in, she'd just lost her husband. We didn't want to upset her none. Then she grew more plain-spoken. We tried to bear with her, thinkin' she was still a-grieving."

"You mean you just put up with it?"

He drew in his breath. "Hannah, every day I go up and work on the House of the Lord. I give all my strength, all my skill as a craftsman. And I think, I'm doing this for the Lord, and for his people. Not just those who are pleasant and pretty, but all of them. Even ones like Sarah, who don't know when to keep their mouths shut."

She spoke quickly. "Oh, I understand, Nat. Believe me, I do."

His eyes shone in the pale light. "To tell the truth—I seem to be her main target. Somehow she found out I had a feeling for you—I reckon one of the boys told her. I surely didn't. But now that it's settled—"

"How do you know it is?"

"In the first place, we're going to be married. Second, I saw her expression when I stood up to leave. She knows she went too far."

"So you figure she'll leave us be. What if she doesn't?"

He drew a breath, then let it out again. She spoke lightly. "Don't sigh at me. Are you master of your own house, or not?"

"Hannah—" He held his cheek against hers. "You see—if she attacked one of the others, it'd be different. If she said mean things about Eb—his being a freedman, for example, or his dark skin, or Gabe being raised Catholic, I—I reckon I'd be riled. That kind of talk I can't abide."

She nodded. "Oh, I agree."

He kissed her hair. "Well, her mind doesn't seem to run in that direction."

"Are you sure it runs in any direction?"

"Oh, Hannah." He brushed his lips against her forehead. "I know it's hard, with so many under one roof. But there's not enough houses for families to live separate. And prices being what they are—"

"If we could just get her to be polite at dinner, it would be a first step."

He said, "The Shakers had blessed silence during meals. Now I understand why."

"Speaking of which—we should go back to our dinner."

"I reckon. It's time we told the others." He turned toward the house.

"Wait." She leaned close to him. "Let's act like nothing's happened. I'll go first, if you want. You can follow in a few moments. When we're finished eating, you can ask Papa for my hand. It would please him. Then we can announce it."

When Hannah looked back through the mist of years, she remembered the frantic activity that followed the announcement. Amazing, that a group of eight people could accomplish what they did in such a short time.

Nathaniel came home early the next day. "Brother Rigdon agreed to do it. He'll be here two o'clock Saturday."

"Four days from now," Rusty said.

Hannah examined her best dress, which looked as if it had seen one meeting too many. Then her father remembered the small trunk he'd carried to Missouri and back in the wagon.

"I kept thinkin' maybe we'd meet up with you."

"And the trunk's here? My old clothes?"

With cries of joy, she and Bethia opened the trunk and rummaged through the contents. A bit of lace here, a pair of sleeves from another garment, and they would have a wedding dress. With the materials laid out, they prepared to work. Nathaniel came and took her aside.

"What, dear?"

"Bid her help you. Sarah. She'll help if you ask."

Hannah hesitated. "Well—"

"Do it for me. It'll bring peace to the household."

"All right, Nat. I suppose."

"And don't be forgetting—the silverware and fancy candlesticks are all hers. She's kind enough to let us use them—we have very little."

"Oh, I know, Nat."

She asked Sarah, who accepted willingly. "I reckon I've sewn enough hems in my time."

With three people, the work went fast, and they were able to add little frills that Hannah hadn't thought of at first. Sarah even remarked that, once they'd finished, Hannah would make a lovely bride.

Eb and Rusty set to work decorating the keeping room and parlor with pine boughs and bits of ribbon. Together Gabriel and Hannah made cookies and the fancy little cakes they remembered from their French childhood. Nathaniel spent most of his time in the shed fashioning a large bed frame out of scrap lumber.

They planned to convert the parlor into a bedroom, but it would have to wait until after the ceremony.

"When your father and Sarah be married, they can have the big room upstairs," Nathaniel said. "Then we'll move into where Sarah and Bethia are now, and we can have a parlor again."

He intended to build a chest and wardrobe to match the bed. Since neither of them had many clothes to store, she figured they could make do without the furniture for the time being.

The day of the wedding, the house appeared transformed. Festooned with pine branches, the windows looked ready for a Christmas feast. The table, draped with a linen cloth, sparkled with silver candlesticks and trays of cookies and little cakes. Brother O'Neill, Nat's friend from the public house, made him a gift—extra jugs of cider for the occasion. They lined the parlor with chairs and borrowed a small gate-leg table from the neighbors. This they decorated with a lace tablecloth and an arrangement of pine cones and bayberry candles. Since candles were a precious commodity, they planned to light only a few of them to burn during the ceremony.

Hannah, descending the stairs in her wedding dress, felt she was entering a magical place of lights and sweet scents. Her father, wearing a coat and trousers of homespun, waited for her at the foot of the stairs. She took his arm and they entered the front room.

To her surprise, the room held more people than she'd expected. Their own little household was there, of course—Gabriel and Eb dressed for Sunday meeting, Rusty in his best work clothes. Sarah sat in the first row, clad in checked gingham, with Bethia beside her. There were neighbors, the ones who'd lent them the table, and men from the public house. But there were at least a dozen others whom Hannah had never met—men and women in varying degrees of finery. Nathaniel had mentioned inviting other people he knew.

In the front of the room, Brother Rigdon stood in a proper suit of black broadcloth, with Nathaniel at his side. Nathaniel wore a new suit made for him by the women who sewed for the workmen. She smiled—she'd never seen him in such good clothes. He in turn stared at her as if he were beholding her for the first time. He didn't smile; his face had an anxious, determined look. He took her hand, and they sat down in the chairs reserved for them.

Brother Rigdon regarded them both with deep-set, intelligent eyes that seemed to radiate sympathy and good humor. A portly figure, he had white whiskers extending around the bottom of his chin. He moved his lips in what Hannah interpreted as a smile. She began to feel more at ease. She stole a glance at Nathaniel, met his eyes, but still he didn't smile. He gave the impression of wanting the whole thing to be over.

They began with a hymn, followed by a prayer by Brother Rigdon. Then he spoke to them and instructed them to be considerate and treat each other with kindness, no matter in what circumstances they might find themselves. He said that life would not be easy—it never was—but that they were to be each other's friend and companion in spite of any blows of fate they would have to endure. Above all, they were to remember that God would always be with them.

With that, he had them stand with hands joined, and led them through the marriage vow:

"Hannah and Nathaniel, you both mutually agree to be each other's companion, husband and wife, observing the legal rights belonging to this condition—that is, keeping yourselves wholly for each other, and from all others, during your lives?"

They assented, and he pronounced them man and wife. Hannah found herself wondering if even the Quakers had a simpler ceremony. The group sang a final hymn, something about earth being dressed in beauty. Brother Rigdon gave the benediction, and then people crowded around to wish them well.

Hannah embraced her family members, then the rest of the household. Sarah kissed her and bustled out to help with the refreshments. Maybe the woman wasn't such a witch after all. In a daze, Hannah tried to concentrate as Nathaniel introduced the guests.

"These are Brother and Sister Crawford—I boarded with him

when I first came from the Shakers."

Brother Crawford shook Nat's hand. "Right glad to see you married at last. And a lovelier bride I've never set my eyes on."

Sister Crawford said, "We brung you some flour and potatoes."

"Thank you."

She met Sister Rigdon, and murmured her thanks to Brother Rigdon for the service. Then Nathaniel took her by the elbow.

"There's someone special you should meet. One of our leading citizens."

She gave him a puzzled smile as he led her over to a group of people by the refreshment table. He stopped in front of a tall, broad-shouldered man. "Brother Joseph—"

She tried to conceal her surprise—how could she have failed to notice him? She looked up into the face she'd seen once before, the high forehead with auburn hair brushed back. He had the same open, forthright expression she remembered. Nat was saying, "I'd like you to meet my wife—Hannah."

Joseph took her by the hand. He gave her a long, intent look. "It's a pleasure, Sister Hannah. In fact—haven't I met you before?"

She spoke quickly, still recovering from her initial surprise. "It was some time ago—before I even joined the church. I visited here with my aunt. It's good of you to remember."

"And what was your aunt's name?"

"Elizabeth Brighton Manning."

A shadow crossed his face. "Ah, yes."

"She came out here to—I guess, to set you straight about religious matters. But I'm glad to say, you didn't listen to her."

He laughed then. "I remember. And so—this is an interesting twist. She intended to enlighten us, and instead, you became converted."

"That was much later—back in Allegheny County."

"As I recall, Brother Rigdon grew up there. Did you know that?"

She didn't. He turned and gave Nathaniel a firm handshake. "Well, Brother Nat—let me congratulate you on your choice of a bride. I must say, it took you long enough."

"I wanted to make sure I had the right one."

"I don't think you could have done better." Joseph introduced his wife Emma, a tall, dark-haired woman. Emma gave her a warm smile.

"I hope you'll both be very happy. It was a beautiful wedding."

"Sidney does some things well, doesn't he?" Joseph said.

Nathaniel clasped her hand and drew her away to meet other guests. Out of the corner of her eye she saw Joseph talking to the group clustered around him. Whatever he was saying, he no longer seemed serious. As he laughed and gestured, expressions seemed to cross his face like degrees of light and shade. She saw Gabriel and Rusty laughing close beside him, and her father smiling with Sarah on his arm. Even Sarah looked amused.

As people started to leave, Joseph spoke to her again. "Nat tells me you've been out in Missouri."

"I—I spent some time there."

"Not the safest place to be right now, I understand."

"I reckon not."

"Well, we're glad to have you here with us. I'm sure Nat couldn't be happier."

It was candlelight before all the guests had left. The neighbors folded up their gate-leg table and carried it out the door. Hannah turned to her husband.

"Why didn't you tell me Brother Joseph would be here?"

"I wasn't sure he'd be able to attend. He said he didn't know how much work he'd have to do."

"I didn't know you'd even invited him."

"And why not?" Nathaniel said. "He's one of my favorite people in Kirtland. And he enjoys a good gathering as much as anybody."

"'Specially now," her father said, "when he has all them law suits and vexatious things to deal with."

Hannah nodded. "I hope he wasn't disappointed. We didn't have a lot of fancy fixin's."

Gabriel said, "I reckon he had a right good time. Bethia kept him supplied with cakes and cookies. And he told enough jokes for ten people."

"I tell you, he's good entertainment for any wedding," Sarah said. "I hope he can come to your father's and mine."

"And when is that?" Hannah asked. They gathered around the table to nibble on what was left.

Her father lifted a glass of cider. "As soon as she figures enough time has gone by. We don't want to be disrespectful of old Jake."

They poured cider to toast the bride and groom. "We have a special present for you," her father said. "You get the whole upstairs, at least for tonight. Then we'll make the parlor into your bedroom tomorrow."

The newlyweds gratefully accepted. They retired upstairs to the big room while the rest began the work of putting the house back to rights.

As Nathaniel opened the door, the sweet scent of balsam and bayberry greeted them. Their friends had decorated the room with the fragrant boughs and candles.

25

Hannah realized soon enough that her trials had prepared her well for her marriage to Nathaniel. She viewed him with greater appreciation and devotion than she might have had with a more placid history.

He in turn seemed to treasure her; often she surprised him looking at her with an expression of pride and wonder. At certain times she wished they had a home all to themselves. She wondered how it would feel to be alone, just the two of them, wrapped up in each other's company. But that would have to wait till later, like the feather bed he'd promised her.

Then she felt disloyal—she would miss the others, especially Rusty and Gabriel. Her father too. As for Sarah—she took some getting used to.

"Land sakes, girl. Can't you stop thinkin' about your ol' man long enough to help me with this bread? We'll all go hungry at this rate."

Hannah could not define when the transformation took place, but after a while she began to find Sarah's comments both funny and true.

"Eb, you git out there and clean off them boots. If I wanted chicken ditty on my floor, I'd go bring it in myself."

She became accustomed to the rhythm of life around her. The main concern of family and neighbors seemed to be the stone walls rising on the hill behind them. Most people referred to it as the 'chapel.' Even Nathaniel talked of little else. But opinions differed.

"If they ever git that thing built, it'll be a whoppin' miracle," Sarah said.

"Yes, and you'll be sorry you didn't give us more help," Nat replied. "We'll finish it anyway—blamed if we won't."

"I'll believe it when I see it."

Saturdays were hauling days. Everyone who had a team and wagon went to the quarry and hauled stone. Joseph Smith himself acted as the foreman in the quarry. Nat and the other males in the household worked at the hauling until the daylight faded. Then they came home to a supper of stew and cornbread.

On Sundays everyone went to meetings in the new schoolhouse, just to the rear of the Lord's House. Sometimes in the afternoons they attended weddings or other gatherings. At night there were more meetings and classes at the schoolhouse, which also doubled as a printing office. On class-free evenings, they sat around the fire and talked, or pored over a borrowed copy of the new monthly paper, the *Messenger and Advocate*.

On week-days, Nathaniel and Hannah's father went off to work at the construction site. Gabriel and Eb found smaller jobs in town, doing repairs and maintenance work for anyone who would hire them. The two were able to bring in enough to sustain the household.

Rusty, being only fifteen, stayed home and attended to domestic chores such as chopping wood. He helped the three women with housecleaning and laundering the clothes and bedding. He also helped with the making of soap, candles, and the other items they needed, like brooms and wooden bowls. In addition to their regular duties, Rusty, Eb and Gabriel managed to spend one day in seven working on the House of the Lord.

"You'd think we'd have enough," Sarah said. "But lots of times, you take your money in and they refuse to sell to you 'cause you're Mormon."

"Oh." Hannah hadn't heard of this kind of persecution. "What do people eat?"

"It's like to be beech leaves, string beans, and maybe a wintered-over chicken that's starvin' to death."

"I see." Hannah felt an ache in her stomach. How would she grow a baby on such puny fare?

"Don't forget the dry cornbread," Rusty said. "As long as we have that, we won't starve."

Prepared for the worst, Hannah marveled that there always seemed to be enough. Several times Nathaniel brought home sacks of corn meal parceled out to the construction workers. Once the neighbors left half a ham at their doorstep. Gabriel and Eb often received payment in kind, and returned with bacon and flour.

People took advantage of the winter weather to go to classes in the schoolhouse. Designed to prepare the elders for the ministry, the classes drew people of every age. Women studied along with their husbands; Hannah went with Nathaniel to learn penmanship, arithmetic, English grammar and geography. So many flocked to the classes that fifty of the younger students had to be turned away so that the elders could attend.

"English grammar, indeed," Sarah grumbled. "You'd be better off at home, makin' clothes. Here it is the middle of winter, and Nathaniel's pants are so thin he don't dare set down."

Nathaniel did have one good suit. He wore it for his ordination service, just after the first of the year. Hannah remembered the schoolhouse crowded with people, and Nat sitting pale and solemn in the front of the room. Two men, one of them Oliver Cowdery, stood behind him and laid their hands on his head. During the statement and prayer of ordination, Nat stared at the floor. His lips moved as if he were unsure, a bit frightened. It was the same expression she'd seen at their wedding. But then he recovered and bore a look of humility and dignity befitting a new elder.

Later in the month, Gabriel and Eb were both ordained to the office of priest. One of their primary duties consisted of teaching people in their homes. They practiced on their communal household until Sarah had enough.

"If they ask me if I pray over my food one more time, I'm like to throw a chamber pot at them."

Nathaniel officiated at the wedding of Sarah and Calvin in late February, and her disposition took a decided turn for the better. They moved into the upstairs bedroom, in effect taking over the entire second floor. They gave Bethia the small upstairs room next to the chimney, where Hannah had spent her first nights in the house.

Nat and Hannah had the downstairs. They elected to keep the front room as their own. Gabe and Eb shared the room vacated by Sarah and Bethia. Rusty slept contented in the little room nearest the kitchen, where he could look over the food supply any time he wanted. Everyone shared in the cooking and housekeeping chores. Bethia took care of the few chickens, and Rusty saw that the horses were fed and watered.

"*Tiens*, I reckon there's room for my sister now," Gabriel remarked.

"And my wife," Eb said.

Sarah raised her eyebrows. "Why don't you just invite the whole neighborhood in? Any stranger you see. We could sleep 'em on the floor by the hearth, the table. Stack 'em in the shed."

"Now, Sarah," Nat said. "Don't be crushing their spirits. You know we'll always welcome kinfolks."

"Might as well open up an inn."

In the early spring, all five men helped prepare their bit of land for planting. When they had finished, most of the area between the back step and the shed had furrows for corn, beans, squash and potatoes. In the adjacent field they sowed wheat and barley.

The women gathered to help with the final efforts. As they worked, they talked about the latest news—the choosing of the Twelve Apostles. In addition, forty-five men had been called to serve in the First Quorum of Seventy.

Eb remarked, "I reckon we be like the New Testament church now, with all them seventies and apostles and such-like."

Hannah's father wiped his hands on his shirt. "They're not all ordained yet."

"Beats me why they waited this long," Rusty said.

Nathaniel straightened up. "What do you mean?"

"Well, from what I heard, they knew there was gonna be apostles as early as 1829. It seems like they coulda chose 'em earlier-like."

Nathaniel gave him a long, searching look. "The trouble with you, Rusty—you're too impatient. How do you know what the Lord intends?"

Rusty shrugged. "Well, I just figured—"

Gabriel said, "As near as I can make out, they were all chosen from those who went with Zion's Camp."

Nathaniel said, "That's right. That should tell you something right there."

Gabriel's dark eyes narrowed as he frowned. "Oh, you mean—well, like they had to pass through all those hardships to prove they were worthy?"

Nathaniel sounded impatient. "Not 'worthy.' Strong enough."

Rusty said, "What about them that died? They weren't worthy? Or strong enough?"

Nathaniel glanced around at the others. He waited before he answered. "Well, I can tell you what Brother Joseph said. Brother Brigham told me. It was something like this: 'Brethren, I have seen those men who died of cholera in our camp; and the Lord knows, if I get a mansion as bright as theirs, I ask no more.' Then he broke down and wept."

Rusty didn't speak; he looked uncomfortable. After a moment Gabriel said, "Interesting, how they were chosen—Joseph asking the men if they would have the Spirit of the Lord dictate in the choice. Then the three witnesses drawing up the list of names."

"Witnesses?" Bethia asked. She moved up close beside Gabriel. Hannah began to feel faint. She left the field and walked over toward the shed. Behind her, Nat was explaining about the three who had seen the plates from which the Book of Mormon was translated, and how they had been promised that they would help choose the Twelve.

She put her hands on the top rail of the fence and leaned against it. The sound of their voices washed over her. Too far away to catch the words. Nat arguing with Rusty. Rusty answering back. Her father defending one of them. The voices seemed to blend together into one. She took deep breaths of air. Strength returned to her.

At first she'd felt perplexed at the way Nat seemed to single out her brother for special questioning. That was before she realized he was seeking to instruct Rusty—in fact, trying to teach them all. She turned to look. Nat stood astride the furrows, his boots and trousers caked with mud, his hair tousled by the wind. Perspiration glistened on his face; his hands sliced the air as he expounded some point. She smiled. Acting like the head of a clan at the ripe age of twenty-five. To be sure, most of his listeners were younger, three still in their teens.

She thought of someone younger than any of them—the new life within her. Aware of it for three weeks now. So far, no one knew, not even Nat. She longed to tell him, yet held back. What if she were mistaken? She thought of Pandora, who had lost every child she'd carried. Best to keep silent a while longer.

But Sarah suspected. "If it were any of my business, I'd allow you were in the family way. Well, I won't say a word. But I reckon Nathaniel's planted more than wheat and barley this spring."

With the crops in the ground, Nathaniel and Calvin returned to the construction of the Lord's House. Their leaders gone, the others gathered around the table for a rare break in the daily routine.

"I vow, that building's goin' up faster than I figured," Sarah remarked. "That stonework's close to being completed."

"They be workin' on the rafters now," Eb said. "Gettin' ready for the first part of the steeple."

Gabriel drew his long fingers across his chin in a nervous little gesture. "When you think about it, it's amazing. I mean, that we could get this far on what we've got. If you figure it all out, I bet that final cost is gonna be over forty thousand dollars."

Bethia gasped. "That much?"

He leaned closer to her, his eyes amused. "Of course. You figure in all the work, the hauling, the lumber—"

Bethia gave a little sigh. "That's something, for people poor as us."

"Maybe some ain't so poor," Eb said. "Rich folks be helpin' too."

"Didn't know we had any," Gabriel said. Hannah was watching

the way he looked at Bethia, as if he had trouble keeping his eyes off of her. Bethia in turn was smiling at him. A warning bell sounded in her mind. *Too soon. Both of them too young. Especially Gabriel.* She wondered if she should mention it to Nat.

Rusty said, "Well, like the Lord said—if we keep his commandments, we'll have power to build it."

Gabriel laughed. "Who do you think you are, quoting Scripture at us? Nathaniel?"

They all laughed. A deep flush spread over Rusty's face; he was looking at Bethia with an intent, pained expression. *Not him, too.* Hannah bit her lip, more troubled than she cared to admit.

"Besides," Gabriel said. "It's not power we need—it's money. Come on, Eb. Let's practice your reading."

How to get Bethia out of the house and away from Rusty and Gabriel? Hannah thought of the women who provided clothes for the craftsmen at work on the House of the Lord. She took Bethia and joined them. To her surprise, Sarah wanted to do it too. Soon all three were engaged in knitting, sewing and spinning, dressing cloth and cutting it up, stitching it into garments. Sarah had plenty of comments after the work sessions.

"Sister Emma, now—she's nice enough. But she's too patient with some of them women. Like that Sister Penelope. The Lord knows she couldn't sew a straight seam if her life depended on it.

"And that other one—Sister Agatha. Blind as a bat, and twice as ugly. Clumsy—trippin' over the wool and falling into the spinning wheel. Everyone thinking, why don't she stay home? And Emma not saying a word against her."

They worked long hours. Hannah felt strangely tired. Most evenings she came home exhausted, glad for the two others to heat up the stew and bake cornbread.

****

> *...and no one can assist in this work, except he shall be humble and full of love, having faith, hope and charity, being temperate in all things, whatsoever shall be intrusted to his care.*
>
> —1835 Doctrine & Covenants, Section 38

In later years, if anyone had asked Nathaniel when he had been most content and satisfied, he would have said it was when he had helped build the House of the Lord.

A strange thing to say, considering the hardships—the back-straining labor, the self-denial which reduced most of them to poverty. And the setbacks. He didn't like to think how many times the board kiln had caught fire and destroyed a load of lumber. Finally they had to contract with a non-Mormon businessman to furnish seasoned wood.

As if the physical difficulties of erecting the building weren't enough, they had to deal with anti-Mormon threats and raids on the construction site. They posted guards to keep off marauders. In fact, so many threats were made against the lives of the church leaders that they were forced to assign bodyguards for their own protection.

"It's enough to try the patience of Job hisself," someone remarked.

But Nathaniel had both strength and tenacity. Newly married, he felt blessed with intense personal happiness. In addition, he considered himself at the height of his skills as a craftsman and wood-worker. As he worked, he sensed all his talents coming together with force and purpose—was this the supreme effort which would serve as an expression of his devotion? If it were true, then his early dream had become a reality.

In the same way, the varied skills of his co-workers were uniting to form the completed whole. One of at least a hundred men who labored on the building at any one time, he believed that in their collective strength and determination, they were presenting a sacrifice to the Lord.

He had worked on most phases of the construction—the quarrying of the sandstone, the plastering of the interior, the carving and finishing of the wood. It pleased him that the wood came from the surrounding area—white poplar, oak, and walnut. He liked to think how the fluted columns were carved, with a yoke of oxen pulling steel plates across the wood to cut the grooves.

With painstaking skill, he helped in the carving of patterns in the wood—the 'ring without end or beginning,' also called the 'never-ending circle.' He also worked on the 'Grecian key' moldings above the doors, and the 'egg and dart' and 'guilloche' designs.

"All symbols of life," he explained to Hannah as he showed her what they were doing. She clung to his arm and leaned against him as he spoke. Heavy with child, she took small, careful steps. Behind them, Rusty stumbled over a board.

Nathaniel looked over his shoulder. "Take care, lad. Lord knows, if there's anything to trip over, you'll find it."

Rusty caught up with them. "I still don't see why there's two floors of chapels."

Nathaniel said, "The first is a place of worship. The second is for school and classes—it's not as elaborate."

"Seems like we coulda made do with one."

Nathaniel looked at him. "Well, you're not the one directing things."

"I know, I know—it's all according to revelation."

"Then I don't reckon I need to say anything else," Nathaniel said. Hannah's hand tightened on his arm, and he remembered his promise to treat Rusty with more patience. "And the third floor has five rooms—for classes and quorum meetings and such. Maybe an office or two."

Their child was due in October, about the time of his own birthday. Nathaniel wondered if the baby would have October colors like its mother, all red and gold. He fretted for Hannah even though he looked forward to the birth. But she didn't seem worried.

"The midwife says I'll have no trouble. And if she can't be there in time, Gabriel will. He promised."

Nathaniel didn't like to think about Gabriel bringing the baby. Not that he resented another man seeing her give birth. But Gabe was so young, as she had pointed out on more than one occasion. Would he be able to care for her properly? Nathaniel remembered the conversation a few weeks after the spring planting.

...Hannah sitting on the edge of the bed, brushing her long hair. A ritual he loves to watch.

"Nat, I think you should know. Gabe and Rusty both have eyes for Bethia."

"What? They do?" He is amused. Sitting down beside her, taking the brush in his hand. "Well, I reckon they're of an age to be interested."

"No—you see, I'm afraid of trouble between them. There's a rivalry already. And she's not helping any—she cottons up to one, then the other."

He doesn't know what to say. "Well, they be growin' up. Gabe's almost eighteen now." He begins to brush her hair.

"But he's too young for any romantic attachment."

"And how old were you, my dear, when you first set eyes on Dan Perry?"

She frowns, then looks away from him. "Nineteen. But I was mature for my age."

"Ah, I see. All of nineteen. Well, there you are."

When she doesn't respond, he continues. "I wouldn't worry none. Folks have a way of workin' things out. I don't reckon Gabe has anything like that on his mind."

Straightening up, her eyes on his. "Still—I think you should speak to them."

He pauses. "I will if you want me to. But, Hannah—I don't know what to tell them. Rusty's father should be the one—"

"He won't. He never tried to discipline us, or teach us. My mother did everything."

He swallows. "I see. As for the others—I can't make them stay apart. That's what the Shakers did—it was most unnatural. Gabriel's in the priesthood now, and I don't look for him to do anything irresponsible. I think both boys are growin' up just fine."

She gives him a look of discontent. He sighs. "I'll be watchful, I promise. Come—let me finish brushing."

With the baby coming, Hannah found other things to think about. Nathaniel watched, but aside from the usual bantering and teasing, he could see no signs of questionable behavior among the young people. Rusty, now sixteen, alternated between work on the Lord's House and laboring for wages with Eb. Gabriel began to spend more time at home with Hannah as October drew closer.

Under the supervision of master-builder Jacob Bump, and Artemus Millet, a Canadian convert, the work on the building progressed. At times Nathaniel found it tedious; things seemed to take forever. Standing on the scaffold in bad weather, his fingers numbed by the cold, he thought how he should be out earning money for his household instead of working for nothing.

"I reckon if things come too easy, they're not worth much," Calvin remarked.

"Why, you're right." Nathaniel hoisted his end of the plank with new vigor. At least he had friends and family working alongside him.

October came. Life continued in its ordinary routine. No change in Hannah's condition. Difficult for Nathaniel to concentrate on what he was doing. His temper grew short; he snapped at both Rusty and Calvin.

"That baby better get here soon," Eb said. "Nat's ready to take the place apart."

On a day in mid-month he left Hannah sleeping and tramped to the construction site. The work seemed to be going well. As he carved the designs on the wood, he remembered how they had all received special blessings back in March under the hands of the First Presidency. Maybe his blessing was for such a day as this, when he would accomplish more than he usually did. Encouraged, he didn't stop to eat the bit of cornbread which served as his midday meal, but kept working into the afternoon.

"Brother Nat!"

He turned at the sound. Gabriel stood at the foot of the scaffold. "Come down. You too, Calvin."

Nathaniel descended. For once Gabriel's face looked impassive, as if he were very tired. *Something wrong.* Nathaniel felt a heaviness in his chest, his throat tightening as he reached the ground. *Hannah dead? The child stillborn?* He met Gabriel's eyes.

"What is it? Bad news?" Whatever it was, he didn't feel ready for it.

"No. Wait."

Calvin joined them. Gabriel took each of them by the arm and led them out of the construction area. "We're going home."

"Well, lad, what's the word?" Calvin mopped the perspiration from his forehead.

Gabriel paused before he spoke. “Hannah—her pains started early this morning. I stayed with her, and finally I sent Bethia for the midwife. Then things started happening mighty fast, and I—”

“Well, speak up, man!” Calvin grasped him by the shoulder. “What’s happened?”

Gabriel blinked, as if startled by the outburst. “You have a son—a grandson. He’s healthy and strong, from all I can make out.”

Nathaniel’s voice sounded harsher than he’d intended. “And Hannah?”

“She’s fine.” Tears stood in Gabriel’s eyes. “It’s just that I—well, I never delivered a baby before.”

“*You* delivered her?” Nathaniel asked.

“I—there was no one else. Bethia went for help, and the baby was out, just like that. I’d read about how to do it—I knew a doctor with a heap of books. But, hang it all—when it comes right down to it, it’s—it’s like—”

“Like what?” Nathaniel demanded.

“A—a religious experience. There’s no other way to describe it.”

Calvin gave a cough. “Oh, for heaven’s sakes. Well, pull yourself together, lad. You’re looking worse than Nat, here.”

“Why did you leave her?” Nathaniel asked.

“I never left her alone. Bethia and the midwife finally got there. They started bathing the baby and bustling around—telling me what to do.”

“And where was Sarah?” Calvin asked.

"She went off after breakfast to sew with the women. Bethia wanted to stay, and it's lucky she did. Both mother and child seem to be doing well, and Sarah's back now. I left to fetch you soon as I could."

Calvin clapped him on the back. "I'd say you did just fine."

"Praise the Lord." Nathaniel began to weep as he stood in the road.

A faint smile played on Gabriel's lips. "Amen to that."

"Let's praise him later," Calvin said. "I want to see that grandson."

They began to run along the road, Calvin and Nathaniel on either side, Gabriel behind them. They rushed through the stalks of corn and onto the back porch. They threw open the door. Sarah stood by the hearth, her finger to her lips.

"Shush! What's got into you? Make enough noise to wake the dead!"

Nathaniel started toward the front of the house. "Hannah—"

Sarah hurried to block his way. "Are you out of your mind? You can't see her now."

"Why not?"

"She's exhausted. She's never worked so hard in her life. 'Course I wouldn't expect any man to understand that. She's sleeping—a hard-earned rest."

"But—" His voice trailed off as he glanced around. The place looked in complete disarray, with white cloths everywhere, sheets crumpled on the floor. Bethia sat holding something in a blanket.

Calvin came up beside him, breathing hard. "We rushed over as fast as we could."

Gabriel, the last inside, let the door slam behind him. Sarah whirled to face him. "How many times have I told you not to slam that door? The poor child won't get any sleep in this house."

"Where is the 'poor child?'" Calvin said. "Let's see him."

Nathaniel just wanted to see Hannah. When Sarah refused again, Gabriel looked up from wiping his boots. "Oh, let him go in there. It won't hurt none—it's a special occasion."

Bethia stood up with the strange bundle in her arms. "First he should see this."

Before Nathaniel could move, she handed him the blanket. He stared at it, open-mouthed. A tiny red creature reminiscent of a boiled owl looked back at him. Nathaniel gasped and swallowed. "This is it? I mean, him? I—somehow I thought he was with his mother."

"He was," Sarah said. "She just put him to nurse for the first time."

Since it was his first confrontation with one so young, Nathaniel felt at a complete loss. The baby opened and closed his mouth in a continuous motion and strained his head back against his father's arm. Gabriel stood close and peered down. "Derned if he doesn't look more awake already."

"What's that white stuff on his face?" Nathaniel asked.

"Oh, it's nothing—it's from the birth. It'll go away before you know it."

Nathaniel handed the baby to Calvin, who seemed to know just what to do. He cradled the bundle in his arms and looked into the wrinkled face. "Hello, there, young man."

"Why does he have a lump on his head?" Nathaniel asked.

"He won't stay that way," Gabriel told him. "Give him a day or two."

"I vow, I'll be the first to say it," Sarah said. "He's a beautiful baby. Better looking than his father already."

"Well, he ain't been kicked in the face by a horse yet," Calvin said.

"And he won't be." Nathaniel made another attempt to reach the room where Hannah lay. This time Sarah didn't stop him.

Hannah gave him a weak smile as he moved toward her. He sat on the bed and reached for her hand. As he picked it up, she squeezed his fingers. He put her hand to his lips and kissed it.

"Have you seen him yet?" she asked in a soft voice.

"Oh, yes. He's—" He searched for the words. "—just beautiful. I mean, he's the best-looking baby I ever did see."

She closed her eyes, content. He didn't bother to say that he hadn't seen too many.

Toward evening, Eb and Rusty came home. They pronounced the new-comer 'first rate' and took turns holding him.

"He do look like a sleepy little puppy-dog, the way he put his head on the side like that," Eb said.

Rusty watched as the baby grasped his forefinger. "I can't believe it. I'm an uncle."

Nathaniel didn't feel prepared for the sudden change in the

household. Everything revolved around young Joseph Nathan, for that was the name he and Hannah finally chose. The young people argued over who was going to hold him next, and when they had to stop for their usual chores, the older generation took over. Calvin never tired of holding his grandson and rocking him. Nathaniel began to fear that the child would grow up thinking Calvin was his father.

"Well, you can hold him all you have a mind to," Hannah said. "But I reckon he'll do just as well in his cradle."

The same friends and neighbors who had attended their wedding now brought gifts of food for the family. A ham came from the Crawfords, and the neighbors next door sent over a pail of milk every week. To Nathaniel's surprise, Rusty insisted that Hannah have most of it.

"He be growing up at last," Nathaniel said to Calvin.

"It happens, sure as spring follows winter."

Nathaniel thought he had never seen anything prettier than Hannah nursing the baby. He wished he could turn into an artist and paint such a picture. But he knew he could never capture the intent looks between the mother and her child, as if they were the sole occupants in a world completely their own. He concentrated instead on his carvings for the interior woodwork.

In November, the finishing work began on the exterior. They placed a heavy stucco over the mortared stone in a technique known as 'rough cast.' The stucco had a mixture of pebbles, river sand and even pieces of broken china and glass to make it glisten in the light. Artemus Millet sent men and boys to scour the neighboring settlements for old crockery and glassware. Nathaniel heard that some women of the church had donated pieces of their own china, but he didn't know first-hand of any who had.

When the stucco exterior was finished, it shone with a faint bluish cast like a New England building. The workmen painted lines on it to look like brick-work. They placed the inscription on the front: 'House of the Lord. Built by the Church of the Latter Day Saints.'

Jacob Bump oversaw the plastering of the interior. Nathaniel remembered the fires built on the earth floors to heat the building so that the plaster would dry in the winter dampness.

When the walls were dry, the windows and woodwork all in place, Brigham Young supervised the painting of the interior with a pristine white paint. Nathaniel labored with the others as they added the finishing touches.

The day came when he stood at last in the finished sanctuary on the first floor. The sunlight streamed through the windows onto the gleaming white walls and woodwork, and he thought he had never seen any place more beautiful.

26

Gabriel the skeptic. The man of science and reason, sitting huddled in the southeast corner. He could see the pulpits for the Melchisedec priesthood with the elaborately carved window arching above. Sounds upstairs—work still being done on the upper auditorium and classrooms. He glanced around—the sanctuary on the lower floor harbored no one but himself.

He ran a hand through his unruly hair and tried to assume an attitude of prayer. But his mind was racing. *Forty thousand dollars!* Enough to free half the state of Virginia. He had to admit, the structure glowed with beauty, the elements flowing together into a harmonious whole. And at times on a bright day, the entire interior appeared flooded with light.

A board creaked behind him. He looked—no one there. Would those in charge be displeased if they discovered him? Probably. He'd managed to sneak past the guards—they assumed he'd come to work. He shrugged. Whatever happened, it would only enhance his reputation as a rebel, one who did things differently.

He looked at the lettering on the pulpits—Nathaniel had tried to explain what each one meant. "M.H.P.—that's for Melchisedec High Priesthood, or High Priests' Quorum. P.E.M.—that's for the Elders' Quorum." Everything labeled in orderly fashion. Gabriel sighed—if only the details of his own life could fall into such order. But he felt too much restlessness and discontent, due no doubt to his association with Dr. Beauchamps.

With his ordination to the ministry, he felt a deeper empathy with all created beings—especially human ones. He couldn't bear to see them in misery. Sometimes it seemed that he suffered more on their account than the sufferers themselves. He wondered at this strange quirk of mind, and wondered even more at his own passion to make things better than they were now.

First, Eb. He wondered if he'd done the right thing, to come north with Eb. Better to stay and lead more people to freedom. But there were many others doing that—the work would go on. Besides, Eb had been hurt, and needed him. And he himself was seeking freedom of a different kind.

They'd come north and found the new religion, the restored Church of Christ which was to bring freedom to all people who accepted it. Putting lofty ideals aside, they'd engaged in a pseudo-military maneuver, marched and fought mock battles, survived a flood and a cholera epidemic, endured poverty and privation, and helped build a house of worship.

But was this really what they were supposed to be doing? All the misery in the world, and they put up a building. Oh, yes—he'd delivered a baby too, for a couple whose union seemed happier than most. And that led back to Eb, whose only hope of seeing his wife again depended on money which they didn't have.

In addition, now there was Bethia. Her image flashed before him, as if mocking his thoughts. Gentle, brown-eyed Bethia. Knowing her had brought feelings he had not sought or anticipated. That he cared for her, he knew already. He couldn't ascertain how much he cared, but he knew he craved her company and felt jealous when anyone else, like Rusty, tried to divert her attention.

She reminded him of the companionship he'd known with his sister Marie, although his feelings for Bethia were very different. She loved animals the way he did, and seemed to care for people with the same concern. So adamant against slavery and discrimination that she'd asked Eb to officiate at her baptism. She said she would feel "honored to be baptized by a freedman."

Sighing, he shook the hair out of his eyes. Because of his upbringing, he felt a degree of guilt whenever he thought of her. It made his yearning for her even more painful. At the same time, he felt joy, anticipation, a newness of life in her presence.

Was it supposed to happen like this? He'd thought of asking Nathaniel for advice, but Nat had enough on his mind with wife, child, household, garden, and repairs to the shed and house from the winter. Not to mention the lack of money.

Gabriel bent forward and leaned his elbows on the wooden rail. A shadow fell over him. He looked up, startled. At the end of the bench stood the senior Joseph Smith, father of the prophet.

Gabriel straightened up. “Oh—good morning, sir.”

Father Smith regarded him with a faint smile. “Why—it’s Brother Gabriel, isn’t it?” In spite of his age, the man stood straight, with a kingly bearing. Tall like his sons, he had the same open, earnest expression as they did. Gabriel knew that the people of the community considered him one of the most handsome older men they’d ever known.

Was he about to be evicted? Gabriel mumbled an excuse. “I was just—”

“You’re a bit early for the Hebrew class. Don’t tell me you’re looking to see angels, like some of the others.”

“Oh, no, sir. I—that is, I know folks are talking about the spiritual manifestations. But it’s not angels I look for. It’s order and—and harmony.”

“I see.” The older man nodded. “I reckon there’s plenty of that here.”

“Oh, there is, indeed. It’s a good place to try and get one’s thoughts in order—if that’s possible, in my case. And to think about the reasons for things.”

Father Smith unlatched the door to the pew-box and sat down beside him. “Another good purpose for this building. ‘The glory of God is intelligence, or in other words, light and truth.’ And what have you discovered, in your meditations?”

The man’s eyes sought his in a direct, questioning gaze. Gabriel could not look away. “I had just decided that I know very little.”

Father Smith smiled. "Ah—the beginning of wisdom."

Then—Gabriel didn't know how it happened—he began pouring out his thoughts and feelings to this man, as if he were the father Gabriel had known for too brief a time. As he spoke, he remembered that this was indeed the Patriarch of the church, the father to his people. When he had mentioned his concerns—he left out the part about Bethia—he stopped. Perhaps he'd gone on too long; Father Smith surely had more to think about than the troubles of Gabriel Romain.

Father Smith drew a deep breath, then looked out in the direction of the pulpits. "In the first place, I feel you should be commended for the care you have for others. The spirit of the Lord confirms it as I speak."

Gabriel shrugged. "Caring is one thing. Actually helping them is another."

"Well, I hope you realize we can't help everybody. Sometimes we can only stand by and sympathize."

Gabriel sat in silence for a moment. "Doesn't seem like that's much to offer."

"But you don't know. I don't reckon anyone knows how much help and comfort one person can give." After a silence, Father Smith said, "I hear you delivered the Givens' baby. Folks tell me you helped tend the sick in Zion's Camp. And people be coming to you now for advice about their health."

Gabriel paused as he considered. "It's true—I know a little bit. And I was there when Hannah's time came. But, you see—if all goes right with the birth, most anyone can bring a baby."

"I'm not so sure. I hear you handled things like an expert physician."

"Well—"

"And I'll bet both Hannah and Nat were mighty glad you were there."

Caught off guard by the turn of the conversation, Gabriel smiled. "Oh, I hope to tell you."

"Now—as for Eb. It doesn't look like you can help him with money any time soon. But you can sympathize—stand by him in his trouble."

"But—"

"I know how you feel about slavery. You don't have to say it again. It's of Satan—we all know that. But it's not something any of us can help right now."

"You mean—"

Father Smith went on. "I'd say you done your part, leading all those folks to the safe houses. And teaching Eb to read and write—I heard about that."

Gabriel turned in his seat, his hands moving as he spoke. "We all did that. Nat and the rest of them. But I hardly made a dent in this—this thing that's so monstrously evil. I—"

"So, in time it will fail. A doomed institution. It can't last forever. But it's going to take more than you and I realizing that it's wrong."

"You think—when enough people—"

"It may take terrible bloodshed—more than anyone's ready to risk right now."

The words sent Gabriel's emotions rushing to the surface; he found himself wanting to weep. But Father Smith hadn't finished.

"Now—for the building. You think the money could've been spent for something else—feeding people, I suppose, or buying their freedom. And no doubt it could. But when it was all gone, we'd be right back to where we started.

"Consider, Gabriel. The whole idea of the House of the Lord is not just to 'put up a building.' All these spiritual manifestations, the organization of the quorums, the classes—don't you see? God is preparing an entire people—us—for something extraordinary. Something we can't even begin to understand. The power we're witnessing, the endowment—we'll be able to go out into all the world with the strength of this message. And with this spiritual power, we'll be able to accomplish—what? Miracles. Healing. The building of Zion, a community where there is no war, no destruction. Maybe even the end of slavery, for all time."

"You mean—when this endowment comes—"

"The endowment is happening even now—even as I speak to you. Don't you feel it? Others see angels; you'll see order and harmony, as you desire. It's all part of what will sweep the earth like a flood. Remember—it won't all happen at once. It can't. But know this—we're being prepared, even now, for things we can scarcely comprehend."

Gabriel swallowed, not willing to admit how much the words moved him. "But—those are wonderful sentiments, sir. I—I do believe—but when I look around, I see such misery—poverty—people with more trouble than they could possibly deserve."

Father Smith let out his breath in a sigh. "It's true—so much we don't know. You mentioned thinking about the reasons for things. I lost my son, whom I loved more than I can tell you—Alvin, my first-born—and the home we worked to build. I struggled with it, and I finally decided that I would never understand fully—at least, not in this life. We walk a fine line, a journey between bliss and sorrow. The best we can do is try to help each other through it."

They both looked at the sunlight shining on the white woodwork. Gabriel had the feeling that the Patriarch had a greater concern for him than he was worth, that the sense of caring and love emanating from the man went deeper than his own petty troubles warranted.

"Thank you, brother, for all you've said. I—I do see things differently. I—well—"

"You're going to do just fine, Gabriel. It's good to have the passion for humanity that you do—young as you are. Don't forget the importance of your skills as a healer."

"Oh, I won't."

They could hear footsteps behind them in the vestibule, people going upstairs to the Hebrew class. The young professor himself, Joshua Seixus, looked in at them. Hired especially to teach the Hebrew language to the assembly of church leaders and anyone else who was interested, he wore a dark suit with a gold watch chain. He appeared out of place among his students, many of them in plain work clothes. He gave a brief, embarrassed smile and turned to follow the others upstairs.

Father Smith got to his feet. “I reckon it’s time to go learn something else.”

“Thank you again, sir.” In his haste to get up, Gabriel dropped the papers and pencil he’d brought for the class. By the time he retrieved them, Father Smith had left.

“*Shalom.*” Eb was standing in the doorway, an amused look on his face.

“*Shalom*, yourself.” Gabriel stuck the pencil behind his ear.

Eb said, “Well, come on. You gonna be late for class or what? I been lookin’ all over for you. I never thought to find you here.”

“*Tiens*—life has some surprising turns.”

“I ’spect so. Soon you’ll be seeing angels like the rest of them.”

“That’ll be the day.” Gabriel unlatched the pew-box door and stepped out into the aisle.

****

“Me, get married? What are you saying?” In his astonishment, Gabriel dropped his pencil in the road.

Eb stopped while Gabriel picked it up. “Well, you be almost nineteen. And look at you. You can’t even sit in class without fidgeting. Jumpy as a frog on a spring evening. It would settle you down some.”

Gabriel gave a short laugh. They began walking again. “I daresay it would. But why would you suddenly—”

"I seen the way Sister Bethia makes eyes at you. And I seen you lookin' back at her. *I* say, ask her before someone else does."

Gabriel wiped the pencil on his shirt sleeve. "You think so?"

"I reckon you can at least get her promise."

"Well, that's a thought. I don't actually have to marry her right away."

Eb rolled his eyes. "Why not? What's the matter with you? She'd make you a right good wife."

"But—but what about our plans? Savin' up enough to get your own family back together."

"Well, I don't see us doing it any way soon."

"That's just it. With one more person to take care of—"

"What difference do it make? We'll do it, whether you married or not. Don't you see the elders going out all the time, leavin' their families? Even Nat—he be traipsin' off to Cincinnati after the chapel's dedicated."

"So he will." Gabriel frowned as he stuck the pencil behind his ear. "Well—it's not that I haven't thought of it. Let me study on it some."

"I wouldn't wait too long. Some other feller might get in there and steal her while you're a-studyin'."

Gabriel thought of the conditions at home. "I reckon us getting married wouldn't make that much difference."

With people crowding in for the dedication, they'd rented out the basement to a family of five. Two men were sleeping out in the shed, and Nat and Hannah had given up their room to an older couple. The

Givens family slept by the hearth in a pile of blankets, with the dog Nell curled up at their side. Jody's cradle stood a few feet away.

"I hear Joseph and Emma Smith be doing the same thing," Eb remarked. "Spendin' nights on the floor while visitors sleep in their bed."

"At least it's temporary." They climbed the back fence and skirted the freshly-plowed field. "I know—I'll ask her to go to that dedication service with me. Then I'll get some notion of how she feels about me."

"Do what you want," Eb said. "But I 'spect you already got all the notion you need."

The trouble was, she'd promised Rusty she would sit with him at the dedication. Gabriel consulted Eb, fuming.

"Rusty! He's not even dry behind the ears! What do I do now?"

Eb said, "Take her to something else—that display of Egyptian truck over in the prophet's house. You know—the mummies and scrolls and such."

"That museum? I reckon she's seen it. Most everybody has. Besides, you have to pay some money to get in."

Eb shrugged. "So don't do it. Know what I'm beginning to think? Getting you married is a lost cause."

As it happened, most of the communal household managed to sit together for the dedication. They waited with the crowd early Sunday morning, March 27. When the doors opened at eight o'clock, they were all ushered in as a group. Joseph Smith himself led them to a pew-box halfway down and unlatched the door for them.

In his rush for a seat beside Bethia, Gabriel stepped on her foot. Embarrassed, he stammered an apology. Joseph put a finger to his lips. Too late, Gabriel remembered the rule about no whispering during meetings in the House of the Lord. Both Rusty and Bethia glanced at him with suppressed mirth, and Eb shook his head. Gabriel felt his face growing hot; all he needed, at this point, was to do something stupid in front of the President of the church.

Nat and Calvin, entering the row just behind him, gave him stern looks, but Hannah caught his eye and smiled. He turned to face the front, glad Hannah had attended instead of Sarah. In spite of her complaints about too many people in the house, and her refusal to give up her room to anyone, Sarah had finally done an unselfish act. She'd agreed to take care of Jody and two other infants while their mothers went to the dedication.

"I'd just as soon listen to babies than all that hoopla."

But Gabriel suspected she knew how hard Nat had worked on the building, and what it meant for him to have Hannah there. Out of the corner of his eye he saw Nat reach for Hannah's hand and clasp it. Did he dare take Bethia's hand? If he did, she couldn't make a big fuss because no talking was allowed.

He dismissed the thought and tried to fill his mind with things of a loftier nature. He looked up at the rows of pulpits gleaming as if new-washed in light, and concentrated on the words carved over the great window: *Holiness to the Lord.*

****

Bethia had almost twenty minutes to ponder what was wrong with Gabriel. As the sanctuary filled with people, she sighed and looked down at her hands folded in her lap.

She'd worn her best dress, one they'd remade from Hannah's collection of old clothes. The color, a soft gray, was one especially becoming to her. Both Hannah and Sarah had exclaimed over it. But the person she'd wanted most to impress refused to even look at her.

What possessed him now? She knew his mind worked in strange leaps and excursions—it was one of the things she liked about him. Always ready with some unusual comment. She'd enjoyed his friendship, had even come to rely on it. She'd thought they shared similar feelings and opinions—almost as if they were of one mind. But now—

Ignoring her, even avoiding her. When he did speak to her, the feeling of awkwardness, of hesitation—as if he wanted to be somewhere else. She tried to think when his behavior toward her had changed. She'd begun to notice it just after the new year. At first she was puzzled, then hurt. She searched her memory. What had she done? Had she said something to offend him?

There he sat, staring at the high window. She wondered that he'd even wanted to sit next to her. Most likely he'd felt anxious about getting a seat. The auditorium, now crowded with people, could not begin to hold those still waiting to get in. She followed his gaze upward. Maybe he was admiring the curtains or 'veils' which hung from the ceiling on rollers. They could be raised or lowered at will, and could enclose the pulpits or divide the room into compartments. She and the other women had helped with the making of them.

The doors closed behind them. Joseph Smith and Sidney Rigdon took their places in the center pulpit. Bethia shot a glance at Gabriel; their eyes met. Then he reddened and looked away.

Hurt to the core, she fixed her eyes straight ahead. Gabriel was a friend to her no longer. A puzzle she could not begin to understand. Henceforth she would stop trying. He could act as peculiar as he wished. In time her own disappointment would fade away. But at that moment she felt the pain of loss in full force. Why hadn't he sat someplace else? She tried to concentrate as Brother Rigdon stood up to read the first psalm.

"'Oh sing unto the Lord a new song; sing unto the Lord, all the earth. Sing unto the Lord, bless his name; show forth his salvation from day to day...'"

By the time he reached the second psalm, Bethia felt restored. "'The earth is the Lord's, and the fullness thereof; the world, and they that dwell therein...'"

Brother M. C. Davis rose to direct the choir which had been rehearsing for weeks. She'd heard that the first selection would be a new hymn by Parley P. Pratt. The voices, coming from the four corners of the building, filled the air.

"Ere long the vail will rend in twain,
The King descend with all his train..."

At first she felt enthralled with the sound, the voices flying from everywhere to meet in wonderful harmony. Then she listened as the words swirled around her.

"Behold the church, it soars on high,
To meet the saints amid the sky;
To hail the King in clouds of fire..."

The Second Coming...in clouds of fire would the Lord return at last, to a people willing to receive him... She sat scarcely breathing as the choir finished, and to her it appeared that the very walls of the building glowed with an unearthly brightness. The strains of music died away, but in her mind they still echoed. Then she heard something else, like the sound of rushing wind, and it seemed as if she stood on a high hill all alone, with wind brushing past her face and hair.

Had anyone else felt such a thing? She glanced around. Hannah and Nat looked at ease, settling against each other for an address by Brother Rigdon. Gabriel had an aloof, skeptical expression, as if his thoughts were wandering. Rusty wore his 'Oh, no—not three hours of sermon' look.

Sidney Rigdon, an articulate speaker, took the eighth chapter of Matthew for his text, saying that at last the Lord had a dwelling place. Bethia always enjoyed his discourses, and at the end she learned to her surprise that he'd spoken over two hours.

"Well over," Rusty informed her at the intermission. "But who's keeping track?"

"Apparently, you are."

"The most important thing we've done is to sustain Joseph as prophet and seer," Gabriel remarked. Bethia wondered if his observation was directed at her. Then she decided she no longer cared.

"Took a while," Eb said.

"Well, all the quorums had to vote their acceptance."

Hannah left during the intermission to feed Jody. Some of the other women left too. Hannah returned just in time for the opening hymn of the afternoon. Just before the singing began, she leaned forward and whispered, "Angels! Sarah—would you believe it? Sarah saw angels on the top of the building!"

Nat motioned her to be quiet. But everyone in the little community had heard, not to mention those on either side. Rusty and Bethia exchanged glances, and Eb raised his eyebrows. Even Calvin looked mystified. Bethia didn't look at Gabriel, but she knew they were all thinking the same thing: *Sarah, of all people.*

****

Angels, indeed. Gabriel glanced at Bethia to see if she shared his amusement. She didn't meet his eyes. He shrugged. After all, it was her aunt who was seeing things; likely she felt embarrassed. He wondered what Sarah had found to drink back at the house. Lord knows they had little besides milk and corn syrup.

They sang a hymn and went through the business of sustaining the various quorums. Curious, he looked to see any dissenting votes; as far as he could tell, there were none. The next hymn must have had a softening effect, for when the prophet rose to offer the dedicatory prayer, Gabriel felt caught up in a strange hush which seemed to fill the room. In a rush of heightened perception, he sensed the words coming to him from a great distance.

"...And now we ask thee, holy Father, in the name of Jesus Christ, the Son of thy bosom...we ask thee, O Lord, to accept of this house, the workmanship of the hands of us, thy servants, which thou didst command us to built; for thou knowest that we have done this work through great tribulation; and out of our poverty we have given of our substance to build a house to thy name, that the Son of Man might have a place to manifest himself to his people..."

All true. Gabriel thought of what Father Smith had said to him, and how the words of the prayer reinforced it. What most moved him was a pervading sense of truth, the rightness of what they were doing. For Gabriel, who had resigned himself to a lot of nonsense concerning religion—the 'angels on the roof' kind of thing—it was like a breath of cool air on a summer's day.

Under the influence of the spirit of calm and reason, he began to believe that all things were possible. Somehow they would build an enlightened community, a society of justice and equality, where nothing like slavery would ever exist again. Perhaps even Eb's family would be reunited, and he himself could study medicine, if that was his intended calling.

"O hear, O hear, O hear us, O Lord, and answer these petitions, and accept the dedication of this house unto thee, the work of our hands, which we have built unto thy name; and also this church to put upon it thy name..."

It was a lengthy prayer, and as it drew to a close, Gabriel marveled that he could traverse the journey from skepticism to fervent belief during the delivery of it. Something about the place...the surroundings, the people waiting in expectant awareness as the final words were said...

"...and let these thine anointed ones be clothed with salvation, and thy saints shout aloud for joy. Amen and Amen."

Then the choir began a hymn, and the strains echoed from the four corners of the room.

"The Spirit of God like a fire is burning,
The latter day glory begins to come forth..."

Stirring words, with music to match. He glanced around at his communal family, at Hannah and Nat both in tears as they clasped hands. Calvin looked shaken, his face as pale as when he was recovering from cholera. Rusty was wiping his sleeve across his eyes, and Eb stared straight ahead, his eyes blinking. Others were sniffing and holding handkerchiefs to their eyes. On an impulse Gabriel reached for Bethia's hand.

She turned and gave him such an astonished look that he almost let go. He smiled and held on. She began to weep, the tears filling her eyes and making paths down her cheeks. He trembled—shook with the spirit as the Quakers did. *What had he done? Would she be weeping anyway?* Everyone else was.

The quorums, being asked, accepted the prayer of dedication, and then they all partook of communion. Gabriel continued to hold her hand, but he found himself wondering when he should relinquish it. Whatever he did, it would be awkward, possibly misconstrued. He felt bound to Bethia now—he knew it—whether he desired it or not. He would not turn back.

As the leading men of the church stood up to give testimony of the work and their part in it, he began to feel at ease. Holding her hand seemed natural, as if not to have done it would have signified some lack in himself. Brother F. G. Williams related how an angel of God came and sat between him and Joseph Smith, Sr. while the house was being dedicated. That was enough for Gabriel. If Father Smith claimed an angel was there, then it was indeed. Sidney Rigdon concluded his remarks, asking them to rise for the final prayer.

Keeping Bethia's hand in his, Gabriel stood with the others. He found himself thinking not only of the society they would build, but the community they had already, all from separate, diverse groups—people who would not associate with each other under ordinary circumstances. Shakers, Seekers, followers of Alexander Campbell. Freedmen and ex-slave owners. New Englanders and frontiersmen. Huguenots and Catholics. Their coming together a miracle in itself.

Then they were all shouting with one voice: "Hosanna! Hosanna! Hosanna to God and the Lamb! Amen, Amen, Amen!"

Three times the shout echoed, filling the room. Finally President Smith dismissed them with prayer.

"Past four o'clock," Rusty said. "Way past."

No one paid any attention to him. The doors opened, and people started to leave. They walked slowly, in little groups. Some lingered inside, as if they were reluctant to depart. Gabriel understood; he wanted to stay, to remain in touch with what had just happened. He looked at the other members of his household. They said very little, but he sensed a silent bond, the sharing of a common experience too deep for words. Then he realized he was still holding Bethia's hand.

Finally Nat nodded and led Hannah out into the aisle. The rest followed.

"I reckon Sarah's gonna be sorry she missed this," Calvin said.

"Why? She got to see angels." Rusty unlatched the pew-box.

"They're having another dedication service," a voice said from behind them. "Someone said Thursday. Too many folks couldn't get in."

"Won't be the same," Nat said.

Gabriel looked at Bethia as he released her hand. He put his hand on her shoulder and spoke in a gentle, teasing voice. "Shall we go see if the angels are still on the roof?"

She returned his look, this time smiling through her tears. "There might be more angels around than you can imagine."

He laughed. "I'm sure they dance around you all the time. Leastways I would, if I was one."

They went out into the late afternoon sunlight. Brother Joseph, who made it a point of greeting every visitor, even the youngest child, now waited to shake their hands.

27

"That's what I understood him to say." Nathaniel shakes out his napkin and tucks it under his chin. "I'm surprised you didn't hear it. Now, Rusty—if you'll pass me a biscuit..."

Rusty, hoping to snatch a fourth one, reaches for the plate. Too late. Gabriel's nimble fingers catch it up and speed it to the head of the table.

"You had enough anyway," Eb tells him.

Nat takes a biscuit and breaks it in two. Calvin speaks from the other end of the table. "Well, I admit I missed it. Joseph really said his work was finished?"

Nat bites into the biscuit. "What he said was that he'd completed the organization of the church and we'd passed through all the necessary ceremonies—the endowments and so forth. He'd given us all the instruction we needed, and we were now at liberty to go forth and build up the kingdom of God."

"When did he say this?" Gabe asks.

Nat's mouth is full. "Why, last Wednesday, when the quorums met."

"Another meeting?" Sarah asks.

Nat swallows the bit of biscuit. He explains, his voice patient. "About three hundred of us met to attend to the washing of feet and to have communion."

Gabe shrugs. "So the work of church organization is finished—not anything else he might do."

Nat wipes his mouth. "So I would assume."

Bethia looks at Gabe. "My, you're particular," she says in a teasing voice. "You want to pick apart any statement you hear."

Eb laughs. "He's just mad 'cause he hasn't seen any angels and such-like."

Rusty watches as Gabe gestures with his long fingers. "That's not true. I don't give a hang whether I see supernatural beings or not."

"Well, some sees 'em and some doesn't," Eb remarks.

Gabe's face reddens. "I haven't noticed *you* seeing any."

Eb picks up a biscuit. "What I see is my own business."

Rusty judges it best to keep silent. From his vantage point as the household's junior member, he manages to learn a good deal as quiet observer. But some things puzzle him. To begin with, he is still trying to figure out if Bethia and Gabe really care for each other. Or are they simply play-acting? If the former is true, than he has serious troubles of his own. For he finds himself liking Bethia more and more.

While he realizes they are both older than he is, he also knows that, at seventeen, he towers over Gabe by at least six inches. Not only that, he is still growing. And Hannah's cracked mirror reveals an incredible change in his appearance. Instead of the clumsy boy with freckles, he looks purposeful, serious, grown up at last. He has dark eyebrows arching over blue eyes, thin lips and an aquiline nose like his father. He considers himself much better-looking than dark, wiry Gabriel. Surely Bethia can see the difference.

Sarah says, "I'm not the only one to see angels on top of the House of the Lord. Prescendia Huntington told me just the other day—a little girl came to her door and called, 'The meeting is on top of the meeting house!' She went to look, and she saw angels clothed in white covering that roof from end to end. They walked about; they appeared and disappeared. The third time they appeared, she realized they were not mortal men. In broad daylight this was—in mid-afternoon. Even the children could see them."

Bethia says, "I heard there was prophesying and speaking in tongues that day. Someone said, in the interpretation of tongues, that the angels were 'resting upon the house.'"

Gabe raises his eyebrows. "Now, where'd you hear such a thing as that?"

"Sister Huntington told us."

Calvin says, "I was there at that one prayer service—remember, Nat? Father Smith prayed for the spirit of the Most High to be poured out on us like it was at Jerusalem on the day of Pentecost—that it might come like a mighty rushing wind. And when it did come, he looked about astonished, as if he'd forgotten. He even said, 'What? Is the house on fire?'"

Nat puts down the butter knife. “I must say, I never thought to hear of all these wonderful things. Healings, speaking in tongues. Visions, prophesying. Lights, heavenly music—choirs of angels.”

Later they hear that Joseph Smith and Oliver Cowdery, at prayer in the House of the Lord, had received a vision of the Lord himself.

Nat’s eyes gleam as he relates it. “They said he was standing upon the breastwork of the pulpit, right in front of them, and under his feet was a paved work of pure gold, like the color of amber!”

Calvin continues. “They said his eyes were like a flame of fire, his hair white like pure snow!”

“And his face shone above the brightness of the sun!” Gabe gestures, his fingers shaping the air.

“So—what did he say?” Sarah demands.

“Say?” Gabe looks puzzled.

“Yes. He must’ve said something.”

Gabe looks at Nathaniel, who sits with six-month-old Jody on his lap. Nat says, “Well—he accepted the house, and said that thousands and tens of thousands would rejoice because of the blessings which would be poured out, if his people were faithful and kept his commandments.”

“That’s right,” Gabe says. “I think he said a heap of other things too. I wasn’t sure right where to begin.”

“Well, let’s hope we’ll be faithful.” Nat holds Jody close to him and kisses the top of the child’s head.

Along with the spiritual blessings comes a relative prosperity. Their gardens flourish; there is plenty to eat. Eb, Rusty and Gabe are in demand as builders and laborers. As new houses go up, they bring home cash and payment in kind. They become so affluent that Calvin and Sarah vacate the upper floor and move into another house close by. To the dismay of Rusty and Gabe, they take Bethia with them.

"Don't be ridiculous," Sarah tells them. "It's not proper for a girl like her to be under the same roof with a bunch of menfolk."

"We're not menfolk," Rusty protests. "She's like our sister."

"When did it suddenly become improper?" Gabe asks.

Rusty and Gabe take turns going over to visit. Rusty, who has chosen to stay with Nat and Hannah, begins to feel unwelcome at the second house. The chilliness comes not from Bethia, but Sarah.

"Like as not, she's right," Gabe tells him. "Here we be, growing up. I reckon they all need their privacy."

"But derned if it isn't my own father's house," he says. "I'm supposed to be family."

Gabe looks at him, and the dark brows knit together. "That part is strange. Let me study it some. I reckon maybe we're taking it too serious-like."

A few weeks later, Hannah tells them about the clothes. "Sarah went out and bought a whole bunch of material to make dresses for her and Bethia."

"I thought they had dresses," Gabe says.

"Not fancy ones. These are for parties, like rich folks' weddings and such."

"Oh." Gabe looks at Rusty; their eyes lock. "Why would they want to go there?"

"I reckon the food's good," Rusty says.

Gabe shakes his head and looks away. "Bethia likes to read and do quiet things. She likes feeding the horses and taking care of Jody. She'd be bored at a fancy doing."

Hannah smiles. "That may be true. But I hear they be going to a big dinner at Brother Rigdon's house come Saturday, with all the community leaders."

Gabe stares off into space as if he hadn't heard. His mouth twitches at one corner.

"Don't fret none," Eb tells him. "There's more than one fish in the river."

Calvin and Nathaniel go off preaching together in southern Ohio. Eb, Gabe and Rusty continue their work as carpenters and handymen. Eb and Gabe find hauling work, but when they go to harness the team of horses, Sarah hurries to stop them.

"Those horses belong to my husband, and you're not to touch them!"

Rusty walks across to remonstrate with her. "They be our family's team. Hannah and I have as much right to them as anyone."

"I don't care! Calvin left me in charge, and I say you're not to use them! They're for pulling a handsome carriage, not plowing or hauling."

Rusty stomps back, shrugging. "If that don't beat all. She liked it fine when we was feeding both her and the horses."

"If only Calvin were here," Gabe says. "Or Nat. They'd soon settle her hash."

Eb scratches behind his ear. "Nat would say to keep bein' friendly, just like we always has."

Acting on that sentiment, Gabe takes over part of a ham that they were given in payment. He returns, so angry he can hardly speak.

"Well, stop sputtering around in French and tell us," Eb says. "What did she say?"

"She—she slammed the door in my face! Said she didn't need anything from the likes of us. Said—"

"Wait a minute. Sarah said that?"

"She said all I wanted was to see Bethia, and Bethia was too busy to see me. Can you beat that? *Busy!* Doing what?"

Eb raises his eyebrows. "Sewing clothes, I expect."

Hannah tries to bring peace to the troubled household. "Nathaniel won't be away much longer. He'll set things to rights."

"Look at it this way," Rusty says. "They're not starving—they say they aren't in need. We should be glad. It means more food for us."

Hannah looks worried as she sets out a meal of ham and cooked apples. Rusty is suddenly watchful, wondering what's wrong with her. She hands Gabriel the bread to slice. Finally she speaks. "I reckon you should know, if you don't already. I was hopin' you would figure it out by this time. But Sarah—well, see, she's bound and determined that Bethia find, well—someone important. To marry, I mean. A church leader. Someone with standing in the community."

"Someone of property?" Rusty asks.

Gabe puts down the bread knife. He looks distraught. "Why don't you just come right out and say it? A rich man. Someone who's not dirt-poor, like us."

A look of pain goes over Hannah's face; she looks close to tears. "Now, Gabe, don't take on so."

"I don't reckon I know any rich Mormons," Eb says.

Rusty reaches for his napkin. "There be some—not very many. But they don't come visiting the likes of us."

Gabe blinks, looks down. Hannah takes a deep breath and continues. "So it's just as well that you don't think of her in that way. Bethia, I mean. If you ever did."

Rusty tries to act casual. "Who does she have in mind? I mean, everyone I can think of is married."

Hannah sighs. "I can't see that it matters."

Gabe finds his voice. "But—her choice. Bethia has her free will—she has to have her choice."

Hannah takes the bread knife and begins to cut slices of bread. "That's what I be tryin' to tell you. I'm awful sorry. I reckon this *is* her choice."

Gabe's face reddens; he glances down at the wooden table top. Rusty feels a pang of sympathy; he doesn't realize Gabe cares this much. In that moment, his own feelings for Bethia take a different turn. He likes her well enough, but he sought her approbation mainly because Gabe seemed to put such a value on it.

"It's no matter, Gabe," he says. "I reckon she'll come around. And if she doesn't, someone else will."

"That's it." Hannah passes the breadboard full of bread slices. "In time, someone will return your affection. And she'll be worth the wait. You'll see."

But Gabe does not look comforted. Hannah exchanges glances with Eb, and Eb shakes his head. Rusty stands up and puts his hand on Gabe's shoulder in passing.

"I reckon I'd better let the dog out."

From where he stood hoeing corn, he could see the two figures as they made their way up the hill—his father and Nathaniel, home from the missionary journey at last. Their clothes looked dusty, their feet kicking up little puffs of dust from the road. From what Rusty could tell, they'd stopped at the public house already to hear the latest happenings in the community. Nat brandished a newspaper, either the *Star* or the *Northern Times.* He gestured with it as he talked to Calvin.

Rusty's first thought was to run and meet them. At the same time he felt he should alert the others. Hannah would want to know. And Gabriel had been acting especially moody; this would raise all their spirits.

Indecision slowed him down. By the time he reached the shed with the hoe, they were already climbing the fence.

"If it isn't Rusty," Nat said. "Actually working. Caught in the act. Don't put the hoe away on our account."

Rusty went to put his arms around his father. Calvin held him close. "How is it with you, lad?"

"Oh—everything's fine, except—" He turned to embrace Nat.

"Except what?" Nat grasped him by the shoulders.

"Oh, well—nothing."

"Everyone's well? Hannah, Jody?"

"Yes."

"And there's enough to eat? You don't look starved."

Just then a frantic barking and scratching came from the back door. Hannah opened it, and the dog Nell shot out like a white cannonball. She began sniffing at Nat's feet, her tail describing wild circles. He patted her; she began a process of investigating every inch of his boots and pant legs. She followed him, sniffing, as he hurried to enfold Hannah in his arms.

After the initial excitement of greeting, they gathered around the table, Nat with Jody on his lap. Calvin, instead of rushing home to his own wife, sat down with them. Rusty thought at first that his father had forgotten about the move.

Calvin unfolded the newspaper and put it on the table. As Rusty had guessed, it was the *Northern Times.*

"Things is gettin' right political," Calvin said. "I was just sayin' to Nat, it's like we're all aimin' to court ol' Andrew Jackson."

"I wouldn't pay that no mind," Rusty said. "I reckon it's just talk."

His father patted the newspaper with his forefinger. "It's more than talk. It's written words."

Gabe raised his eyebrows. "No church should get mixed up in politics. Look at the history of Europe."

"Well, this one sure shouldn't. I reckon we got us enough troubles," Calvin said.

Nat looked at Hannah. "You hear about the Saints in Missouri?"

"What's happened?" Hannah asked.

"They've been asked to get out of Clay County—to go further north."

A shadow went over her face. "But—but there's nowhere else—"

"So the Missouri legislature has gone and created another county, just for us. Caldwell."

"Called well?" Rusty asked.

"The name of the new county. The people be gathering there, even as we speak."

"Oh." Rusty tried to smile. "For a moment I thought they were all fixin' to come here."

"Not a chance," Eb said. "I reckon most folks in Missouri be wantin' to stay."

They talked about other things—last year's boycott, when the local miller had accumulated a quantity of grain and refused to sell any of it to Mormons.

"That was clever—us sending to Portage County for grain," Rusty said. "Come harvest time, those gentiles had more grain than they knew what to do with. Served 'em right."

Nat stroked his chin. "Things are a lot different now. New buildings going up all over town. We got the brickyard in operation, the printing office, the shoe shop, the lumber kiln."

"Don't forget the ashery and tannery, and the steam sawmill," Calvin said. "In fact, I hear there's even talk of a bank. Think of it! Our own bank, like a proper civilized town."

Hannah said, "Joseph and Emma have another son, born in June. They named him Frederick, after the good doctor."

"A fitting tribute," Nat replied. "Dr. Williams should be right pleased."

Then Gabe told about the horses, gesturing as he spoke. Rusty noticed that he tried to choose his words carefully, so as not to offend Calvin. In fact, Rusty considered it a little masterpiece of understatement, with emphasis on the lost hauling jobs instead of their being forbidden to use the horses.

"We coulda made ourselves a heap of money."

Nat and Calvin looked at each other. Calvin drew a breath and opened his mouth, as if he were about to speak. Nat smiled. "Well, I don't see anyone going hungry. I think you've done right well."

"But—"

Nat went on. "I reckon she's right about the team. Those horses can't haul too much anyway. What you need is oxen." He paused. "Come to think, I know a man over in Mentor who owes me money. He once offered me a pair of oxen, but I didn't think we could afford to feed two more animals. Times have changed. I reckon I'll pay him a visit tomorrow."

After a moment, Gabe spoke again. "From what I hear, Sarah and Bethia been travelin' in some highfalutin company."

Calvin looked puzzled, then laughed. "What've those crazy women done now?"

Hannah said, "I reckon they're being invited to social gatherings with the best in town."

Calvin shrugged. "Well, I figured that's what she wanted. Is that all?"

Rusty said, "I hear she wants a fancy carriage like the Rigdons."

"Oh, she does, does she? Well, more power to her. If she can find a rig like that, I'd like to see it."

When Calvin had left, Gabe said, "I must say, he took it light enough."

Nat looked at him. "Sarah has her whims. They come and go. I wouldn't worry none."

In the fall, Joseph Smith returned from a mission to the east with plans for the new bank.

"They're calling it the Kirtland Safety Society Bank," Nathaniel said.

"That's a fine, proper name," Hannah remarked.

"I hear they're fixin' to replot some of the town," Rusty said. "Make it more orderly-like."

Nat looked at him for a moment. "I reckon most anything'd be an improvement."

"They want to get rid of some of the poorer houses—the shacks and shanties."

Nat said, "I agree. No more people living in boxes and such-like."

Rusty tried to choose his words carefully, so as not to betray his fear. "Well, I sure hope they don't make us get rid of our house."

"They shouldn't, now that it's painted and all."

Calvin came to tell them about Sarah's newest whim. "It beats me—she's bound and determined to put all our savings into that new bank. She wants us to buy stock in it first thing."

Nat smiled. "Well, Brother Calvin—like as not you'll be a rich man."

"And we be gettin' our fancy carriage too. Derned if she didn't go and find one."

Nat raised his eyebrows. "I reckon you won't even want to talk to the likes of us."

"Don't be ridiculous. I vow, she's only doing it to impress some of them high-society folks. First, clothes and parties, and now a rig for everyone to stare at."

Nat gave a short laugh as he reached to pick up Jody. "Land's sakes, Calvin. If prosperity knocks, don't bar your door. Go and enjoy your new carriage. Maybe when she's off somewheres else, you can take us all riding."

Calvin left. When the door had closed, Gabe spoke. "Well, I'm not going to set foot in it."

Nat sighed. "Like as not, they won't ask you to."

Gabe gave him a dark look and left the room. Hannah said, "Are we going to buy shares in the bank?"

Nat tightened his lips. "I would if I could. Right now, I'd say no."

They had the team of oxen now, two gentle, young beasts called Buck and Handsome Jack. Both were reddish in color, with white between the eyes. Buck's coat was a solid color; Jack had white patches on his back. Nat hitched them to the wagon, which they pulled to the various construction sites.

In early October, they met Bethia and Sarah on the road. Rusty and the others were returning from a day's labor. Rusty remembered how Nat was walking beside the team, next to Buck, the lead ox. Eb walked on the other side, and Rusty sat in the wagon with Gabe. Gabe's work shirt, besides needing a wash, had split down the front while they were working; his bare chest glistened with perspiration.

A cloud of dust appeared ahead of them. Out of the dust trotted the two bay horses and the prettiest rig they'd ever seen. It had green and gold trim, and green cushions. In it sat Sarah and Bethia, both dressed more elegantly than Rusty had ever seen them.

"Good afternoon to you, sisters," Nathaniel said.

Sarah replied, "Good afternoon," but her voice sounded strained. She gave them a look which Rusty could only call disdainful. But it was Bethia who drew his eye. She didn't answer; her eyes grew wide as she looked at them. Her lips parted in an expression of bewilderment and concern.

Beside him, Gabe gave what sounded like a low groan. Rusty watched him through half-closed eyelids. Gabe looked at her briefly, then cast his eyes down. His face reddened, his dark brows drawing together. He blinked, as if he had something in his eye. At first Rusty thought he might be weeping, but it was only beads of perspiration from his forehead. Then Rusty became aware of Nathaniel watching both of them.

Nat seemed deep in thought as they plodded the short distance home. In the shed, he filled the trough with hay. "I've studied some about what's best for us to do. And I've decided not to put any money in the bank—at least, not right off. I have another plan. Gabriel?"

Gabe looked up from the traces. He was sniffing, as if he had a cold.

Nat said, "I know an older gentleman in Mentor, a physician—did some work for him once. When I went to fetch the oxen, I stopped in to see him. I took the liberty of asking him if he could use an apprentice—someone who wanted to learn about medicine and the healing arts. This man is a gentile, but he's friendly to us. He agreed to take you—that is, if you'd do household chores for him and pay something for your room and board. If you be willing, that is."

An elated look rushed over Gabe's face. Rusty thought it was like the sun coming from behind clouds. In his excitement, Gabe began to stammer.

"You—you mean that I—*mon Dieu*—that I would go—"

Nat said, "Let's get your things together, and tell Hannah what we're about. It's best we do it now, before the cold weather sets in."

"But—" Gabe glanced around. "But, Eb—"

"I be just fine right here," Eb said from behind the wagon. "You go, and learn all you can."

Gabe shook his head and ran his fingers through his hair, as if he were still trying to get used to the idea. Rusty stepped over and clapped him on the shoulder.

"Well, if it isn't the future Dr. Romain."

Gabe gripped Rusty's hand in a firm grasp. "I don't know what to say."

After a few moments he found plenty to say, eager questions

directed at Nathaniel.

"Why didn't you mention this before? I mean, you got the oxen weeks ago."

"Well, lad—I wanted to be sure it was the right thing to do. And I wanted to have enough money in hand so's you wouldn't have to return after only a month or so."

"*Tiens*—I understand. But won't he wonder why I didn't come earlier?"

"He said you could start any time you were ready."

"Yes—I see." He smiled then, and for the first time since Bethia had left, he had a purposeful, cheerful expression. Until the time he packed up and prepared to leave with Nathaniel, he didn't mention her name again.

28

In May of 1837, Nathaniel and Calvin returned from preaching assignments in southern Michigan. Nathaniel felt a wave of weariness as he climbed the last hill.

"I'm about wore out."

Calvin gave a half-smile, more like a grimace. "What's the matter? Feeling old already and you're only twenty-six?"

Nathaniel noticed Calvin breathing hard. "Let's stop in for a mug of cider before we head home."

"Fine, if he'll serve us on credit. We got nothing left."

Soon they were sitting in the public house with a page of the *Messenger and Advocate* which someone had left. O'Neill put a pitcher of cider and two mugs in front of them. "Just don't try to pay fer it with them bank notes."

"What?" Calvin said. "What's wrong with bank notes?"

"Why, ain't you heard?" said a man at another table. "Them notes ain't worth chicken ditty."

Calvin turned pale. "But—but that's impossible."

O'Neill said, "We might as well face it. That Kirtland Safety Society Anti-Banking nonsense was one of the biggest mistakes we ever made."

"But—the prophet assured us—"

"You think *he* knows anything?" said the man at the other table. "Start up a financial institution when banks are failing all over the state."

Calvin gave a low groan. Nathaniel looked at him, alarmed. "Come on. Drink some cider."

The man at the other table spoke again. "Where you been, anyway? No one's takin' those notes any more. Even your know-it-all prophet is warning people to be careful."

O'Neill said, "While the prophet's been fighting law suits, they been out preachin' the word."

"Well," the man said. "The word is, we've all been hornswoggled. And we know who's to blame."

"Let's drink up and get out of here," Nathaniel said. As he raised the mug to his lips, he caught sight of the words in front of him. *'...guilty of wild speculation and visionary dreams of wealth and worldly grandeur, as if gold and silver were their gods, and houses, farms and merchandize their only bliss...'*

"That scoundrel, Joseph Smith. It's all his doing," the man said.

Nathaniel stood up. "Watch your mouth, brother, or I'll shut it for you."

O'Neill hurried around the end of the counter. "You fellers better go now. I don't want any trouble here."

Nathaniel folded the paper and put it under his arm. Calvin seemed confused; Nathaniel took his coat sleeve and led him toward the door.

"I'm ruined," he said in a dull, low voice.

"Nonsense. Let's go home and find out what's really happening. Rusty will know, and Eb. Hannah, too."

"Everything we had was in that bank."

"Maybe it's not as bad as they said."

In fact, it was worse. Sarah and Bethia had moved back in with Hannah, Rusty and Eb. Sarah, no longer haughty, ran weeping to embrace Calvin.

"It's all gone! There's nothing left! No one will take our notes for anything!"

"I know, love." Calvin held her and patted her back. "I'm sorry."

Not only were the bank notes worthless, but the women were hard-pressed to buy provisions with the little cash they had. "No one wants to sell to us anymore," Hannah said.

Nathaniel smoothed her hair back from her forehead as he hugged her. "Then we'll have to do the best with what we can find."

Sarah looked at him, her cheeks tear-stained. "You didn't invest anything in the bank, did you?"

Nathaniel sighed. "The truth is, we didn't have that much. What we had went to something else—let's call it an educational venture."

Sarah gave him a blank stare, but Bethia lifted her head and smiled.

In the morning Nathaniel took Eb and Rusty and went out looking for hauling jobs. To his surprise, some of their fellow Saints refused to hire them.

"If you still believe that man's a prophet, you can work somewhere's else."

Nathaniel looked at Eb, bewildered. "What are they saying?"

"That's the way it's been," Eb said. "If they think you're loyal to Joseph, they're makin' it harder than ever."

"Who's 'they?'"

"Oh—dissenters. Mostly folks who lost their money."

Everywhere he went, he heard talk of the bank failure.

"Why, Brother Cowdery just declared the bills weren't legal tender. And he's justice of the peace."

"Derned if I didn't lose everything."

"But it's not a bank. They couldn't get a proper charter. It's an anti-banking society."

"I don't keer what they call it. It's failing anyway. And I don't have nothing left."

In spite of the troubles, Joseph managed to send off missionaries to England. In the latter part of June, Heber Kimball, Orson Hyde, Willard Richards and some others left Kirtland. Nathaniel, whose missionary efforts had been concentrated on areas closer to home, could only wonder at the sacrifices which these men and their families were making.

"I reckon we better keep those families in mind," he remarked.

"Why?" Sarah said. "Those women can sew and clean and wash as well as anyone. I reckon they'll survive. We got troubles of our own, in case you haven't noticed."

They stowed the fancy carriage behind the shed. Nathaniel shook his head as he looked at it, wishing he had the money they'd spent on it. He no longer had funds to send to Gabriel—he dreaded writing to inform him. He put off doing it.

As the summer progressed, the discontent grew. Someone estimated that at least a third of the leadership was in the process of withdrawing. There were numerous dissenting groups, people uniting under various leaders. Nathaniel went to his friend O'Neill at the public house in an effort to sort out the different factions.

"Well, let's see, there's the bunch that think they're the real church, except they no longer acknowledge the prophet. They claim the House of the Lord belongs to them, and they're even holding meetings in there. Then there's Warren Parrish and his 'Parrish Party'—about thirty people. And something called 'The Independent Church.' And—I dunno—scores of others."

"Amazing," Nathaniel said. "When you think of all they went through, and now—"

"Tough times. It'd surprise you—all the leading men who are out there stirring up trouble. Why, I could name you names that'd knock yer hat off."

"You don't have to."

"Why, there's William E. McLellin, Luke Johnson—Lyman, too—John Boyington, F. G. Williams, Oliver Cowdery, David

Whitmer, Martin Harris—"

"That's enough." Sick at heart, Nathaniel turned to leave.

"Sylvester Smith, Warren Cowdery, Joseph Coe..."

What was happening to them all? Nathaniel went outside and paused beside his team of oxen. He stood there a long moment fingering the leather straps, patting the lead ox. Then he led them home, the wagon rattling behind them.

"It's apostasy, that's what it is," he said to the lead ox. His mouth worked as he wondered what to do. All his family needed was to be denied sustenance because he was backing the wrong faction.

To add to his troubles, Hannah felt unwell, at the beginning of a new pregnancy. Luckily Bethia was able to take care of Jody, while Sarah cooked for the household on what little the men could provide.

In August they heard distressing news. Joseph Smith and Sidney Rigdon had been set upon by a mob as they returned from a mission to Canada. The two were taken to Painesville and secured in a tavern where their persecutors intended to hold a mock trial. But the housekeeper, a member of the church. let them out the kitchen door.

"Derned if they didn't search for 'em all night with lighted torches," Rusty said.

"But they could see the torches, and that's how they escaped," Eb said with a laugh.

Nathaniel sighed. His worst fears were coming true. If the prophet's life was in danger, then they, too, were no longer safe.

Good news came from Gabriel. Before Nathaniel could tell him they were out of funds, they had a letter.

'Dr. Newton told me this morning that he figured he had taught me everything he knew. He also said he had never had a more receptive apprentice. These remarks made me feel very good. He invited me to stay on as his partner, saying he would share the proceeds from his practice with me, and I would benefit from the experience.

'I agreed to stay with him at least till the end of the year. Accordingly you need not send any more money; I am now able to earn my own keep.

'He had an earnest talk with me and encouraged me to give up anything to do with Mormonism. He said, "I hear they are even rioting in that temple now—how can you continue to believe in such folly?" I told him I didn't know what was happening in the building, but I would always treasure the Book of Mormon since it had opened a door in my mind and set me free.

'What is happening? Are you rioting too?'

"What'll we tell him?" Rusty asked after they heard the letter. "People are jumping out of windows and pulling knives on each other? They took a dagger away from one fellow."

Eb said, "Wait'll he reads about Father Smith being accused of starting a riot. Him and the sixteen others, all because of that fight between Parrish and William Smith."

"We won't tell him anything," Nathaniel said firmly. "He doesn't need to know, unless things get a lot worse."

"But he asked," Hannah said in a soft voice.

Nathaniel closed his eyes as he thought. "A few simple words about apostasy will do. He'll understand."

Rusty said, "Then he's ahead of us, 'cause I'll be blamed if I can figure it out."

While Nathaniel was finishing some repairs at the public house, O'Neill said, "I'd be mighty careful if I was you, Nat. Most everybody knows how you feel about Joseph Smith. I hear them dissenters is even seizing folks' property, saying it's being sold to pay off the prophet's debts."

"I'm not afraid," Nathaniel said. "I haven't got much property to speak of."

"You got your oxen and wagon. Did you know people are hiding out at certain houses, waiting for their chance to clear out of here?"

Nathaniel swallowed. "No—I didn't."

"They even had to hide the mummies and the Egyptian stuff, so it wouldn't be destroyed. I won't say where it's hid, but those mobbers ain't gonna find it."

Uneasiness stalked Nathaniel as he headed home. Not for himself, but for Jody and Hannah, now big with child, and the others all looking to him for leadership. Bethia. Rusty. Calvin. They sat like solemn presences in his mind. How could he keep them safe, and get them out in a hurry if he had to? Whatever happened, the dissenters wouldn't catch him unprepared. He tried to think what to do.

To add to their woes, they now had a full-fledged economic boycott to deal with. Since the miller refused to grind their wheat, they ground what they needed in an old coffee-mill. Just as well, Nathaniel thought. Get them used to being self-sufficient.

"Johnny-cake for supper again," Sarah said. "And not even milk to moisten it with."

Then the thing happened with the Crawfords. Brother Owen and Sister Polly appeared at their door.

"Hard times, Brother Nat." Owen's voice broke. "I can hardly believe what I have to tell you."

"Oh, tell him," Polly said. "I'll do it. My nephew, who was living with us—we took him in, can you imagine? He went and joined those dissenters. They got up a lawsuit against us—hatched it up—entirely false!"

"They took our farm and everything we had," Owen said. "Left us an old horse and a rickety wagon."

Polly said, "And all because he was too stubborn to denounce the prophet, the way they wanted him to. If he'd a just done that—"

"Come in," Nathaniel said. "Don't stand there gettin' cold. It's the dead of winter."

They put Eb and Rusty together in the little room by the back porch. They gave the Crawfords the room where Sarah and Bethia had once slept. That evening, as Owen and Polly mourned the loss of their property, Nathaniel led them all in prayer.

Soon after the first of the year, they heard that Joseph Smith and Sidney Rigdon had fled for their lives. Their families left for Missouri a few days later.

"Other folks is leaving," Crawford said as they fed the horses. "I hear Brigham Young's already gone."

Calvin said, "Another home burned last night—just up the hill. Eb came in and told me. The family got out in the nick of time."

"Seems like they won't be content till they run us all out of here," Nathaniel said. "Here's my plan."

As he was outlining it to Crawford, Sarah called him from inside the house. Hannah lay in pain, bleeding months before her time.

"Send for Gabriel," Hannah said between breaths. "He'll come. I know he will."

Eb went off to Mentor in a snowstorm to fetch Gabriel.

"She fell," Sarah explained. "She was dragging crates around, and she fell."

"Why was she dragging crates around?" Nathaniel demanded.

"She thinks we're aimin' to leave. She was trying to help."

Gabriel finally arrived. He threw off his coat and rushed to the front bedroom where Hannah lay. Nathaniel could tell by his expression that Eb had told him everything, even about the persecution and the lack of food. With sure hands he probed Hannah's belly. He frowned as he examined the sheets full of blood.

"Let's have some more towels," he said to Sarah. His tone had more authority than Nathaniel had ever heard from him. Sarah started in surprise, then hurried to get what he wanted. To Nathaniel he said, "I'm awfully sorry—she's had a miscarriage. But as far as I can tell, she'll recover just fine—there's nothing left that shouldn't be."

He gave her something to help her sleep, then left Sarah and Polly to do the cleaning up. He took Nathaniel out into the main room.

They embraced each other.

"About six months along, wasn't she?"

"About that," Nathaniel said. He felt numb, drained of all energy.

"I couldn't have stopped it, even if I'd been here. You'd be surprised how often it happens. And lots of times, no one knows why."

"They say she fell."

"It would have to be quite a fall. I'm sorry I had to come home like this. I was planning to leave next week anyway."

"You want to go back to Mentor?"

"Not now. Not after what I've heard." He looked down at his clothes, soft gray trousers with vest to match. "I feel out of place in these. The doctor bought them for me, so I would look proper."

"You look just fine," Nathaniel said. "At least one of us has something good."

While Hannah rested, they packed up things of value, mostly clothes and dishes, and stowed them in the two wagons. Nathaniel built make-shift frames and stretched tarps over them, to cover the wagons. They brushed the snow from Sarah's carriage and loaded it with goods.

On the night of January 16, an arsonist set fire to the schoolhouse and printing office, just behind the house of worship. Nathaniel saw the flames rising from the House of the Lord, and he knew. Better to brave the winter in a wagon than stay any longer.

****

The wagon bounced as it hit a rock, then settled into the ruts of the road. Hannah, huddled in a blanket, looked at the woods on either side, the evergreens dusted with snow. Snow lay in patches under the trees; the road stretched ahead, firm and clear. She glanced at Nat beside her on the front seat. He had a determined, resolute expression as he clicked to the oxen.

Sorry for him. He must be weary, after all he'd had to bear. Her illness and loss, among other things. And now—leading another expedition, in the middle of winter.

His eyes met hers, and his look softened. "Be you tired? You know there's a place you can sleep, back in the wagon."

"I'm not tired."

Gabriel, Eb and Rusty walked beside the wagon. They moved without speaking, their boots crunching in the gravel. Behind them, the two bay horses pulled the carriage with Sarah, Bethia and Jody. Her father walked beside the horses. At the end came the Crawfords and their horse and wagon, with Owen walking alongside while Polly rode.

Hannah felt something nudge her back—the dog, who refused to leave Nathaniel. If he walked, she trotted beside him. Now she lay curled up just behind the seat.

Hannah looked out at the forest, where sorrow lay like a pale, washed-out light under the trees. She tried to remind herself that she was not the only one who grieved. She'd lost her baby, but others had lost homes, possessions, farms, means of livelihood. And through it all, her family had sought to sustain and support her with love and gentle words. Not just her immediate family, but the larger household.

She'd asked Gabriel to tell her whether the dead child was a boy or a girl.

"My dear sister—even if I could, I don't think it would be wise. It wasn't what I was looking for, to tell the truth. My main concern was for you. You'll have other children—I promise you. And I'll be there next time—I swear I will. *Eh bien*—I'll watch over you from the start."

Hannah felt curious as to how the new, mature Gabriel would affect the household, especially Sarah and Bethia. Would he propose to Bethia right away? To Hannah's surprise, Bethia and Gabriel began a game of ignoring each other. Yet she caught them sneaking looks when they thought the other was unaware.

Sarah's first reaction was to treat Gabriel with awe and deference. Later, just before the departure, she devised ways for the two young people to be alone together. Gabriel, as if sensing how greatly the tables had turned, managed to ignore both women.

As they reached a bend in the road, a doe stepped out of the underbrush and stood statue-like in a patch of sunlight, head up, ears alert. From the carriage, Jody let out a cry of delight, so full of pure joy that everyone smiled. Hannah longed to go back and take him in her arms. To live through all the deprivations they had known, and still be able to make a sound like that.

Then she realized—life went on. She was no longer the girl of nineteen who had ridden into Kirtland with her aunt to stumble onto love and a new way of life. She was a woman who had known unspeakable grief and had survived to find a kind husband, bear a son. She belonged to a community of people so close they were like one family.

And now—a new journey. Leaving all they had known, even the House of the Lord, to follow their prophet to another beginning. The patches of sunlight took on a soft, magical glow. Did it exist just ahead of them—the place of peace, the shining city, the holy mountain where no one would hurt or destroy? It seemed that the promise lingered in the golden light, brighter as the day advanced—beckoning them, waiting for them in the hills of Missouri.

They had reached the summit of a hill, a gradual ascent. Nathaniel stopped to let the animals rest. He glanced at Hannah and their eyes met. He smiled. Then he clicked to the oxen, and she looked ahead to where the road curved south into the woods.

About the Author

Elaine Stienon grew up in Detroit, Michigan, and attended the University of Michigan, where she majored in English and American literature. In her senior year she won a Hopwood award (a prize in creative writing) for a collection of short stories.

Since that time, she has had stories published in literary magazines such as *Phoenix, South,* the *Cimarron Review,* and the Ball State University *Forum. In Clouds of Fire* is her fourth published novel.

She has had a life-long interest in history, especially the history of the early Mormons and the difficulties they experienced on the American frontier. She lives in Glendale, California, where she devotes her time to writing and teaching.

The cover photograph was taken by Sam Rose.

Printed in the United States
19075LVS00004B/34-306

9 781418 447670